ON THE ACCOUNT

ON THE ACCOUNT

THE FIFTH VOYAGE OF CAPTAIN JESAMIAH ACORNE

BY

HELEN HOLLICK

www.penmorepress.com.

DEDICATION

Acknowledgements

First, thank you to Michael and Penmore Press for republishing the *Sea Witch Voyages*. We met a few rough seas during the re-editing and converting the files from their original editions, but here we are, at last, safe in harbour with all the existing books back in print.

Thanks to Cathy and John Millar of Newport House, Virginia, for words of wisdom regarding eighteenth-century ships and sailing, but in particular for guiding me through the romantic steps of the folk dance, *Well Hall*. If you would like to see a version there are several examples on YouTube, just 'search' for *Well Hall*, although these reproduced dances do not have the erotic frisson that occurred between Tiola and Maha'dun as depicted in this story.

A quick thank you to Mark Evans for helping me with various Arab information and to Jo Field, not only for her editing skills for the original editions, but for allowing me to link Jesamiah to her own fictional characters in her English Civil War novel, *Rogues & Rebels*, which I sincerely hope she will republish one day. My appreciation to Carol Turner, who copy-edited the original version and nautical author James L. Nelson for his sailing advice—I hope he did not laugh too loud at some of my silly errors. Any that remain are my fault.

My thanks to the splendid readers who volunteered to fine-tune *On the Account*—authors Anna Belfrage, Elizabeth St. John and Caz Greenham and to Lisa Adair, Sue Bloom and Richard Tearle—all very fine crew indeed! Cathy Helms, my dear friend and graphics designer, must be First Lieutenant, though. Thank you, Cathy, for your friendship and your company.

Finally, as always, thank you to my family who do not complain when my fictional characters take precedence over the everyday happenings of real life

Helen Hollick

2021

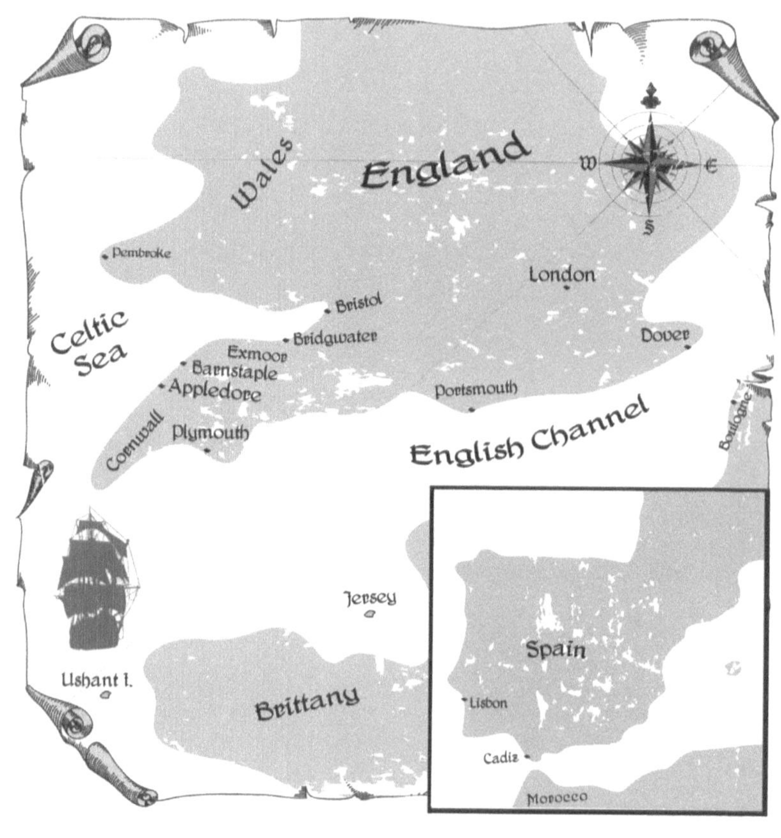

MAP OF THE ENGLISH CHANNEL AND WEST COUNTRY ENGLAND

'On The Account'

– to become a pirate or commit acts of

piracy

THE WEST COUNTRY, ENGLAND

CHAPTER ONE
Exmoor, Devon

Death was indiscriminate. There was nothing that the Wise Women and those of the White Craft could do to avert it. Even with her gift of healing, Tiola Oldstagh, the last of her kind, could not intervene with that omnipotent finality, however unwanted, frightening, painful, or sorrowful its presence. But the Shadows of Death were not all-consuming. Some souls remained Behind for they had no desire to cut the threads that bound them to the memories of mortality, or were curious about the ones who followed after. Others could not pass through the Portals of Eternity for their cries were too desperate to release their hold on what had once been. The desolation of their agony, or the necessity for revenge, was too great. Yet others refused to bow to the power of Death and defied its coming, but always, always, as day follows night and the sun rises and the moon sets, Death awaits its turn.

What of that empty place Between? The place that was not Behind or Beyond? That dark place where souls wait in hope, or fear, before journeying on—or returning? Waited for the Way Through to open, to be breached by the heat of love, the gentle caress of compassion or the satisfaction of revenge? What of those troubled souls who wait, entombed, desperate for release...

March 1719

An hour after dusk had settled into the star-frosted night, Tiola fed another stick into her meagre fire. The wood was damp and it gave off more smoke than heat, but it was better than nothing up here on the windswept openness of Exmoor's exposed coast. She was sheltered in the hollow behind the magnificent tor of rocks that separated the valley from the sea three hundred feet below. A place steeped in myth, legend and mystery. There was nothing left, now, of the wooden circle, or the standing stones erected by the people who had lived here long ago. It was said that the Devil had resided in a castle of rock with his many wives, but angered at their infidelity, he had blasted the eyrie to pieces. All that remained were the bare, jagged bones; the skeleton rocks piled stone upon stone. Nothing but a story, an old tale to explain the strangeness of a natural glacial formation —the Devil did not exist, but Tiola was aware that something was lurking out there in the darkness, watching her.

The stick flared into flame and the light caught the glint of an eye a few yards off. Tucking a loose strand of her black hair behind her ear, Tiola calmly added more wood to the fire and smiled to herself. This was the Valley of the Rocks, known also for the herds of feral goats that thrived on the coarse sea-salt grass. A huffed snort and a stream of misted breath evaporated into the cold air. A wild pony then, not a goat; one of the distinctive two-thousand-year-old Exmoor breed with their thick, weather-resistant, shaggy coats and light-coloured muzzles. Had she borrowed such a pony from the stables at Tawford Barton she would be at her destination by now, but her mission was secret and she wanted to know who had been watching her these past seven days, and had followed her, this night, up on to the moor. Had she asked for a mount her dear friends would have insisted on a servant to accompany her—young ladies were not supposed to wander the lonely moors on their own, but had she such an escort her strange accompanying shadow would not reveal himself.

The pony moved away, uneasy at the smell of fire; she heard his hard, little hooves clatter on some scree, then the sound of him cantering away, the drumming thudding as if the very ground was hollow. She fed the flames with yet another stick.

"You are welcome to share my warmth and light," she said as she moved her hand slightly in a figure-of-eight motion and the sulky fire leapt into vigorous life.

A shape approached from the opposite direction to where the pony had disappeared. Tall, lean and lithe of figure, he was dressed immaculately in breeches and knee-high black leather boots. A sumptuous dark green velvet longcoat and an exquisitely embroidered waistcoat covered a linen shirt, the froth of a French lace cravat precisely knotted beneath his chin. At his left hip, a rapier scabbard delicately engraved and inlaid with silver and lapis lazuli enamel, a gentleman's slender weapon sheathed inside. Draped rakishly across his shoulders a hooded, ankle-length sable-lined cloak fastened across his chest with a gold chain looped to two diamond-encrusted clasps that glistened in the starlight. An elegant man, his fastidious apparel incongruous out here on the open moors.

He pressed his slender-fingered, manicured hands together as if in prayer and bowed, his bright, sapphire blue eyes gazing at her from beneath lustrous black hair.

"*Namaste*, Lady."

She returned the greeting, but did not rise from her seated position on the frosted grass. "Well met, Maha'dun of the Night-Walkers. Are you alone, or does a companion accompany you?"

Maha'dun bowed again, smiled. "I am alone."

Tiola was certain this was technically untrue, but the Night-Walkers did not lie. Maha'dun, however, was adept at skilfully circumnavigating the truth. He had answered correctly, no Night-Walker accompanied him, but Tiola was aware, on the periphery of her senses, that another presence lingered somewhere out there in the darkness. Was Maha'dun unaware that he, in turn, was being watched and followed? Unlikely, for the Night-Walkers' sight, hearing and smell were highly sensitive. His answer had been literal; perhaps she should rephrase the question to be precise? Had there been two of them on the moors? Did she need confirmation of what she already knew? Leaving the matter, she asked instead; "I would know why you have followed me so closely while I have been about my business this last sennight, and now, this night up on to this desolate place? What is it you want of me?"

Smiling still, showing perfect white teeth, he indicated the fire, seeking permission to sit.

When Tiola nodded, he sank effortlessly down to sit cross-legged opposite her. "Am I not old friends with Tiola of the

White Craft? Do I not owe her my life? Do I need a reason to be in her company?"

"That you do not, but there is a reason behind this meeting and I would know what it is." Again her fingers made the figure-of-eight sign and a small escape of breath left her mouth on a soft *hieshh* whisper.

Maha'dun's smile remained intact, but he tilted his chin a little higher, a subtle indication of defiance. "Your gift of magick does not work on me, Lady. If I tell you what is in my heart and in my mind, then it will be through my own wanting, not your trickery."

She inclined her head in acknowledgement of the mild chastisement and feeling in the basket beside her for the bottle within, passed it to him. "It is brandy; a distillation you enjoy, if I recall correctly."

Eagerly he prised open the cork sealed with wax and drank deeply, then dabbed his mouth with a silk kerchief which he withdrew from his coat pocket. "And if I recall, there is little that you remember incorrectly, for you are the Wising Woman and you know everything."

Tiola laughed and brought out a muslin-wrapped pasty filled one half with meat and vegetables, the other with apples and blackberry preserve; a more than adequate meal for a growling stomach. She peeled aside the hard pastry casing and bit into the succulent meat within, offered none to her companion for she knew he did not eat the charred flesh that a man would savour; Maha'dun had his own preferences for sustenance.

"If I knew everything, my friend," she said between mouthfuls, "I would not have need to ask why you are sitting beside my fire."

As a tactic to receive an answer it failed, for Maha'dun

sampled the brandy again, then exchanged the kerchief for a cheroot and lit it with a burning stick from the fire. The scent of strong, sweet Virginia tobacco filled the air.

"For myself," he said, "I wonder why you, a beautiful young woman, are out here alone scampering about. It can be a dangerous place among the rocks and heather where robbers and murderers lurk."

And Night-Walkers, Tiola thought, but answered: "There are few footpads up here on the tracks of Exmoor, beside those who remain of the Doone clan in a valley yonder, and I have no reason to fear them."

Maha'dun puffed on his cheroot, sending spirals of blue smoke into the cold night air, the tip of it glowing red like a minute star as he inhaled. He replied, as if it were the most casual of statements, "I have been in the service of a man called Doone these past few months." Pretended not to see her frown.

"And since when," she said, "have you been in the employ of men?"

He remained silent, only the glow of his cheroot and the firelight illuminating his pale, expressionless face, his blue eyes studying the woman seated opposite. He saw a young woman who appeared to be some eighteen or nineteen years of age, with flawless skin, bright, intelligent eyes and a curved mouth that fell easily into a smile. Her figure was willowy—not so slender that it was nothing more than skin and bone, not so full that it could tend towards plump. But he knew her to be older, as old as the hills, as old as the sky, for she was one of the Old Immortals who had passed through Time from one reincarnation to another, from grandmother to granddaughter. Tiola was a living, breathing woman of these the early years of the eighteenth century, but she had also been the same woman in a time when humans were no more than apes existing in the trees of the African Savannah; when the Great Stones were erected; when Persia had ruled and Rome had fallen. When kings had followed the calling of their Church to take up the symbol of their Christ to wage a long, bloody, and ultimately pointless holy war.

At last, stubbing the cheroot out on a stone and immediately lighting another, he answered her question. "Since we discovered that he has knowledge of something the Night-Walkers want."

In her own turn, Tiola was quiet as she contemplated his words. She finished the pasty, tossing the hard and inedible pastry shell into the fire while savouring the remains of the sweet fruit by licking the sticky sweetness from her fingers. She thought she knew what he was alluding to, but could not be certain; if she was right the implication was unsettling.

"Are you going to reveal more of that cryptic comment?" she asked, ensuring her voice remained neutral with no hint of alarm or intention of control.

He smoked the cheroot halfway through, flicking ash into the fire, and gazed up at the myriad of stars sprinkled liberally across the vast night sky. Two planets hung there, Mars and Jupiter. A shooting star fell to the Earth; still he inhaled the tobacco, spiralling the smoke from his lips and nostrils.

"A long time ago," he finally said, shifting position to make himself more comfortable, "in the summer heat of the Spanish Alhambra, that pearl set among emeralds, ten of my kind were betrayed and taken prisoner. They were stripped naked, beaten, tortured and raped—the males as well as the females— then dragged to the town square and chained to posts. We are night creatures. Our skin blisters and burns in the strong sunlight, and our eyes are blinded. My friends were left thus in the scorching summer heat for many days." He shuddered to a halt, finding the words difficult, his throat and chest tight with grief. Very quietly he managed to add, "It took them a long while to die."

Tiola knew the story, had witnessed some of it herself. Compassionately, she reached out to touch his cheek, a gentle, healing gesture of sympathy and condolence, but she withdrew her hand. Maha'dun often disliked the feel of others, unless invited.

He noticed, smiled, offered his hand for her to take, his fingers entwining into hers for comfort. "When they were dead," he continued, "their corpses were left to rot. For many months carrion birds and rats feasted on their sun-roasted flesh and organs, and then the elements cleansed the remaining bones, which unlike a human's are not brittle or fragile. Eventually, the king of those merciless people ordered everything to be disposed of. The one who had originally betrayed my friends gathered the charred bones up and using his skill, carved and fashioned them into ten boxes. He kept one and gave the other nine as gifts to his favourite concubines to keep their trinkets in."

Maha'dun withdrew his hand and, fists clenched, spat his contempt into the fire. "Over time his whores lived to an old age, and gradually the story was told that whoever possessed one of these boxes, made from what they called the Bones of the Devil's Own, would live forever. The man who made them, it was said, became an immortal, for the spirits of the dead Night-Walkers penetrated his skin and saturated into his blood, heart, and his very being. But their hatred also seeped inward, and the man became possessed by cruelty and vindictiveness. So cruel and hated did he become that he was driven from Spain and no one saw him again. On nights when the moon is full and runs blood-red, The Carver's laughter can be heard on the wind, drowned by the curses of those he tortured and killed." He spat again, the spittle sizzling in the flames. "Hah! Humans and their stories!"

Tiola knew the stories, and the truth behind them, but the sadness of this telling did not dissipate by its familiarity. "And these caskets," she gave them their correct name, "over time became highly valuable, as The Carver knew they would, for it was he who began the tales to gain fortune from his greed."

Nodding, Maha'dun observed, "Wealthy humans will do anything to obtain one, for the legend of the stories and the value of the bone-boxes. But there are now only three left—we have recovered and destroyed seven. With the destroying, the souls within are released. They no longer writhe in pain and scream for help in that fearful place where they were trapped between life and death. And with each bone-box destroyed, a part of The Carver is destroyed also, for he put his power into the making of those boxes. But we have lost him; for more than fifty years now, we have been unable to sniff out his trail."

Taking another draught of the brandy, Maha'dun washed the foul taste of the story from his mouth. He smiled at Tiola. "I have told you my tale; are you to tell me why you are out here on these moors?"

Amused, Tiola smiled. He had not quite told her what she wanted to know; the Night-Walkers' search for the bone-boxes did not indicate why he was following her, but she let that point go. "I follow the wild pony and red deer tracks to visit the man you mentioned, Sir Ailie Doone, in order to beg his assistance in freeing my husband from gaol."

Raising one eyebrow, Maha'dun gazed at her quizzically. "You have a husband? You trust a mortal man not to reveal what you are?"

"This one I do. Jesamiah would give his life to protect

mine."

The faint snort of derision from Maha'dun's nostrils gave away that he did not believe her. No man could be trusted with such a secret, or be willing to give so much.

"If he is stupid or careless enough to get himself locked up, he does not seem, to me," he said slowly, "to be as reliable as you assume him to be."

"Seven nights ago," Tiola answered, "his ship ran aground at the place they call Crow Point where the mouths of the River Taw and the River Torridge meet. The excisemen and Devon militia were waiting for him; someone had informed that a cargo of contraband was to be brought ashore. That someone was your master's son. He was killed there. I do not feel any remorse for his passing, his treachery caused the death of several of my husband's crew, men who were my friends. Nor do I know who killed him. Possibly my husband did so. Many of his crew escaped and they are being safely sheltered by various good people, but as many were arrested and taken to Bristol to face trial. My husband among them. The last I saw of him he was being led away, tied and bound."

She did not add any of the other details; that her husband had been attempting to smuggle ashore a man who claimed to be the rightful Jacobite king of England, and that one of the passengers, an accomplished spy, had been a heavily pregnant English woman with a Spanish name. Or that Jesamiah had been the father of the expected child.

Tiola cocked her head to one side. "But you know all this for you were there, hidden, watching from a distance."

"Ah," was all Maha'dun said.

"You were there, yet you did nothing to help—not even the Doone men. You ran away, in fact." She tried hard to keep the censure from the words, but the hurt that her husband was incarcerated in gaol and she could do nothing to help him, scalded her pride and heart.

Maha'dun shrugged, a gesture that revealed he was embarrassed by her accusation. "I was there to observe. I do not involve myself with the trivial matters that men get themselves mired in." His steadfast gaze bored into her face, daring her to imply he was a coward a second time. "Aside, I had no wish to entangle with those red-coated soldiers. I..." He paused, looked away then boldly stared at her again. "I was afraid of being captured. I am afraid of dying in a prison."

Tiola dropped her hostility. For Maha'dun that fear was a genuine one—as genuine as her fear for Jesamiah. She said, "My husband is in gaol and will be hanged if he is found guilty. That is not a trivial matter to me. I go to Sir Ailie Doone, who was the master behind the idiotic venture, to beg him to ensure my husband does not go to the gallows."

Contemplating lighting another cheroot, Maha'dun sniffed. In his opinion any of the Doones were as likely to put the noose around the necks of those arrested that night for their abysmal failure, but he kept the thought to himself.

Making a decision, he thrust the cork back into the bottle and standing, slid it into his pocket. He offered his hand to Tiola to assist her to her feet. "I suggest, then, that we continue our journey, for it will be light soon and I would reach Doone Valley before daybreak." He grinned, "Else, I will have to seek an undignified shelter grovelling beneath dead bracken, and you will need to travel alone. Which," he bowed solemnly, "I cannot permit for this remarkable husband of yours is not here to lay down his life in the face of cut-throats or highwaymen. My humble service will need suffice in his stead."

Supressing a smile—Maha'dun was anything but humble in

all that he did—Tiola refrained from pointing out that she was quite capable of seeing to her own protection. But it would be good to have company, and she might as well accept that Maha'dun had no intention of turning away from his determination to follow her.

If she was lucky, or skilful enough, she might even discover the real reason why.

Chapter Two
Bristol

"No." Jesamiah Acorne folded his arms and glowered from beneath an untidy forelock of curly black hair at the stout but dapper man standing before him.

"No? Without knowing what it is I am asking of you? Without knowing what is in it for you?" Captain Henry Jennings was finding it difficult to control his temper. But then, that was often the case where Captain Acorne was concerned. Especially when he was in one of his more belligerent moods.

"Aye, an outright no. I have done enough for you, Henry. I have lain my life on the line once too often for your inane scheming and plotting. And now, because of you, I've lost m'ship, m'freedom, and probably m'wife as well!"

Not very successfully keeping the irritation from his voice and expression, Jennings answered with a brave attempt at civility. "There are other ships. If you help me, your freedom from this gaol will be secured, and your wife..."

Jesamiah took a menacing step forward, his right fist raised. "Don't you fokken dare suggest there will be other wives!"

Patting the air with his hands in supplication, Jennings

stood his ground. The hour was late and his foot ached abominably from the gout. He had no wish to spar verbally for much longer with this very angry young man. "I was not going to, lad. I was going to say that Mistress Tiola would not, in my opinion, abandon you."

"Well, in *my* opinion, your opinion stinks." Jesamiah turned away, clenched his fists around the iron bars of the cell window. The view beyond was as dismal as that inside the prison. Grey stone walls surrounding a square courtyard, where even the weeds were ashamed to grow. A place that could chill the soul to the bone. With the onset of night, the temperature had dropped and the cobbles in the courtyard were frosted white. The brackish drinking water in the provided jug would soon freeze, as would the miserable inhabitants of these miserable premises if they were unfortunate enough not to have the luxury of a blanket or mouldy straw to sleep on. At least Jesamiah had his own coat, and Jennings had provided a hat; somewhat shabby and obviously second- or third-hand, but it fitted well enough.

"If she has not abandoned me," Jesamiah said forlornly, his fingers fiddling with the gold acorn earring dangling from his right ear, "why has she not tried to contact me? It has been seven days now." He looked over his shoulder at the man he would, ordinarily, have called a friend. Did not attempt to wipe away the threat of tears from his eyes. Said; "I have not heard a word from her." The pain was there, twisting at his soul, the words that had been churning in his thoughts and guts spilling out, unbidden. "What if she'd been caught in the crossfire on that beach, Henry? What if she is dead?"

Jennings gripped Jesamiah's shoulder, gave a reassuring squeeze. Older than Jesamiah's twenty-five years, he had seen more of the world, had known more heartbreak, faced death more often, but, even with his experience as a seaman, he would readily acknowledge that Jesamiah Acorne held the edge where ships and the sea—and women—were concerned.

"Jes, it is not easy getting letters written and sent. Or getting them to where they should be delivered. Nor is it easy to bribe guards to obtain visiting passes. Maybe she has tried. Maybe she is delayed in North Devon? It is a fair trek from Barnstaple to Bristol."

"You manage to bribe whoever you need to. You got a pass. You're here."

"Yes, but I..."

"I don't want to hear it!" Jesamiah swung around, the anger returning. "I do not want your lies, your platitudes, or your bloody help. I want to be left to live my own life. Savvy?"

Slamming his fists against the bars, the frustration increased then dissipated as fast as it had risen. Jesamiah sighed, removed his hat, raked his fingers through his hair then rested his forehead against the unyielding iron. How could he tell Jennings that his relationship with Tiola Oldstagh was different to those between other men and their wives? How could he confess that she was a witch and had the ability to talk to him inside his mind? Hah! To say as much aloud would set him swinging on the noose quicker than a foremast jack spends his wages ashore!

Releasing an uncomfortable groan, Jennings eased himself down onto the hard wooden bench that served as seat and bed. "Help me and I will help you. Do this thing for me and you could be out of here within the hour. And when it is done you will be able to ask your wife for yourself why it is that she has not visited you. Though I would wager there is a reasonable explanation. I do know that she had been assisting Señora Escudero through her labour."

Looking at him critically, Jesamiah raised an eyebrow. Those last few moments when *Sea Witch* had run aground and they'd had to abandon ship had been one of his worst nightmares; a situation not assisted by the señora's onset of labour. As casually as he could he asked, "And the child? Was Francesca safely delivered?"

"I believe it did not survive the birth."

The words hit Jesamiah like a blow to the belly. Another secret, another matter he could not discuss with this man who was supposed to be a friend. How did you express the uncertainty that this dead-born child was possibly your own son? Daughter? 'Cesca had stated quite clearly that the babe she had carried was not his, but Jesamiah had not believed her. Or was that because he had not wanted to?

"What was it?" he asked.

Jennings shrugged. He had more important things on his mind than the birth and death of by-blow squabs. "I never asked, all I know is that the señora has been incapacitated, which is a nuisance for us as we have been left with several dilemmas that need tidying away."

The guffaw that erupted from Jesamiah's mouth was eloquent in its meaning. "Hah! Now that you have a dead uncrowned king on your hands, you mean?" He leant forward, his face almost pressing into Jennings'. "Let me guess; you want me to sort out the unholy mess you've got yourself into. You tried smuggling King James Francis Edward Stuart into England in order to rouse the populace into Jacobite rebellion. Only the stupid man got himself shot by someone who preferred to keep Fat George on the throne." Jesamiah laughed again. "To be frank, Henry, the man I brought ashore was a whimpering oaf, you are well rid of him."

Fumbling in his coat pocket, Jennings brought out a

leather flask and, unstoppering it, took a sip of its contents. He wiped the spout on his sleeve, offered it to Jesamiah.

Nodding his thanks, Jesamiah took a hefty gulp. Strong, dark rum. He took another swallow, handed the flask back.

Jennings took a swig. "But there is more to it than that. You see, the man you thought was the king was an imposter, a decoy. The real James was to meet the invasion fleet at Cádiz and sail in via the back door while the rest of England was chasing the man they thought was the king."

"Ah well, that's that plan scuppered then, ain't it?"

Pushing the stopper firmly back into the flask, Jennings grimaced. "More than you think. The armada never made it to England. The storm that grounded your ship did a lot more damage to the Spanish. Early reports indicate that it is gone, it's likely only a few vessels will manage to limp back to Spain. Most of the fleet is wrecked on the English coast, or in the Channel. And if King James was aboard..." Full of despairing gloom, he let the sentence trail off.

"The Dons never were keen on learning lessons from history." Jesamiah could not resist the sarcastic observation; despite his mother being Spanish, he had no liking for the country or the people. Probably because most of the Spaniards he knew would be quite happy to see him dead—by various unpleasant methods.

"At least," Jennings confided with a sigh, "there is no evidence to confirm treachery or rebellion on your part. The militia assumed those Spanish soldiers aboard your ship were tars." Jennings grinned. "A shrewd move on your part to ensure that disguise. I commend you for it, although most of them either drowned or managed to vanish into the night. A few were picked up along with your crew but none of them speak English so we are safe enough from wagging tongues."

Jesamiah frowned. Soldiers? He had not been aware that any of those dagos put aboard his ship had been military, he'd assumed they were all genuine seamen. Had he been duped again? Did it matter? Said, "And the men waiting for us? Your friend Ailie Doone's supporters?"

"Clean away. They're locals, they know the hiding places."

Jesamiah scowled and murmured, "Conveniently leaving us as fodder for the Excise."

"Unfortunately, yes." Resting his elbow on his knee, Jennings cupped his chin in his hand. His skin was pale, drawn, with black shadows beneath his eyes. He had lost weight too; could lose a lot more of everything. Forlorn, he shook his head, ruin staring him in the face. "Look, lad, we can try to get you a pardon—prove that all this was a mistake, that you were not running contraband, nor involved in any way with rebellion, weaponry or soldiers."

"Try? That's not what you implied just now, is it? I ain't no fool, Henry; even tryin' will be hard to do. The militia were waitin' for me. Jacobites came ashore with me. The only good thing about it is the bastard who betrayed us is dead. An' who do you mean by 'we'?"

Grunting with the effort and the pull of pain on his knees, Jennings got to his feet, picked up his hat from where he had put it down on the bench. "Myself, a few others and Sir Ailie Doone. He holds great influence in various places. All I need do is inform him you are willing to do something for us."

"You trust him? With his own son being your sod of a traitor?"

Jennings sighed. "Sir Ailie is as distressed as we all are. We knew there was a turncoat in our midst, were not sure who it was, but..." Jennings spread his hands defeated, "but we never suspected it to be Winnard Doone."

"You were blind fools to even attempt such a plan knowing you had a traitor." Suddenly suspicious, "Or was I as expendable as that poor bugger you conned into pretending to be James?"

"You are never expendable, Jesamiah. You—your talents—are too valuable to us."

Jesamiah laughed outright. "Oh, aye? Yet I'm sent off on a fool's errand then lured back straight into the arms of the Excise men? If that's not expendable, I'd hate to be in the boots of someone you don't care for!"

The retort from Jennings was indignant; "We are doing all we can to get you and your men out of this mess!"

"Didn't do much to stop me gettin' into it in the first place, though, did you? And I ain't daft. You want me out of here because you need me for something. Well, without a ship or a crew I can't do anything to help, so it ain't worth askin', is it?"

Setting his hat on his head, Jennings hobbled towards the cell door. He rapped on the bars with the knob of his walking cane, alerting the guard that he was ready to leave. "We are doing our utmost to ensure their release. If you are found innocent of these charges, then so must they be."

That meant bribing the right people with the right amount. A financial commitment that could involve Jesamiah digging deep into his pockets.

When he received no answer, Jennings added; "Very well, you know how to strike a hard bargain. Sir Ailie will cover all financial costs that are required, including repairing *Sea Witch.*"

Delight flooded Jesamiah's face, rapidly replaced by dark suspicion. "She ran aground. Her keel will be smashed to pieces."

Scratching at the itch of lice beneath his wig, Jennings

shook his head. "No, she has relatively minor damage—masts mainly, broken by the sudden stop of forward momentum. Her bow came to rest in wet sand that cushioned her nicely. Emptied of all weight and with the tides remaining high, your first mate, Claude de la Rue, and John Benson—a master shipbuilder, I might remind you—managed to salvage and refloat her. She is being repaired at Benson's yard. He is as anxious as I am to see you declared innocent at your trial."

Jesamiah snorted derision. "I bet he is. He was on the shore with the reception party. I saw him. Good for him for getting safe away, but now he wants to see me safe because repair costs will take a hefty purse of gold."

"I agree, but that is not Benson's concern. His son was arrested along with you and the remainder of your crew. The little fool got separated from his father and was caught on the headland. If you hang, then so does young Thomas."

That news stung. Was Jennings serious? "The boy is twelve years old! He has nothing to do with any of this, Henry. What is the matter with these government tosspots? He was not one of my crew. Have they not seen my logbook? The crew lists?"

"Not yet, they haven't. Documentation will be produced as evidence tomorrow."

"Tomorrow? A trial's to be that quick, is it?"

Jennings gave a knowing smile. "The Quarter Session Assizes were due to end today. The judge wants to leave Bristol as soon as he can; he is keen to get back to London for personal reasons. You have, unfortunately, become an inconvenience as he is obliged to clear the gaol of prisoners before he can leave. Sir Ailie hopes that we may be able to influence a quick and agreeable solution to this mess."

More bribery.

"The need for speed might work in our favour, Jesamiah. A

short, to-the-point trial with the right evidence produced could bring us satisfactory results. There again, hurrying things might work against us."

"You've got it all planned out then?" Jesamiah said grimly.

Jennings nodded. "We will try our best. Assuming you are willing to cooperate. For the sake of the boy and your crew, if not for yourself."

"You are a bastard, Henry Jennings."

"Oh, I learn from you, lad. I learn from you."

It was only after the outer door had slammed shut and the bolts rattled home that Jesamiah realised he had not asked what it was Jennings wanted him to do. Not that it mattered. Once he was out of here, he had no intention of doing anything except collect his wife—and maybe his ship if what Jennings had said was true—and head for a very distant horizon.

Chapter Three
Exmoor

The path that meandered down into Doone Valley was long and steep, dropping precariously in places through knee-high clumps of heather and winding through fierce stands of thorny gorse that was beginning to burst into yellow spring flowers. It was little more than a deer track, although the ponies and sheep often used it—and men, for Tiola spotted the occasional boot print in the cleavages of muddy frost-encrusted hollows. More than once Maha'dun graciously offered his hand to steady her as she descended, apparently oblivious to the fact that dawn was lightening in a thin line along the cloud-raked eastern skyline. The wind had swung from north-east to south-west, lifting the temperature, but threatening rain to scour in behind the frost. The weather these last few days had been like a pendulum; rain and sleet followed by a sharp frost; miserable wet to bitter cold and back again within the span of hours. With the land saturated and the rivers nigh on swollen, there would be flooding soon on the lower levels.

Without appearing to do so, Tiola quickened her pace. Maha'dun's robust clothing would protect him from the approaching daylight to an extent, but to walk in this rough terrain with his face swathed by his cravat, the cloak's hood drawn well forward and his hands encased in the leather gauntlets tucked through his belt, would not be comfortable. There were places out here where he could burrow beneath the undergrowth, but it would be an unforgiving hideaway. Even with the protection of his garments and in the half-light gloom of a possible storm, his skin would be vulnerable.

"It is a form of *cutaneous porphyrias*," Tiola had once said to him, "from the Greek πορφύρα—porphyria, meaning 'purple pigment'."

He had shrugged. "I am a Night-Walker, a creature of the night," was all he had replied, "and I am quite content without knowing, or caring about, an explanation."

"We have a mile or so more," he said, holding out his hand to help her make a small leap over a particularly boggy patch of ice-rimed sphagnum moss. "Plenty of time before sunup."

There wasn't, but Tiola held her council. Maha'dun always had been reckless, lacking a practical mind—Jesamiah would say he sailed overladen too near shallow waters.

They crested a rise and stood looking down on the Doones' personal empire of Badgeworthy. Nestled between the steeply descending heathland and woodland dominated by ancient oak trees, the village was set close to Badgeworthy Water, a river marking the boundary between Devon and Somerset. The higgle-piggle hotchpotch of thatched cobb-built cottages, barns and farm buildings were all constructed with, apparently, no regard for neighbours; several of the rugged houses were almost back to back, while others stood alone within forlorn, untended gardens. Apart from one stone-built, larger and grander dwelling where smoke was rising from one of its two chimneys, the place looked deserted.

The hold that the Doones, a family of notorious outlaws, cut-throats and thieves, had mastered over Exmoor and the surrounding area of Somerset and Devonshire had collapsed with the passing of old Sir Ensor. Unrest brought by the fear of the Doones had been compounded by the warring between the heirs of Charles II and had culminated in the subsequent horrors of royal reprimand. Hanging had been the fate of too many good men who had supported the Duke of Monmouth and not King James II; a foul death brought about by the assizes presided over by the Lord Chief Justice Jeffreys. Men, women and children were found guilty of insurrection, most being transported in slavery to the American colonies, while other unfortunates were executed by drawing and quartering. The lucky few, those who had rich relatives to pay bribes, had faced the noose instead of quartering. Nearly all who had died were innocents. Those remaining—among them the Doones—were often dangerous, for they were the ones who knew how to survive.

Exmoor was a lonely place where few travelled unless they had reason to; it provided ideal seclusion for those who had no regard for the laws of whichever king sat his royal arse on the royal throne—and for those who held a hankering for their own lucrative rule. The vast solitude of the moors suited those who, for whatever reason, sought distance from the turbulences created by princes and governments. Had suited the Doones.

Their reputation, like most tales spread by gossip, had been exaggerated of course; tales of callous murder, vicious rape, and kidnapping of children for the reward of ransom. Any traveller found dead anywhere near the high moors was presumed butchered by them, and Tiola, gathering her skirts to crab sideways down a particularly steep slope of tufted grass and dead bracken, could well believe some of the stories as she glanced at Maha'dun, striding sure footed ahead of her. He was no Doone, but nor was he innocent where murder was concerned, for the Night-Walkers had a reputation for killing, for ripping out the throats of young men in the silent darkness of night—and as the sensational rumour had it, for drinking the blood and eating the flesh of their victims. Such horror was not the truth, it was merely the stuff of embellished tales and was abhorrent to Tiola, but then, she reflected as she reached firmer ground and lengthened her stride to catch up with him, who was she to judge? Was Captain Jesamiah Acorne, her beloved husband, not formerly a pirate? A man who had killed without mercy, and would kill again if he needed to?

"Someone, at least, is astir," Maha'dun said, pointing to the single line of chimney smoke. "As well," he added in a louder voice as thunder grumbled in the distance and a cold sleet started to lash down, "for we are likely to drown if forced to remain out here!"

He grinned at her. Offering his hand for her to take, they ran the distance across the sedge-grass to the front door of the main house, their boots splashing in the puddles, their breath gasping mutual laughter as they stood within the shelter of the porch waiting for someone to answer the summons of the door knocker that Maha'dun had rapped loudly and forceful. Tiola tossed back the woollen hood of her cloak and shook some of the rain droplets from her plaid skirt. Her boots, she noted, were mud-splattered, and on discreet inspection, so too were her stockings.

Maha'dun knocked again, three curt bangs, but no footsteps were heard within coming to answer. A low growl rumbled in his throat as he impatiently lifted the door latch, the metal stiff and rusted beneath his pressing thumb, the hinges protesting as he swung the door inward. Beyond, a gloomy rectangular room with one narrow window that would give little light, even on the brightest day, for it was so dirt- and dust grimed. Square red-and-white tiles on the floor, several of them cracked, three missing. Beside a closed door on the right, an ornate wooden chest; opposite, another closed door alongside a high-backed dark oak bench. Between the two, and directly ahead, a staircase rising to a first-floor gallery. Weapons of various types and ages adorned the walls: blunderbusses, muskets, pistols; swords and pikes. An armoury as well as an entrance hall.

A door opened and closed somewhere upstairs; a moment later a man appeared, his hand gripping the banister rail, a scowl distorting his unshaven face.

"Zur Ailie be nait ple'sed ye've nait been 'ere these past foo days," he drawled, his heavy Devonshire accent echoing around the hall, the tone as gruff as his sour expression.

"As I was not pleased to be here," Maha'dun answered, looking up at him with an indifferent shrug. "Mistress Oldstagh has come to see Sir Ailie."

The man leaned over the rail, his aggression menacing. He ignored Tiola. "Ye be s'ppos'd t'serve our maister. Dis'ppearin' wi'out leave be nait service."

"He is your master, not mine. I do not require his leave." A slight smile tipped one side of Maha'dun's mouth—the sort of smile an adult wears to indulge a belligerent child.

Tiola removed her cloak and shook some of the rain off it. She had seen Maha'dun show that same smile before, knew it to be most extremely dangerous. Jesamiah possessed one exactly the same.

"Sir," she said, dipping a slight curtsey, "I have come especially to see Sir Ailie. If he be still abed, may I perhaps wait before a fire to dry the dampness from my gown?"

Transferring his scowl from Maha'dun to Tiola, the man

studied her a moment, then jerked a whiskered chin towards the right-hand doorway with no intention of coming down the stairs. "Kitchen be thro' thar," he grunted.

"I am to my bed," Maha'dun said, turning his back on the rudeness and sweeping Tiola a courteous bow. "I trust we shall resume our companionship come the fall of evening? When you are ready to return to Instow I have a carriage at my disposal; I would be honoured to escort you home. Assuming my driver is not too drunk to harness the horses."

"Thank you. I shall look forward to this evening." Tiola smiled as he bowed and lightly kissed her palm.

With a swirl of his cloak that sprinkled a shower of raindrops, his boots tapping on the tiles, he crossed the hall casting an uneasy glance at the breaking daylight seeping through the grimed window as he hurried away.

The man upstairs was about to spit, but swallowed the saliva, muttered instead beneath his breath, but loud enough for Tiola to hear, "Bast'rd d'vil spawn!"

"Sir Ailie?" Tiola persisted, politely reminding him of her presence.

"Bain't 'ere, 'e be gone up Bris'ol t'see tha 'angings."

Tiola blanched and felt sickness rise in her gullet. "When did he leave?"

"Day a'vore yes'dy."

Setting her cloak back around her shoulders and tying the laces close and firm, Tiola headed to the door. "I would be obliged if you would inform Maha'dun that I am returning to Instow, and will be taking passage to Bristol as soon as I can."

She heard the retch of spittle come into the man's mouth, closed the door behind her before he gobbed it over the rail onto the worn and disintegrating tiles.

~ *Jesamiah?* ~ The words formed; the special, secret way

they had of communicating, mind to mind. ~ *Jesamiah?* ~

There came no responding warmth of his husky voice in her head. Perhaps he was asleep?

As she started upward through the wet heather, her head bowed against the buffeting wind and scouring rain, she pushed aside an alternative, darker reason.

That he was already hanged and dead.

* * *

The sea heaved over the tumble of rocks many feet below the edge of the cliffs, lashed by the wind sweeping in across the Atlantic Ocean, and a driving rain that alternated between sleet and hail. Tiola glanced at the white-topped rollers and hoped there were no ships battling their way through the storm. Unless they were under the command of a good captain, few vessels would have much chance of survival beneath this battering.

Cresting the rise, she peered ahead, barely able to see more than a few yards through the dense rain. The sky of low, sullen clouds was slate grey, dusk-like although it was almost noon. In the lee of the Devil's Rocks, near to where she had lit a fire and met with Maha'dun, she paused to retie her bootlace. The wretched thing had snapped and, too short to knot securely, kept coming unfastened. Her muddied stockings, she noticed, were torn beyond repair. Three times she tried to tie the lace; in exasperation she sat on the sodden grass and, pulling the boot off, flung it away in a wide arc over the edge of the cliff. She watched it sail into the air, then plunge down out of sight towards the angry waves below. She sat there for a few minutes, gazing at the white-capped grey sea and the even greyer sky. Almost, she wept. The tears were stinging behind her eyes but if she were to give in to despair, she would not be able to get up and go on. She was tired, scared. What if Jesamiah was dead?

Impatient with herself, she brushed the unwelcome stray tear from her wind-chafed cheek. Jesamiah was alive. She would know if he were not, but time was spilling too quickly through the hourglass and she could run the quicker barefoot. She removed the other boot, then her ruined stockings, flung them all into the void of space beyond the cliff. Scrabbling to her feet, she hitched her gown to her knees—tempted to take that off as well and proceed in only her undergown petticoat. That raised a smile. She would cause enough stir when reaching Instow boot- and stockingless; a state of undress would cause more than raised eyebrows!

She walked on, uphill now, following the faint tracks that parted the bracken and heather. The moorland here was steep with high upward climbs and sharp downward drops, but the wind was a little calmer. Twice she slipped as she half ran, half slid, the wet grass like ice in places on the downward slopes. It would be sensible to walk, to take care where she placed her feet, but desperate to reach Instow and transportation, she did not heed caution. Wished, now, that she had brought that pony, for sure-footed and sturdy she could have galloped him across this rough terrain without fear of him falling.

A boat had been her original plan, but that was out of the question; nothing would be leaving harbour today. She could take one of Tawford Barton's horses and ride to Bristol, but the coach from Bideford would be the better option. Tiola cursed her blind stupidity; she should have borrowed Maha'dun's coach, why had she not asked? Or what of the Bristol Flyer that departed daily from Porlock on the Somerset side of the moors? Could she go back? What would be the quicker?

She halted, trying to get her sluggish mind to think

sensibly. Turning to look at the way she had come, the Devil's Rocks now a few miles behind, she lost her balance, fell, her foot bending beneath her as she tumbled down. With a cry she tried to grasp a tussock of heather to save herself from sliding further down the slope but the roots, loose from so much sudden rain, came away in her hand and she slid for several yards, her wrist crunching against a protruding granite rock.

Her skirt almost over her head, her petticoat torn and mud-covered, she lay, winded, in a ragged heap, her eyes closed against a sky that was spinning above her. Pain ripped up her right leg. She lay in the grass, the rain beating at her face, cooling the red heat that was flushing through her. With great effort she slowed her breathing, inhaling and exhaling with controlled calm, fighting against the threatening scream of pain and panic.

She concentrated on the feel of the wet earth beneath her back, calling on her knowledge of healing to flood her blood system, spinal cord and brain with her body's natural opioids. She understood these things about the functions of her body because of her gift of Craft, but took great care to keep the minutiae of detail to herself. Not even Jesamiah was aware of the extent of her knowledge.

Ignoring the cuts and grazes she struggled to sit up, the bruising to her wrist as painful as the fractured bone in her ankle, both injuries rapidly swelling with throbbing heat. She needed help but no one would be travelling this path in this storm. Her only hope was that Maha'dun would be as obsessive as he always was and follow in her wake. But that would not be until nightfall. Her only comfort; darkness would be descending the sooner because of this tempestuous weather.

Chapter Four
Bristol

Bristol Courthouse was full to capacity for the last trial of the Spring Quarter Assizes. The benches, set as if they were church pews, were crammed with men wearing their Sunday best and clutching their hats in their hands. More men were ranked at the back, leaning where they could against the wall or the marble pillars supporting the high ceiling. Even more were crowded outside, heedless of the drizzle. There was something fascinating about watching bedraggled, filthy men being led, hands bound, ankles shackled, from the gaol to the courthouse, and there was entertainment in hurling abuse, rotten food, mud and dung at them. Spectators came as well because of the possible multiple hangings—even if it was unlikely that those accused would be immediately sent to the gallows if found guilty, but there was always that chance. It did, sometimes, happen.

Jesamiah himself had escaped the unpleasantness as Jennings had paid good gold to ensure that he had been escorted into the courthouse by a side route. He had also paid for hot water, a barber and a clean set of clothes. Jesamiah appreciated the gesture, but was aware that this was all part of the proffered bribery. His answer remained no, the stubbornness confirmed when his crew were hustled into the courtroom. No payment for privileges for them, they were all unwashed, unshaven and wearing torn, muck-covered clothes. Several were still grimed with the dried blood from untended wounds.

The babble of conversation increased from the spectators, a few hisses were tossed towards the prisoners. Grim, jaw clenched, Jesamiah gripped his hat tight in his hands, his knuckles white with anger. The men were chivvied in to sit side by side along the rows of benches set for them, their feet shuffling on the wooden floor, the chains at their ankles clanking. Several men had deep, dry coughs. All looked gaunt and haggard.

"Has no one attended you?" Jesamiah muttered to the man seated alongside him.

"Nay. Who'd be bothered with the likes of us?"

"I damn well would, Finch, had I known!" The growl rippled through Jesamiah's words as he twisted around to inspect the sorry rows of men, his eyes narrowing in fury. How dare these English bastards treat his loyal crew so badly! How dare Jennings not see to them!

"We're a lot missing," he observed, doing a quick headcount but leaving aside the Spanish for whom he had no interest. As far as he was concerned, let them hang; he had not wanted them when he left Spain, did not want them now. There had been sixty-three of his regular crew, now there were a mere thirty-seven.

Chippy Harrison sat in the second row; Skylark was three men along from Finch. No sign of Crawford. Good, Jesamiah was glad to see the back of that troublemaker.

"Where's young Jasper? Did Jansy make it?" he snapped suddenly. "And Isiah?"

Finch, who had been Jesamiah's steward for some years and knew all his captain's moods, hesitated before answering. "I didn't see Jasper. The others didn't make it, Cap'n. I saw Jansy in the water. Isiah took a bullet to 'is 'ead. I saw 'im go down. At least it were quick fer 'im."

Jesamiah gripped his hat even tighter. Both men had been his friends. He breathed in, released the air slowly; wished to God that he could hear Tiola in his mind. Where the fok was she? Why wasn't she communicating with him?

The conversations along the spectators' benches had muted again. Jesamiah caught occasional snippets; exchanged opinion of how the trial would go, of what punishments befitted pirates the best. A few guffaws that had nothing to do with the court, but referred to the pleasantries of bedchamber sport. A well-dressed man was sitting in the front row, his hand curled around a silver-topped walking cane. Sweat beaded his brow beneath a slightly askew wig and he gazed steadfastly ahead to where the judge would be seated once he entered the room.

John Benson. His son, twelve-year-old Thomas, sat stiff-backed, eyes wide with fear, at the far end of the first row of prisoners. They had shackled him as well.

"Is the lad all right?" Jesamiah asked Finch, nodding in the boy's direction.

"Scared shitless, but it'll teach the li'l bugger to stay in bed at night an' not go where he ain't got no right t'be, won't it?"

That it will, Jesamiah thought, *as long as he has a life to learn lessons in after this debacle.*

Next to Benson, Captain Henry Jennings and Sir Ailie Doone, self-styled Earl of Exmoor. Jennings had said that he would try to ensure the accused were acquitted. Hah! How he planned to do so was anyone's guess; Jesamiah was convinced the man would fail miserably.

He'll have to find himself another idiot to do his dirty work, won't he? Jesamiah thought to himself.

All conversation ceased as the court was ordered to rise, the chatter replaced by shuffling feet, coughing, and one or two of the extra chairs at the back scraping on the floor. A door opened behind the judge's bench and, flanked by his court officials, Baronet Sir Abraham Elton, Mayor of Bristol—and possessor of several other such dignified titles—entered with all the pomp and ceremony of his rank. A man in his early forties whose father had made the extensive family fortune through the merchant trade of slaves. A man who, Jesamiah guessed from experience, had no compassion for anyone who was not of his own rank or skin colour, and who held an intense dislike for smugglers and pirates. It was an odds-on bet that he had a cellar or two full of illegally imported goods, though. These rich-gills wanted their tea, brandy and various fripperies and fancies at low, untaxed prices but soon forgot how they had come to possess them; sneered at the men who risked all to provide them.

Arranging his papers, Elton sat, smoothed his heavy gown and glowered beneath his wig at the dishevelled men arrayed before him; '*Hang the lot of them now*', a clear expression on his face.

The buzz of conversation was rising again, albeit more muted than before. Gruff, Elton ordered the bailiff to call for silence and begin proceedings.

As always with anything involving legal matters, the initial ramble was interminably long. Jesamiah, and a few of his crew, had heard the reading of the King's Commission before, knew it to be extremely boring.

"George, by the Grace of God, of Great Britain and Ireland, King, defender of the faith..."

Jesamiah did not listen to any more of the secretary's droning voice. He had a theory that this ritual was specifically designed to influence a prisoner to admit guilt. A quick hanging could seem an attractive alternative to being slowly tortured to death by this monotonous drivel.

Chapter Five
Exmoor

The smell of the moors was overpowering. The natural, earthy aroma of peat and grass, of bog and rock. The tang of the sea, the dank mist in the air. Over it all, the distinctive scent of spilt blood and the stink of fear.

The Night-Walker stood, clad in cloak, hood and leather gloves, face covered as well as may be against the damaging light even though it was grey and sullen from the rain. Stood, sensing the cries of pain, the desperation for aid. Those who had been chained and left to die in the blaze of the Spanish sun had so pleaded. Their cries, too, had been of agony. Their tortured souls continuing to writhe and scream these many years later, imprisoned within the tombs of boxes carved from their bones. Their desperate cries unheeded, unheard. Only the Night-Walker Seekers, charged with finding and destroying those foul caskets, could end that continuing torment. Only the Seekers... and the last Wising Woman of the White Craft. But she had failed, and now, in Cara'mina's mad-minded opinion, it was Tiola's turn to suffer.

* * *

The rain had eased slightly, the thunder grumbling off towards the distant coast of Wales, although another bank of cloud was building in the south over towards Dartmoor. Wet through, cold and tired, Tiola had lain as still as she could to minimise the pain that darted up and down her leg and arm. Both limbs were bruised and swollen. At least her ankle was a simple fracture and would heal tidily, not that this fact was much of a comfort to her. If she could not get help soon, she would be in desperate trouble, not from her injuries, for she had the ability to heal herself, but from the speculative gossip that would follow. With her use of Craft the bones would knit and become strong within three or four weeks, less time than an ordinary human. How did she explain that to those who knew her? And unless she was found soon it would take some skill to explain why she was not dead. Few survived nights out here with injuries such as she had sustained.

Tiola groaned and controlled her breathing through another wave of pain. She needed to find somewhere sheltered where she could tuck herself away, like any wounded animal, and create a plausible reason for her survival. Unable to move, that was not going to happen.

She could have slipped her soul from her body, allow time for the damage to heal, but she dare not do so, for if she was found it would be assumed, with her body apparently lifeless, that she had died. There would be mourning and sorrow, a funeral. She would be buried beneath the earth and there would be no one to stop it. No one to tell them that she was not dead, that to bury her alive would condemn her spirit to eternal wandering, unable to return, unable to pass on.

Tears meandered down her cheeks at the thought. Not for

her own fear or sadness, but for Jesamiah who would never learn of her fate. When it was necessary for him to pass over, he would grieve again, for her promise that she would be waiting for him on the other side would be broken. She would not be there to greet him, nor would he ever be able to find her. Why had she not been able to contact him in their own special, secret way of mind to mind? Whenever she had tried, it had been like wading through a quagmire morass. She could not pierce through that thick, sticky barrier.

~ *Jesamiah?* ~ She tried again. Nothing.

Another wave of pain swept through her. "Sweet Universe!" she murmured as a flash of lightning from many miles away reflected lurid pink on the grey clouds, the light penetrating her closed eyelids. She counted beneath her breath, very slowly but with rhythm: "One and, two and, three and, four and… " Reached one-and-twenty before the distant thunder rumbled. Some miles away, then.

Movement nearby. Animal? Human? Eager with hope, Tiola opened her eyes, saw a veiled face staring down at her. Maha'dun! Slipping from her rigid control, her heartbeat increased with a mixture of relieved joy and the return of pain, only to lurch with dismay as she realised the eyes were not Maha'dun's deep, sapphire blue, but a dark, sea green.

Cara'mina. High-born Lady of the Night-Walkers. The most arrogant and dangerous of all her kind. There were only a few ways that Tiola could die: her throat torn open by this female monster among them. The thought hurtled through her mind that at least now, if anyone eventually found her, her remains would be truly dead; there was no fear of her wandering as a lost soul for eternity. Cara'mina could see to that.

"I would know, Tiola of the White Craft, what it is you do

here on the moors? Why do you walk with that scut, Maha'dun, who has so disobeyed me? Is he swiving you as he does with every male and female of my kind?" Her words were filled with more venom than a cobra could spit.

"Maha'dun's honour is beyond the reckoning of your crude spite, Cara'mina."

The retort of laughter was devoid of humour. "Honour? Maha'dun does not know the meaning of it! He is the lowest of our low. Even the fetid scum that floats upon stagnant water is of more value than is he." Cara'mina leaned in closer, her breath smelling of old copper pennies, "You are tainted, Witch-Woman, because you were foolish enough to save his life. You should have left him to drown. There were others more worthy who died, yet they were not saved."

A suspicion crossed Tiola's mind. Was this the reason for Cara'mina's resentment against Maha'dun? Had she been involved in his attempted murder? Tiola shuddered. She would not put such a despicable act past this grotesque.

How many years ago had that incident taken place? Tiola had existed within a different incarnation then, had been practising her Craft of healing in the jewel of India's mountain terrain beside the beauty of the lakes. Men had captured Maha'dun, beaten him almost unconscious, then bound him with chains, put him into a boat and, paddling to the centre of the lake, thrown him into the deepest part of the water. Except Tiola had been watching their laughing cruelty from the shelter of the trees. Deep water was nothing to a white witch who could hold her breath. For that act of kindness, for saving him, Maha'dun owed her his soul—an obligation of gratitude redeemable only through repayment of kind; no easy task when Tiola's life was difficult to destroy. She had also saved Cara'mina's life once, but that, in hindsight, had been a mistake for the creature followed her own rules and saw the act as a failure, not as a kindness.

Now, Tiola thought, *would be a good time for you to fulfil your vow of life-for-life, Maha'dun, my friend.*

"I tried to save those others," she said, knowing her words would fall on closed ears. "I suffered for that trying, and I grieved then and grieve still for their souls, as much as do you."

"You suffered? Hah! You are still alive, they are not!"

"I died in that past life, Cara'mina. I too burnt, my woman's body chained to a stake, faggots set around my feet. Most memories from our previous lives are removed when we incarnate into the new being that is our embryonic granddaughter. That memory has never left me. By chance, the daughter of the woman who was then me was newly pregnant. Had she not been, my soul would not have transferred and my line would have ended with that wicked burning. I died because of those Night-Walkers, Cara'mina. I tried to save them."

Cara'mina thrust her face into Tiola's. "You did not try hard enough! I find it abhorrent that you could not save them, yet years later you saved that runt."

There was no point in arguing. Sense would never win over narcissistic insanity.

"I want the casket," Cara'mina said, curling her gloved fingers into Tiola's black hair and jerking her head backwards to expose her throat.

"It is already destroyed. I set its captive soul to rest some weeks ago."

Viciously, Cara'mina kicked at Tiola's foot, sending a scream shuddering through her victim. "I know of *that* casket. The one those stupid women tried so uselessly to hide in their shabby little house at Tawford Barton. Do you not think the tortured screams trapped within it and pleading for release did not reach my senses? Do you not think I tried to reach it, to destroy it myself?"

Tiola gazed steadily into Cara'mina's cold eyes, masking the fear that was pounding through her. The good ladies of Tawford Barton had kept what they thought to have been an ebony box discreetly hidden. It had contained papers that had revealed Jesamiah to be their close kindred, unravelling more hidden secrets, answering questions and tangling yet more that would need answering one day. Lady Jennet Dynam, now passed into eternal rest, had held a small amount of Craft, enough to shield the household from harm and keep the likes of Cara'mina away. And then Tiola had arrived, and with her Craft had strengthened the circle of protection. Tiola had instantly recognised the box for what it truly was and had ritually burnt it at her first opportunity, murmuring the incantations necessary for unfettering the spirit incarcerated within.

Cara'mina made a sound that was part hiss, part growl. A sound of vapid malevolence. "Do you not think I know what you did? I sensed the deliverance. It is another casket I seek."

A thank you would not go amiss, Tiola thought, but considered it unwise to say so. "I know of no other casket."

"I speak of the one your husband possessed. For many weeks I watched that house where you now reside, unable to reach what I wanted. Then you came with that man, whom I discovered to be your husband. He has the residue smell of a casket upon him. I want to know where he, and it, is."

Tiola remained silent, could not risk giving any sign away, no matter how slight. With her beside him Jesamiah was safe, and for much of the time when without her protective presence he had been aboard *Sea Witch*—unreachable by this vicious female, for the Night-Walkers, as earth-bound creatures, were afraid of open water. Not one of them could swim, and only when necessity dictated did they dare endure the shortest distance across the English Channel between Calais and Dover.

When Jesamiah had secretly sailed to Spain, to Cara'mina he must have simply disappeared. Was she aware he had now returned to England? Had Maha'dun informed her? But then, Maha'dun did not know that Tiola's husband was Jesamiah, did he? Maha'dun had not been near Tawford Barton while Jesamiah had been there, for Tiola would certainly have sensed him—as she had sensed Cara'mina, but had dismissed her presence once the casket had been destroyed. A mistake on Tiola's part, it seemed.

"I know not the whereabouts of another casket," she repeated. "Nor has my husband possessed one."

"You lie!" Cara'mina cried again, her fingers tightening around Tiola's throat—and then she shrieked in rage, her hand clutching at the black pendant Tiola wore. She yanked at its silver chain, snapping it. "Where did you get this? Why are you wearing it?" She kicked Tiola again, her anger tipping over the edge of reason into insanity, where Cara'mina most often resided.

All Tiola could do to save herself from more excruciating pain was detach her spirit from her body. As she sank into unconsciousness, memories fluctuated in her mind. Not seven days since, Señora Francesca Escudero, the English widow of a Spanish nobleman, 'Cesca, Jesamiah's lover, had given Tiola the pendant necklace. She had taken it from her own neck; a small but pretty gift for assisting with the birth of a dead-born son. Tiola frowned. How, why, had she forgotten about it?

With that memory, another: 'Cesca had once possessed a casket. In Hispaniola. It had contained rare, precious diamonds. And Jesamiah had, for a short while, taken care of it, still had several of those diamonds. He had told Tiola part of the story during the long sea crossing from America to England. Not all of it, though! He had failed to mention that he had made love to 'Cesca and had given her a child.

Thoughts drifted, pieces of a broken puzzle slipping into place. Somehow, the Night-Walkers must have discovered the connection between a casket and Francesca. If she still possessed it, but had secreted it somewhere, they would have had need to follow her, or use another way to track her movements. Ah! The pendant! More things began to make sense: only men carried the residue scent of those boxes on their skin, not women, the pendant was an effective alternative. But who had given it to Señora Escudero? There were no Night-Walkers in the Americas—none had ever found courage enough to cross the vast Atlantic Ocean, so was the connection through someone in Spain? It had to be! Thinking it nothing more than a pretty trinket, Francesca had, in turn, passed the pendant on as an innocent and grateful gift.

Sleep beginning to overtake her, Tiola allowed herself to sink deeper into approaching oblivion, a nagging question remaining unanswered; what in all the Universe had possessed her to accept the thing from 'Cesca? She had known precisely what it was! Had she perhaps hoped that it would be Maha'dun tracking the English woman? And where was 'Cesca now? Tiola drifted further into the in-between shadows of nothingness. Was she with Jesamiah? In his arms, making love with him? Where had she gone?

"Gone," she murmured, "gone to Bristol."

Chapter Six
Bristol

A buzz of voices and renewed shuffling jerked Jesamiah from his reverie about the most efficient way to store hogsheads of tobacco in a hold. They had been sitting in the courtroom for over two hours now—had, one by one, been named and called to stand at the bar, swear on the Bible, and state their case; all had pleaded, "Not guilty."

Jesamiah had protested once, when young Benson had stepped forward. The boy was clearly terrified.

"Your Honour," Jesamiah had stood, spoken politely, "this lad is not a member of my crew. Beyond misguided curiosity, he was not involved in this incident. He deserves his backside given a whipping, but no more."

Elton had peered from beneath his wig and studied Jesamiah a moment. "And you are?"

"Jesamiah Acorne, gentleman, merchant trader and Captain of the *Sea Witch*."

"Then as a gentleman you should know that prisoners in my court are only permitted to speak when they are spoken to. You will be seated."

"But…"

"You will be seated and be silent, sir!"

Feeling like a chastised schoolboy, Jesamiah had sat, twiddling his hat around and around between his fingers, and despite the inner fuming, was silent.

The proceedings rambled on, several of the crew were asleep, Finch included. Jesamiah was almost nodding off into a doze when Henry Jennings stepped forward.

Sitting upright and folding his arms, Jesamiah thought, *this might be interesting.*

Jennings started with the usual banal compliments, the 'blah, blah, blah' bits, as Jesamiah thought of them.

"My lord," Jennings eventually cut to the chase, "you mentioned a curiosity of treasonous implications towards a connection with rebellious allegations, but Captain Acorne is no soldier, nor is his vessel, *Sea Witch*, a warship. Indeed, I wish to make it known he carried a woman heavy with child aboard. Would he deliberately endanger the life of a lady and her unborn infant?"

Elton looked down from his bench with stern deliberation. "If there was no intention of hostility, may I ask why there were cannon and armed men aboard?"

"The seas between Spain and England harbour hostility, sir. As we now know for a certainty, James Stuart had the audacity to attempt to attack our shores by means of an armada of some nine hundred ships. The lady in question has a status of importance, and the *Sea Witch* had a legal cargo of some value aboard. Would not any sensible captain take precaution of armament against attack?"

The number of ships in the armada fleet had been exaggerated, but otherwise, Jesamiah thought Jennings was putting forward a good argument of defence. It was just rather a shame that Elton was not looking as impressed.

Jennings rumbled on for another twenty minutes; after ten, Jesamiah considered that he was somewhat over-egging the pudding and Lord what's-his-name Elton had slid off into his own little reverie. He was sitting there palms together as if in prayer, his lips and chin pressed against fingers and thumbs, his eyes closed.

Contemplating the last fox hunt of the season or the next tumble with his whore, I'd wager, Jesamiah thought. Then, *When was my last romp?*

With Tiola. He had made love to her that night before he had assisted with breaking her brother and several of Ailie Doone's men—his grandson included—out of Barnstaple Gaol. He should have guessed, then, that Doone's son, Winnard, was not to be trusted. He had been the traitor, he had been the one to tip the Excise men off about when and where *Sea Witch* had been expected to return, and of the real value of her cargo—the man impersonating James Stuart.

A large black spider was dangling on a thread above the judge's head; Jesamiah watched it swinging to and fro. Like a man on a rope on the gallows. The web broke and the spider dropped onto the piled papers on the desk.

Lucky sod, Jesamiah thought, *how often does that happen to the poor bastards having their necks stretched?*

His thoughts returned to Tiola. That blissful lovemaking, their bodies entwined in the ecstatic crescendo of mutual sexual pleasure. He spent time with whores to sate a passing need, but there was no feeling for those working-girl pieces of laced mutton, not even for the young, fresh, game pullets. His flagpole might enjoy their handiwork but there was a difference between sex for need and sex for love. Jesamiah bit his lip, regretted thinking of the topic. Now was not the time or place for arousal.

Elton coughed loudly, suddenly either coming awake or completing his daydream. "All very interesting, Captain Jennings, but smugglers are smugglers. I have no patience with them. You may sit down."

"Aye, my lord, but..."

Lord Elton peered at Jennings as if he were a slug crawling over a cabbage leaf. "I have no patience with 'aye butters' either, sir!"

Taking the hint, Jennings bowed, sat.

"Is there anyone else wanting to speak for these ingrates?" Elton enquired in a tone clearly indicating that he sincerely hoped not.

Sir Ailie Doone got to his feet, flourished a respectful bow. There came further shuffling from the spectators as they all turned in their seats to stare at him.

"My lord, I wish to be granted permission to speak for one of the prisoners if your compassion would permit me to do so."

The men of Jesamiah's crew glanced at each other. To speak for only one of them? Which one? They all glowered, suspiciously, at Jesamiah. The threat of a protest settled, however, when Doone indicated the boy, Thomas Benson.

"My lord, this lad is, as Captain Acorne previously mentioned, innocent of these charges. He is a high-spirited, wilful boy..." Doone looked around at the people crowding the court, smiled, spread his hands. "Who among us, as grown men, does not recall those mischievous adventures of our boyhood? And our resulting tender buttocks!"

There were a few chuckles, some nodding heads. Even Elton partially smiled.

"My lord," Doone continued, "I will take personal responsibility for the boy and find him an apprenticeship where he can learn some adult morals. He is twelve years of age, I believe, old enough to set aside these silly pranks." He glanced at the boy's father, John, sitting red-faced with anxiety. "If his father so permits, that is?"

Benson stood, nodded vigorously. "Indeed so, my lord. After I have ensured the boy will not be sitting down for a good week or two."

Again the courthouse rippled with amusement.

Tidying some papers into a neat pile, and without noticing it, Elton knocked the spider aside. The mood of the courtroom was a hard one to gauge. From the outset they had wanted a hanging, but the good nature towards the boy was belying that undercurrent. He sat there, pondering. It would show compassion to set the boy free, and gainsay those Tory asses in Parliament who whispered about judges becoming as notorious for hanging innocents as some others had been.

"Is there a ship's log?" he asked of the clerk, who searched through the paraphernalia on his desk and handed *Sea Witch*'s official documents to the judge.

Jesamiah assumed that Benson had salvaged the ship's papers, hoped that perhaps his beloved ship was not as badly damaged as he had feared. He watched Elton leaf through the pages; he would be reading a more-or-less accurate account of the passage from England to Spain and back again, complete with a full list of cargo and crew. He would find the Spaniards there as foremast jacks, but not young Thomas Benson's name. And, if he looked further, he would see a full inventory of wine and Spanish brandy, which Jesamiah had genuinely intended to declare as legal cargo. Bad enough smuggling the supposed king of England ashore without added complications of contraband.

Looking up, Elton beckoned to the boy. "Come forward to

the bench," he said in his severest tone.

John Benson broke out in a fresh sweat as his youngest son, encouraged by one of Acorne's crew, hesitantly stepped forward.

"Boy. What have you to say for yourself?" Elton asked peering down at him through slightly myopic eyes.

"N...nothing sir, except I beg the pardon of Your Highness and of my papa." Thomas risked a glance at his father, and blushed. "And of my mama who is, I expect, most severely distressed."

"That she is!" Benson interrupted. "It is selfish and unthinking of you to put the dear lady through such pitiful worry!"

Moving his papers aside, Elton leant forward to stare at young Tom. "This is a court of law. You are under oath to God to speak the truth, so tell me true, were you waiting on that beach to assist in bringing contraband goods ashore?"

Thomas looked direct back at Elton, said without hesitation, "No, Your Highness, I was not."

A smile twitched at the corner of Jesamiah's mouth. The boy had not lied. They had been there to welcome that idiot imposter ashore, no other reason.

Elton's expression became darkly serious. "You have come very close to being hanged alongside these ruffians. Think yourself fortunate that I am of a lenient disposition. Get yourself gone from my court—but be warned, if I should ever find occasion to see your face again at any time in future years, you shall be hanged by the neck without any qualms. Is that clear?"

Thomas nodded fervently and his father stepped forward to grab his arm and hustle him away, fearing the judge may discover the truth and change his mind. His chastising lasted as long as father and son were within the building. Once outside, Benson scooped the boy into his arms, hugged him close and did not care who witnessed his intense relief.

Feeling satisfied that his leniency would receive approval from his peers, Elton picked up the next document and stifled a scream as the spider fell into his lap. He threw the paper aside as he leapt up, brushing frantically at his gown. Because the judge was on his feet, everyone also rose, but it was not long before laughter began to ripple around the courtroom.

"Court is adjourned until ten of the clock on the morrow," Elton barked as he fled through his private door, slamming it behind him.

The clerk and bailiff were both confused, but shrugging his indifference, the bailiff repeated the order and the courtroom began to clear with much chatter and amused guffaws. Earl Judge Abraham Elton, it seemed, was not at all squeamish about sending men to die on the gallows, but he was clearly perturbed where spiders were concerned.

Jesamiah grinned as he and his men were led from the courthouse to face another night in their squalid cells. It was good to know these pompous pisspots had their vulnerabilities the same as any common man.

CHAPTER SEVEN
Exmoor—Doone Valley

"Up! Wake up, you imbecile!"

A sharp-nailed hand slapped at Maha'dun's face, and with a snarl, his own hand shooting out to grasp at the offending wrist, he thrust aside the blanket covering himself and sat up, ready to strike in retaliation. He was met with a hiss and another slap from his assailant's free hand, and he shrank away, releasing the clasped wrist and withdrawing his instinctive reaction of defence. More blows to his face, head and body; the slaps and punches hard and merciless, the accompanying torrent of verbal abuse foul and degrading.

"How dare you be so incompetent, you idiotic fool! How dare you encumber me with your inane stupidity!"

Maha'dun had no idea what Cara'mina was raging about, but it was pointless to ask; she would only scorn him the more. From experience he knew it best to take the blows and stay silent. He remained none the wiser when she struck his face with a silver chain, the pendant dangling from it catching the corner of his eye and drawing blood.

"You followed the wrong woman! You oaf, you dolt! Can

you not even manage the simplest of orders? Wait for the woman with the bone-stone to come ashore, then follow her. You feeble-minded dotard! Could you not even do that?"

Realisation dawned. "But I did! I did as you bade me! I have followed the woman with the stone these last seven nights."

Another blow, but with a clenched fist this time, crunching into his cheek. Maha'dun reeled, almost knocked unconscious.

"You were following the witch-woman; you were supposed to follow the other one. The English woman with the Spanish name!"

A final blow did numb his senses; he fell back, his ears ringing, head reeling, redness alternating with blackness. When the room stopped whirling he opened his eyes to find the chamber empty, the door open with daylight from the outside spilling in.

Hastily, he covered himself with the blanket, lay there curled up, shivering with fear. His orders had been to go to the shore with Winnard Doone and to watch for a ship returning from Spain. He was to locate the woman aboard the ship who would be wearing the bone-stone, and follow her. He had done that. Admitted he was surprised and disconcerted—confused— to discover the woman to be the Lady Tiola, but then Cara'mina never deigned to explain her orders, so how was he to know he had got it wrong?

The bruises and cuts to his face stung. Cara'mina was a vicious bitch with a temper like a roused bear. He rose from the bed, and kicking the door shut with his foot, went to the washstand to pour water into the laver. Tentative, wincing, he soaked the washcloth and bathed his injuries. Not for the first time Maha'dun regretted the Night-Walkers' rigid code of honour forbidding the killing of each other. He would very dearly like to kill Cara'mina if ever he had the chance. And then it occurred to him. If Cara'mina had the bone-stone that had been hanging around Tiola's neck—what had happened to Tiola?

* * *

The moors of an evening, when the rain had been falling for most of the day, were a dismal place. Grey and desolate, the mists rose from the gullies and hollows, settling over everything like the breath of a brooding dragon.

Tiola lay, shivering, only half-conscious as the daylight drained into early dusk. Something had alerted her, bringing her back from the semi-suspended state she had put herself into. A noise... Something, someone, brushing through the wet gorse and remains of last year's bracken. The mist dampened and confused the sound. Was it distant? Close by? Cara'mina returning to try again for information she, surely, knew she would not get?

A splash, a hissed curse. "Bloody moors! I loathe this wet, dismal, dreary, muddy, foggy, bloody country!"

Maha'dun? Oh, thank the stars! Maha'dun!

Tiola tried to move, but the pain, now she was fully aware, was too intense. She tried to call out, but her throat was dry, nothing but a hoarse groan emitted from her lips. It was enough, though!

With his sensitive hearing and enhanced olfactory ability, Maha'dun located her. He was there kneeling by her side, uncaring now of the wet grass as he moved his gloved hands gently over her body, exploring her injuries. He removed his cloak, laid it with care over her, the sable of its lining bringing her some warmth.

"How long have you been here?" he asked. "No, hush,

Lady, do not answer. Long enough is all I need to know." Then, "You were attacked?"

"I fell," Tiola mumbled. "Down the slope."

Maha'dun snorted. "You did not receive these hideous bruises from a fall." He leant away a little, sniffing as a dog scavenges for crumbs, his nose wrinkling with distaste, his suspicions confirmed. "Cara'mina was here." He all but spat the name.

Tiola nodded. "She wants my husband's life."

"I must get you to human help. These injuries are bad. Will you be able to bear me carrying you?" He was now regretting not travelling here in his coach—but then, a coach would have had to stay on the rutted cart-tracks, and he had found her the quicker by scenting her trail and following on foot.

"I would know of Cara'mina first," Tiola insisted.

"Later. I will tell you later."

"Now, Maha'dun."

Rocking back onto his heels, assessing the best way to lift her, Maha'dun shrugged. "I do not know, Lady. That bitch despises me, tells me none of her secrets and schemes. Why should she? I am nothing to her. All I know, she heard of a bone-box some weeks back. I assumed it was the one Doone has been attempting to purchase, but I am not so sure now; perhaps they are different bone-boxes?"

"One was at Tawford Barton, but it was not for sale, no one knew of it and I destroyed it in the proper way. This other, I know nothing of."

Maha'dun cocked his head to one side, his sapphire-blue, night-sighted eyes glinting in the half-light of approaching dusk. There was more to what Tiola had said, but now was not the time to continue the conversation. "I must get you to where it is dry and warm, to where you can be helped. Those people at Tawford Barton seem to be your trusted friends. I will take you there. We can discuss this other matter later."

About to protest again, Maha'dun silenced Tiola by placing his mouth over hers, his lips a butterfly touch as his tobacco- and copper-tasting breath drifted into her body and eased her to sleep.

"Cara'mina commands me," he said aloud to himself and the moors as he lifted Tiola's inert body, carefully tucking the sable around her. "I am honour-bound to obey her, even if she has the madness of a froth-mouthed rabid dog about her."

As the dusk darkened into night, and with no further necessity to shield himself, the Night-Walker loped with long, steady strides straight across the moors, not needing to follow the trails or stop for breath or direction. His night vision and senses were all he required to travel with the ease and confidence of any wild creature.

"On the other side of the argument," he muttered as he descended the final slope onto the rough mud-track road that would lead to Instow, "you, my dearest Lady Tiola, are precious to me and I owe to you more of my life, love, and honour than do I to that tainted, sadistic bitch."

* * *

Tiola recalled Maha'dun carrying her down from the moors and the flurry of consternation when they reached Tawford Barton. Pamela's ashen face, Rue's furrowed concern. Vaguely, she remembered flickering candles and soft-glowing lamps, the crackle of the fire in the hearth and the bitter poppy juice mixed with sweet honey. Remembered too, a gentle-handed doctor attending her injuries, setting the bones while soothing her with soft-spoken kind words. She recalled her brother's worried voice as well. Someone must have sent to Appledore to fetch him. Was he here still? *Carter?* Did she say his name? Perhaps she had merely thought it, for there came no response.

Beyond the bedchamber window, a weak early-morning sun was trying to push through the grey clouds. The Bar, that sandbank and shale barrier between the tamed estuary and the wild sea, was a distant froth of white foaming water. It was hard to picture the storm that had raged so mercilessly that night a sennight since. To look out at this tranquillity of a calm morning and remember *Sea Witch* foundering and muskets firing, men dying... Tiola closed her eyes, dozed, opened them again, a minute, half an hour later? She could not judge how long she had slept, except the shadows had altered and the sun had moved round.

Where had Maha'dun gone, she wondered, then forgot him; he was quite capable of looking after himself—he would have found somewhere away from the daylight to rest and sleep. Without moving too much she could see the low-tide spread of the estuary and, as the sun came out again, the sparkle of the narrow ribbon of the River Taw, its sullen grey turning a sudden blue. With the sunshine too, the green hues of the headland opposite and the shore where *Sea Witch* had gone aground. Where Francesca had delivered her dying baby, where Tiola had given the child to the sea, and where, to almost the exact same spot those years before, Jesamiah himself had been born.

By craning her neck slightly she could see Benson's shipyard and the hulk of a ship set inelegantly on her side, her masts unstepped, her keel exposed. The sun glinted on her copper-clad underside; Tiola smiled, the ship was like a brazen maiden lifting her skirts to show off her expensive silk under-petticoat. She had been careened—cleaned and scraped of weeds and barnacles. Tiola smiled again: fresh-washed laundry, bleached and starched and left to dry in the sun. Ships looked so forlorn, so vulnerable, when they were not as they should be—riding proud under full sail upon a white-crested sea. *Sea Witch*, Jesamiah's beloved vessel. Did he know that she was nigh on repaired?

Three people were walking arm in arm across the garden heading towards the beach and the little boat used for ferrying across the water. Carter, Pamela and Rue. Ah, so she had not dreamt it; her brother had been here. When Jesamiah came home the other two planned to marry, although Tiola was uncertain whether that was wise, for Rue was a sailor, he would find it hard to give up the sea. As would Jesamiah if ever she asked it of him. Yet Pamela and Rue would make a fine couple and the future was their life, their choice.

The two men dragged the boat through the mud to where the river was deep enough to float it. Climbing in, they dipped the oars and pushed off. On the grassy bank, her shawl gathered around her shoulders, Pamela waved as they rowed across the estuary. Tiola watched a while then closed her eyes. She was tired, her energy had been spent on controlling the pain, now, all she wanted was to sleep.

CHAPTER EIGHT
Bristol

Typical. Jennings did not come, and Jesamiah desperately wanted to talk to him; the man was too damned unreliable! Strictly speaking, Jesamiah wanted to talk to John Benson, not Henry Jennings, but it was an odds-on wager that Benson had scurried back to Devon with young Thomas on the fastest coach.

He gathered the flimsy blanket around his shoulders, trying to get warm. The bed was as hard as a rock, and as cold. He wanted to know about *Sea Witch*. Was she repairable? Was she afloat, salvageable? And Benson might know of Tiola. That was the thought niggling at him. If John Benson could travel from Appledore to Bristol, why was Tiola not here as well?

The gaol's lamps had been extinguished two hours ago, but the noise of muttered talk, coughing, belching and farting of restless men in the other cells had not entirely ceased. At least Jesamiah had the luxury of a cell to himself. Courtesy of Jennings' bribery. He rather wished he was with his crew; they could talk, exchange opinions, ideas—agree, disagree, argue.

But it seemed that this Bristol gaoler liked to keep his pockets lined with Jennings' silver and had flatly refused to move anyone anywhere. The irritating thing was that Jesamiah was wealthier than Jennings could ever hope to be, but Jennings had ready coin to slip secretly into a man's hand; Jesamiah did not. And very probably the reason Jesamiah craved companionship was the same reason the gaoler had refused it. Discussion between a captain and his crew could well consist of other things beyond general conversation. Plans to attempt escape, for instance.

Aside, would the crew talk to him? It was for him to make the decisions, be they good or bad, and although men like Finch, and old Jansy and Toby Turner—both now gone—might be cantankerous and crotchety old buggers, it was not their place to tell a captain what to do or not to do. Not that any of them ever took note of propriety and were always voicing their opinions, usually in opposition to his orders.

Jesamiah gave up trying to get warm, went to the piss bucket to relieve himself, the blanket still around his shoulders, then wandered to the window, his hands clamping around the bars. For the first time in a couple of weeks he noticed the stab of discomfort from his left hand. There was just enough light creeping under the door crack and from one lantern swaying in the wind out in the courtyard to see the scars and mess of his fingers. A Spanish cannon had ripped through *Sea Witch*'s upper deck, taking down rigging and sail, shattering bulwarks and spars. Killing and injuring good men. Toby Turner among the dead, Jesamiah one of the injured.

He looked at his hand. The skin across the knuckles was puckered and torn, obliterating the tattoo of Tiola's name and blasting away his little finger and half of the one next to it. Strange how he could still feel those missing digits, how, unless he looked, he forgot that they were no longer there.

'Cesca had tended him, seen to his injuries and the inevitable fever that had followed. 'Cesca had been there in Spain, had stopped him and his men from being hanged as spies and prisoners of war. Except at the time, officially, England and Spain had not been at war. But who gave a toss for treaties and platitudes between countries that were always at each other's throats?

What had 'Cesca been doing there? Where was she now? The questions flooded his thoughts, followed by a probable answer. Because it was Francesca Escudero who was the spy.

He looked again at his disfigured hand, felt again 'Cesca's gentle touch as she had cleaned and salved the torn mess. Tiola did not know he was disfigured. That there were bits missing. Huh, if he was to hang soon it would not matter, would it? Then another maudlin thought. Would having two fingers missing make a difference to his lovemaking? Oh, for heaven's sake! He stomped back to the wooden bench, lay down again. How would losing fingers affect sex? It wasn't as if he had lost his essential bits, was it!

Another rain squall. The courtyard lantern swung a little wilder as a gust of wind tramped against it, sending wild shadows dancing over the cell wall. The wick fluttered and went out. No moon to light the skies above the clouds. Darkness. Solitude.

"Tiola? I miss you. Want you so much." He spoke aloud, the sound of his own voice providing some, small, company. He turned over, fidgeted to get comfortable. He was cold outside and in. An ice feeling deep in the pit of his stomach that no blanket would cure. Only the love of a woman would chase the cold of grieving loneliness away.

Why had Tiola not come? There were only two reasons.

She could not. Or would not. If she would not it was because she no longer wanted him, had taken her love to another man's bed. And why would she do that? Simple. Because she knew he had been unfaithful to her. Oh, she might have guessed about his infidelity with 'Cesca last year, but she would not have been certain. How many times had they fucked in those woods that night? Two, three? Did it matter how many? They had shared the delights of sex and he had given her a child. She had denied it was his, but he knew she was lying. Just as Tiola always knew when he lied to her.

Tiola had been there—on that beach—that much he knew, but had she helped the child into the world? Had she held him, or her, for that short length of existence, trying to breathe life into the helpless little thing? All the while knowing who its father was? For Tiola would have known, Jesamiah had no doubt of that. And that was why she had not come to Bristol, had not even attempted to talk to him in their special, secret, mind-to-mind way.

She did not want him anymore. He didn't blame her.

Jesamiah rolled onto his other side, heaved the blanket over his head and drew his knees up to his chest. He stuffed his injured fist into his mouth, bit down on the scarred and scabbed knuckles, not wanting any of the men in the adjoining cells to hear his sob of despair. He had lost his ship and now, it seemed, had lost his woman as well.

* * *

As with everyone else in the courtroom, Jesamiah shuffled his backside round on his bench to see who it was making such an intrusive attempt at entering. Court had been called to order more than half of an hour since, although nothing further than yet more shuffling papers, mumbled legal jargon, and sour looks from Spider-legs Elton—as he had been swiftly and irreverently dubbed—had occurred.

The place was packed to capacity, the enticement of seeing a judge squawking like a girl at a mere spider had become more of a draw than the prospect of witnessing men hanging. John Benson's place, Jesamiah noticed as he had scanned the faces to see if he knew anyone beyond Jennings and Doone who might speak out for him, had been taken by a man who kept grinning and making annoying gallows motions. Crawford. He thought death by slow strangulation amusing, did he? More than once Jesamiah's fingers had strayed to the blue ribbons laced into his hair. If ever he got out of this situation, he would show Crawford his error of judgement by unthreading one and pulling it tight round the turd's scrawny neck.

Someone was making an Anne's Fan of a fuss at the courtroom door. Craning his head to see who it could be, Jesamiah gave up. It was not Tiola, so what did it matter? He caught a glimpse of someone standing at the back in the shadows, frowned as he returned attention to the judge. Why would a cowled monk be interested in a hanging trial? If the fellow hoped to save Jesamiah's soul he was going to be unlucky!

A part cheer, part growl of disapproval broke out, rippling from the back of the room to the front like a wave rolling in over the sea. A glide of silk rustling on the polished floor, the tap of shoes, and a whiff of lavender perfume. Dressed in a forest-green gown with a contrasting spring-green stomacher panel, both of which complemented her red hair and green eyes, the woman swept into the courtroom with all the stature of a royal barge being rowed in great state and ceremony up the

Thames to Hampton Court Palace. Francesca, Señora Escudero, looked more beautiful than Jesamiah had ever seen her, no sign of recent travail, of near drowning or childbirth, though a tight-laced corset would efficiently see to that last small fact.

She came to a halt before Elton's bench and sank into a reverent curtsey. When she rose, with elegance and grace, her head was held high and her direct gaze was locked into that of the outraged judge.

"Madam!" he stated with curt abruptness, "unless they stand accused before me, I do not permit the female sex within my court. Be gone with you, or do I order my bailiff to remove you and have you whipped for insolence?"

'Cesca was made of sterner stuff. "You may so do should you wish, my lord, but King George of Hanover would be most disapproving should he learn of it." With great solemnity she handed a small scroll of parchment to the court secretary. "Your Honour, I am here by the royal command of His Majesty. I am the Lady Frances Fitzroy, daughter of Lady Charlotte Fitzroy, acknowledged daughter of King Charles, second of that name, of England, and the Duchess of Cleveland, Lady Barbara Villiers." She smiled, indicated the scroll. "My credentials are within that letter of instruction."

Even Jesamiah gasped.

The frown of disapproval not leaving his face, Elton held out his hand for the parchment, broke the seal and read, his face turning a pale ash grey as he did so.

"May I politely suggest, my lord," 'Cesca said sweetly, with another, shallower curtsey, "that we retire to the privacy of your chambers to discuss this issue?"

For a full minute after Sir Abraham Elton and Lady Fitzroy —as 'Cesca was apparently now calling herself—had departed, the entire court sat in stunned silence. When the incredulous talk eventually erupted, the bailiff's gavel banging on his desk and his stentorian voice calling for silence was drowned to useless avail.

"Gaw' blimey. Who'd 'ave thought it!" Finch declared.

Jesamiah could not have put it more succinctly himself.

The sun shining with gentle spring warmth outside the courtroom was unexpected after days of frost alternating with rain. It was cold, another hard frost would soon claim the air, but everything sparkled and smelt fresh, even the streets that were usually fetid with rank detritus. Cheers tumbled upward to a clear blue sky as the courtroom emptied; Jesamiah was surprised, given the previous expectation of it all ending with the spectacle of the gallows. The crowd had been cheated of men kicking and squirming through their last moments of life, but it seemed this turn of events had proven as exciting. It was not an everyday occurrence here in Bristol, he supposed, that a ship's crew walked free from court. How often did a trial end with the judge announcing in a few terse words; "There is insufficient evidence for this trial. Case dismissed."

The crew were almost dancing as they descended the steps from the courthouse, slapping each other on the back, whooping their pleasure, tossing hats into the air and shaking hands with anyone and everyone. Jennings' and Sir Ailie Doone's faces looked as if they had been searching for pebbles and found pearls, their triumphant grins as wide as the Atlantic Ocean.

"We are off to the 'Trow!" Jennings called to Jesamiah above the noise. "Drinks for you and your crew; and I will secure you a room—and a..." He was about to say 'whore', but Francesca Escudero was standing at Jesamiah's side. Jennings grinned. Acorne already had a woman far classier than any street doxy.

Interpreting the grin as exultation at the verdict, Jesamiah waved an acknowledgement, and grasped 'Cesca's elbow to steady her as she was jostled by the crowd. He shifted the grip to clasp her upper arm, shouted in her ear; "All right, madam. Are you going to be good enough to tell me what the fok this is all about?"

She laughed at him, her eyes sparkling with elation. "I managed to free you, does the detail matter?"

"It does!" he retorted, attempting to steer her away into a side street, failing because the entrance was blocked by a group of women prancing a hearty jig. Bristol had gone mad.

The Llandoger Trow was a short walk away, on King Street to the far side of Queen's Square. Jesamiah was tempted to turn right around and march 'Cesca in the opposite direction but the pressing crowd made the idea impossible; they were wedged into the crush, Jesamiah's back and shoulders beginning to ache with all the patting and thumping.

"I ain't a bloody horse!" he growled at one man who was overenthusiastically slapping his back. He recoiled as a woman planted her mouth firmly on his for a kiss. She smelt of gin, urine and breast milk. He pushed her away when her hand groped at his crotch. Sheltering 'Cesca from the worst of the crush, he managed to steer her towards an alley and hastily ducked down it.

"Not the most pleasant of places," 'Cesca said, wrinkling her nose at the stench. "Bristol is not exactly comely where aroma is concerned, is it?"

"Few ports are, especially when they are as big as this one."

They passed a warehouse with doors locked firmly and a man sitting on a stool cradling an old matchlock musket that had seen better days. He stood as they approached, brandished the weapon.

"What you want 'ere?"

"Nothing, nothing!" Jesamiah responded, making it clear they were merely passing through. He indicated his hip, showing he had no sword. "I carry no weapons, we are taking a shortcut, that's all."

"To where? This backwater ope don't go nowhere worth goin' to."

"Llandoger Trow."

The man lowered the musket, sat down again. "Then ye'll be 'eadin' in tha contrary direction." He pointed to another alley to the right. "Take that'n, then the next."

Jesamiah nodded his thanks, felt in his pockets for a shilling and was dismayed to recall that not only did he have no weaponry, he had no money either.

'Cesca felt with her hand through the narrow pocket opening in her gown for the cloth poke bag hanging beneath. She found some coins, held them out to the man with a smile. "Thank you, sir. Most kind."

He propped the musket against the wall, leering, got to his feet again. "You can keep yer silver if'n I can 'ave a squeeze o' them plump titties o' yorn." He had moved closer, his hands outstretched ready to grasp at 'Cesca. Jesamiah was quicker.

He had noticed the dagger poked into the man's belt the moment he had first stood up, within a heartbeat it was in Jesamiah's hand and at the man's throat.

"Now then, mate, you have got the rare opportunity to make an important decision. You can apologise to the lady and sit your arse down on that stool of yours, or you can take a journey to meet your maker. What is it t'be?"

The man glowered, weighing whether this fellow meant what he said or not, decided, when the blade pricked into his skin, that he did. "'Scuse me, missus, I meant no 'arm," he muttered.

It would do. Jesamiah grunted and, slipping the knife into his own belt, offered 'Cesca his arm and walked off without a backward glance. A few yards up the alley he uncurled 'Cesca's hand and, removing the coins, put them into his coat pocket. "I feel somewhat poor without a single penny to my name," he said.

"I would lend you more, my dear, but alas, those were the only coins I have at this precise moment. I am now the penniless one."

"Well, then, I will have to play the part of Robin Hood and relieve old Henry Jennings of 'is silver, won't I?"

* * *

The Llandoger Trow's timber-beamed gables soared upward from the wash of people grabbing for tankards of ale that the landlord was attempting to serve as quickly as he could. Jennings was standing on a table trying to calm everyone, shouting that he had meant drinks for the crew of the *Sea Witch* not the entire town—an exaggeration, but there were a lot of people here Jesamiah did not recognise. A rotten egg flew through the air, caught Jennings squarely on the chin. Laughter rippled, joined enthusiastically by Jesamiah.

'Cesca was concerned, however. "Jesamiah, should we not help the poor man out of his predicament?"

"What, and spoil the fun? Don't think so." Then Jesamiah saw Crawford punching and elbowing his way towards Jennings, intent on clearing the unwelcome crowd. Jesamiah watched as he picked on a couple of the crew, nodded satisfaction as Skylark responded with a threatening dagger.

"Do the bastard," Jesamiah muttered, but Skylark, mindful of the penalty for murder, pushed Crawford out of the way and sat down again.

"We will find somewhere more congenial," Jesamiah said to 'Cesca, skirting around the tavern's open courtyard, one hand firmly grasping her forearm and pulling her along behind him, the other pushing and prodding revellers out of his way.

"Excuse me... Mind yer back... Shove over, mate..."

"But we need Captain Jennings. We have no money!" 'Cesca cried several times, each shout louder as Jesamiah had apparently not heard.

They came out into a cobbled side street, turned right and walked along beside some warehouses.

"God's breath, but something stinks in there!" 'Cesca said, wrinkling her nose at the stench emanating from within.

Jesamiah sniffed once. "Slaves. The poor buggers are probably packed in like herrings in a barrel. The dead and dying along with the barely alive."

"Slaves? Here?"

"Bristol's making its money on the trade. Merchants get a lucrative fat profit buying an' selling the black people. The savvy traders are avoiding Bristol now, though, shipping the wretched sods straight to the colonies. They work better in places like the Carolinas than do the indentured white Irish."

"Do you transport slaves?" she panted, trotting to keep up with his long stride.

"Nope. They stink the hold out."

"No other reason? No conscience of morality?"

He stopped, stared at her; said, "You say the oddest things, woman," and walked on, dragging her after him.

"I also said we have nothing to buy food or drink with!" 'Cesca snapped, pulling her hand free of his to retrieve her left shoe that had caught in the cobbles. "Slow down, I have lost my shoe!"

"Take the damn things off then," was all he growled.

"I will not! These stockings are silk."

"Take them off an' all."

"Do not be absurd."

With a sigh, Jesamiah stooped, hefted 'Cesca into his arms and carried her.

In alternative circumstances Francesca might have protested, but the shoes were not hers and too tight, were pinching. She looped her arms around his neck and kissed his cheek. "A thank you would be nice," she whispered.

"For what?"

"For saving your life?"

"Huh."

Dumping her none too gently onto a wooden bench in the centre of Queen's Square, he stood over her, arms folded, watching critically as she smoothed her gown and inspected a stain on the intricate embroidery of the stomacher panel.

"Well?" he said after a moment.

Francesca had not recalled that stain being there when she had squeezed into the gown. "Well what?"

"Are you going to explain that little burst of acting skill in the courtroom or not? You once told me your mother was a nobody from nowhere, and you ran away to become an actress. You met with a dashing Spaniard, married him and became a Don's wife. Was it all lies, then? I certainly don't believe the packet of cow shit you sold Elton."

'Cesca looked up at him, her head cocked on one side, patted the bench next to her. "Sit down, Jesamiah. Please."

As belligerent as ever, he remained standing.

"Please, Jes. Sit."

With an exaggerated sigh, he sat. Kept his arms folded.

"You know very well that my marriage was legitimate; you met my father-in-law. Alas, the poor man died not long after you left Hispaniola."

"Oh, I am sorry to hear that. He was a good man."

"Indeed he was, but he was in constant pain from the torture he had suffered and I do not begrudge him being free of it all. Except…"

"Except?"

"His passing has left me homeless and penniless. I need money."

Jesamiah grinned; who didn't?

"I came to England for a reason," 'Cesca snapped, irritated by his determination to not take her seriously. "To get what I am owed. Most of the information I gave to Judge Elton is correct, although the letter itself is a forgery, I grant, but he will never discover that fact. It was composed by Robert Harley, who is titled Earl of Oxford and Earl Mortimer. He is the political spymaster for the government. My controller. These clothes belong to his wife."

If he was supposed to look impressed Jesamiah did not respond as required.

"Robert is in ill health since a recent disagreement with Parliament and the old Queen Anne. He retired from government, but he still, secretly, handles the reins of political intrigue and, preferable to George of Hanover, supports the return of James Stuart."

"This despite his public opposition to Catholicism and the Jacobites?"

"Oh, so you have heard of him!"

"I read the news sheets when I can get them."

"He has a hope to improve the Country Party and to

oppose both the High Tories and Whigs, neither of whom serve England well. He deplores corruption and dishonesty."

"Yet you tell me he is spymaster? Is that not somewhat contradictory?"

'Cesca glowered at Jesamiah; he always had been too glib with answers. "Robert is a conscientious, highly educated man. He has negotiated many successful treaties and steered the union of England and Scotland to fruition. He passionately supports the arts and literature—without his patronage we would not have the likes of Swift, Pope, and Defoe."

"Not that we would be any worse off without them. Especially Defoe. Was Harley behind that ridiculous idea to smuggle an imposter king into England?"

'Cesca prudently made no answer.

They sat in silence a moment, listening to the raucous carousing from taverns and brothels in the side streets radiating from the higher quality buildings surrounding the square.

"What was the child?" Jesamiah asked quietly, reaching over to fold 'Cesca's hand within his own.

"A son," she whispered, tilting her head to rest it on his shoulder. "A boy. He was born dead."

Tenderly, with his thumb, he caressed her cheek. "And was he mine?"

She shook her head.

Leaning forward, Jesamiah kissed her. A kiss that he had intended to be given in chaste friendship, but her response of wanting was erotic, stirring his own passion. Reluctant, he eased her away.

"Are you hoping to woo me with kisses and an invitation to sex?" he asked cynically. "So soon after giving birth? Or is this the next act in your dramatic play?"

"It is no act, Jesamiah. I love you. I have done since that day we first met at the governor's palace on Hispaniola."

"You love me so much you cannot resist continuing with the lies," Jesamiah retorted with abrupt scorn. "What purpose is all this serving, 'Cesca? To lure me into the scheme Jennings wants me to accept? To bail you all out of the armpit-high pile of dung you find yourselves in?" The anger increased; he stood, waving his arms about, almost shouting. "Between you, you feed me lie after lie. The Duchess of Cleveland's granddaughter? That clodpoll tosspot aboard my ship the real king? The child was not my son? What do you take me for? The ship's idiot?"

There seemed to be some sort of argument overflowing from the direction of the Llandoger Trow. Finch, Skylark and four other crew members lurched into the square, followed by several townsfolk, some of whom Jesamiah recognised as courtroom gawpers.

"Bloody tavern's closed its doors, ain't it?" Finch grumbled as he came abreast of Jesamiah. "Landlord says we ain't good enough for his mutton tart whores. Bloody cheek! We're 'eadin' fer somewhere more afflable."

"Affable," Jesamiah corrected. Added, "The landlord being particular about his girls might be because you stink higher than a slaver's hold. I suggest, find yourselves a barber and a bath, then try somewhere more appropriate to your status—but where the girls do not carry the pox." He reached into his coat pocket and tossed a small bag that chinked with coins to Finch. "And do not spend it all at once."

The men grinned, cheered their thanks, but were cut short by Jesamiah saying with stern sincerity, "Do not get too drunk, I want to leave on tomorrow's tide for Devon, assuming I can find us a passage. Anyone not ready to come with me stays behind, savvy?"

Nodding that they understood, the men lurched away, arms around each other's shoulders, singing heartily.

"And from where," 'Cesca asked, "did you obtain that coin pouch?"

Grinning, Jesamiah took another from his pocket and hefted it in his palm. It clinked satisfyingly. "Similar place to where I got this one."

"Which was?"

"Some drunken revellers' pockets."

'Cesca frowned. "That is immoral stealing. You can be hanged for a thief."

"There's usually a pretty lady to rescue me from that fate, and I thought you'd realised by now, I ain't got no morals." Jesamiah grinned. "But I do, now, have some money!"

Despite her disapproval, 'Cesca laughed.

* * *

With interest in the hanging trial diminishing, Bristol was getting back about its business. The tide was not far short of being full in, and the docks along the river were busy with cargo being loaded or unloaded—a rush to be finished before the ebb; but even with the dock workers and merchants seeing to their trade the taverns were still brim-full. Several groups of men and women were drifting into the square, most on the wrong side of sober. A state of drunkenness was all too often the only way to make it through the day, inebriation the means of blotting out the wretchedness of the living conditions, the maggoty food, the violence, the disease... The list went on for most people in most towns. Life was short and harsh and had to, somehow, be endured.

Jesamiah watched one particular rowdy group; a drunk took a swipe at another and within moments a fight had broken out between six men, the women cheering them on.

Perhaps it would be safer back at the Llandoger Trow after all? Jesamiah thought. "Jennings has reserved me a room," he said aloud. "We can talk there without interruption—and I'm hungry." Add to that, he needed weapons, hoped Jennings had acquired some for him. He had brought nothing from *Sea Witch.* Abandoning ship, with a miscarrying Francesca, had been the priority, not arming himself. Of course, had he known the militia were there waiting for them... A nuisance to be here in Bristol without weaponry, but he could acquire new stuff. It would not be the first time he'd been in this position. And maybe John Benson or Rue had his possessions safe? If, as Jennings had suggested, *Sea Witch* had not been damaged too badly, and water had not ruined everything in his cabin. If, if, if!

"I would prefer to stay here," 'Cesca said, feeling uncertain of being alone with Jesamiah in a bedchamber where anything could happen. Where, despite not that long after giving birth a little bit of her, in her mind although not her body, rather wished something would.

Ignoring the protest, Jesamiah took hold of 'Cesca's hands, winced as a stab of pain reminded him of his injured fingers, but urged her to her feet, steered her in the opposite direction of the escalating fight, growing uglier as others, uninvited, joined in.

As they walked, sidestepping piles of horse dung and the occasional drunk, 'Cesca limping slightly from the pinching shoes, she expanded her innocence; "I have nothing to do with any plan of Jennings', Jesamiah. There was a disagreement at Nassau between him and Governor Woodes Rogers, Jennings left in a huff, but I know nothing more than that. For the other, King James could have saved many from bankruptcy, myself included. He promised that once crowned he would be helping many in dire need of financial aid."

"Ah, good old-fashioned bribery. Maybe I like the man after all. Pity he might be dead."

She stopped, stood with her hands on her hips as he continued walking. "I did not come to England because of King James, Henry Jennings or any other scheming bastard. I came because of my son!"

Turning back, Jesamiah retraced his steps, confused. "Your son? You have just told me he was born dead."

"Not your son, *my* son. My son by my Spanish husband. Leandro is nine years old, and I want to ensure he sees his tenth."

The memory clicked into place. She had a son on Hispaniola; presumably, the Spanish were not too happy with 'Cesca's involvement in the downfall of the island's previous governor. Not that his death had been her doing, Jesamiah had been the sole cause—he had personally blown the governor's ship to pieces. With Don Damián on board.

"As much as I would like to be of help, darlin', I have no idea what I can do about it. Take him somewhere, hide him. Stop this meddling in lost-cause political affairs and become the homemaker mother you are supposed to be." He encouraged her to keep walking—the fight seemed to be following in their wake. "Could your Spanish friends not have assisted you?"

Her response was terse. "Why do you think I was there, in Spain, Jesamiah? Antonio Calderón was most helpful, but it was not enough. I do not want my son and I to be forever running and hiding."

Jesamiah could see the sense in that. "So, who is this barnacle threatening you both?" He held up one finger as a caution. "But mark this, do not get me involved in killing him. I have no interest in your, Jennings', Calderón's, Doone's or this Harvey person's political intrigues!"

"Harley. And it is nothing to do with politics or intrigue, it is to do with my son's life—and mine."

All she received as reply was a sceptical grunt.

"I made enquiries while I was in Spain. All I could discover is that there is a list of names of people who are to be eliminated."

Jesamiah rolled his eyes. "Lists? We've 'ad all this before, if I recall. You personally told me that a list of traitors was a false ruse to flush out Winnard Doone. So, what sort of fanciful list is this one? In my experience, most of them ain't worth the scraps of paper they're writ on. Go fetch your son, find somewhere quiet to live, stay clear of men like Harley and Doone, and you will be fine. Trust me."

"Your name is also on it."

"Darlin', my name is on lots of lists!" Jesamiah laughed. "They usually relate to cuckolded husbands or the hangman's noose. Probably on a few fatherless brats' lists as well." As he said that, a vague thought regarding something 'Cesca had recently said tapped at his mind, but it slipped away.

'Cesca stamped her foot in frustration. "Be serious. If you cannot be concerned for my safekeeping, then at least be considerate for my son!"

"I am being serious. Being wanted for hanging or to be beaten up for swivin' someone's wife or virgin daughter is a very serious matter."

Closing her eyes a moment, taking a deep breath—fighting the urge to slap him—'Cesca tried again. "Please, Jesamiah, I am worried sick about this. I have travelled all the way to England—with child—because of it." She did not add *lost the baby because of it*, but the words hung there, heavy and precarious, like a badly placed cannon ball resting on its brass monkey.

Relenting, Jesamiah kissed her cheek. "I'm listening. Reluctantly, but I'm listening."

The fear and frustration were clear as 'Cesca fought down her anguish. "If I knew who was threatening me, I would do something about it."

Jesamiah puffed his cheeks. "So why, then? Can you answer me that one?"

Spreading her hands, sighing, 'Cesca shrugged. "Take your pick of reasons. I have been a spy for England for many years. Along the way I have upset a lot of people." She attempted a smile, "Though most of the blame is set at Francis Chesham's feet, and fortunately the connection between him and me is unknown, even, I might add, to Harley. He never knew that I was also Chesham. No one alive knows, apart from yourself, that is." She raised an eyebrow, questioning his integrity.

"No one will hear of it from me," Jesamiah answered. "Maybe someone wants you to spill the secret of his identity? Jennings seemed to think Chesham was still alive, he said something about he'd sent warning of that armada attempt?"

"Oh? When?"

Jesamiah shrugged, "Dunno, can't recall. Couple of months ago?"

'Cesca laughed, the sound pleasant. She had a lovely laugh. "Chesham did send word, but well before he 'died'." She linked her arm through Jesamiah's and they began walking slowly away from the increasing noise of the rabble, 'Cesca steadfastly ignoring the discomfort of her shoes.

"No," she said with finality, "all this has to be something else. Harley is dying. He is fond of his drink and the drink is killing him. Or at least, something is." She paused while several people, yelling and shouting, pushed past. "Do you remember that box I had? The one from the nunnery with the diamonds in it?"

Jesamiah nodded. Remembered it very well. Black ebony, about five inches long, three deep, four wide. The carvings on it had been exquisite, if somewhat macabre; the face of a man with scimitar fangs inlaid with ivory. Delicate, thin-cut slivers of what could only be sapphires had formed the eyes. For all that this was obviously a depiction of the Devil, the creature was most wondrously beautiful. "The one we were attacked for? The one that one of the attackers ran off with? The one that had a king's ransom of Russian diamonds hidden beneath a lead gold-painted crucifix?"

She nodded, had to smile. "How did you know it was lead?"

"Wrong weight. I assumed those fellows were after the diamonds?"

"The ones you pocketed?"

"You had a share of them, madam."

'Cesca gave a small nod, acknowledging the truth. "Alas, they were few and their value has long been spent, but no, those men wanted the box. It is worth more than twice that many precious gems. I suspect someone is somewhat annoyed that I managed to retrieve it from them, and subsequently kept it."

Jesamiah waved one hand, flippantly. "So hand it over and be done with this."

"I do not have it with me."

"Where is it, then?"

"I hid it. I want to use it as a bargaining tool to find out who wants it enough to put me and my son in this position."

"Ah. Is that wise?"

"No, but a message came from Harley ordering me to come to England because, as I said, he is dying. There are things—secret things—that he wants me to see to, with it was a second addendum message reminding me to bring the box. This one was not from Harley, although it was meant to look like it was; the code had discrepancies which he would never had made. A lot of people want that casket box because it is supposed to prolong life." Her voice quivered with a mixture of anger and sadness.

Lengthening his stride, Francesca hobbling to keep up, Jesamiah said, "So it could be Harley himself who wants it?"

"Maybe—please slow down. Ailie Doone wants it, but perhaps so does Jennings—he is in financial difficulties. Or maybe your wife threatens me, wanting you back?"

"Tiola's not like that," Jesamiah snapped, annoyed at the suggestion and quickening his pace, not slowing it.

More than two dozen men were now brawling, a few women as well, settling old scores rubbed by old jealousies, their cat screeching shrill. An excited audience was gathering, the added shouting of enthusiastic encouragement and placing bets on winners and losers adding to the overall noise. Instead of altering course to remain in the wider thoroughfare, the fight had squeezed into the narrower cobbled street that led to the Llandoger Trow.

Jesamiah glimpsed the burly doorkeeper coming forward, cudgel in hand, to break the fracas up before it came too close to the tavern. Hesitating, he was in half a mind to assist him, in the mood for a fight that he had a chance of winning, but 'Cesca would be in danger out here and his priority was to keep her safe.

"Let's get inside," he shouted, steering Francesca forwards. They managed a few yards but the fight was upon them, enraged and inebriated men beating the hell out of each other; hair pulling and cat-scratching women clawing at rival whores and mistresses. Thinking quickly, Jesamiah swung 'Cesca towards the wall and stood in front of her, his back outward, protecting her from the crush and unguarded punches.

"Where did you hide it?" he asked.

"What?"

"I said," he shouted into her ear, "where did you hide the box?"

Someone lurched into him, hitting him with a solid thump in the small of his back. 'Cesca gasped, her eyes widening, and, grasping the lapels of Jesamiah's coat, swung him around, hurling him hard against the wall. He cried out as his elbow jarred against the solid brick, put his other arm out to grasp 'Cesca who was falling, held her upright a moment, then as she sank to her knees, went down with her, held her close.

The crowd had passed by, spilling into the inn's open courtyard, where, abandoning their drinks, various patrons were joining the affray. Vaguely, Jesamiah was aware that the monk he had noticed in court was among the crush.

"You all right, darlin'?"

'Cesca's head was against his chest, his arms around her. She nodded.

"What you want to put yourself in danger for, you daft woman?" Heard Jennings shouting for calm above the receding crowd heading onward up King Street.

"'Cesca?" Jesamiah pushed her away from him in an attempt to help her sit up. "'Cesca? You'll ruin that soddin' gown if you sit there." He moved his hand to brush hair away from her face, left a trail of blood. "What the...? Where...?" Blood covered his hands; he wiped his fingers on his shirt, turned 'Cesca over, saw the blood soaking through her gown looking black and evil as it seeped into the green silk. He let go of her, she toppled towards the wall and he promptly vomited.

Jennings was there, kneeling also, looking to see where all the blood puddling the cobbles was coming from. "My God! She's been stabbed!"

Embarrassed at his reaction, Jesamiah swallowed more bile and, cradling her with one arm, clamped his other hand over the raw, bloodied hole that was in the woman's side; pressed hard.

Her head on his shoulder, her eyes fluttered open and she smiled up at him, with an effort of movement, touched her palm to his cheek. "Your wife is a lucky woman," she said in a hoarse whisper, "I am so envious of her." Her breathing was becoming laboured. "See my son safe, Jesamiah. Please, see Leandro safe."

Blood dribbled from her mouth, her words fading. "Promise me?" She looked direct into his eyes, looked deep, as far as his soul; repeated, "Promise me."

"I promise." Unable to speak further, Jesamiah gently kissed her lips and looked, helpless, at Jennings who was looking into the dispersing crowd. No one else seemed bothered about a dying woman sprawled on the cobbles soaked in her own blood. Most of them were too drunk to notice.

"Harley's going to be so bloody cross about this," Jennings said quietly, then, louder, pointing. "It was that monk fellow, Jes, lad—look! There he goes!"

"See to her," Jesamiah said quickly, getting to his feet and shouldering the few stragglers aside, ran. The monk saw him. Ran faster.

CHAPTER NINE
Instow, Devon

Tiola opened her eyes to see the sky beyond the window ablaze with a glorious sunset. She lay watching, entranced, as the colours flared across the scatter of clouds turning them gold, pink, red and then purple before fading into dark grey. She drifted asleep, woke again to see a star-studded night. After all the rain, it had been pleasant to admire the sunset, as pleasant to see the stars, those thousands of distant suns sparkling against the ebony-black vault of the night sky. Her ankle and arm ached; she vaguely recalled a soft-spoken doctor tending her, was grateful to him for he had been skilled at his job, a fact which would help explain why her broken ankle would be healing quickly. Even then, it would be difficult, she would have to be very careful.

Had anyone told Jesamiah that she was injured, she wondered? Then another thought, what if he was no longer alive to be told? What if he had already been hanged without her knowing, without her there? Her heart rate bounced in a moment of panic. She had not been there to help or save him!

~ *Jesamiah?* ~ Tentative, she nudged the silent call into

her mind, met with a fluctuating blankness. He was not dead, surely she would know if he was dead?

Suddenly thirsty, Tiola glanced at the table beside the bed, lit by only the flickering fire. She reached for the glass of elderflower cordial, but even that small movement hurt. Her pearl earrings next to the glass, the only jewellery she regularly wore, aside from her wedding band.

The wonder of nature, she thought. *Something so exquisite formed from a tiny granule of sand caught within an oyster shell.* She stared at the fire. Someone must have been in recently for the logs were not yet charred through. She frowned, trying not to fall asleep again, to think clearly. There had been something else... A necklace? Her hand went to her throat—and horror hit her with all the force of a wielded poleaxe! That pendant! How could she have been so utterly stupid? What idiocy had clouded her senses? Why in all the names of everything sensible had she not taken notice of what that black pendant was? Idiot! Idiot! *Idiot!*

Her only—somewhat feeble—excuse, she had been concentrating on Señora Escudero, on the difficulties of afterbirth and the grief of losing a newborn child. Oh, who was she fooling? She had been angry, furious with Jesamiah for betraying her with his infidelity. The child had been the result of him rutting with that woman—his bastard child, and she had been glad that it had not survived the birth, which in turn had shocked her and brought in yet another wave of anger to add to the guilt and grief. No child deserved to be tainted because of the frailties of father or mother, and there should never be that gloat of jealous gladness when a child or its mother did not survive birth.

"Take this token," Francesca had said. *"It is jet, it will see you safe."*

Was that how whoever had given it to her in the first place had ensured the señora would wear it? By telling her it was a blessed relic to ward off evil? Or had she been fully aware of what it was, and had taken the first opportunity to be rid of it? No, that was uncharitable; if she had wanted that she could merely have dropped it overboard. Francesca had erroneously thought it would keep her safe, and had genuinely given it to Tiola—except Tiola had no need of amulets. But Francesca would not have been aware of that.

Tiola's prevailing question was why had she blithely accepted the wretched thing, knowing it would inhibit her ability to transfer thoughts? All these days worrying why she could not mind-speak to Jesamiah—and she had completely overlooked the pendant! Jet? It was not jet, but bone. Black, sacred bone. Bone similar to those wretched caskets, except this bone had been from the cremated remains of warrior heroes who had died fighting for the honour of the Night-Walkers. They were used as very effective tracking devices. The carbonated bone gave off a residue of sound, unheard by human—or a Wising Woman's—ear. High pitched so that only the Night-Walkers could hear. But Francesca Escudero would not have known that either. Again the thought; or had she? Few humans knew exactly what the Night-Walkers were and what they could do. What if Francesca Escudero was one of those few?

The door opened, accompanied by the familiar aroma of cheroot tobacco. Maha'dun.

"Ah! You are awake. Good. Did you call?" He came into the room, frowned. "Has no one been in to close the shutters and light the lamps? Never mind, I will do it. Mistress Pamela is preparing chicken broth for you. I have strict orders that if you were awake I was to fetch it and to ensure you ate it all." He had his back to Tiola, was carefully folding the shutters over the draughty window, shutting out the night.

"I will have the broth in a moment."

"But Mistress Pamela said..."

"In a moment, Maha'dun. Not now."

The Night-Walker glanced at her. He knew Tiola well, she rarely spoke with such abrupt sharpness. He latched the shutters and, playing for time, took a spill from the box on the mantelpiece. He lit it from the fire and went from candle-sconce to candle-sconce, bringing light into the room. The last one flaring into life, he considered smoking a cheroot, thought better of it and, blowing out the spill, tossed it into the grate. He turned to face Tiola with an apologetic smile, his palms pressed together made a bow of obedience.

"Have I offended you, Lady? Have I inadvertently done something amiss?"

Solemnly Tiola touched her throat. "Who gave the bone-stone to the English woman with the Spanish name?"

Maha'dun shrugged. Not *her* again! "I know no such woman."

"That you might not, but you know *of* her. You watched me help her through her labour on the night of that storm."

He pursed his lips, shook his head, feigning innocence.

"Very well, I will ask a different question. Were you meant to have followed the English woman with the Spanish name?"

Preferring not to answer, he shrugged again.

"It must have been bewildering for you to have discovered that I had the pendant. Did you not realise you were trailing the wrong woman?"

Maha'dun remained silent, wishing he could slink away but his pride kept him standing beside the mantelpiece.

"Who gave it to her, and why do you need to track her?"

Regretting his decision not to smoke, Maha'dun slipped his hand into his pocket to feel the cold silver of his cheroot case. He forced his hand to withdraw; now was not the time for she would see his hand shaking and his desperate need for tobacco.

"Lady, I do not know this woman you speak of, aside from that she was here with you for a few days. But she has gone now, and she was, is, no concern of mine."

"Was Cara'mina angry that you got things wrong, Maha'dun? Is that why you bear the marks of scratches and blows to your face?"

Maha'dun made no answer. The silence stretched out. Tiola could hear the longcase clock in the hall downstairs, *tick... tock, tick...tock,* its rhythm like that of a slow heartbeat. Maha'dun stared, unblinking, at her; his chin high, head erect, then he lowered his gaze and admitted the truth.

"I was told to watch for a certain ship coming in, and that on the ship would be a woman I had to follow. I would know her by the call of the bone-stone."

He could not resist the temptation of tobacco any longer. Removing the case and taking out a cheroot he lit it; that first satisfying pull of nicotine steadying his rising anxiety. "We waited many nights for the ship, but it did not come."

"We?"

"Winnard Doone and his men." Maha'dun shoved one hand into a pocket, uneasy at remembering. "Doone was angry with me because I had not followed his orders to stay with his son, Ascham—but the idiot had gone aboard a ship and I was too frightened to go with him."

Tiola cocked her head to one side, questioning. "What ship?"

"Before you came here. The one going to Spain. Winnard Doone did not want it to get there. He arranged for it to be lured ashore to where the militia was waiting. I tried to get Ascham away safely but I was captured as well." He shuddered, it had been horrible, horrible, in that Barnstaple Gaol. "Winnard was furious when he discovered that Ascham had disobeyed him and had been aboard. Someone broke us out of gaol, though. Winnard's men. Then it happened all over again when that second boat was wrecked. I was with Winnard then as well. I thought the other men hiding in the dunes were all his men. I did not know they were militia. I had not expected that ship to come in like it did—hurled upward by the rage of the water!" He took his hand from his pocket, wiped his palm around his face, remembering. As with all Night-Walkers, he avoided boats and the sea as much as possible; such wrecks and disasters served to confirm an inherent fear. "And then the men hiding sprang up, shouting and firing guns, and there was a lot of fighting and killing. The smell of blood in my nostrils! A few men attacked me, I dispatched them, then took advantage of the night to get away."

He paused, contemplated what more to say; decided to continue with the truth. "I was confused by something else as well..." He went across to a chair, sat, and inhaled the sweetness of his cheroot. There had been the scent of a bone-box on the man who had helped them escape from Barnstaple, but too frightened, too desperate for freedom, Maha'dun had ignored the matter. Regretted doing so ever since. That same man was there that night... But then, how could he have killed the one who had set him free? He waved cheroot smoke away from his face, dismissing the memory with the same gesture.

"I located the call of the bone-stone but did not expect to see you there. I was too far away to discover who was wearing it, you or the other woman, and..." He started talking faster, the unsettling memory of that evening returning with unease to his mind; "And then Ailie Doone's son, Winnard, was killed, and men were being bound by ropes and marched away. I did not know that one of them was your husband. I was frightened of being captured. I ran."

The thought of being restrained terrified Maha'dun. He shivered, the memories of that night haunting him, along with other similar nights where the fear had taken hold of his soul and strangled all sense from his brain.

"I sheltered throughout the next day beneath a pile of musty bracken in an old shepherd's hut. When night eventually fell, I returned to the shore. The ship was afloat but deserted. The bone-stone called to me from the far side of the estuary, and I found that you wore it." His eyes were pleading for her to believe him. "I do not know who gave it to this woman you speak of. I do not know her. If it was hers, as you say, why did you have it?"

Why indeed!

Tiola persisted. "Someone in Spain must have given it to her. Who, Maha'dun? Why?"

Becoming further agitated, he stood, walked around the room, shook his head, genuinely did not know.

Seeing his distress, Tiola relented. He did not know, she would have to accept it.

"Where is the bone-stone now?" she asked. "Does Cara'mina have it?"

Again he shook his head. He felt in his pocket, withdrew the chain and pendant. "She did not take it with her, I have it."

Ah, Tiola thought, *its closeness explains why I can still not converse using my thoughts.* It had been responsible for clouding her mind that night on the beach and after. Had muddled her mind enough to make her forget she wore it. Such things were dangerous, to her and to others.

"Throw it into the fire, Maha'dun. Destroy it."

He gaped at her, astounded; stammered, "But I, I cannot! It is not mine, it belongs to the High-Class. It is sacred, it is forbidden for me to harm it."

"It is also forbidden for the Night-Walkers to inhibit the Craft of the Wising Women. Because I have touched and worn it, the call of that bone-stone is suppressing some of my abilities. It is causing me great discomfort."

Maha'dun hesitated, swallowed hard. What to do? If he obeyed the witch-woman he would be disobeying the honour of his own kind. But then, his own kind had once abandoned him, left him to drown at the bottom of a lake. It had been Tiola who had saved him, not the Night-Walkers. Not Cara'mina, who had watched and laughed, who, he suspected, had betrayed him to those men in the first place. He took a deep breath and with a swift decision hurled the pendant into the fire. It burnt quickly with an uprush of bright red and orange flame, which turned yellow, green and blue, then diminished and was gone, gone to ash, lost among the glowing embers already in the hearth.

Tiola clutched, one-handed, at a stab of intense pain shooting through her head, a cry of tearing grief wrenching from her. Her own desperate voice mingling with Jesamiah's howl of despair.

~ *Jesamiah?* ~ She called out to him, her captured mind set free, extreme anxiety plunging through her thoughts instead. ~ *Jesamiah! There is death, I can feel it! What is wrong?* ~ Then she slammed her thoughts shut as someone else touched her mind.

Tiola gazed at the Night-Walker who was standing eyes wide, mouth open. *Fishified*, Jesamiah would have said.

Shielding herself from Jesamiah, she said in her mind, ~

You heard my thought, Maha'dun? ~

Elation swept over his face, pure, utter joy. "I thought you were angry with me, I thought you no longer desired my friendship and love, I thought..." His face crumpled into something resembling a child upset at the loss of a favourite toy. He raised his chin, defiance replacing the chagrin. He stared at her, blew a perfect blue smoke ring into the air and discarded the remaining stub by throwing it into the fire.

"I followed you discreetly all those nights and days, never daring to go nearer or make my presence known. You would have mind-called me had you wanted me. But you did not. Not until up on the moors did you summon me, with spoken words, to your side." He looked down at his feet. Looked up again, defying his own cowardice. "I assumed you were angry with me after our last parting. You never said goodbye, you just left. I did not hear your mind-thoughts again. Until a few nights ago I had not seen your face, nor heard your dear voice in my head for many, so many years."

~ Distance of place and time separated us, Maha'dun. I have had several reincarnations since we last met. And then the bone-stone set a barrier between us. Now it is destroyed the wall has been breached. ~

He smiled, came to sit on the edge of the bed, joy coursing through him. "I thought I had lost you forever. Those days when we were together were the happiest of my long life."

~ I would never have been parted from you for eternity, my dear, but circumstances, until now, did not permit our paths to cross. ~ She took his hand, held it lightly within her own, said with actual words, not as mind-speak: "I would like to know how you have the ability to hear my mind-words, though, Maha'dun. No one outside of my own kind has ever been able to do so." *Except Jesamiah,* she thought in a deep,

shielded area that Maha'dun would not be able to access, both being facts that she wanted to keep secret.

His sapphire eyes were similar to the melting gaze of a dog staring with devoted, unconditional love at his mistress. "I heard you in my mind from that night you saved me from drowning, from when you pulled me out of the lake and breathed life into my lungs. I remember looking up into your eyes and feeling as if I had been reborn. A night of horror and fear and pain became something exquisite. I have never, since then, seen the moon so bright, smelt the jasmine so strong, felt the grass so soft. You were, so, so beautiful. I assumed you had breathed your thoughts into me with that gift of life and then, after, through the love you gave me."

Unintentionally, she possibly had, but everything that had happened on those long-ago nights had been unintentional.

~ Can I trust you, Maha'dun? ~

He looked up sharply, hurt. "Implicitly. Need you so ask?"

~ Enough to do anything I request? ~

"Yes."

Again she contained her words, she needed to confirm he could not hear her concealed thoughts: *~ Enough to kill Cara'mina? ~*

Puzzled, he spread his hands. "Ask me anything, Lady, and I will serve you if what you ask is within my ability to perform."

Openly, she said, "Can you speak your words into my head, Maha'dun?"

He gazed at her astonished. "How would I be able to do that? I have none of the magick you possess."

"Apart from the ability to hear my mind-words, and the magic of exquisite sexual pleasuring?"

He laughed at that, "The first is an ability you gave to me, and the second is what I do, is it not?"

Tiola relaxed, it appeared this was a one-way transference, unlike her unity with Jesamiah, who could communicate back. All the same, and more worrying, did Cara'mina know of it?

~ Does Cara'mina know you can hear my mind-words, Maha'dun? ~

He rose from the bed, tossed two logs onto the fire sending sparks shooting up the chimney. Disgust infused his expression, his nose wrinkling, lip curling. "Of course she does not! Why would I tell that bitch of something so precious? Why would I tell anyone? This thing I share with you, and you alone." Disappointment again suffused his features. "Or, at least, I thought it was something I alone shared with you." His lip trembled. "You called to your husband. Does he, also, hear you?" Hurt was there along with jealousy.

Tiola nodded. "I will not lie to you, my friend. *Ais*, I have unity with my husband. For, as with you, he is very, very dear to me."

"He can hear your thoughts?"

"*Ais*. Yes."

"You breathed the gift of thoughts into him, as you did with me?"

Again, "*Ais*. Yes." It was not quite the truth, that was too simple an explanation, but it was near enough.

She held her breath, willing Maha'dun not to ask that other question, for she did not want to lie: *Can he mindspeak to you?* But he did not ask; the possibility that Jesamiah—anyone—could do so had never occurred to him.

"I have one last question, Maha'dun. Where is Cara'mina?"

He shook his head. "I do not know. Do not care. Far from here, I hope. I hate the bitch."

Tiola repeated her question. "Where is she, Maha'dun? It is important that I know."

"Very important?"

"Very, very important."

He paused, wondering whether he should answer or not. He had a good idea where Cara'mina was, and why she was there, but how could he lie to Tiola? "I think she went north."

With great difficulty Tiola kept the anxiety from her voice. "To Bristol?"

"I am not especially concerned about where Cara'mina is, as long as she is a long way away from me." He felt for his cheroots.

Not suppressing her rising panic, Tiola stated, "If she is in Bristol, Maha'dun, my husband, Captain Jesamiah Acorne, is in mortal danger from her." Was now the time to test the depth of Maha'dun's loyalty and love? A test that could end in death for at least one of the players in this nightmare game of violent murder?

"You must follow her as swiftly as you can, Maha'dun. I entrust to you the life of my husband. If he dies, so shall I die, and my death will be as if it were at the doing of your own hand."

Chapter Ten
Bristol

The cobbled Bristol streets were hard on the feet and legs, especially where running was concerned. Jesamiah leant his back against a brick wall, closed his eyes. He was tired and frustrated. All afternoon he had traipsed up and down looking for that bastard monk—if he was a monk, Jesamiah had started doubting that fact soon into the search. Twice he had glimpsed the hooded figure, once in a crowded tavern, the second time at the far end of an alley, although now, standing here utterly exhausted with evening setting in, he was questioning the sightings. Why would a murderer disguise himself to kill someone, then remain in the vicinity while still wearing the disguise? Maybe all his assumptions had been mistaken, maybe his mind was playing tricks? Maybe. Maybe, maybe... He groaned, realised he needed a drink and something to eat. It had been a long day. A long week.

This whole runaround was pointless, this monk-murderer who stabbed women was probably long gone by now. Yet, if this was the case, why this inner certainty that he was still nearby? If it had been him that Jesamiah saw, why had monk-man been waiting beside a window in that tavern? If he was supposed to be hiding, trying to lose himself, a window was not a good place to be. And that alley? Jesamiah had been walking along its narrow cobbled length, uncertain of the shadows, had spun round, the feeling of being watched sharp in his brain—he hated people coming up behind him, a legacy of when his half-brother had bullied him in childhood. The monk had been there, behind him. Watching. Or at least, Jesamiah thought he had. He'd only caught a glimpse of someone moving aside quickly—by the time he had hurried back along the alley into the wider street at the end there was no one to resemble even vaguely a monk-clad, tall person—only the street girls, drunken sailors and ragged children.

Using the wall to push himself into motion, Jesamiah limped along the quay, barely bothering to dodge the effluent and rotting detritus. His lower back ached where the monk had punched him. It must have been a heavy blow for it to ache so; probably there would be a bruise. He rubbed at the spot, felt what seemed to be a rip in his coat. He took it off, inspected the damage. A tear about one inch long. Investigating further he found a matching rip on his waistcoat. He could not strip off here in the street, but his linen shirt had stuck to his skin, and when he tugged at it he felt fresh blood trickle down over his hip. No punch then. It had been a knife, badly used, doing little damage beyond bruising and nicking the skin. Either this monk-man was not a skilled killer or luck had been on Jesamiah's side. The luck had run against 'Cesca instead.

Replacing his waistcoat and coat, Jesamiah walked on, feeling the soreness even more now he knew the cause. Another realisation: 'Cesca had seen the knife, that was why she had swung him around, had taken the blade herself. She had given her life to save his. For a moment he was overwhelmed by grief. It hurt, deep inside, hurt like his guts were being ripped out. He leant against the wall, eyes closed, head back, allowing the pain to sweep through him. Then he unclenched his fists, took several deep breaths. Another uneasy thought tormented him. Was this monk-figure trying to find him, not the other way around? Waiting for an opportunity to strike again? The thought was disturbing, but made very clear sense.

The tide would be full out in another hour or so, and when the flood came back in again the beleaguered vessels settling on their keels as the water ebbed would be afloat again. The taverns would empty of dockside workers and fill with shore-leave crew; the endless round of load, unload, high tide, low tide, would start again.

Bristol never slept. For every store—be it chandler, sail-maker, rope-maker, candle-maker, baker, leather-worker, ironmonger—there were three taverns and two brothels. For every keg of rum or brandy, or bottle of gin—for every whore—there were four or five men. The River Avon on a flood tide was crowded with ships and boats of all sizes and shapes, the town as crowded with the men and their families who worked on the sea and river or by it. The bustle was never quiet. The stench never sweet.

Turning into the nearest doorway, the Crowing Cock, which seemed by the sign hanging above to refer to an engorged intimate part of a man's anatomy, not a plump cockerel, Jesamiah changed his mind. Did he really want to get drunk in a squalid brothel? Then he turned back again. Why not? What else was there to do?

With the flat of his hand he pushed the door open, from the corner of his eye caught sight of movement from behind a man-high pile of barrels at the end of the nearest wharf. He spun on his heel, drew his knife and, grim-jawed, walked forward, body slightly bent, eyes and mind focused. Stepping quickly, he rounded the barrels, dagger ready to thrust or protect—to find no one. He could have sworn—sworn—a brown-clad figure had been there!

"I can't do this!" he cried aloud, sliding the dagger back through his belt. "'Cesca, how can I take revenge when I cannot find the heap of shit who killed you?" Despair took him as he slithered down the side of the barrels to squat on his heels in the mire gathered at their base. He removed his hat, ran a hand through his hair; this was all hopeless, utterly hopeless.

~ Jesamiah? Jesamiah! What is wrong? ~

His head shot up, eyes wide, breath catching in his throat. *~ Tiola! Tiola darlin', where've you been? I thought I heard you earlier, but you went away, I thought I'd imagined it. ~*

~ I have been unwell. What is wrong, Jesamiah? I am drenched in your grief, what is it? ~

Jesamiah felt her concern, the image of a hangman's noose flickering into his mind. God's teeth, did she think he was about to swing?

~ I am fine, sweetheart. The trial's over, we were acquitted, all of us. There's no need to worry. ~

Her relief flooded his senses, to be replaced by a different anxiety.

~ There is something wrong, Jesamiah. What is troubling you? Tell me, I might be able to help. ~

He stood, and began walking in the direction of King Street and the Llandoger Trow.

~ I'm tired, that's all. ~ Then he realised what she had said, blurted, worried, *~ What do you mean 'unwell'? ~*

~ I have sent a messenger, an old friend of mine, to tell you... ~ Jesamiah heard her casual laugh. *~ I cannot say more*

in this private way of ours, my luvver, for how will you explain knowing of these things to others? ~

Suspecting there was more here that he ought to know, despite her reasoning, he was about to ask questions but the street lamplighter appeared from a side alley and almost cannoned into him. The man cursed, raised his fist to cuff Jesamiah aside.

Jesamiah swiftly bowed, gabbled, "M'apologies, mate, I weren't lookin' where I were goin'."

"Thy shud open thy bleedin' eyes then!"

"Quite right. Again, I apologise." Digging into his pocket, Jesamiah found a coin and handed it to the surly old goat, touched his hat and walked on. The lampers were notorious for their bad tempers and bruising fists, the last thing Jesamiah wanted was an unnecessary fight. It was the necessary one he was looking for.

~ Jesamiah? ~

~ Still here. I'm looking for someone. Someone who... ~ He paused, uncertain whether he should divulge the truth, but then, Tiola always knew when he was lying or hiding something from her.

~ 'Cesca is dead, ~ he said flatly. *~ Someone killed her. ~*

He heard Tiola gasp and a private thought scurried into the back of his mind. *'Cesca thought you would kill her, Tiola. Because I made love to her, gave her a child. Was she right?* He had learned long ago to keep some things secret from their exchanged mind-talk. Hastily he damped this one down but he had not been quick enough.

~ I remind you, my husband, that unless for reason of defence, I cannot cause deliberate harm to any human. ~ It was gentle, but still a rebuke.

He coughed to hide the ensuing pause, changed tack.

~ *The blade was meant for me.* ~ There, he had confirmed it, had faced the thing that had been tormenting him all day. That knife had been intended for him, not her.

~ *Do you know who it was?* ~

~ *No. He was dressed as a monk. I did not see his face.* ~

Tiola went very quiet, he felt her stillness and again thoughts entered his mind; *Did you know the killer? Did you send him?* Gods, this was ridiculous! Tiola would never harm anyone, except in dire need... But would disposing of her husband's lover count as need? No! Tiola was never petty or jealous. Or was she?

~ *'Cesca asked me to take care of her son. I'm sorry, I know this is going to be hard for you, but I promised I would.* ~

Still that grave quietness, and then Tiola said, gently into his mind as if she were touching him with the lightest caress, ~ *The boy died, Jesamiah. I could do nothing to save him. He was born too early into this world.* ~

Jesamiah was about to correct her but King Street was ahead, and welcoming light shone from the windows beneath the three gables of the Llandoger Trow. The entertainment of the fight was forgotten—even the murder of a woman causing little concern where violent death was a common thing. Singing drifted from the open doors and there were several groups of men and women sitting at the tables on the cobbled yard outside. Two people had appeared—Jennings and another man. Jesamiah raised his hand in acknowledgement as Henry saw him and waved him forward. Jesamiah scowled when he recognised the other man to be Crawford. What was he doing here?

~ *I have company, sweetheart. When will this old friend get here?* ~

~ Tomorrow evening. ~
~ Then we will talk tomorrow. ~

* * *

Henry Jennings hurried towards Jesamiah, his arm outstretched to take his sleeve as soon as he came within reach. "Jes, lad! We've been looking for you all over, where've ye been, eh? I were about to send Crawford out to take another look." He gave Jesamiah a small chastising shake, "Come inside, there's a bottle of brandy waiting and a mutton stew. A room, too."

Irritated, Jesamiah brushed his clasping hand off. "What has happened to Señora Escudero? Where is her body?"

Crawford answered. "She is lying in St Mary Redcliffe Church up yonder. The clergy are taking care of her. Burial's tomorrow morning."

Ignoring the man, Jesamiah spoke to Jennings. "She was Catholic. She ought to have a Catholic funeral."

"Aye, aye, I know, lad, but things have already been arranged."

"Who by?"

Jennings patted Jesamiah's shoulder, part in sympathy, part as encouragement to get him inside the tavern. "Someone has taken care of everything, but can we talk about it later? After we have eaten."

"Someone? Who?" Jesamiah persisted. "Tell me Henry, I need to know."

"Robert Harley. He is—was—a prominent politician; Speaker of the House, Lord High Treasurer. Queen Anne's prime ministerial advisor, he..."

"Aye, all very interesting. I know who he is. What about

'Cesca?"

"He knew her well. Let's leave it at that, eh, lad?"

"No. Let's not. Are there monks at this church?" Jesamiah spoke direct to Crawford, a lazy troublemaker he had never liked, even as an unwelcome crew member aboard *Sea Witch*. And now that Jesamiah had discovered the rat was also one of Jennings' bone-scut spies, the dislike deepened.

The feeling had always been mutual. "Monks? Shouldn't think so. They're confined to monasteries, ain't they, not churches." Crawford laughed, an unpleasant licentious sound; "I'd have thought you'd be more interested in asking after nuns! All them innocent virgins begging for you to do them."

Jesamiah punched hard and fast, direct into the belly. Crawford dropped like a rock tipped into a well, lay gasping on the cobbles.

Jennings tutted a rebuke and, taking a firmer grip, steered Jesamiah away. No one else seemed to have noticed the brawl. "You are tired and angry, lad. Come and eat, have a drink. Rest."

"I don't need rest, I need to find the bastard who murdered a very special lady."

"We will."

"Don't lie to me, Jennings, you've no intention of doing anything. Why was 'Cesca here? What was she up to? What are you and Doone up to?"

Jennings took Jesamiah's shoulder in an attempt to steer him inside. "My dear fellow, we are up to nothing at all. You are distraught, tired. Come and eat, have a drink."

Angry, Jesamiah shook him off. "Where does this Harley reside? 'Cesca went to see him. Where is he?"

Rubbing his whiskered chin, shaking his head, Jennings frowned. "My apologies, lad, I cannot help you."

"He's the head one, the big wig—he controls all the spies who scuttle around under rocks gathering secrets and gossip for the government. He controls you."

Again Jennings shook his head. "I know nothing of spies or spying. I am a Jacobite, but I am not a spy. Let us eat, talk inside, eh?"

"You're lying. You are involved in this rat's nest nonsense as much as 'Cesca was."

"No, I..."

Chopping the air with his open hand, Jesamiah cut Jennings short. "Oh, forget it. You are not goin' t' help me. Fine, but don't ever ask me to help you with anything ever again. I need weapons, a pistol and cutlass. Where do I get 'em?"

"All in good time, lad, all in good time."

"Now, Henry!"

Jennings sighed, relented. "Crawford, go find suitable arms for Captain Acorne." Indicating Jesamiah's bloodstained shirt, added, "Clean clothes, too. Nothing with crawlers in, mind. Make sure you check."

Sitting on the cobbles, his hand cradling his sore belly, Crawford scowled. "An' what am I supposed to purchase weaponry and such with, may I ask?"

Jesamiah guessed that the son of a bitch had good gold secreted about his person, but he was not looking for charity, nor did he relish being beholden to a man like Crawford. He tossed one of the heavier pouches from his pocket towards Crawford. It clattered to the ground with a satisfying chink. "Use that. I want what's left back."

Touching his forelock, Crawford grabbed the pouch and scrabbled to his feet. His lazy smile as he scuttled off conveyed there would be very little to return.

Already annoyed, Jesamiah was not especially delighted to discover Sir Ailie Doone sitting at a table in a discreet corner inside the tavern. Jennings seated himself next to the self-titled Earl of Exmoor and indicated for Jesamiah to seat himself also. Tossing his hat onto the bench, Jesamiah sat opposite the two men and poured himself a large brandy from the bottle on the table. His question of why that rusty-gut pimp Crawford was involved going unanswered by either of the men, he concentrated on ordering and devouring two servings of mutton stew and a good deal of the brandy. The varied conversations between Jennings and Doone occasionally gained his attention but he refused to be drawn or appear interested.

On the whole, the talk consisted of Jennings bemoaning the spreading gossip that James Stuart was dead. Rumour varied between drowned with the foundered Spanish fleet, or shot on a headland in Devon. Did tittle-tattle matter? Fat George had his arse square on the throne and it was unlikely that the bumbling attempts of incompetent Jacobite rebels would remove him. By all accounts, the real James Stuart was a feeble and sickly weakling—Jesamiah was still unsure whether that man aboard his ship had been an imposter or not; one way or the other he did not particularly care.

"King James," Jennings remarked, feigning casualness, "is betrothed by proxy to a Polish princess. Unfortunately, the lady has been captured en route to their marriage nuptials. Until an act of procreation can be fulfilled, no legitimate heir will be produced. Which is why she has been imprisoned by our opponents, of course." He paused, expecting a reaction from Jesamiah. Nothing was forthcoming.

He doggedly continued his tale of woe. "She is being held at Innsbruck Castle, but we are certain we can get her out." He leant across the table, lowered his voice. "All we need is a skilled captain and a fast ship to take her safely to James in Spain." Added, "Assuming he *is* safe in Spain."

Ah! So this was what they needed him for! Clearly that weakling booby aboard *Sea Witch* had indeed been a decoy. The one sentence Jesamiah uttered was droll. "Last I 'eard, Innsbruck was in Austria which, if I recall, don't 'ave no 'arbours or coast to its name."

"We can get her to the Italian coast. Would that suit you, Acorne?" Doone interjected, clearly irritated by the ongoing lack of cooperation or respect.

"Don't care where you can get her Princess-ship too, your problems ain't nothing t'do with me. An' I'm keepin' it that way." Jesamiah stood and stepped out from the bench he had been sitting on, tossed a handful of coins onto the table and picked up the almost empty bottle of brandy along with his hat.

"If you will excuse me, I will leave you both to your scheming. I want nothin' t'do with it, I have my own things to sort. I'm t'bed."

An hour later, in need of relieving himself, Jesamiah's irritable mood was increased when he discovered no chamber pot in the room. On hands and knees searching under the bed, he moved too quickly and banged his head on the wooden frame. Cursing and rubbing a sore scalp, he got to his feet and stalked to the door, shouting for Finch, remembering as he pressed the door latch that he was not in his cabin aboard ship.

"You want something?" Crawford was sitting cross-legged on the wooden floor on the opposite side of the corridor, a pistol resting on his lap; beside him, a pile of clothes, a cutlass and hanger, and a pistol with powder and cartridge pouch. In his hand, a bottle of cheap rum.

"What are you doing here?" Jesamiah snapped.

"Waitin' t'give you these things you wanted me t'get, and I've orders t'make sure no one cuts your bleedin' throat in your sleep," Crawford answered, a slight drawl giving away that he was on the wrong side of sober. "An' before you says it, I am not p'tic'lar 'bout nannying you neither."

Jesamiah stared at him with hostility, collected up the weaponry and clothes, then ordered, "Fetch me a pisspot. I ain't got one."

Returning the hostile glower, Crawford got slowly to his feet, tucked his pistol through his belt and, belching loudly, wobbled slightly as he ambled off down the corridor towards the adjoining room. The door was locked, he tried the next.

Not waiting, Jesamiah returned to his room and, after shutting the door, dumped the stuff in his arms on the bed. He considered using the washing jug and laver to pee into, opened the window instead and pissed his stream of urine out into the night, not caring if anyone happened to be in the street below.

The door opened, closed. "You don't need this then?"

"Shove it somewhere, then shove yourself off."

Placing the china utensil under the bed, Crawford joined Jesamiah at the window and, reaching for the catch, took a good look outside before securely closing it. "Can't do that, Cap'n. Doone's payin' me for this job, you will just 'ave to put up with me." He raised the bottle still in his hand in a gestured toast, and then finished the contents.

Jesamiah pointed to the armchair beside the fireplace. It was not a warm spot as the fire had not been lit, but, relenting, he scooped one of the blankets from the bed and tossed it at Crawford.

"If you snore," he threatened, "you will follow my piss out that window."

* * *

He did snore. Loud and deep. Not that Jesamiah could sleep anyway. Usually he dropped off the moment he closed his eyes, but tonight he lay on his back staring up at the moon shadows sweeping into the room and illuminating the cobwebs that hung from the beamed ceiling and faded drapes of the tester bed. He was cold, the temperature had dropped, and he wished he had not given Crawford that blanket. His thoughts were too busy for sleep; they were running around and around like an eddying whirlpool. He had thought of trying to mind-speak to Tiola, but it was almost midnight and she would probably not be awake, and anyway, he had never been able to initiate their private conversations. What was that she had said about being unwell? He had not asked for details, he should have done. Nor had he clarified that 'Cesca had an elder son. What had she said? *See my son safe.* What had she meant by safe? And where was he? Still on Hispaniola? Somewhere else? Where? The thoughts, restless and relentless.

A particularly loud snore rippled from Crawford's open mouth.

"Bugger this," Jesamiah muttered as he swung from the bed and felt for his boots that he had dumped on the floor. He was fully dressed, apart from boots, hat, and weapons. By the glow of moonlight he buckled on the new cutlass and powder belt. Tucked his pistol through it. Crawford's pistol had fallen to the floor, Jesamiah picked it up. Either too drunk or lazy, the idiot had not kept it in good condition. Nor was it loaded—not much use for reliable on-watch duty! Inspecting the weapon, Jesamiah wrinkled his nose in disgust. The thing was clogged with powder residue which was eroding the inside of the barrel and the lock mechanism. The gun was useless, more like to harm the person firing it than the person it was aimed at. Angry at the slovenliness, Jesamiah aimed the gun at Crawford's temple and, flicking the hammer home with his thumb, pulled the trigger.

"Bang!" he muttered as the only response was a dull click. Even the flint was damaged. Too drunk to hear, the man did not wake.

"You're dead, mate," Jesamiah added heading for the door and tossing the useless weapon onto the side table. He paused, changed his mind. What if Jennings came by, wanting another go at browbeating him into helping with whatever stupid plan those two bleeders were hatching? Something was needed to put them off the scent a while... Ah!

As carefully as if lifting a sleeping child, Jesamiah manoeuvred Crawford onto the bed, and manipulating his arms removed his coat then put his own discarded, bloodstained, shirt on him. He covered the dead-to-the-world man with blankets; anyone peering in would assume the occupant was Jesamiah sound asleep—and it was quite likely that Crawford would sleep on for several hours. He had not even roused. Leaving one lamp to give a low glow, enough to silhouette the shape in the bed, Jesamiah doused the other two and slipped out of the door.

With lamps sparingly placed along the corridor, and three guttered out, the hall outside was in semi-darkness. With his sailor's night vision, Jesamiah walked quickly to the stairs and hurried down, stopped short at the last bend as he saw that Doone and Jennings were still seated at their table deep in discussion. The tavern was almost empty, sensible men had gone to their own or their whore's beds, he would not be able to slip out unseen. As he stood there pondering what to do, a woman came in and went up to the bar. Dressed impeccably in expensive silk and brocade, she had sleek, glossy black hair, pale skin, and was exceedingly beautiful. The sort of woman whom, not that many months ago, Jesamiah would have considered coercing into bed. The landlord pointed towards the stairs, the woman turning in the same direction. Jesamiah hastily ducked out of sight and retraced his steps upward. There had been a servants' door at the far end of the corridor if he had not been mistaken... Yes! He could hear the tap of shoes and the swish of silk as the woman came up the main stairs; he opened the door, went through and ran downward, his palm firm against the wall to guide him as the only light filtered up from the kitchens below.

He emerged into a scullery to find a startled maid in a state of half undress staring with alarm at him. Her lacework cap, plain overgown and petticoat lay across a truckle bed beside a finer set of clothes more suited to her night-time occupation. She stood there in corset and stockings, her auburn hair, unbound from its daytime confinement, cascading over her shoulders and partially exposed breasts. Another woman Jesamiah would not, in the past, have thought twice about bedding. She opened her mouth to scream; Jesamiah moved quickly, grasped her hair, planted his mouth over hers and kissed her. His free hand felt in his pocket for some coins and, smiling as he pulled away from her, poked them down into her cleavage.

"I am just nippin' out for some fresh air," he said. "Don't worry yourself, Sir Ailie Doone, the Earl of Exmoor, and Captain Henry Jennings are taking care of m'bill."

He touched his hat, gave her another kiss and was off, hurrying through the kitchen. He flicked the bolts of the courtyard door open and was out and away, walking quickly along the dark cobbled streets towards the River Avon.

It occurred to him that he had not attempted to find a ship to take him and what remained of his crew to Devon, but how could he leave now? He had unfinished business to take care of here in Bristol.

* * *

Perhaps the church of St Mary Redcliffe was not the most suitable place, comfort-wise, to spend the night, but given the circumstances, Jesamiah welcomed the quiet solitude. Not being a particularly religious man, he was usually uneasy within holy buildings; his mother had been Catholic, his father Protestant, and with the division of belief the whole concept of worshipping God and Sunday church had been set aside during his childhood. Uncertain of the protocol and the ever-present feeling of being watched from on high, Jesamiah had hesitantly entered through an unlocked side door. A few candles had provided pools of light on the altar, near the doorway, and at strategic points along the nave, casting long shadows that flickered and danced on the stone walls and tiled floor. The rest of the church, with its echoing emptiness and high, vaulted roof, remained in secluded darkness. The air was heavy with stale incense and the musty smell peculiar to old buildings. There appeared to be no one else around. Jesamiah considered calling out, but the revered silence of the place almost seemed to forbid the disrespect of such a violation.

Lifting a candle from a wall sconce with one hand, Jesamiah removed his hat with the other and walked slowly into the church, uncomfortably aware of the loud echo his boots made. He stopped at a black tombstone set in the floor, holding the candle so he could read the inscribed name of its occupant.

Sir William Penn. A Bristol-born man, remembered by many as a sailor, for it was he who had drawn up the first code of battle tactics for the navy. In indebted lieu of which, King Charles II had handed American land to Penn's son. Jesamiah recalled a childhood tutor telling him how Penn Junior had named the new colony Pennsylvania, and had, as a Quaker, been an early champion of democracy and religious freedom. Under his direction, Philadelphia had been developed. Jesamiah had never been there. Perhaps he could take Tiola, set up home together, become Quakers and champion democracy and freedom of choice? As if he could see himself doing that!

He turned towards the south transept, the great south window partially illuminated by a three-pronged candelabra. Within the stained glass the ship *Matthew*, captained by the Italian John Cabot who sailed the Atlantic Ocean in 1497 and discovered parts of the North Americas and Canada. Jesamiah laughed. All these history lesson memories buzzing like busy bees through his mind. He felt as if he were a professional traveller taking in the sights. The Grand Tour of Bristol! And yes, there, tucked into a corner, the main feature that he had come to see. Two tall candles, the width of his wrist, burnt in sconces at the head and foot of a coffin laid across two trestles.

He walked slowly, holding his candle high, suddenly afraid at what he might see, but the coffin lid was closed, nailed shut. He considered prising it open and, setting the candle down, looked around for something to use, slid the dagger from his belt and fitted the blade into the gap between lid and coffin. Halted. What was he doing? What right had he to disturb her sleep? And would it not be best to remember her as he had known her, vibrant in life, not cold in death? He folded his arms on the coffin, rested his head on them.

"Oh, 'Cesca; what am I to do? It should be me lying in

there, not you."

He remained there a while, mind numb, but his back and legs were aching, he needed to sit down. He settled himself into a pew, tightened his coat around his body, folded his arms, and stared at the coffin. They could have done better for her than that cheap thing made of shabby wood. A poor man's box, not something fitting for the woman Francesca was—whether she had told the truth about her lineage or not. Should he make a fuss come morning? Demand something more elegant? To what purpose? It was merely a box, something in which to bury the dead. At sea, a corpse did not even have that. Sewn into a canvas shroud, weighted with a cannon ball, a body went over the side into the deep to await corruption and Judgement Day when the angels sang and trumpets blared. The way he was feeling this night, that event could not come soon enough.

A door opened way up the nave and a priest came in, did something near the altar and went away again, not noticing Jesamiah down at the southern end of the church. Did they have vespers, or nones—or whatever it was called—in these places? Matins? That was an early morning service surely? Strange how he could recall those history lessons, but had only vague memories of his mother muttering her private prayers whenever Father had been away. She had knelt at a little carved walnut table on which she had placed a candle, a crucifix, and a statuette of the Virgin Mary. Sitting there, in the quiet solitude, Jesamiah could picture her clearly, her black hair covered by a lace veil, her head bowed in prayer. She had not had Catholic prayers spoken over her grave, as 'Cesca would not. Did it matter? Tiola would know. She would probably say it did not. He hoped so. Hoped it didn't.

In the silence, where only the soft light of a few candles glowed, the tears began to fall. Tears for the memory of his mother, for the crew, friends he had lost. Jansy, Isiah—the others. For Tiola who he wanted so badly to be with him through this night of lonely vigil. For 'Cesca. A woman he knew not a single truth about, yet who he could have loved had life been different. And for words that he suddenly remembered. The words she had said before she had died.

"Not your son, my son. My son by my Spanish husband."

Not *your* son, my son... *Your* son...

That boy born dead in the sea. She had lied then, throughout. Had lied until that one slip had imparted the truth. He had—*had*—fathered her child.

And now they were both dead, mother and son. Two people he could have, would have, loved. And that other son of hers, perhaps he too was dead. Did he care about this other boy? This Leandro?

Sitting there, with the cold of the stone walls and the damp from the river mist seeping into his bones, Jesamiah realised that he did care. For her sake, for 'Cesca, he did care. And he had promised.

How could he explain all this to Tiola? Would she care as much? That was a different matter completely, one he would have to think about soon. But not yet.

* * *

Jennings was asleep. Being roughly and rudely awakened by Jesamiah before the sky had turned properly light beyond the somewhat grimed window was not his idea of how a morning should start.

"What the...? Acorne! What the bloody hell are you doing in my bedchamber? Are you drunk? Get you gone this instant!" Scrabbling at his nightcap to ensure his short, very grizzled hair was securely covered, Jennings sat up abruptly and shoved Jesamiah's hand from his shoulder. "Desist shaking me, man! How dare you burst in here, uninvited, un..."

"Shut up, Henry. Crawford's dead. His corpse is in my bed."

"What?"

Partially amused that there was another mound beneath the covers showing the top of a woman's tousled head of hair, Jesamiah tossed a log onto the pile of ash in the grate and half-heartedly poked at it in the hope there might be some stirring of life and heat. The old dog still had it in him then!

"You heard. His throat has been cut."

Indicating that Jesamiah was to hand him his clothes, Jennings swung his legs from the bed. "Who would want to kill Crawford? He is no one important."

Jesamiah could think of one or two people, himself at the head of the list, but judiciously remained silent.

With half the bed growing cold, the girl roused. Not realising they were not alone, she sat up and, squeaking a small scream when she saw Jesamiah, hastily covered her nakedness.

"I want it made clear, here and now, that I did not kill him," Jesamiah said. "He was drunk and asleep, soundly snoring, but alive and well when I left around elevenish last night." He nodded towards the girl, "as she will confirm, won't you, darlin'?"

Frowning, Jennings paused with his breeches halfway over his backside. He glowered at the girl; had she been spreading her favours elsewhere? "How so?"

The girl blushed. "He came through the kitchens, sir, shortly afore I were summon'd up 'ere."

"That is not confirmation of your innocence, Acorne. You could have returned any time, or killed him first."

Jesamiah ignored the implication, said, "Crawford is well dead. He's as solid and cold as stone. Whoever killed him did it hours ago. And my bet is on the woman who came up the stairs shortly before I left. Ask the landlord, he sent her up."

Pulling on his stockings and boots, Jennings tucked the long flap of his shirt through his legs and finished fastening his breeches. Jesamiah handed him a waistcoat, then, solemnly, the wig draped over the back of the chair.

"It is also my opinion that this woman could have been the same person who murdered Señora Escudero."

His cravat partially tied, Jennings turned to gape at Jesamiah. "Woman? Francesca? You said you saw a monk."

Jesamiah nodded. "I have been thinking about it all night. It was a woman who killed Crawford, an' I'm wonderin' if the same woman murdered 'Cesca." He paused, gathering his thoughts. Looking Jennings direct in the eye, said quietly, "And both times, the blade was meant for me."

Jennings frowned, not convinced. "How can you be certain?"

"Coming for me? I think I am right; 'Cesca said my name was on an executioner's list. For the other," shaking his head, Jesamiah admitted he could not be sure. "Both tall, both wore gloves. That is all I've got. Could have been a young man, maybe?"

"You did not see this monk's face?"

Again, Jesamiah shook his head. "No, he—she—wore a scarf wound around the face, but it weren't a monk. Just someone wearing a monk's habit."

Several hours later Jesamiah finally got to eat some breakfast and enjoy a cup of steaming black coffee. Various authorities had come and gone. Various questions had been snapped and snarled at Jesamiah, with the answers plainly not being believed but the evidence, on this occasion, in his favour. The kitchen maid confirmed he had left the tavern. The landlord confirmed that a woman had asked for Captain Acorne by name—he'd had no reason not to direct her upstairs, assuming she was an expected whore plying her trade.

So, twice now an assassin had attempted to kill Jesamiah. He ate his breakfast, drank the coffee and walked with Jennings, Doone and several men of the crew to a solemn funeral held in a cold and wind-tormented cemetery.

"This funeral is taking place in some haste, is it not?" Jesamiah had remarked to Jennings earlier in the day. "Should there not be an enquiry or something? The whys, wherefores, hows, ifs and buts?"

All he had received by way of reply was a pat on the shoulder and a not very convincing reassurance. "Things will be looked into, lad, but all in good time."

"Why not now, Henry? There's a bad smell here!"

"Captain Acorne," Ailie Doone had whispered, coming up behind him, "Francesca Escudero was a spy for our Jacobite cause. Do not ask further questions, for there are too many that will not be answered."

And that was that. 'Cesca was to be swept away like dust under a carpet.

A bleak day, a bleak service. Jesamiah recalled little of it, for his mind was as numb as his fingers and his dog-tired body. He was aware of a coffin—he had elbowed one of the pallbearers aside and insisted on carrying it. Recalled being surprised at how heavy it was. 'Cesca was not as small or slender as Tiola, but neither was she plump or big-boned. He vaguely remembered a mumbling priest and a hole in the ground, but could not place 'Cesca anywhere within the surreal events of the dull, grey morning. She would come breezing back into his world soon, creating mayhem in his life—and his breeches. It was wrong, he was a married man and he loved his wife—but he wanted 'Cesca. Wanted her so much...

There was no one Jesamiah did not know except the attendant priest and sexton. He had hoped that this illusive spymaster would be there, but supposed that high-ranking officials did not attend the funerals of the scum they controlled.

He again asked Doone for information, received nothing beyond a terse, "She supported our cause, that is all I know of her."

Jesamiah did not believe him. "You are here at her funeral?"

Doone had a simple answer: "Jennings asked me to come. As I am of the same faith as the deceased, Jennings thought my presence would comfort her departed soul."

Knowing, privately, that Jennings himself was Catholic, that excuse was plainly untrue. He could not very well say so, though. Instead Jesamiah asked a more pertinent question. "Do you know where her son is?"

"My dear fellow, I was not aware she had a son." About to turn away, and leave the gravediggers to their task of completing the burial, Doone paused, said, "Might I ask your interest in the lady? Was she perhaps an acquaintance of your wife?"

Jesamiah swallowed a corrosive answer—the question had been deliberately prying, said instead; "Do you know where the Earl of Oxford and Earl Mortimer is residing?"

Ailie Doone shook his head. "I have not heard of either of them."

Smiling indulgently—Doone knew exactly who he was talking about, but if he wanted to play silly-bugger games —"One person. A prominent politician, I believe. So prominent that as Earl of Exmoor you would be familiar with a fellow peer."

Doone's false smile remained fixed. "I suggest you ask Captain Jennings; your line of enquiry is more suited to his expertise." He touched his hat, walked away, his cane tapping on the flagstones as he left the churchyard. Jesamiah watched him go. If nothing else, he had Doone rattled. That was better than nothing.

CHAPTER ELEVEN

It took Jesamiah an hour to find where this illusive and secretive Earl was lodging. A futile effort, for when he reached the place, a footman informed him that his lordship had returned to London that very morning. It was a lie. There seemed to be all too many lies lurking in the filthy streets of Bristol these past few days. Jesamiah tried to insist, to force his way into the house, but was threatened by the footman and a supportive cohort with some unpleasant consequences should he persist.

Jesamiah gave up, turned away. No one was going to answer his questions. No one wanted to know. He had paid the Llandoger Trow landlord—via a loan from Jennings—for food and drink to honour the tradition of a wake, and a drink, a lot of drink, suddenly seemed a very good idea.

A person stood discreetly to the side of an upstairs window watching Jesamiah trudge away.

"Captain Acorne asks too many questions. He needs to be stopped before he blunders into places he should not be going."

Seated in the shadows within the room, Lord Harley smiled benignly at his companion. "On the contrary, if we can harness him, he could be most useful. He has an agile mind and knows how to use it. A most suitable replacement for Francis Chesham, do you not think?"

"It is a great pity we lost Chesham. He was good."

Harley's answer was droll: "And a great pity we no longer have my lady Francesca Escudero either. After Chesham, she was my best spy. Was that blade meant for Acorne or her?"

The person at the window shrugged. "How should I know? As you frequently remind me, you are the spymaster, not I."

Harley hrrmphed, finished his large glass of brandy. "Acorne's father was also one of my best spies, he trained Francesca, and possibly more than trained. But then he, in turn, was trained by the *very* best, his French mother, Arabella Béjart. Francesca's death has left us somewhat bereft; I am most disappointed by it. I will not be lenient with the perpetrator should I discover who it was."

"I understand Acorne shares a similar sentiment."

Harley got to his feet and joined the man at the window, watched Jesamiah disappear around the corner. "Jennings told me that Francesca, with her dying breath, asked our pirate friend to pledge her a promise."

"Indeed?" His companion raised an eyebrow.

"Mm. She asked him to see to her son's safety."

"I was not aware her son was in any danger."

Harley went back to the couch, seated himself with a loud sigh. "A pity Francesca is dead; I would very much have liked that casket she had possession of."

"As would several others, if the whispers can be believed."

"It is also a great pity she did not bring it here to Bristol. Could the son have it, do you suppose? Or Acorne? Alas, we do not know either beyond surmise, nor do we know where the boy is, or who killed her. Or why. We are, it seems, most short of information. And that is a situation I do not sit well alongside. I do trust," Harley's tone became harsh, "you had nothing to do with her death? Or that the intended victim was, indeed, Acorne himself?"

The man turned towards him in astonished innocence. It took a moment to swallow down indignant annoyance. "I have made no secret of my dislike of Acorne. I disapproved of your sanctioning his acquittal. It would have suited me well to have had the law hang him, but no, I know nothing of an attempt to kill him." Barely concealing his fading patience, he walked to a nearby sideboard and poured two generous measures of brandy. Handing one glass to Harley—even though he had consumed enough already—said, "Why did you not force the señora to tell you what we want to know in exchange for Acorne's release?"

Harley's retort was vicious. "There were other bargains I needed to make with her first; and do you think me such a fool? I agreed to save Acorne's life for the delivery of that casket! She agreed to fetch it, except some damned idiot managed to stab her in the back before we completed the deal. You want Acorne dead and I do not. I want him to work for me, and you do not. As I said, I need a replacement for Chesham. Acorne will suit me well."

"I disagree."

Harley swallowed his anger with the brandy. "Unfortunately, as you have already pointed out, sir, you are not Spymaster, I am. The lady hid that casket somewhere. I suspect it is with her son. Acorne can start in my employ by finding him, and it."

His companion laughed, sceptical. "And just why would he do that? Are your wits addling, Lord Spymaster?"

With extreme patience and talking slowly as if he were

explaining some complicated mathematical equation to a child, Harley said, "Acorne and Jennings believe the boy's life to be in danger—although I do not know why this is so. Henry was also fond of Francesca; I am not certain that, as with Acorne's father, the swiving old sod was not more than merely 'fond'. It is entirely possible her son is the bastard brat of either of them. I do know he is not of the Spanish husband's seed."

Harley's companion was not interested in paternity issues, nor was he convinced about the relevance of the casket. "I have heard these nonsense myths about the black boxes. They prolong life, they cure ills—it is all fairy tale."

"Then you would also have heard they are extremely rare and extremely valuable. Of course, I do not pay heed to the silly stories, but the king, our blessed most noble, intelligent, fart-arsed George of Hanover, who cannot speak a single word of English, does believe." He snorted, "The man cannot pronounce the 'Th' in London's great river, so those who grovel to him are now calling the *Thames*," he emphasised the *Tha*, "as the 'Tems'. What nonsense." He *hrrmphed* again. "But I too need to grovel, so I need this casket to give it to him as a gift. With it I can reclaim my lost power, buy my way back out of this damned back-room wilderness and return to running this godforsaken country as it should be run. God willing, I live long enough to do so."

"What of James Stuart?"

"What of him? It makes no difference to me, or you, what popinjay idiot sits on the throne."

"Do we know if he lives? He was supposed to have sailed with the Spanish fleet."

Harley leant back in his chair, belched, his stomach full of acid. "I heard yesterday eve. The fool man never even reached Spain. He is still somewhere in Italy as a guest of the pope. The fleet sailed without him."

"How fortuitous for him. Perhaps it is just as well your imposter is also dead."

Narrowing his gaze, Harley tossed another question; "Aye, perhaps it is. Did you shoot him as well?"

The other man placed a hand on his heart. "No, I did not. I was not even there!"

Harley waved the indignation aside. "You are too quick to defend your actions, my friend. Your enemies will never believe you. All this is as may be, but we must work with the tools we have got, and what we have is flatulent King George. What we have not got is the one thing that will buy us into his permanent favour."

Grudgingly, "Very well, I agree, but I do not see why Acorne need be involved."

Harley ignored the tone of disapproval. "Jennings is with Acorne, but he has dull wits for this sort of business. Aside, I have another task for him. I am ordering him back to Nassau—he will just have to sort out that damned silly quarrel he's had with Woodes Rogers. I could knock their bloody heads together at times. Call himself a governor? Rogers could not govern a dung heap without offending the worms within it. He should have soothed the situation and not let Jennings leave. He is too valuable as my ears and eyes—I need him back there."

"Forgive me, but is a backwater colony and a brothel-bound rum-stack of drunken pirates really so important? Why the devil are you concerning yourself with Nassau, Rogers and Jennings?"

Harley exhaled a patient sigh. "You are, for the most part, highly intelligent but at times you can be more dull-witted than that fool Rogers. Spain wants Nassau. It is a key harbour for the Bahamas. We also need to keep the pirates under control, for, if we do not, the revenue from the colonies will collapse, and anarchy will take precedence. The scum have, for the most part, taken advantage of the amnesty offered them—give Rogers his due, he is implementing that well, for while the dregs of the pirate world are partaking of Nassau's rum and its cunny-squint whores, they are not having a disastrous effect on our mercantile shipping. Another year like the last few and many of us will be ruined financially. We need the rum, the sugar and the tobacco here in England. We need to improve and expand the growing cotton trade. We do not want the wealth handed over to Spain or those bloody pirates!"

Harley's companion nodded; that all made sense. But he did not see why or where Acorne came into it. "Acorne? What role has he to play, then?"

"He knows the pirates; he is a pirate! Rogers will never be able to control them, Acorne will. Jennings too, that is why I have ordered him back."

Harley's companion laughed. "Ordered?"

"Bribery then. It cost me only a few acres of land. I gave him one of my Bahama estates. It is nigh on worthless, but he knows not that fact yet. Jennings will encourage Acorne to look for the boy and the box, and then invite him to Nassau. To fight pirates, you use a pirate. Acorne will suit very well."

"And you think you can trust him?"

"I do not trust him in the slightest. Which is why I want you to keep close eye on him. It will stick in your craw like a fish bone, but I want you to see he stays alive, finds me that casket, and..."

The other man made a dismissive, discourteous noise, "I have no taste for such a task, I..."

Harley hissed an annoyed growl. "I have no concern for what you do or do not like. Remember this, I am unwell, I am not in immediate danger of dying but if I do not rise to the surface of power soon, then neither do you. This is my—our—chance to take back what I, we, have lost and now that Francesca has been so inconveniently murdered, Acorne's assistance could well be the only key to opening the locked door that is keeping me, us, out. Acorne must be accompanied as close as a shadow. And you will be that shadow. If anyone gets in your way, dispatch them. Is that clear? Set your personal grudge against Acorne aside. I need him alive."

"And I want him dead."

"You have my word when Acorne is of no more use, you can be the one to finish him."

"And how long into the future will that be?"

Harley flapped his hand, "A few months, a year, who can say? But as long as he is useful to me, he will be as useful to you."

That was not a satisfactory answer. Harley's guest had no intention of traipsing around after a degenerate former pirate—and heaven forbid—going to sea with him! No. A flat no. He changed the subject.

"And how are you feeling now, sir? Your health issues have given us a bit of a scare, you know."

"I am not going to turn my feet up just yet."

"I am glad to hear it." *But that is not what your doctor implies,* he thought. *When you are gone, soon I trust, I will do things as I see fit. Especially now that Francesca bloody interfering Escudero is out of my way!*

Feigning giving ground, Harley's companion sat, capitulated to the spymaster's request—with no intention of complying. "It will not be easy to tame Acorne, you know."

"It will not, but I am optimistic that, while shadowing his every move, you will find the right rope to tie around his neck to tether him to us; the right lever to convince him to cooperate. I have every confidence in you, every confidence."

* * *

After several pints of ale, washed down with brandy and rum, the laughter at the Llandoger Trow had risen along with the lewd chatter. It all seemed insensitive. Beyond a few half-hearted toasts of 'may she rest in peace', there had been no mention of 'Cesca by name or memory. It was as if she had never existed. Perhaps she hadn't. Perhaps her varied disguises were all make-believe.

Jennings had been elsewhere, making arrangements for Crawford's burial. He slid onto the bench beside Jesamiah and helped himself to what was far greater than a simple tot of rum. He wiped his mouth with a kerchief. "Ah, that's better."

"It's not better for your gout," Jesamiah replied. "Where's Doone?"

Jennings poured more rum. "How should I know? I am not his gaoler, nor his molly boy."

They sat for a while in silence, the rowdiness around them growing louder as the free drink flowed. There would be fighting before long. Sick of it, and beyond exhaustion, Jesamiah informed Jennings that he was going to bed. It was only an hour after noon, but he could not remember when he had last slept.

"I will be using your bed," he stated. "Mine is soiled—and as for the bastard who soiled it, you can go to his burial on your own. I had no liking for Crawford in life, I ain't goin' t'start liking him in death. Even if he did die instead of me."

Chapter Twelve

"What are you doing here, scut?"

Maha'dun was a Night-Walker; his reactions did not include jumping with startled surprise, although on this occasion he very nearly did. Controlling his anxiety, he took another sip of the Cogniack brandy he held in his hand and, not looking round, answered, almost lazily, "Is it not obvious, Cara'mina? I am minding my own business while enjoying a drink and observing the company here present." He nodded towards a group of young sailors rapidly becoming over-inebriated in one corner of the Llandoger Trow tavern, their shouts of laughter and lewd jests clearly audible to even those without the Night-Walkers' heightened hearing ability.

"Those young men seem particularly delicious, do they not?" He grimaced. "Or at least, they would be if they did not stink so much. I have found sailors do not have a propensity to wash, either themselves or their clothes."

Ignoring his fastidiousness, Cara'mina leant closer and hissed in his ear, "Why are you here? How did you get here?"

Maha'dun took another mouthful of brandy, its fire-taste sliding easily down his throat, flooding him with courage. "I came in my carriage; how else would I travel? With Sir Ailie Doone here, I assumed I had no further reason to stay on the inhospitable dredge of land these humans call Exmoor, so I decided to join him and partake of a more civilised way of life for a few days. I was unaware that you also were here, Lady."

"You are a fool," Cara'mina snapped. "You have made a mess of things as you always do; you are useless to me. Go back to Europe, back to your usual lascivious stalking grounds."

"It seems to me," he drawled with unexpected bravado, "that the mess is yours, Lady. It was not I who made a mistake and killed the wrong person." He turned to look at her, his sapphire eyes meeting directly with her sea green. "You killed the woman we were supposed to question. She is not going to give us answers now, is she?"

Cara'mina's eyes narrowed with hatred. "I do not make mistakes." She changed the subject. "Doone is aware the English woman with the Spanish name knew where a casket is. You have failed me in this. You will make him divulge more information."

The brandy was giving Maha'dun confidence. "I have already tried. He knows nothing."

"You? Tried? If you tried to tie a bootlace, Maha'dun, you would fail."

Her insults rarely stung, for she delivered them so often Maha'dun was almost immune to them.

Almost.

He had caught the faint scent of a casket, here in this very tavern. She would not have picked it up yet, for there were too many other, stronger stenches, but it was the same aroma that had clung to the man who had freed him from that Barnstaple gaol. Maha'dun regretted not following the man that night, nor finding out from the Doones who he was, or where he had come from—gone to. To have offered him as a gift to Cara'mina would have salved several outstanding issues, but at the time Maha'dun had considered it prudent to flee for his own safety. Should he tell Cara'mina of it, him, now? Perhaps if he did, she would give more respect? Stupid! That was as unlikely as the sun shining at midnight!

I ought to tell you, but I did not notice your assistance in freeing me from that gaol, Maha'dun thought with loathing. *You make a habit of leaving me to suffer. So why should I share my secrets with you?* Wished he had the courage to say so aloud.

Unaware of his thoughts, there was a malevolent glint in Cara'mina's eyes as she announced, "Aside, I have completed my mission; the witch's husband is dead. I slit his throat while he slept in his bed last night."

The glass of brandy empty, Maha'dun leisurely refilled it from the bottle. Should he show some reaction? Alarm? Regret? But that was what Cara'mina wanted; she knew he was fond of Lady Tiola. Fond? Ah, it went deeper than that.

"He might have led us to the bone-box," was all Maha'dun said. "If he was this English woman's lover, she might have told him of its whereabouts. We needed him alive."

"Pah, you are a fool. Immerse yourself in your frivolities, waste your time drinking, smoking and whoring—leave the serious work to me."

He gave Cara'mina an almost insignificant bow. "You have your work, Lady, I have mine. Shall we leave it at that?"

"Your work? Looking for virile lovers to carouse with? You are a foolish lowlife, and nothing more. Useless at everything except sex." Cara'mina snorted derision and swept away out into the night, her hood pulled low over her face, although few people noticed her; tonight, instead of a hooded cloak or expensive silk and brocade, she wore drab clothes and hunched her back to appear old and insignificant. She had not had a real answer as to why Maha'dun was in Bristol. She smiled, a smug, self-satisfied leer. If he was here on behalf of the witch's husband, then he had failed that too. No surprise there; outside of sexual pleasuring, Maha'dun failed at everything. Sweeping her faded and patched grey cloak close around her, she turned down a narrow alley and disappeared into the night, with only one small doubt niggling at her like a flea bite. That man she had killed. She had done it quickly, ripping his throat in the darkness while he slept in a drunken stupor, there had been the smell of the English woman's blood, and his own, but he had not smelt of the witch. Had not smelt of a casket either. Why not?

She dismissed the anomaly, what did it matter? She was Cara'mina, Lady of the Night-Walkers, and she did not make mistakes.

Maha'dun finished the brandy, and putting some more coins on the bar, indicated for the bartender to fetch another bottle. Despite his apparent air of nonchalance his hands were shaking. Cara'mina terrified him; she would tear his entrails out if she knew the real reason why he was here in Bristol. But he was more scared of failing Tiola than of Cara'mina. Or so he told himself.

He toasted the air in mock salute to a sham confidence, and drank a glassful of brandy straight down. Despite being frightened, he was finding it quite exciting to be knowing things that Cara'mina did not. Had she not been so arrogant, she would have heard the buzz of gossip that was still high on everyone's lips. Bristol, as with any port or large town, had more than its fair share of depravity and murder, but this tavern, the Llandoger Trow, apparently had something of a good reputation. Spoilt by the death of a man in his bed last night, his throat cut from ear to ear. But the name everyone mentioned was Crawford; Maha'dun knew that Lady Tiola's husband was named Acorne. Captain Jesamiah Acorne, and he, according to the landlord, was alive, and asleep, in a room upstairs.

Maha'dun smiled, smug, to himself. Cara'mina had killed the wrong person.

Again.

* * *

Possessing sensitive hearing, a crowded tavern was not always the congenial occasion it appeared to be when you were a Night-Walker. Maha'dun had a third bottle of brandy in front of him, and was smoking yet another cheroot. There were quite a few stubs and a pile of ash at his feet. His head ached. It could have been the drink, but it was more likely the cacophony of noise. Men, especially men associated with the sea or the docks, were not known for their quiet speaking. Did no one here in Bristol ever talk without shouting?

Stubbing the cheroot out and draining the bottle into his glass, Maha'dun came to a decision. He could not continue to disobey Cara'mina. He would do her bidding and return to where he belonged. Paris, Milan, Venice, Florence, Cádiz. Not here, not England. If she ever found out that he had considered going against her, his life—as sorry as it was on too many occasions—would not be worth living. She would make it hell. He would suffer, over and again he would suffer. Misery and pain, taunting, deprivation, humility—all that and more would be his fate if he did not stand up and leave this tavern now. Right now. This very minute. He should go. Depart. Be gone. Yet he sat there, staring into the liquid that was his drink. How could he go? How could he disobey Cara'mina? But if he obeyed, he would betray Tiola. And did he not love Tiola beyond his own life? He drank the brandy down. What to do? He did not hear the first call, so deep was his despair and faltering hesitation, but the name shouted again caught his attention.

"Acorne! Hie, Captain Acorne, come and join us!"

Maha'dun did not turn around. He had been sitting all evening in this shadowed corner of the Llandoger Trow, several other men had attempted to sit opposite him on the far side of the table, but his surly grimace and low growl had seen them off. Deliberately he had sat with his back to the crowded room, figuring that if he genuinely did not see Tiola's husband, then failure would not be his fault, would it? Whether Tiola would accept such a pathetic excuse was another matter entirely. Here it was, the final chance to make a decision; to go or stay. To do as Cara'mina ordered, or as Tiola had asked. But still he sat there, his back to the crowded room, his hands gripped tight around an empty glass. A voice answered that shout.

"No, ta, I have other things to do."

And Maha'dun felt his skin tingle, his blood surge. His hearing followed the sound of the man pushing his way through the rowdy scrum. Heard his boots thudding on the wooden floor, heard him speak to a few men as he pushed past. Heard the door open, close, as he went out into the night.

For thirty heartbeats Maha'dun sat there, caught frozen like a mouse sheltering from a circling buzzard. *Leave it, leave him,* one side of his thundering mind advised. *Go! Follow him,* cried his thudding heart. That voice, that deep husky voice. He had heard it before. Had so wanted to hear it again!

Without thinking further, he was on his feet, elbowing two men aside, thrusting his way past another—was at the door, through, outside... For a moment he panicked. The man he was supposed to find, Tiola's husband, Captain Acorne, the man who... the man who... He had gone. Maha'dun was too late, he had lost him.

No! There he was! Maha'dun ran, ignoring the sting of cold, frosted air, not hampered by the darkness of the ill-lit cobbled street—scrabbled to a halt as Captain Jesamiah Acorne suddenly whirled around, a cocked pistol in one hand, a glinting cutlass with a rasp of steel against its protective sheath coming into the other.

For almost a minute they stared at each other, Jesamiah with knees bent, one leg slightly more forward than the other, body poised to spring forward and fight, his chin tucked into his chest, eyes narrowed.

Maha'dun, too stunned to reciprocate with a similar stance, recovered first. He smiled, spread his hands, palms outward to show he was no threat.

"You are Captain Acorne? Captain Jesamiah Acorne?" His heart was hammering, the rich blood hurtling through his veins. Surely this man was not Tiola's husband? He could not be? Could *not* be!

Remaining suspicious, Jesamiah narrowed his eyes further, tilted his head slightly upward and to one side. "Uh huh."

"I have been sent by your wife to find you. By Lady Tiola."

Another suspicious, "Uh, huh?" Jesamiah sheathed the cutlass, kept the pistol aimed. Said, "And you are?" Thought, *This cannot be the 'old friend' Tiola was sending? He ain't old at all!* Added, "I've seen you before? Where?"

Maha'dun placed his hands together, bowed, his mind racing, his stomach feeling as if it were going to leap up out of his throat. *This* was Jesamiah Acorne? The man Cara'mina thought she had killed? The man who had, not so long ago, been in possession of a casket and should therefore die? The man who had released him from that foul gaol. The man he had been seeking these past weeks to offer his gratitude to? The man Tiola wished him to protect? The same man. All those were the same man?

Maha'dun had assumed that Tiola's sea captain would be older, grey-grizzled, smelling of tar, sweat and rum—gruff, bad tempered; all other captains he had ever met had been like that. What was he to do? This man standing before him was young, virile, handsome. He did smell of the sea, of tar and strong liquor —but it was a pleasant, enticing aroma. He smelt, too, of a casket. That distinctive scent of sandalwood and copper. He was a carrier—Maha'dun wanted to sink to his knees, curl into a ball, wish for the sun to frizzle him to a cinder—by the Blood of Life, what the damn was he to do!

From somewhere down in his boots he summoned the courage to speak. "I am Maha'dun, an old friend of the Lady's. She sent me because she has suffered an accident."

Jesamiah's head shot up, anxiety overriding suspicion. He lowered the pistol, took a step forward. "What kind of accident? Is she hurt? Is she in danger?"

Ah! That told Maha'dun all he needed to know. The concern was genuine and deep-rooted. This man loved Tiola. What she had said about him was all true; Acorne would give his life for her. Maha'dun bowed again, offering unequivocal respect. "She is in no danger, but she is bruised and battered, her ankle is fractured and her wrist sprained. She needs you to return to her as soon as you can, for she has personal concerns that might endanger her."

Jesamiah uncocked the pistol and slid it through his belt; how could he return? He had unfinished business here, a murderer to find and finish. He exhaled, tilted his head back, to look up at the star-studded night sky. He needed a shave, a wash. Needed to let go of futile vows. The killer was probably long gone, but if he—she—was not, and the premise was correct that he, Jesamiah, had been the intended target, then this person would try again. Let him, her, do the bloody seeking!

He closed his eyes, exhaled, letting a held breath seep from his lips. It was over, he had let go. He opened his eyes, lowered his head, half smiled and stepped forward, offering his hand. "I thank you, Mahardun, for bringing this news." He stumbled over the pronunciation of the unfamiliar name.

"Ma-h-dun; a bit of a breath in the middle. As if you were breathing quickly on glass or warming cold fingers."

"Maha-dun? Maha'dun," Jesamiah repeated.

The name in question nodded.

"Then, Maha'dun, I will, naturally, return as soon as I can find transport." The suspicion was still there, but diluted a little. He was grateful for the message, although perturbed by the messenger. Tiola had implied her friend was an elderly man, this fellow was young and beautiful—handsome did not seem the right word. Was he, had he been, a lover of hers? Ah, stupid, jealous thoughts! She had meant old as in long-term. From childhood, perhaps?

It occurred to him, fleetingly in that moment of hesitation, that he knew very little of Tiola's private self. Beyond the few basic facts, he knew next to nothing of her existences during other eras of her life—lives. There was a lot—a lot—that he did not know about her distant past. In truth, there was probably even more that he did not want to know.

"My wife believes herself to be in some sort of danger?" Maha'dun took the proffered hand, unaware that he was breaking that silent, somewhat insidious thought of doubt from the man opposite him. "It is not my place to say," he said, "but her injuries heal quickly. Too quickly for a mortal woman?"

Jesamiah drew back, suspicious again. No one beyond himself knew that Tiola was a witch. No one.

"I have a carriage, Captain." Maha'dun said, aware he had uttered something amiss, but not sure what. "We can leave at once."

The fellow's skin felt cold to touch as Jesamiah shook hands, but the grip was firm and confident, and his own hands were no warmer. *Old friends*, Tiola had said. Was this Maha'dun chap one like herself?

"Maybe we'll start out at dawn," he suggested. "I don't much fancy being jolted and jumbled on rough roads for several hours at night." Did not add that nor did he fancy the company of a rather odd stranger.

Maha'dun grinned; "I also have an excellent coachman, who has always assured me that it is safer to travel by night because of footpads, highwaymen and the like. Aside, would the Lady Tiola not be delighted to wake come daylight, to find you beside her bed?"

Returning the grin, Jesamiah admitted, "Beside her bed? I would be more delighted to be in it!" Added hastily, lest his new companion took a wrong meaning, "For the warmth, you understand. It's getting bloody cold out here. I don't mean for any other reason if, as you say, she is injured. That would be most unseemly and ungentlemanly."

Maha'dun laughed. He liked Acorne. Liked him very much.

Explaining that he had to find some of his crew to leave orders, Jesamiah headed towards Broad Street where he knew the majority of them to be billeted. He hoped to find Skylark, the most reliable of the lads, but met with Finch first—in somewhat of a compromising situation. The surly bugger was swiving a street whore up against a warehouse wall.

To Maha'dun's amusement, Jesamiah leant against an opposite wall a few yards away, legs and arms crossed, watching intently.

"Do you sailors not prefer privacy?" Maha'dun asked, adopting the same pose.

"For making love, aye, but not for a quick rut with a street doxy. What's the point of wasting good coin paying for a bed? These street pullets demand enough silver as it is."

"He is not in, you know," Maha'dun observed. "She's got him between her thighs."

Jesamiah was impressed. "How can you be so certain?"

Maha'dun grinned. "Experience. And the fact that he is too drunk to notice." Added, "Why do you seafarers make such disgusting grunts? It sounds more like a pig at a trough than an act of sexual pleasure."

Jesamiah laughed. "In Finch's case, even a pig would be better mannered! You finished, Finch, you brandy-faced buck-fitch?"

The girl, for she could not have been much older than fifteen, pushed her skirts down, dropped the coins Finch gave her into the pocket bag inside her grubby gown, and sauntered away looking for more custom.

Finch turned around unsteadily, fumbling at his breeches. "Cain't a man even dip 'is wick wivout you bloody pokin' yer nose in?"

"Not when we are about to weigh anchor, you can't," Jesamiah answered, pushing away from the wall. "I am returning to Devon. My wife has had an accident and needs me. I expect you, and any of the crew who want to stay with me, to be at Instow by Sunday noon. Is that clear?"

"We goin' somewhere then? Where?"

"If you're not there you won't find out, will you?"

* * *

Walking along the cobbled, dimly lit back lanes of Bristol, turning into Small Street, Jesamiah casually mentioned that his new companion had not answered a previous question.

Wrinkling his nose at almost stepping into a pile of human waste, Maha'dun wondered whether to ignore the question again, but Jesamiah repeated his curiosity.

"Where've we met before? I never forget a face."

Maha'dun relented, he might as well answer for this Captain Acorne was likely to remember anyway. Besides, was it a secret? As lightly as he could, making little of it, he said with a laugh, "Barnstaple gaol. You blew out half the wall with a wad of gunpowder. I thought it a little excessive; just the window would have sufficed as a makeshift exit."

Laughing as well, Jesamiah nodded, remembering. "We created quite a stir in the town that night. My second in command, Rue, blew the front off a bank—purely to distract attention from what I was doing, of course."

"Seems a shame to gain entrance to a bank but not reap any benefit of reward. But then, I understand they tend to keep the money in secure vaults because of people like you."

"That they do."

"And gaining access to the vault would have required more gunpowder?"

"And more time." Jesamiah laughed again, "I agree, though, a shame."

There was a long silent pause as they turned into another lane; the Llandoger Trow was not so far ahead now.

"A pity Winnard Doone turned traitor. Was his defection anything to do with why you and Doone's grandson were banged up inside?" Jesamiah asked.

Maha'dun made no answer to that. The experience had been dreadful for him; the squalidness of the gaol, the difficulty of keeping out of the sunlight—albeit a meagre few rays slanting through the barred windows. The embarrassment of people gawping at them, throwing rotten vegetables and detritus. His clothes had been quite ruined. "I was waiting on the shore but the Excise men turned up and I stupidly managed to get myself captured along with young Doone." It was near enough the truth.

Beyond a snorted *hrmph*, Jesamiah made no reply. Arrest happened. It had happened to him. Were it not for 'Cesca would he still be in gaol here in Bristol? Or hanged?

"So, you work for Doone?" Jesamiah repeated, but Maha'dun laid a hand on his arm, whispered, "We have company." He tipped his head slightly, indicating over his shoulder. "Behind us. Five of them."

"I've been embroiled in Ailie Doone's scheming," Jesamiah continued, his right hand going to his cutlass hilt, "I ain't sure I want any further contact with him. I thought he was decent enough when I first met him, but he seems to bring trouble..." He drew the cutlass, spun around, Maha'dun echoing the action, his rapier appearing as if by magic in his own hand, glinting in the lamplight.

The five men, rough-looking scubbers, stopped, grinned. The one in the middle, the tallest and eldest, spread his hands, showing he held no weapon.

"No need for a fuss, squire. We be makin' our way 'ome for t'be along our dear wives after an 'ard day on the docks."

Jesamiah did not believe a word of it. He could see a pistol tucked, not quite hidden, through one man's belt. Saw the hefty rings on another's hands. Innocent adornments or a fighting man's useful weapons?

"If ye be s'kind as t'let us'n pass," said the one on the far right, "m'young tib 'as tha bed warmin' for I. Pity t'let it grow cold."

By way of answer Jesamiah nodded, stepped aside and stood with his back against the wall, his cutlass still in his right hand, with his left he fumbled slightly to click his pistol hammer home—not so easy with one and a half fingers missing—although he did not withdraw the gun from his belt. Maha'dun followed his lead, standing alongside closely examining his rapier. He ran a thumb lightly along the blade, emphasising its sharpness and lethal potential.

"Thank 'ee kindly, squire," said the first man, a crooked smile showing a row of broken and blackened teeth as he touched his forelock and sauntered past with his companions. The one on the far left, a stocky, bald-headed man with only one ear, sniggered; "May'ap thy tib'll keep us'n all warm for an 'our or two eh, Pierce?"

"Spec'lly if'n we take 'er a shillin' or two," offered the man in the middle, hooking his thumbs through his belt, his fingers elaborately framing his crotch.

"That she might, Nobs," said the one called Pierce.

They walked on for a few yards—Nobs shouted as he whirled around, "An' I guess these sea crabs'll provide the silver fer us!"

Five against two. The first moments of the fight were more of a scuffle. Grunts, punches, poorly aimed kicks that fell short of their mark as each man jostled for a good position or brought a weapon into play. Jesamiah quickly evened the odds as he shot one of the gang through the guts. The poor sod had not primed his own weapon fast enough. He threw the spent pistol at one of the other men, concentrated on using his cutlass to best advantage.

With his left arm, Maha'dun parried a blow from the one with the knuckle-rings, simultaneously thrusting with his rapier and slicing the razor-sharp blade through the man's eye and cheek, cutting to the bone. His severed eyeball dangling by sinew and muscle, the man screamed, covered his face with his hands. Maha'dun kneed his victim in the groin—causing him to grasp at his stinging genitals, then ripped his blade through the man's exposed throat. It would only take a few minutes for him to bleed to death, but too busy to witness his end, Maha'dun immediately turned attention to the one called Pierce who had two daggers, one long, one short, in his hands.

The grin on Maha'dun's face held nothing of humour about it, but oozed calculated menace. He was skilled with all weaponry and had no trouble removing the short blade along with a couple of Pierce's fingers. Pierce was a tougher fighter than his friends, and ignoring the blood, he feinted to one side then kicked, catching Maha'dun's shin. With Maha'dun momentarily off balance, Pierce slashed with the other dagger, ripping a gash in Maha'dun's coat, then leapt back as his opponent countered the move. Outraged at the damage to the velvet, Maha'dun forced Pierce back, step by step, driving him into an unlit side alley.

Jesamiah was struggling with the other two. Nobs; the gang leader, and the bald-headed ruffian with one ear. One slash of his cutlass precisely aimed and half of the man's remaining ear skimmed across the cobbles. Baldy bellowed and turned to look for his missing appendage, giving enough momentary distraction for Jesamiah to deal with just the one assailant. But Nobs also had a cutlass, and was almost as skilled as Jesamiah at using it. The blades clashed, steel grinding against steel. Evenly matched, they exchanged blows, neither gaining the advantage. Then Jesamiah slipped, his foot skidding on an ice-rimed puddle. He lost balance, almost went down—Nobs advanced forward, rammed his boot into Jesamiah's belly and followed through with a left-handed punch to his chin. Head reeling, black and red dizziness sweeping through his brain, Jesamiah staggered back against the wall and Baldy waded in, blood streaming down his jaw and neck, both men drumming heavy, relentless blows to Jesamiah's body. He fell onto one knee, almost losing his grip on his cutlass, and then Baldy stamped on his arm and the cutlass spun across the cobbles, leaving Jesamiah without a drawn weapon. This was it, the moment when he knew he had only a few moments to live.

Nobs yelled, a bull roar of pain and rage as Maha'dun's hand clasped his shoulder and spun him around, followed immediately by the rapier blade slicing through his throat. Blood gushed from the severed jugular artery like the spout of a red-wine fountain, and Nobs fell face down, his dying body twitching.

Baldy abandoned kicking Jesamiah and, realising his own life was now threatened, turned to face Maha'dun, who smiled laconically and with one finger beckoned him forward. Jesamiah's cutlass was at Baldy's feet; he bent quickly, snatched it up, his face snarling a leering grin. The cutlass was a weapon that was hefty and solid, the rapier agile and flexible. Lunging forward, Baldy drove an attack home, using the cutlass two-handed, swinging it from left and right. He was short, but had weight and muscular strength behind his shoulders and Maha'dun very soon realised that he was in trouble. The rapier was a crafted weapon, deadly if used for stabbing and slashing but against a cutlass, it was like striking an oak branch with a willow frond. For all that, it was made of quality steel by an expert craftsman, a magnificent blade when used by an experienced swordsman. But Jesamiah's cutlass was also a good weapon, and despite it not being supposed to happen, Maha'dun's blade shattered.

Shocked, he stared at the stump in his hand, disbelieving what he was looking at. Never had he known a rapier to break, not unless it was flawed or already damaged, and he took great care of his weapons, always.

His opponent's attention distracted, Baldy plunged the cutlass towards him in a sweeping arc that would have taken his head off had Maha'dun not possessed the ability to dodge aside. As it was, Baldy caught his upper arm a glancing blow with the edge of the hilt which numbed the nerves all the way down to Maha'dun's fingers.

Baldy leered expectant triumph as Maha'dun backed away, the leer becoming a grin as solid wall hit against his victim's back. "Nowhere to run to now, boy," he sneered, making ready for that final, finishing touch. He raised the cutlass, his eyes widened, mouth opened but no words came out, only a strangled gurgle as something tightened around his windpipe.

Jesamiah pulled the blue silk ribbon tighter, crossing his arms and locking them together at the elbow to gain more purchase, his feet planted wide apart, knees bent, spine arched away slightly to avoid a backward kick. As with most victims of strangling, Baldy dropped the cutlass and instinctively clawed at the garrotte, trying to loosen it with his scrabbling fingers. But it was too late. He had wasted his time. With a sharp twist, Jesamiah jerked the tightened cord and thrust his knee into Baldy's back, pushing his body forward, his head back. Baldy's neck snapped.

Five men dead. Four laying grotesquely in the lane, one out of sight in the dark side alley. There was quite a bit of blood puddling in the cracks of the white-frosted cobbles.

Jesamiah was bending over, his hands on his thighs, regaining his breath. The whole fight had been short lived but, what with the events of these last days, he was exhausted. "I reckon we ought to move these four to join that one over there," he pointed towards the alley, "just in case anyone comes."

Maha'dun grimaced. "Can we not leave them? They will be found eventually anyway, wherever they are."

"Aye, but not so quickly." Jesamiah straightened and re-laced the ribbon into his hair then retrieved his pistol and cutlass, wiped the bloodied blade on the nearest corpse. They served a purpose, his ribbons: useful for emergency repairs when there were no straps, twine or cordage around; a keepsake for the ladies after a night of pleasure; and a handy garrotte for sticky moments. Bending down, he picked up his hat, knocked off in that first flurry, settled it on his head before grasping Baldy's ankles. The man had pissed and shit himself in those final moments. A lovely mess for someone to find come daylight. Jesamiah dumped the body in the alley, came back for another.

"Aw, c'mon!" he snapped at Maha'dun, "don't just bloody stand there. If we are caught, we'll hang for murder."

"But the scum attacked us!"

"Try telling that to a judge." Jesamiah panted as he grasped the wrists of the first man he had shot and hauled the corpse across the cobbles.

"You're leaking," Maha'dun observed. "From your nose."

Jesamiah dabbed at his nostrils, discovered he had a nosebleed. He pinched the tip with his fingers, tipped his head back, then doubled forward gobbing a clot of blood from his throat. At least the bleeding had stopped. "You've your own share of blood," he observed, pointing at Maha'dun. "Your mouth's bleeding."

Maha'dun licked his lips, tasted blood and fished in his pocket for a linen kerchief. He felt his cheroot case, fancied a smoke. Tobacco was always good after a killing feast.

Frowning at the lack of assistance, Jesamiah ordered, "Help me get these last two out of the way, then we will find somewhere to clean ourselves up, in case we draw too much attention. And gather up those weapons, hide them somewhere."

Pulling a disgusted face, Maha'dun dragged the one called Nobs into the alley, then between them, disposed of the last body, Maha'dun picking up the dislodged eyeball as they moved the corpse and throwing it into a pile of rotting debris.

"My rapier's broken," Maha'dun complained as they left the lane and turned into a wider street where more people, mostly drunks and whores, lingered.

"We'll get you a new one. Better your rapier in two bits, not your head," Jesamiah answered. Heading for a horse trough, he removed his hat, dunked his face into the freezing water. Straightening up, his hair dripping, he felt in his mouth, removed a loose tooth. More blood, another dunking.

A couple went past, the man already busy at the whore's bodice, unlacing it, eager for his money's worth. She took little notice of him, her attention on Maha'dun and Jesamiah, her expression plain; *When I've finished with this dolt, would you two gentlemen fancy a quick poke?*

They disappeared into the lane, Jesamiah discreetly followed. Seeing the whore take her client into the darkened alley where the bodies had been dumped, he cursed.

Replacing his hat, Jesamiah hurriedly steered Maha'dun away, nudging him to stop mooning over the broken weapon. A loud, high-pitched scream from the alley made him take hold of Maha'dun's elbow and walk off, faster.

The whore ran into the street, her skirt still hitched around her waist. "Murder! His throat's ripped open!"

Not looking back, Jesamiah lengthened his stride. "You say you've got your own coach?"

Maha'dun nodded.

"How long to get the horses harnessed and on our way?"

"All I have to do is rouse my coachman. We can be on the road in, what, half an hour?"

"Let's make it twenty minutes, shall we?"

CHAPTER THIRTEEN
Instow

Fever had set in. Tiola had been expecting it, for the body had its own ways of healing and dispelling the invasive impurities garnered through injury or illness. She often thought of it as two entities fighting. Good against bad, the invader against the protector—David and Goliath, as in the Bible story. In battle there was heat. The heat of energy—the fight itself, blow against blow. The heat of emotion—the determination to win over an opponent. The hot heat of sweat and exhaustion as the fight battled on.

She lay sweating, partially delirious, as her vital organs diverted their strength and energies to eradicating the army that had invaded her system. She knew it would alarm her dear friends, Rue and Pamela, and her brother Carter and his wife Pegget, were she to transpose her spiritual self into another plain in order to leave her physical body to heal, but to survive she had to do it. And while her spirit was gone there would be no communication with Jesamiah. She only hoped, as she had made her decision, that Maha'dun was fulfilling his avowed promise.

On The Account

Dreams inhabited her drifting mind. With the living world shut away from her consciousness, the higher plains formed a presence, but with no control over the tides of place or time, all she could do was float as if on a lazy-flowing river and watch and listen to what was shown her. Some of it made no sense; pictures, patterns, the peculiar coupling of unrelated sequences and odd occurrences. Occasionally a face she knew from the past loomed near, then vanished. Old friends, old enemies; those missed, those she had been glad to see the back of. Events trailed a misty path; happy occasions and pleasant memories entwined with the sad or frightening. Gut-lurching things that had happened or she had witnessed raised their ugly heads to leer at her through her enforced sleep, from which there was, as yet, no escape. The faces of the dead lingered: dear friends, casual acquaintances; their calm smiles, their agonised screams. Her former incarnations swam along with her treasured memories and forgotten incidents. Revisited her past lives, those physical existences: the natural deaths of old age; the accidental demise of the not so old—and those pre-existence women who had died innocent of guilt but betrayed by greed or superstitious fear.

She saw her mother hang. Her dear face contorted as the rope bit into her neck and slowly strangled her life away. She had died to protect her daughter—Tiola—accused of murder and witchcraft, but she was not the witch. That was Tiola herself. And then Tiola's grandmother's face, an Old One, a Wising Woman of the White Craft, an old, wizened face with bird-bright eyes, guiding the departed soul to that better place where fear and pain no longer abide. She had been a witch too,

Grandmamma. Her face, as a young woman, no different to Tiola's now. The gift of Craft was passed on, grandmother to granddaughter, down and down through generation after generation, from when Time had first begun and the stuff of the stars had formed into those varied new-created life-existences. The one ongoing reincarnated soul departing the dead and entering the new-created unborn life. The sadness, a grandmother had to die before a granddaughter was born. Conception opened the pathway for the soul to enter. It was not just the male seed joining with the female egg that formed into a new being—it was the fusion of a soul that begat the spark that created the tiny start of a new life and opened the path for an old soul to infuse within it.

In her deep-trance sleep Tiola stirred, the heat pouring from her confused mind and damaged body. She was aware, vaguely, of Pamela attending her in the night-quiet of the bedchamber, afraid that this was the end, calling for Rue to come and come quickly.

For her life-soul to enter her own future granddaughter, Tiola must herself bear a daughter, watch her grow into adulthood and only then pass on. But all she saw was the thread of future life severed: nothing there, nothing more, nothing ahead...

"I can have no daughters!" she mumbled, and Pamela, even more anxious, bathed the sweat from Tiola's forehead and tried to calm her delirious agitation.

"Jesamiah?" Tiola whispered. "Where are you, Jesamiah?" Did not hear Pamela's soothing reassurance that he was coming, would soon be here.

Derisive, the Others laughed; those crowding spirits who had no care for the Wise Women who defeated the Dark Malevolents of evil. They cared not for the discomfort of pain or the tragedies that tore the heart to shattered pieces. Deceptions and hatreds laid their foul-treading paths and twisted the minds of the followers who despised the gentleness of caring love.

He will not come, they mocked. *He has no care for you,* they jeered.

In her entranced sleep she saw the faces of the undead, of those who waited in the Between, where life was no longer theirs but death had not yet claimed them. The sad, terrified faces of those who waited to Pass Through, hindered and held firm by the unheeding cruelties of their tormentors. The Night-Walkers, crying silent pleas for her to help them, please help... She had tried, had saved one alone among them, but had then paid the ultimate price. Death and despair. Agony and heartache. The Carver. A brutal man with a scarred face...

Tiola tried to scream, but no sound would come from her dry, tight throat as she rode the galloping nightmares. Her fever-wracked body quivered and shook as Cara'mina's face contorted into a contemptuous sneer. Maha'dun was there, behind her, watching, unable to move, for his lonely sorrows prevented him from reaching forward to offer protection or comfort to one he loved more than his own life. And then he was naked, his body gleaming with a light filter of sweat, his muscles rippling. He was making love, with passionate devotion. Tiola could not see his partner—it was not Cara'mina, for that evil demon would not condone the pleasure of gentle, love-shared sex.

Jesamiah was there too in her dreams, also naked, also making love; the bed covers were rumpled, his strong hands around the slender waist of the woman straddling him, pulling her down as he thrust in. Her breasts gleaming with the sweat of erotic, indulgent pleasure, her back arching as she rolled her hips bringing him to exultant climax, her head thrown back, long hair cascading to her buttocks. Dark, dark hair that contrasted with the scarlet blood that spread from Jesamiah's torn throat to stain the sheets and puddle the floor. Cara'mina, the craver of lust. The bringer of death.

They were dreams. Nothing but dreams.

* * *

"I think we should summon the physician again," Pamela said, biting her lip to suppress the threatening tears. Tiola was dying, of this she was certain. The fever had been raging for two days, the bed sheets were sodden as soon as she changed them. Tiola's hair was matted and dull, her cheeks sunken, her breath rasped in her chest.

Setting another log to the fire and poking it into place with his toe, Rue turned to Pamela and took her hand. He kissed the palm then held it tight within his rough-callused bear-paw. His own heart was breaking, for her grief and his: Tiola was a dear friend—more, he thought of her as a sister or daughter.

"The physician, 'e can do no more for 'er, *ma petite*." As always when his feelings were heightened by stress or an excess of drink, his accent degenerated into the strong French of his childhood. "It is Jesamiah we need to summon 'ere." *Or a priest,* he thought, but kept those words firmly to himself.

"John Benson said the trial had collapsed, that Acorne had been acquitted," Carter Trevithick spoke from where he huddled in a chair on the other side of the bed. He sat up a little straighter, rubbed at his stubbled chin and tired eyes; "So why has he not come, eh? Why has he not returned?"

Rue shrugged. "Maybe because 'e cannot get transport; maybe 'e 'as things to do, papers to sign—I do not know..."

"Tiola's friend has gone to fetch him," Pamela said, sliding her hand from Rue's grip to wring out a cloth in a bowl of cold water. With gentle care she patted its coolness over Tiola's hot face.

"That devil's oddity? The molly?" Carter was scathing. "I've met some types in my life, but that one beats them all. If he's gone to fetch Acorne then I'm the uncle of a mule." Carter stood up, for want of something useful to do added yet another log to the fire, although it was unnecessary. "He came here to sniff round my sister, that is obvious. Now he's cleared off because she is married and unavailable—married to another devil, I might add." He looked across the room towards the bed and the young woman labouring to stay alive, shook his head, despair clouding his eyes. "What is it with you, Tiola? Why could you not find yourself an ordinary, decent man—not a ruffian of a pirate or this other abomination?"

"Maha'dun seemed a kind, gentle man," Pamela countered, wetting the cloth again. "It is clear that he adores Tiola."

Carter glowered; had he not just said the same? Although he had meant it in an entirely different context.

Setting his hand to her shoulders and steering her to the chair Carter had vacated, Rue forced Pamela to sit down. She looked exhausted. "He may seem kind and gentle to you, *ma petite*, but there is killing in his eyes."

Pamela looked up at the man she loved, her gaze meeting his. "There is killing in your eyes, too," she said, "and in Jesamiah's. That does not make either of you bad men."

Angry, frustrated, Carter punched his clenched fist onto the mantelpiece, making the ornamental clock set there tinkle. "Even if that—thing—this Maha'dun, has gone to fetch Acorne, where are they? Why have they not returned yet?" He strode to the bed, stood looking down at his sister. He had only just found her again after years of enforced exile from England. She had returned unexpectedly a few short weeks ago. Their mother had hanged for murdering the bastard who had claimed to be their father—and for being accused of witchcraft. Tiola would have hanged too, had the mob been able to find her, but Carter had got to her first. His only sister, the only girl among nine brothers, his dear, dear sister... He had sent her off in the safe care of a smuggler's boat. Had never expected to see her again—had definitely not expected to see her return with a knave of a pirate as a husband.

"I would run one hundred miles to be with my wife were she sick," he snarled. "Nothing, nothing, would hold me back."

"Give them time, Carter," Pamela responded with exasperation. "It is a long way to Bristol and back."

Indicating his contempt, Carter snorted disbelief.

"'E will come," Rue stated, "as soon 'e can. I know 'e will."

"And I know he will not!" With one swipe of his hand Carter sent the bedside table crashing to the floor, the water bowl and a vase containing a posy of spring flowers with them. Pamela squeaked dismayed alarm and hurried to clear up the mess, the held-back tears now cascading down her cheeks.

"You imbecile!" Rue roared. "'Ow is your stupid temper to 'elp us 'ere?"

Carter strode across the room, stood direct in front of the older man, not intimidated by his taller height or larger, muscular build.

"He will not return," he shouted, "he has gone off with a whore to poke his prick, hasn't he? He has abandoned his wife, my sister—and it would not be the first time, would it?"

Rue hit him. Once, a blow to the jaw, his anger made all the more potent because he was trying so hard not to entertain exactly the same thought.

ON THE ACCOUNT

* * *

Pamela was dozing in the chair, her head to one side, her feet stretched to the fire.

"How is she?" Rue came quietly into the room, picked up Pamela's shawl that had slid to the floor and placed it around her shoulders. She was pale, dark bruises from tired exhaustion and worry beneath her eyes. Her answering smile was a poor attempt at reassurance.

"She sleeps, but her breathing is shallow and I fear that her soul has almost left her." Pamela welcomed Rue's hand taking hers, welcomed his firm, solid anchorage to life. "She will not, I think, survive for much longer."

Rue went to the window, pulled the curtains open, revealing the pale blue of the early morning sky and the sparkle of a heavy frost on the ground. He stared a while at two swans paddling so apparently calm and serene along river, then hooked a stool nearer to the bed, sat, his thigh against Pamela's, welcoming her close presence as much as she did his. He rubbed at her fingers with his other hand. "Carter has gone to Bristol to find Jesamiah. He left at dawn."

"Then it is a wasted journey," she answered on an exhaled sigh. "Except for the choosing of a coffin, and the burying of one who should not be dying, Captain Acorne will be a widower when he comes."

Rue did not answer immediately, for grief was stealing his words.

"This is not the occasion," he said in French, unable to bring himself to speak in English, *"for it is inappropriate, but..."*

Pamela made no response. She did not speak French, was unaware of what he was trying to say. He cupped his hand

153

around her cheek, turned her face towards his; said in English, "I love you, *ma petite*, and I do not wish to waste what time we 'ave together. *Si peu de temps*. There is so little time. Let us be wed as soon as we can?"

Pamela touched her palm to his cheek. Fighting the need to weep she could do nothing except smile and nod.

CHAPTER FOURTEEN

A few miles after the coach had left Bristol behind, even the jolting on the rutted roads did not keep Jesamiah awake. He was a seasoned sailor—had been to sea as a pirate from the age of fifteen and prior to that, had sailed with his father from young boyhood, but a carriage had a different motion and those first few miles had been somewhat unpleasant. Maha'dun had noticed the green tinge to Jesamiah's face and had handed him a new-filled hip flask of brandy. It had helped ease the queasiness, and had tipped the balance between staying awake and falling asleep.

Vague images and sounds filtered through Jesamiah's sleeping mind; the horses' hooves—four hired post-horses—the crack of the whip, the creak and squeak of the carriage itself; the rumble and mud-splutter of the wheels. The coachman, who apparently doubled as Maha'dun's personal servant and valet, was a noisy fellow constantly urging the horses forward with shouts of, *Get on, you lazy bugger*, and, *You only got three feet, you bag o' bones nag?* All interspersed with various curses at drunkards to *Get out the bleedin' way.*

Once out of Bristol the cussing had then eased, with only

155

the occasional yelled encouragement to the horses. At the first turnpike, Jesamiah briefly roused, but not enough to wake. He was vaguely aware of the coachman complaining at the cost of the toll and the answering bickering from the tollkeeper, but the sweetly acrid smell of Maha'dun's tobacco, mixed with the brandy, was more than enough to send him off to sleep again. When he next awoke the carriage had stopped again, more colourful language was coming from their coachman, accompanied by the anxious neighing of horses and clatter of shod hooves. Unaware of how far they had travelled Jesamiah peered out of the small coach window. They were at an inn, a posting stage, and it was still dark outside; dawn could be half an hour or several hours off for all he knew.

"Where are we?" he asked as he stretched cramped muscles.

Maha'dun, sitting next to him, legs crossed, lit another cheroot. There was already a generous scatter of ash and discarded butts on the floor; a cloud of blue smoke clinging beneath the roof.

"No idea," Maha'dun answered, flicking more ash to join the scatter. "Does it matter?"

"I s'pose not." Jesamiah yawned, stretched again. Various bruises were beginning to feel tender. "Just wondered how long before we reach our destination."

"We've been on the road over an hour. About one hundred miles to travel? Depending on whether we get bogged down in mud, although it is rapidly freezing out there, ten, eleven, hours? If we do not meet too much ice, the hardened tracks will be of benefit to us."

Not too happy with the answer, but unable to alter the facts of road travel, Jesamiah again peered out of the window when a series of explicit oaths tore from the coachman. "Your driver seems to be making an Anne's Fan of a nuisance of himself out there."

"He's fussy about changing horses. The carriage is mine, the horses are not. These fellows at post stations charge a fortune to hire their beasts, but it is more practical than having my own stable as I never know where I may be from one week to the next. A carriage you can put into storage if you are not using it. A horse you cannot."

Was that a hint for payment? Jesamiah felt in his coat pocket. He had some money, but not much. "I will refund your expenses when we reach Instow."

Maha'dun made a sound that was half amusement, half indignation. "No need. I have wealth enough to cover these sorts of paltry costs."

"Then I thank you for your generosity."

"There is no generosity. I do it for Lady Tiola's sake."

The coach lurched, followed by a spate of abrasive language from the coachman as he started the horses up.

"You know my wife well then?" Jesamiah could not resist asking, that squint-eyed monster of jealousy raising its head again. He wanted to ask how long had they known each other, and what depth did 'well' go to? This Maha'dun fellow was an attractive man, he oozed sexuality and an air of mystery. Tall, slim, charming. Rich. Jesamiah doubted that many women would resist falling into bed with him. Men too, he'd wager. But did those things influence Tiola? Had they been lovers? Were they still lovers?

Maha'dun had not noticed the slight hint of hostility in the question, he answered with bland sincerity. "I owe her my life, which is a debt that carries a repayment I am never reluctant to make."

What did that mean, Jesamiah wondered? "Some debts

can mount up, especially those that are limitless."

"Some debts, especially those for a life saved, are, nonetheless, worth paying."

Jesamiah agreed with that sentiment in principle but the value of a life depended on the person involved. For those scubbers back in Bristol, their lives had been worthless. Tiola, on the contrary, was beyond price. For this elegant fellow? Maybe a few gold coins, nothing more.

"You have known her a long time?"

Maha'dun nodded. "Many years."

Again, that niggle of jealousy. How many were 'many'?

The carriage rumbled on up a low incline, down the far side; lurched over several frozen ruts, the horses going no faster than a walk.

"You may have noticed," Maha'dun said with a proud smile, "that this carriage is better than most. When I was in Germany recently I had these thick glass windows put in, and the chassis redesigned. It now also has Berlin springs fitted, and the wheel rims are German made. Very strong, very reliable. The springs make it quite comfortable in here, do they not?"

Jesamiah thought not, but nodded and agreed. It was never wise to belittle a host's pride, and he supposed that compared to other carriages then, yes, this was more desirable. The seats were plush velvet, with matching curtains hiding folded back wooden shutters—that was odd, Jesamiah had never seen shutters on coach windows before. Something else from Germany, he assumed.

The driver seemed to have got the measure of his new team, and the rutted road condition improved slightly so that the horses broke into a trot, and the sporadic lurching settled to a more even swaying.

There was no hint of dawn on the horizon, but the sky was clear with an almost full moon which shone as bright as a lantern. Lengthy shadows from alder and ash trees trod across the flat landscape. The heavy frost sparkled over the marshy fields, ice solidifying in the puddles and ruts. It was cold within the carriage; Jesamiah pulled his coat tighter, thrust his hands into his pockets. He somewhat envied Maha'dun's fur-lined cloak.

Hooves clattered as the horses trotted over a stone bridge, the ring of an iron shoe on stone, a spark flying out like a miniature firework. The moon was reflected in a partially frozen lake of floodwater that covered the lower levels of a field. The river itself was tumbling fast, a froth of gleaming white water, the banks and overhanging shrubs and trees dusted with glittering white frost.

Maha'dun noticed Jesamiah frowning, for he peered out of the window on his side of the carriage. "No need to fear, there is a foot or two before the water reaches the top of the bank."

"A risk of these rivers flooding might depend on the next few high tides, though. With a full moon and spring tides combined, the folk around here are probably getting anxious."

Puffing on his cheroot, Maha'dun said nothing. He did not want to admit that he had no concept of what this fellow sitting next to him was talking about. What did the moon or a spring tide have to do with an inland river?

Another long stretch of lurching and bouncing interrupting intermittent dozing. Vapour streamed from the horses' nostrils and the coachman had huddled himself deep into his coat, his gloved fingers almost frozen to the fistful of reins. But the going had been faster, for the muddy ground had hardened enough for the horses to trot on at a smart pace, their hooves and the carriage wheels cracking through the ice of frozen puddles.

Changing the team at the next post-station inn meant a chance for Jesamiah to climb down from his seat and stretch aching and stiffened muscles; to relieve himself and go in search of a bite to eat. The landlady had provided a jug of mulled wine and a generous portion of bread and cheese. The wine Jesamiah drank down, the bread and cheese he took back to the coach, aware that Maha'dun's coachman at other such stops had been quick to change horses and be off again. He seemed to be lingering this time, however, for the horses were harnessed but the man was leaning in at the coach's open door, engrossed in an animated conversation with Maha'dun. Jesamiah sauntered nearer, head cocked, listening.

"Three of 'em, sir," the coachman waved his hand in an exaggerated gesture back towards the road they had just come down. "Been with us since Bristol, I reckon."

Maha'dun said something—Jesamiah could not hear what.

"Nay, sir, that I could not say."

What can he not say? Jesamiah thought. He looked at the moonlit road, at the still shadows, the sparkle of frost. A shape slunk beneath the trees, but it was only a fox. Another glided above, silent wings spread wide, accompanied by a mournful cry. An owl. Nothing else.

"At least we know they're..." The coachman saw Jesamiah, ceased talking. He touched his hat, said, "We're almost ready to leave, sir, if you would be so good as to take your seat?"

So, the exchange was not intended for his ears? Interesting.

"Everything all right?" Jesamiah asked casually, as he climbed into the coach and hastily settled himself beneath two blankets that had appeared. The coach lurched, the coachman encouraging his new team direct into a swinging trot.

"Of course," came Maha'dun's equally as casual reply.

"Want some of this bread and cheese?"

"No, thank you. I eat very little while travelling."

"Suit yourself." No mention of being followed, then. Jesamiah peered out the window. "Sun will be up in an hour or so. We might be able to push on come daylight?"

Maha'dun grunted unenthusiastically and closed the shutters over the window on his side of the coach. "Would you mind doing the same?" he asked.

"What? It ain't light yet, and when it is I'll not wish to sit in blackness when I've been looking forward to looking where we're going." Jesamiah did not like the prospect at all. Night journeys were all very well, but he preferred to be able to see out, especially if it sounded like trouble was dogging their heels.

"I have a problem with daylight," Maha'dun explained, retaining what was very obviously a false smile. "I cannot allow the sun's rays to touch my flesh, it will burn me. Beside which, closed shutters will retain more warmth for you, will they not?"

"Oh. I see." Jesamiah was a little taken aback by the first statement, saw good reason for the second. There was something most odd about this fellow. Was he serious? He could not tolerate sunshine? Jesamiah peered again at the night sky and the glittering twinkle of frosted stars. The moon was much lower, the shadows longer, more sinister. They could well be in for a bright, sunny day come dawn. "Does Tiola know of this sunlight business?" he asked, speaking with his mouth full of cheese.

Maha'dun nodded. "She does. She says it is called poor-fairy-ear, or something like that."

All Jesamiah could do was repeat an astonished, "Oh," close the shutter, and eat his frugal meal in darkened silence.

Chapter Fifteen
Exmoor

His hat pulled well down over his eyes, hands tucked into armpits for warmth, Jesamiah was dozing, but aware he would need to piss fairly soon. He was growing more uncomfortable than the stiffness already aching in his back and legs. He was jerked awake by the coach slowing down, accompanied by the driver thumping heavily three times on the roof.

Maha'dun cursed and, taking a quick peep behind the window shutters, confirming that it was still dark—although only just—he leant forward to pick up his rapier and scabbard set there on the seat opposite while travelling. He cursed again, had forgotten that his prized weapon was broken.

Jesamiah frowned. "What is it?"

"Trouble," Maha'dun hissed. "Thieves."

"Highwayman?"

"Highway*men*. Three of them. Three knocks."

As he spoke, the carriage stopped and the door nearest Maha'dun was almost immediately opened by a man holding a lantern high in one gloved hand, a pistol in the other. He peered in, the lantern gruesomely illuminating his face. Two other men were shouting at the coachman to climb down, and, refusing, the coachman was shouting back. A shot. More shouting. Another shot. The shouting ceased.

"Step down from the carriage if you please, my friends," ordered the man with the lantern, "and I will have your weapons if you do not mind." His skin was tanned, and he had a strong colonial accent, a slight drawl common to the Caribbean.

"If I do mind?" Maha'dun retorted with a growl.

"Then I will shoot you now, and save myself a lot of bother."

Jesamiah indicated the pistol. "One shot. You cannot kill both of us."

The door on his side jerked open, and a shorter, scruffier man with a kerchief hiding his face leered in. A pistol pointing at Jesamiah's chest. "Two pistols. I suggest ye do as my companion says, or else ye can join yon driver's corpse. 'Tain't no diff'rence to us whether'n we robs ye while ye be alive or be dead."

Solemnly Maha'dun handed the man nearest him the scabbard with the broken rapier and alighted from the carriage. Jesamiah had considered going for his cutlass, covered by a blanket on the seat opposite, but it would not be easy to draw or wield in the cramped confine of the carriage, instead, picked up his pistol from the same seat and discreetly cocked the hammer as, bending low, he followed Maha'dun out into the frosty air. Had he been more of the romantic and not in a life-threatening situation, he might have appreciated the beauty of the white-gleaming landscape, the moon hanging large and round low in the sky, the faint purplish hue over to the east. But all he was thinking about was the pressing need to empty his bladder. And the man who wanted to take his pistol off him.

A ruffian lay dead on the ground, a large hole in the centre of his chest. Neither of his companions seemed concerned at losing one of their number. Maha'dun walked to where the coachman lay dead, dangling from the driver's seat, his fired pistol still clutched in his hand. There was very little left of his head. Brain matter, blood and bone dribbled down the side of the coach, lay scattered, grotesque, on the white ground. Another growl rumbled in Maha'dun's throat.

Jesamiah took a step forward, but the barrel of the first man's pistol prodded him in the belly.

"I asked for your weapon, my friend."

With slow movement of his left hand Jesamiah pushed the pointing gun aside. "We've met before," he said. "I don't forget faces."

"Never seen you before," the man sneered. "Your pistol, if you please. I'll not be asking again."

"What does the name Francis Chesham mean to you?" Jesamiah asked.

No response. Not a flicker.

"How about Francesca Escudero?" Ah, that got a reaction! The man's pupils dilated and a muscle to the side of his face twitched.

"Your pistol. Now."

As if surprised that he was holding it, Jesamiah looked down at the weapon in his hand. "You want this old thing? It's no good. It usually misfires and the pan is always damp. Look, see the firing pin is rusted..." He held the gun out, brought it up quickly as his thumb clicked the hammer full home and fired. His opponent saw the movement, ducked to the side. Quick enough to avoid a fatal shot, not quick enough to avoid the bullet driving into his shoulder and shattering the entire joint. He screamed, fell to his knees, the lantern tumbling from his hand and guttering out as he clamped his hand over the agonising wound.

Maha'dun sprang over the two wheeler horses, vaulting across their rumps, causing them to toss their heads and snort. He landed awkwardly on the far side, went down on one knee, rolled and was up again, but the second man was haring off towards a stand of trees. He became lost in the shadows; a moment later the sound of galloping hooves.

"Not very good robbers, are they?" Jesamiah said, pushing his pistol through his belt and taking a closer look at the coachman to ensure he was dead. A lost cause, for there was no doubt. He unbuttoned his breeches, pissed a stream of steaming urine up against the front wheel. "Can you drive a four-in-hand, Nightm'n?" he asked Maha'dun, hoping that the answer would be to the affirmative.

Maha'dun shook his head. "If I could, why would I employ a coachman? Can you?"

"I'm a sailor, not a horseman. I could manage a simple wagon or trap, but for them..." Jesamiah indicated the horses standing patiently, "I wouldn't know which rein went where or why." He refastened his breeches, withdrew the pistol, and went to kneel beside the man he had shot.

"You've put us in a bit of a spot, mate." He poked the pistol barrel into the man's shoulder, eliciting another scream. "And that's made me a tad annoyed." He mimicked the assailant's accent perfectly as he added, "My friend."

Reloading the gun, taking his time, Jesamiah said, "Now, while I'm busy doing this, why don't you tell me why you and your cock-poxed fatherless whore-monger friends were following us?"

Maha'dun, standing behind Jesamiah, raised an eyebrow, impressed. Ah, so this Captain Acorne was astute?

"I don't know what you are talking about. We were waiting for a coach to pass by. Any coach. We're robbers."

"Were robbers. Your career has just ended," Maha'dun offered.

Jesamiah looked around and waved his hand at the silhouetted outline of the surrounding moors. "At dawn? Out here in the middle of nowhere?"

"There's always a coach..." the man groaned.

"Not on this road," Jesamiah countered. "All I can see are our tracks behind us. We left the main road a good hour ago." He glanced over his shoulder at Maha'dun. "Why would we do that, I wonder?"

Maha'dun shrugged.

"I think our dead coachman was hoping to lose some irritating bum-sniffers who had been clinging to our wake since we left Bristol. Only he reckoned wrong, and whoever set you to following us reckoned wrong an' all." Jesamiah squatted down next to the man. Clicked the hammer of his pistol home. "He didn't take into account that scum like you and your scum partners disobey orders and get distracted by the lure of a possible Prize. An' I ain't talkin' about the present moment, am I?"

The man gazed at Jesamiah, hatred in his eyes.

"Or were you supposed to stop me and kill me? Like you were supposed to do once before in the hills of Hispaniola? You must have been pretty pissed off when you discovered that fancy black box had been emptied of the diamonds it contained."

For answer, the man spat into Jesamiah's face. Maha'dun had gone very still. Very quiet.

Jesamiah wiped the spittle away with the back of his hand. Stood, turned to face Maha'dun. "You got any thoughts on why we were being followed? Has it got anything to do with a woman being murdered, or a man asleep in his bed ending up with his throat ripped open?"

Maha'dun spread his hands in innocence. "I do not know, Captain."

Narrowing his eyes, Jesamiah stepped very close. "Oh, I think you do. Is Ailie Doone behind this? Jennings?" He could not believe it would be Henry, but Doone? Aye, there was every chance this—all of it—was his doing.

Shaking his head, Maha'dun responded with a firm no. "If it is Sir Ailie, then it is a plan I am not aware of. I have not seen or been with him for a while now, nor am I privy to his thoughts or ambitions."

That, Jesamiah did believe. The rest? There was something here he was not being told.

Very clearly Jesamiah remembered that skirmish in the woods above Santo Domingo where he and an army of rebels had been brutally and bloodily ambushed. Two men had grabbed Francesca and dragged her off down through the trees. Jesamiah had rescued her and one of the men he had killed outright; the other had escaped with the box that had held the diamonds—only they had spilled out to be swiftly scooped up into Jesamiah's pocket. The added pleasure had been of making love to 'Cesca. It occurred to him, not for the first time, that she had not made much of an attempt to escape from her abductors. He had always assumed she had wanted those precious diamonds for herself, but now it looked like the box had been the Prize. He needed answers.

"Who were you trying to steal that box for? Who are you working for? Doone?"

The man spat again, the globule landing on Jesamiah's muddy boot.

"Box?" Maha'dun echoed, glancing nervously at the sky lightening rapidly over to the east. "What box?"

"A black ebony box," Jesamiah said, "with the mask of a man on the lid. He had sapphires for eyes." He frowned, squinted at Maha'dun. "Looked a bit like you."

Maha'dun's face was always ivory pale, but it paled even more, went almost translucent. "This man had a bone-box?" He almost whispered the words. Why had he not smelt it? Why was there no residue scent of it on the man's skin?

"Don't recall bones in it, and I don't care much about the box," Jesamiah interrupted. "I want to know who is holding this dog's leash." He kicked the man's shoulder, eliciting a shriek. "Who are you working for? Tell me!"

"I care about it," Maha'dun retorted with venom. "I need to know where it is!"

Suddenly Jesamiah felt very tired, and very annoyed. "It was a wooden box. Someone wants it badly. And that same someone could well be the someone behind 'Cesca's murder."

"I want it," Maha'dun said quietly. "It has a personal value to me that is incalculable."

Jesamiah looked up sharply, anger scudding across his face. "You had better not tell me that you want it bad enough to have killed Francesca."

"And how would I have been able to do that?" Maha'dun retorted, gambling on Acorne being unaware that there was another Night-Walker interested in lost bone-boxes. "I cannot be in two places at once. At the time of that woman's death I was with the woman you *should* have been with, tending her injuries!"

Unable to answer, Jesamiah scowled. All this talk was getting him nowhere, although as he squatted down next to his squirming attacker, he wondered if there was he was missing.

"He does not smell of a bone-box," Maha'dun said, squatting next to him, puzzlement and frustration spilling into his voice. "Every male who touches a box always smells of it."

"He had it several months ago," Jesamiah answered absently, only partially listening. What was this idiot babbling on about? Boxes did not leave a scent!

"No, it remains for many months, many years. The residue seeps into the skin and remains there—like tar on a sailor's fingers."

Jesamiah stared at him, not certain whether to believe him or not, but then some of the things Tiola came out with sounded utterly absurd, one of them being that there was a vast, single continent at the bottom of the world, not just scattered islands as everyone assumed. She said that mountains had been pushed up from the sea; that the stars were millions of miles away. Other nonsense, incomprehensible things. "I had the box for a short while, do I smell of it?" he said inspecting his hands, grimacing at the reminder of losing his fingers.

"Yes," Maha'dun answered simply. "You do."

Jesamiah sniffed his hands again. "I smell tar and gunpowder, and some other things that I've no doubt m'wife will make me take a bath for. But what do boxes smell of?" Then he smiled, slow and nasty. The sort of smile that could freeze the sun and blot out the moon. "I guess they smell of shit, like this bastard here."

He had not heard Maha'dun's soft-spoken reply. "They smell of torture and death."

"Tar on fingers, eh?" Jesamiah leant forward, grasped the thief's hand that was clamped across the blood-soaked shoulder. "Gloves," he said. "He wears gloves. I remember him wearing gloves even back there on Hispaniola."

He yanked the leather glove off. Beneath, the skin was puckered and scarred.

"Burnt your fingers dipping 'em where you oughtn't?" Jesamiah asked. "That's why nothing of this scent-thing seeped into the skin, Maha'dun, my Nightm'n mate. This scum-bummer wears gloves." He tossed the glove aside, stood over the prone man who tried to wriggle away.

There were two sides to Jesamiah Acorne; the calm, reasonable man who preferred to make slow, gentle love to a woman rather than using her roughly or by force. A man who enjoyed good company, good drink, good laughter—and the man, the pirate, who revelled in the pleasure of chasing a ship, bringing her to a halt, boarding and taking what he could for plunder. The other side of his soul, the dark, rarer side that lusted for the fight, and had no qualm about who was killed or how. Jesamiah Acorne, quick to laugh; formidable when angry.

"Was it you who killed Francesca Escudero? You bastard! Was it?" Jesamiah raised the loaded pistol. Aiming carefully, he cocked the hammer full home and fired, the bullet scudding into the frozen ground half an inch from the man's right knee. He screamed, a high-pitched ululation of abject fear as he tried to roll away from the torment.

"I do not know why you are making such a noise," Maha'dun drawled, "he missed."

"I didn't miss," Jesamiah said as he turned away, "and he knows full well I didn't. He has the time it takes me to reload to tell me who he is working for, and why. Otherwise I will adjust my aim."

"Go...piss...yourself."

It was cold out here. Jesamiah's hat was still inside the coach; he leant in, reached out to retrieve it from the seat, turned around to see Maha'dun drawing a knife through the man's throat.

"No! Idiot! Belay there! Don't cut his..." Dropping the pistol and hat he ran the few paces back, grabbed Maha'dun by the scruff of the neck and pulled him away, met with a bared-teeth snarl that was more animal than human.

"Who are you to give orders? He had possessed a bone-box. He had to die!"

Although he was unnerved by the ferocity of the response, the angry retort still burst from Jesamiah's lips; "Die? Because of a soddin' box? I needed him alive to answer questions about 'Cesca! And now we won't find out where that box is, will we?"

Maha'dun's sapphire-blue eyes blazed with the intensity of complete disdain. "This low-life shitbag does not know where it is."

"Oh, so you do know what's going on?"

"I know as much as you. And do not question me again."

About to protest, Jesamiah comprehended the danger he was in. He knew killers well enough to recognise when bloodlust could override reason, and that this creature—he could not, surely, be a man—had not finished killing. He took a step backwards, raised his hands in supplication. There was something else going on here that he ought to know about, but now was not the time to ask. His own anger was surging through his body, pumping his heart, extending his nostrils, increasing his breathing. He wanted to hit, punch—kill—but knew enough of the world to register when anger could drive a wrong move and evoke nothing except more anger and dreadful circumstances. Like ending up dead. It took guts, sometimes, to know when to fight, more guts to know when to surrender. He turned away, retrieved his discarded pistol and hat, walked towards the carriage. Climbed in.

"Wait!" Maha'dun cried in alarm, "it is dawn, you must drive the horses!"

"It's your carriage," Jesamiah retorted, "you drive it."

* * *

The curse was explicit, and even to Jesamiah's well-seasoned sailor's ears, extensively lewd. Another heavy thud followed the first, joined by a further bout of crudities. One of the horses squealed, the coach rocked. What the bugger was that cretin doing out there?

Sighing heavily, more than ready to add his own expletives to those already being tossed around, Jesamiah opened the coach door and stepped outside. The sky was rapidly becoming lighter, the sun would be rising above the horizon very soon. Two travelling chests lay on the ground, a third, along with an array of tangled harness, was dangling from one of the horses unhitched from the team. A fourth chest lay open, clothes scattered about on the frosted ground, a prominent horseshoe-shaped hole through its lid.

"What, may I ask," Jesamiah said, placing his fists on his hips, "are you trying to do?"

"I am playing chess. What the daylight do you think I am trying to do?" came the snapped retort.

"Looks more like you're playing silly buggers to me," Jesamiah answered as he stepped quickly out of the way of an aimed hoof. The horse was not taking kindly to Maha'dun's attempt to secure the chest to its side. Maha'dun, though, was not so quick; the shod foot connected with his thigh. He yelled fury and pain, and kicked the horse back.

Bending down, Jesamiah retrieved some of the scattered clothing and shoved them back into the open chest. He pointed to the others. "Do these all contain clothes?"

"Yes."

He held up a pair of silk drawers. "Yours?"

"Yes." Maha'dun turned to him, glowering. "If you are going to make stupid remarks you can get back into the coach and leave me to figure this out in peace."

Almost, Jesamiah laughed at the absurdity, but choked the guffaw into a cough. "I take it you are trying to use the harness to adapt the horses as pack ponies?"

"How nice to have someone so helpfully observant."

For a moment, Jesamiah stood there, arms folded, watching, sucking in his cheeks to stem the laughter. The rim of the sun blossomed above the horizon, flooding the sky with golds and pinks. Maha'dun flinched, threw his arm over his face and cowered away, the best he could, into the horse's shadow. His hand was exposed, the skin immediately reddened as if burned by a hot poker.

Jesamiah's laughter evaporated. Thinking quickly, he tore off his coat and flung it over Maha'dun's head. He steered the whimpering man to the carriage, bundled him inside and slammed the door.

Maha'dun had at least dignified his coachman by draping the driver's bloodstained leather apron over the corpse. Jesamiah heaved the body down, laid it next to the other dead men then climbed up into the driver's seat and beneath it, found the toolbox where he had expected it to be. Lifting the lid, he rummaged about—was relieved to discover that the coachman had been a conscientious fellow who had kept his tools in shipshape order. He selected the items he wanted, climbed down and worked quickly, well used to jury-rigging broken cordage, spars and stays; familiar with knots and bindings. Within half an hour he had two horses harnessed as pack animals, although he was not certain that Maha'dun would approve of several of his shirts and two coats being used as essential padding. Too bad if he didn't. For the other two horses, he removed the coach harness, releasing all the straps except for the bridle and reins, which he cut to a shorter, more manageable length. They would have to ride bareback, which he did not relish, but the alternative was to stay here and wait. And out here, it could be a long wait.

He rechecked his knots and fastenings, then spoke through the carriage door: "Right, we're ready. You can either cover yourself as well as you can and come with me, or I'll hobble a horse and you can follow on tonight."

There was muffled movement from inside, a few expletives and Maha'dun emerged, swathed in heavy travelling clothes, leather gauntlets and a scarf wound about his face. Only his eyes were visible. He nodded at Jesamiah, a combined gesture of apology and gratitude, and, handing him back his coat, took the adapted reins. With ease, he swung up onto the nearest horse, a chestnut with four white stockings and flaxen mane and tail.

"Can you lead the bay?" Jesamiah asked, putting on the coat and holding out one of the makeshift lead ropes.

"I can." Maha'dun took the proffered rein in his leather-gloved hand. Jesamiah shuffled the other riding horse towards the carriage step and, using it as a mounting block, scrabbled aboard, nowhere near as competently as Maha'dun had mounted. Nudging his horse with his heel, he leant forward and, giving a sharp tug to the tether, released the other packhorse. "Right then. Which way do we go?"

Maha'dun stared at him. Had his face been uncovered his expression would have been blank.

"How am I supposed to know?"

"What was the name of the last place we stopped? Don't

tell me; you don't know that either."

Maha'dun shrugged. "I employed my coachman for these details."

Puffing his cheeks, Jesamiah indicated the corpse. "Did you want to bury him before we set off?"

"What for? He is dead. He is of no more consequence."

"Well, you could argue that he deserves a Christian send-off."

Again a somewhat astonished response. "Why would he want that? He was not a Christian."

"Oh well, then, that's different." Jesamiah nudged his heel into the horse's side, set him to an easy walk.

"What about those other two bodies?" Maha'dun asked after a few minutes.

"What about them?"

They rode in silence for about half of an hour. Jesamiah's thighs were already aching, but at least the horse seemed quiet and content to remain at a walk.

"May I ask," Maha'dun queried, "how you know which way to go?"

Jesamiah wiped the back of his hand across his mouth. He would have appreciated a drink—something warm and comforting; rum or brandy. And food, also warm and comforting. He needed a shave, his moustache and jawline beard were almost vanished beneath the accumulated stubble.

"The sea," he said patiently, "was to the west of us. Now it is to the north. That ahead," he indicated with a toss of his whiskered chin, "is Exmoor. Therefore, I reckon we need to follow established tracks that will take us roughly sou'-sou'-west."

"Sow-sow-west?"

"Aye. Sou'-sou'-west."

They rode on, saying nothing. Maha'dun was most impressed. Had he been inclined, he might have mentioned that he had not understood a word of what this Jesamiah Acorne had been talking about. What had female pigs to do with direction?

Chapter Sixteen

It had occurred to Carter Trevithick that he was possibly being an idiot after riding five miles. After ten, the possibility became fact. The pony was an Exmoor, a hardy, sturdy and solid little breed that, despite the small height could easily carry a man, especially over the rugged terrain of the moors. But the breed was also single-minded, stubborn and strong. The pony wanted to eat grass; Carter's arms felt like they had been wrenched out of their sockets through yanking the animal's head up from repeated attempts to graze.

Carter's rise of temper and the stupid spat with Rue had soon cooled. For both of them, anger had been fuelled by concern, and after a few tots of brandy and dozing before the fire in the parlour, sense had started to get the upper hand for Carter. But approaching sunup a headache and frustration had crept back in, and on visiting the outside privy, awake and already cold, Carter had taken bridle and saddle and borrowed one of Tawford Barton's mounts. Initially, he had been intent on riding all the way to Bristol, but a stubborn pony, and the lure of Porlock and the daily Bristol Flyer coach had soon become a preferred option.

The morning air was cold, but bright and clear, the sunshine sparkling on the frost—heavier set once he reached the higher ground of the moors. With the glistening frost, the rimed trees and shrubs, everything was crisp and white and clean. A red deer stag bounded away, its breath snorting in clouds of vapour as he ran with purposeful ease across the glimmering expanse of last year's heather and bracken, the magnificent creature as much a part of the moors as the wind and the rain—and the frost. Lord and monarch of Exmoor, his coat gleamed, and head still crowned with his full array of branching antlers, not yet lost to the spring shedding. Had he his musket with him, Carter would have been admiring the chance of acquiring fresh venison, not the living animal, but even if he'd had a weapon, the irksome pony would have alerted the stag to the presence of danger long ago.

The only track was clearly defined, no sign of a coach having passed for the iced puddles were unbroken, the frosted ruts undisturbed. He urged the pony to go faster, but yet again the animal refused to canter, breaking only—and reluctantly—into a jerky trot, which ended abruptly after a few yards with a sudden halt and the shaggy head shooting downward for another mouthful of winter-weary grass. Carter's legs were aching from the constant kick-kick to keep the wretched beast moving, and then the last straw. The pony decided he'd had enough of this irritating burden, so when splashing across a shallow but fast-flowing stream, he stopped and began pawing at the water. Too late, Carter discovered what the animal had in mind... He leapt from the saddle with a shrill, angry cry, hauling at the reins, but he was too slow, the pony's legs were gracefully buckling and he was down, rolling in the cold water. The girth snapped. Bliss to get rid of rider, saddle and the itch of a winter-shedding coat.

"Get up, you little sod! Get up!" Carter was knee deep in

ice-cold water, and getting wetter from the pony's thrashing about. He hauled on the bridle—another mistake. The pony did get up, but with Carter heaving on the straps the bridle slipped neatly over the pony's ears. As agile as the stag, and as free, the Exmoor was up and away.

A string of expletives followed him.

Carter blamed his brother-in-law, Acorne. Had the man been more responsible, reliable, likeable, trustworthy—the list went on—he, Carter would not be standing here, sodden, cold, hungry, tired, and facing a long walk home.

Squelching in his boots, shivering, he set off along the way he had come.

If words could kill, Captain Acorne would be well and truly dead.

* * *

"Well, what have we here?" Jesamiah reined his horse to a halt and, leaning his arm on the animal's neck, could not resist a laugh.

"I'm stalking game," Carter replied. "The wife needs more meat."

"'Course you are," Jesamiah answered, pointing at the man's sodden, muddy apparel. "Well-known fact you have to wrestle the wildlife hereabouts to the ground. What did the rabbit do? Fight back?"

"I hear it is a Devonshire sport to catch game with your bare hands," Maha'dun added, his voice muffled by the scarf. "Fish, for instance."

"You took your time fetching this turtle-head. How many brothels did you both visit along the way?" Carter glowered back at him.

"One or two," Jesamiah quipped. "Might have been three."

Maha'dun shook his head. "No, *sahin*, it was four. You forget the brunette with the..." he outlined the shape of a woman's endowed chest.

Carter's expression deepened into a scowl, the mockery unamusing.

"Do you seriously think," Jesamiah barked, sliding from the horse and approaching Carter, his finger outstretched, stabbing at his brother-in-law's chest, "that I would be swivin' women when my wife lies ill abed?" He poked again, harder. "An' why did you not come and fetch me? Bring horses; come by boat? Why send this dim-skull knobhead who cannot drive a coach, or bear the sunlight?"

Equally as annoyed, Carter retaliated; "I did not bail you out of the mess you got yourself into because I wanted to be near my sister who has every likelihood of dying. And it was she who sent that devil spawn, not me."

Maha'dun had slid from his horse and was fumbling with gloved hands for his cheroot box. He found it but then could not take one of the tobacco sticks out, light it or even smoke it because of the scarf protecting his face. He thrust the box back into his pocket, said with annoyance; "That is not true. Until I met with her seven whole nights after the Captain here came ashore and had been taken captive, Lady Tiola was perfectly healthy."

Carter shot him a look that was as grim as congealing lard.

Tiring of the pointless argument, Jesamiah bent one leg behind him and asked Maha'dun to boost him onto the horse. The Night-Walker obliged and swung himself onto his own mount. Fingers gripped tightly to the mane and thighs clamped for dear life to the none-too-secure body, Jesamiah set off at a trot, Maha'dun following, leading the two packhorses.

Enraged that they were heading off without him, Carter

ran after them, crying out and waving his arms. "Hey! Hey, stop, you bastards! How am I to get home?"

"Got two bloody feet, ain't yer?" Jesamiah mumbled, trotting onward.

Maha'dun took pity; he halted, waited for Carter to catch up and held out his gloved hand offering to haul him up behind. It was not a situation he felt at ease with, but they would get home quicker with this man who knew the way riding, not walking, plus there was the practicality that his body would aid as an additional shield against the sun.

Scowling with an expression that could curdle milk, Carter accepted the offer.

The only concession Jesamiah made was to slow to a walk, hoping that his brother-in-law would not realise the gentler pace was a great relief to his own sore and aching thighs and backside.

* * *

"Sweetheart?" Jesamiah walked quietly into the room, went to the bed and laid the back of his hand against Tiola's cheek. The skin felt cool, no sign of heat or fever.

"You asleep, darlin'?" A stupid question. Of course she was.

Pamela, squeaking with pleasure and throwing her arms around his neck on his arrival, had breathlessly explained that since dawn Tiola had taken an enormous step for the better, the fever fading, her breathing easing.

"She sleeps quiet and sound, almost as if she knew you were on your way."

Jesamiah had answered, without thinking, that she did.

Fortunately, Pamela had laughed and said, "Such is the nature of true love."

A response of, *"These things are possible when you are a*

witch," he firmly kept to himself.

"Tiola?" He sat on the edge of the bed, wincing at the discomfort from his sore backside and thighs, took her hand in his, stroking his thumb over her fingers and knuckles. Pamela had gone to prepare something for him to eat; Jesamiah sat in the quiet, listening to the fire crackling, a robin singing outside the window, someone calling to someone else—the two maids who helped around the house he guessed. Mary was one, the other—Sarah, Sally? Susannah? He could not remember; he stood up, walked to the window. Bone-weary tired, he opened it to breathe in the cold, fresh air. The headland opposite on the far side of the Taw estuary was fully in view, dark patches of cloud shadow skidding across the sunlit bright green of the coarse seagrass, the occasional glint of frost lingering in cracks and crevices along the shore where *Sea Witch* had run aground. Where he and his men, and 'Cesca, had struggled ashore. Where his son had been born dead.

'Your son', 'Cesca had said. *Your* son. *My son,* Jesamiah thought. *My* son.

The tide was on the flood, sluicing over the sand and gravel bank of the Bar. Beyond, the blue of the open sea, sparkling in the sunshine. Beckoning.

A voice, distant but clear, carrying across the estuary. Jesamiah would recognise that French bellow anywhere. He craned his neck to see out towards the left. Appledore was partially hidden by the barn and stables, he could see some of its rounded hill and a few of the colourfully painted houses and merchant shops straddling the quay. It was not the scenery or landscape that stole his attention, but the ship.

He had seen her as they had ridden in. There had been several larger boats waiting beyond the Bar to come in with the tide, needing the deeper channels where the Taw met in confluence with the Torridge, but a barque with a shallower draft, her sails flapping as her captain almost lost way to a sudden come-and-gone flurry of wind, had obscured that other ship at anchor. The one with only half the high rise of her masts, with no canvas bent to her yards. From the way she had been riding high in the water, the rim of her copper keel gleaming like painted gold in the sun's glare, her holds were empty. Not even her guns were aboard. As they rode down from the hills, Jesamiah had tried not to look at the figures scurrying over her decks, climbing like monkeys up the network of shrouds and cordage that was starting to appear like expanding spiders' webs. Tried not to look because he ought to be there. How could he? His place was here, with Tiola. But how could he not gaze with longing at his beloved, beautiful ship returning, slow step by slow step to glory beneath the command of someone else? As competent as Rue was, *Sea Witch* was not *his* ship.

The only thing that had stopped Jesamiah from kicking his horse into a gallop, urging it across the mud and into the water to swim across to the far side, was a barely concealed snort of disgust from Carter.

"You covet that ship like you would a whore! Well, if it is more important than your wife, go whoring why don't you?"

Jesamiah had said nothing, had stoically glued his attention to the smoke streaming like fingers pointing into the sky from the chimneys of Tawford Barton.

Carter was in the kitchen warming himself beside the fire. Maha'dun? Jesamiah did not particularly care where he was. He had slid from the horse the moment they had entered the yard and scuttled away. Old Rob, husband to the cook and in charge of everything to do with the farm and the land, had taken the horses to the meadow. Come the morrow he would take them to the nearest post house in Barnstaple.

Another distant shout from across the bay. "Judas!" Jesamiah swore. "Keep hold of that bloody rope, you idiot! What manner of landlubber men are you using, Rue?" He turned away from the window, picked up his hat from where he had tossed it onto a chair, was almost at the door when Pamela came in carrying a tray.

"I thought you would prefer to eat in here, where you can watch over your wife," she said, nodding her thanks as Jesamiah, put the hat down again and took the heavy tray from her. "There is cheese and ham. The bread is from the oven this morning, and the butter fresh churned. The wine is the last of the blackberry and apple. I am afraid we have nothing stronger. I could send Carter to fetch rum or brandy from his tavern if you would prefer that?"

"No, no, this is handsome, thank you," Jesamiah said as he set it all down on the table beside the fire. "A feast for a king, I would say!"

Pamela blushed. "Nay, 'tis only humble fare. I will serve a hot meal later, when the tide turns and Rue returns." She laughed, "You see, I am already learning the ways of the sea. The time and the tide do not wait for dallying over things like putting a good meal into a man's belly at a reasonable, and constant, hour of the day."

"We have our meals at regular times when at sea, always assuming the weather is not so bad that it is impossible to light the cooking stove, or Finch is too drunk to do more than snore in the sail locker."

She conceded his point, although won the round by adding, "But here we have fresh food without weevils and maggots."

Jesamiah bowed, took her hand and gallantly kissed it. "And your talent in the kitchen, ma'am, far outshines Finch's culinary disasters."

She smiled, admitted the truth; "Alas, I would probably match the talentless skills of your steward. It is our cook you must thank; Elsa is a wonder with the meanest scraps."

Nodding his appreciation, Jesamiah seated himself at the table. "Then I had best not insult her by returning this tray with nought but empty platters and a few crumbs." It was all banter; he was so hungry he could eat stewed rat if it were served to him. Which, in the past, it had been.

Through a mouthful of cold meat he asked, "What time does the tide turn?"

Pamela had been bending to add logs to the fire; she straightened, peered out of the window. "It will be full flood soon. Rue has worked hard to restore your ship as well as he can. He says Master Benson made good work of repairing her."

"Master Benson is a skilled shipwright and a fair man."

"He was a'feared for the life of his son, as were we all—for all of you. Sir Ailie did well to secure your release."

About to correct her about Doone, his words were forgotten as Tiola stirred, murmuring a low moan that was part sigh. Both Jesamiah and Pamela were beside the bed quicker than blinking.

"Tiola?" Jesamiah sat on the edge of the bed, his wife's fragile hand clasped within his own. "Sweetheart?"

Tiola's eyes opened. To the other side of the bed, Pamela uttered a squeak of relief.

"Are you a ghost come from the gallows to visit me?" Tiola asked, looking up into Jesamiah's eyes. "You do not seem like one."

"I most likely don't smell like one either. I've not had chance to bathe or change clothes for a day or two."

Apologising profusely, Pamela hurried to the door, a blush

to her face. "I never thought! I will see that hot water is set to heat immediately."

Rising, one hand reaching out, Jesamiah implored her not to concern herself. "I shall attend to the matter of dust and sweat later. For now I would prefer to be with my wife."

Again, Pamela blushed, "Of course you do, and I have household chores to attend." She smiled at Tiola, pale and small in the big bed, "Glad is my heart that you are returned to us. We have spent some fearful days and nights of late."

"Glad I am to be returned, my dear friend."

Alone with Tiola, Jesamiah shuffled further onto the bed and with great gentleness took her into his arms. She felt as thin and frail as a little bird. "I do not know what I would have done had I lost you," he said, kissing the crown of her head.

"Returned to one of your mistresses, I expect," Tiola answered, pulling away from him, the apparent frailty quite gone. "Alicia Mereno in Virginia perhaps, now that Francesca can no longer accommodate you?"

Jesamiah sat there, stunned, speechless, thoughts and acerbic retorts tumbling through his head. In the end he touched one finger to her cheek, said mildly, "It is not like you to be cruel."

With her uninjured hand she slapped his face. Not hard, but enough to let him know she was angry. "It is not like me to resent the whores you couple with, you mean? Am I not permitted to despise them for taking you away from me; to despise you for betraying me?"

There was nothing he could say to that, so he kept quiet.

"I have lived in fear these last days, not knowing whether you lived or were swinging from the gallows. I have walked through lonely shadows and stared at death, and, before that, I helped birth your son," she snapped, "a son fathered on another woman. A son that came from a whore's belly. How do you expect me to react? With joy? With pleasure? To kiss you and say, 'Well done'?"

"I am sorry," he said, moving away from her and back to the window. Her words and the slap stung in equal measure.

"I'm sorry for all of it, except," he found the courage to gaze directly into her eyes, "except, when I was with 'Cesca last year I thought you were no longer my woman. I thought I was on my own, and to me she was no whore."

Tiola sighed, lay back against the pillows. She was not as frail as she was leading Pamela to believe, but still she was tired and had not returned to full strength. The long sleep had almost healed her—almost, but not quite.

With his back to her, Jesamiah stood, staring out of the window at his ship. "I thought you were dying," he said. "I came back as quick as I could."

"It takes more than a broken ankle and sprained wrist to kill me, Jesamiah. And I was frightened. I thought you were dead."

He turned around, could not resist the answer, "Despite despising me?"

"It is not you I despise," Tiola responded with a sigh, "it is the fact that you cannot keep your breeches buttoned that I hate."

"I've told you what happened with 'Cesca, and she's the one who is dead, her and her son, my son; they are both gone, so you've nothing to worry about, have you?" The words came out sounding angrier than he had intended.

Tiola was tired, the tiredness of exhaustion, the tiredness that made tempers short and the wrong words trip with unguarded haste off the tongue. "And had they not died? What then, Jesamiah? Would you be here now, with me, or with them?"

He could not answer. His own anger spilled out, an unwatched pot boiling over. He snatched up his hat, made for the door.

"*Ais*, go on, go to the one you've been staring at since you entered the room. The one you will always, always, put before me!"

"You know that ain't true," he snarled as his thumb pressed the door latch, "but as I have clearly been misinformed about your frail health—you seem to be very far from death's door—she's my ship an' I need to be out there seeing to her well-being."

He opened the door, walked through and slammed it shut behind him. Regretted losing his temper three strides down the hall, but pride forbade him to go back and apologise.

Chapter Seventeen

"This deck's a bloody mess! You there, sailor, coil that line or you'll have someone catch their foot in it. And you..." Jesamiah peered up the mainmast, "if you think that's the place for playin' silly buggers, then carry on, but don't be expectin' any sympathy when you bleedin' fall and break your soddin' back!"

Jesamiah had expected the foul mood to have lifted as he had neared his ship, but it had festered while waiting for the ferryman to return from Appledore, had thickened on discovering the imbecile was the snipe-minded lazy sluggard he'd had reason to cross when last he was in the vicinity. And had turned as black as pitch as he'd stepped through the entry port onto *Sea Witch*'s deck. He had seen wrecks tidier than this!

"An' 'oo do 'e think 'e be?" someone muttered, the sneer not quite soft enough to remain unheard. "The bloody Kraut King or summat?"

Rue was hurrying down the ladder from the quarterdeck. At the bottom he spread his arms, a grin reaching across his face from one ear to the other. "*Mon ami!* Ah, 'tis good to see you!"

The two men embraced, Rue breaking away slightly to look Jesamiah up and down, assessing his well-being, then planting a solid kiss on each of his cheeks. "By those bruises on your face, I 'azard a guess that you 'ave been brawlin'? Can I not leave you alone for more than *un jour*? A day?"

Jesamiah laughed and poked a finger into Rue's stomach. "An' I can't leave you alone, either. Where's this flab of a gut come from?"

Rue scowled, patted his girth. "Alas, although she is modest about it, Pamela's baking 'appens to be better than Finch's."

"Anyone's baking is better than his!" Jesamiah laughed as he embraced his friend a second time then indicated the ship. "Thank you for seeing to her, though she's a bit of a…"

"*Merde* 'ole?" Rue finished for him. "These are Bideford men, not John Benson's own. They resent working on a ship which they say was a pirate vessel. It 'as been difficult to convince them otherwise." Then he noticed Jesamiah's hand, snatched it up.

"What is this? *Dieu du ciel!* This is not an injury from a street brawl!"

"A gift from the Spanish," Jesamiah said as he rubbed the fingers of his right hand over the two stubs and the scarring on his left. "Cannon shot made short work of the taffrail, binnacle box, old Toby Turner's head, and my hand. The Spanish weren't especially pleased to see us, but soon realised their error and made good the damage caused."

Rue murmured something uncomplimentary about Spain and the Spanish, then, concerned, asked, "Where are the rest of our lads? Benson said you were all acquitted?" He peered out over the rail as if expecting to see a couple of longboats crowded with men pulling from the shore. "They are coming, *n'est-ce pas?"*

"They are coming," Jesamiah answered with more optimism than he actually felt. "I gave orders for them to muster here at Instow on Sunday morning, but," he scowled at the tardiness of the deck, the incomplete rigging, the fact that *Sea Witch* was still practically an empty hulk below decks, "but I am not too hopeful about setting sail again soon."

"*Non*, once this rigging is completed, we only need put everything back where it belongs. It is all stored safe in Benson's yard. We lost very little except a few barrels of cargo from the 'old. It will not take us long, *mon ami*, to be *finis. Un? Deux* days? You see only the muck 'eap, not the good soil *le merde* is turning into."

"'Ware below!" The warning shout came from above before a marlinspike fell to Jesamiah's feet, missing his head by a fraction of an inch. He bent, picked it up and hurled it over the rail into the tidewater.

"Dock its value from that man's wages," he growled, "and a shilling from his." He pointed to a bearded ruffian with a red bandana tied around a bald scalp. "What's your name?"

The man glowered back at him.

"I said, what is your name?"

"Perkiss."

"Perkiss what?"

"Perkiss, sir."

"Well, for your information, Perkiss, you insolent tar, I don't *think* I'm anyone, I *know* who I am. I'm owner and Captain of this ship and at this precise moment, therefore, your employer. And if you don't like that fact I suggest you get yourself ashore and bloody stay there. Savvy?"

The man most likely needed the money and the job. More affably he answered, "Aye... sir."

Jesamiah turned back to the entry port. "Rue, I'll take the jolly boat and inspect the hull. Meanwhile, these fatherless whoresons can set these decks straight or they'll all be less more than a shillin'."

There were a few grumbles and protests as Jesamiah descended the cleats and, tugging the painter free, pulled the small rowing boat towards the end of the ladder, but Rue silenced the dissent.

He shoved his face close to the bald man's. "You might be a lubber come new aboard, but I suggest you start learnin' fast, *mon ami*. What *le capitaine* said? It is not true. It would not 'ave been the Spanish who severed the 'ead, but *le capitaine*."

Rue grinned as he climbed up to the quarterdeck and everyone aboard suddenly looked lively. Landlubber dolts believed the stupidest things.

* * *

Candlelight was glowing from several of the downstairs windows at Tawford Barton as Rue and Jesamiah stepped from the jolly boat onto the soft mud and heaved her higher up the shore. The tide was ebbing, dusk was falling, and as much as Jesamiah had wanted to stay aboard his ship, practicality dictated otherwise. Men could not work efficiently in the dark with a ship listing at low water. Time enough to do more tomorrow.

There was light in one upstairs window as well. Tiola's room. Twice he saw a shadow move across the room inside. It would not be Tiola. Pamela? Maha'dun? Was Tiola in a better frame of mind? Was he? He felt ashamed of himself now, for she had been in the right, but these past few days had caused feelings and thoughts to buck and prance about inside him like a rudderless ship caught in a storm. Had he loved 'Cesca? Of course not—at least not in the way or depth that he loved Tiola —but he could have done, would have done, if he had not already had a wife.

"There's my lady come to greet us," Rue said, pointing towards the sandbanks, seagrass and salt-tolerant shrubs that formed what passed as a front garden.

"Pamela is a good woman, Rue. She will make you a wife to cherish. And one to warm your stinking feet nor mind your dreadful manners. Make no complaint at your excessive farting..."

Rue laughed, "*Oui*, that she will; am I not the most fortunate of men to 'ave one so blind-eye devoted?"

Jesamiah slapped his friend's shoulder, and lengthened his stride to be able to kiss Pamela's cheek before Rue could do so. "My friend here," he grinned, "claims that he is a fortunate man to have one so lovely as you as his bride. Personally, I cannot think what it is you see in the old goat to have accepted his proposal. It certainly is not his good looks or genteel manners."

"I will 'ave you know, *mon capitaine*, that *cette belle jeune fille* 'as the good taste and the good sense."

"Added to which," Pamela retorted as, standing between the two men, she linked arms with them both, "I heard that Monsieur Claude de la Rue is rich and an adept lover."

"Who told you that?" Jesamiah guffawed. "If it were Rue himself, he failed to add that he is as much a liar as am I!"

The kitchen door opened, sending a stream of light flooding across the grass as if it were a welcoming pathway, then became muted as Maha'dun stood in the way.

"'E still 'ere?" Rue complained, grimacing. "I 'ad 'oped 'e would remain in Bristol."

"He is good in a fight," Jesamiah countered, touching one of the bruises on his cheek.

"So is a baiting dog or a bear, but neither would I trust outside the pit," Rue answered.

"Who said anything about trust?"

Maha'dun bowed slightly as they approached, stood aside to permit them to enter the kitchen, offering a smile to Pamela as she passed. Her response was polite, a quick smile and a brief-bobbed curtsey; she was afraid of this tall, dark-haired, blue-eyed man who preferred the solitary night to the joy of sunlight. Agreed with Rue that life would be more settled at Tawford Barton had he remained in Bristol, but Tiola appeared to be fond of him and she had no qualm about his integrity. And, Pamela had to admit, this Maha'dun person had fulfilled his promise of bringing Jesamiah home. For that alone she was prepared to tolerate his presence.

"Will you dine with us this evening, Maha'dun?" she asked, broadening her smile to one of a hostess's welcome.

"I thank you, my lady, for the generous offer but I will see to my own fare. I have things to do." He bowed, walked away down the path heading for the direction of Instow.

"'Eading for the tavern, I suspect," Rue observed as he shut the door with a firm click to the latch. "I 'ave seen many a tar drink 'imself as full as a goat, but that one can empty a barrel without wetting a whisker."

"Not that he has whiskers," Jesamiah observed as he helped himself to a slice of the lamb that the cook was carving. She slapped his fingers away and he calmly took another slice before skittering off across the kitchen out of her reach. "His cheeks are as smooth as a babe's bum."

"And you would be knowing about a babe's *derrière* then, would you?" Rue quipped.

Jesamiah laughed as he headed for the stairs. "A wench's bum then!" Rue's guffaw of laughter followed him as he took the stairs two at a time.

Opening the bedroom door quietly, Jesamiah peered in. "Tiola?"

Nothing flew through the air at him—actual or verbal; he guessed it would be safe to enter. She was lying down, her back to him, her long black hair twisted into a single plait that had wisps escaping from it. One shoulder showed beneath the coverlet, bare and round, white-skinned.

"Tiola?" he repeated as he crossed the room, hesitated, uncertain whether to reach out and touch her. She stirred, turned over with difficulty, the bandaging to wrist and ankle hampering ease of movement. It was only then, as her shift slipped slightly, that he saw the yellowing bruises to her upper torso.

"Sweetheart, I am sorry, so sorry."

"For what?" she said, modestly rearranging her shift and heaving herself up to half lie, half sit. "For being an idiot or for forgetting to fetch me up my supper?"

"For being an idiot?"

Tiola smiled. "I will forgive you if you will forgive me? I had no right to be cross with you, and no right to take my frustration out on Señora Escudero either. These bindings," she indicated her bandages, "are weighing heavy on me. They are more of a nuisance than the injuries—which are almost mended, but I cannot allow anyone to know that. I went far away to heal myself and was not properly returned. My words came out as unforgivable spite. It is I who apologise."

Jesamiah sat on the bed, held her to him—gently—his hand stroking her hair and her back. "You never say anything that is not true. You just sometimes say it in a way that bites the deeper because your knife is sharp."

"Help me blunt it." She twined her arm around his neck,

put her mouth to his and kissed him, long and sensuous. "Make love to me," she whispered.

"How can I? You are injured; I would hurt you."

"I have said, I am nearly healed; and besides, gentle lovemaking is as pleasurable as the tumble of high passion, is it not?"

Jesamiah heard Rue call that the meal was served, but ignored him. He had a different hunger that he desired to be fed.

Chapter Eighteen

Maha'dun squatted among the sand dunes looking out over the mudflats of low tide towards the froth of the sea as it spewed over the Bar, the shoal of sand, gravel and mud that caught many a ship that was not captained well or fell foul of weather and tide. He was remembering that night when the ship opposite had come in, too fast, driven by an angry sea. The sound she had made as she had been hurled onto the shore had been terrifying. He was afraid of the sea, of its tempers and vastness. It stretched, so he had been told, to beyond the edge of the world—and beyond again. You could sail on the sea for weeks and never once see or smell land. The only sea he had crossed in all his long lifetime had been from Calais to Dover; a short crossing on a fine-weather night when the waves had been nought but ripples and the moonlit land had never been very much out of sight. He lit another cheroot from the one he had been smoking, stabbed the stub out. Blew smoke up towards the starlit night sky. He was troubled and did not know what to do about it.

The English woman with the Spanish name who was supposed to have delivered a bone-box was dead. Killed, perhaps, by Cara'mina. Another man was dead, one who, as far as Maha'dun was aware, had nothing whatsoever to do with the Night-Walkers or the bone-boxes. His throat ripped open instead of Captain Acorne's. Also Cara'mina's mistake. Was she as yet aware of her error? Of course she was! Who else would have set those apparent robbers to follow his coach from Bristol to Devon? But that was the puzzle. Why employ men to do the skilled work of tracking when she would have been far better at the job herself? And when she would have guessed the destination anyway? No, those men had been sent to kill Captain Acorne, and Maha'dun had a deep suspicion that Doone was behind that sending.

He looked around as something rustled in the marram grass, expecting to see Cara'mina loom up out of the darkness, her eyes spitting rage at yet more of his incompetence. But it was only a cat hunting shrews.

The cat stood a moment, unmoving except for a slight twitch at the tip of her tail, then she hissed, turned away and was gone. Maha'dun wanted another cheroot. That had been his last one. He would have to obtain more. He stood up, stretched cramped legs. He could go to Bideford or Barnstaple to find some smokes. It would be no difficulty to break in and steal what he needed from the right store. He did it often. Bideford would be the nearer. Or would it? Barnstaple was the larger town. Barnstaple had a gaol. Did Bideford? Indecisive, he stood there, hands in pockets, not knowing what to do. He was a creature who followed orders. Do this, do that. Give pleasure, spy, watch, listen. Kill. These were his talents. Sexual skills, and killing. He was a hopeless spy; to be a good spy you needed quick wit and firm decisions. Unless the wit was for entertainment and the decisions for what positions to pursue in bed, the two qualities eluded him.

A light appeared in one of Tawford Barton's upper windows. Lady Tiola's room. Ah! They were awake then! The lure of stealing more cheroots entirely, for now, forgotten, Maha'dun set off at a slow lope. Tiola would know what he should do. She always did.

At the house, Maha'dun quietly ascended the stairs, mindful of the fifth from the top that groaned with even the lightest pressure. The rest of the household were asleep. Candlelight glimmered beneath Tiola's door, a shadow flickered. He moved to the door, put his hand on the latch, pressed down with his thumb. The latch clicked, the door swung open, and Maha'dun stood as if turned to stone. Remained there, thinking nothing, feeling nothing. Numb, frozen. Then his senses returned. He backed away and closed the door even more quietly than he had opened it. He descended the stairs, went through the kitchen, out the back door, and walked to the dunes and the beach, tears dripping from his eyes. Grief filling his heart, head and soul.

* * *

Soon after nine of the clock, Jesamiah had emerged from a deep sleep to find Tiola awake and watching him.

"Whoever tended that hand," she had said, "made a skilful job of healing it."

"'Cesca saw to it. She nursed me through a few rough days," he had answered flatly, aware that he was risking much by talking, again, of his lover.

To his surprise—relief—Tiola had not resurrected her anger, instead she had said, "Then I will send a prayer of thanks to her spirit for her kindness."

And then they had talked, she wrapped in his arms, the

firelight flickering over the ceiling, the household, an hour later, settling with contentment to the night and sleep. He told her everything; the death they had met in Spain, 'Cesca's stopping of his own hanging—and again in Bristol. Of meeting his maternal uncle, the Marqués de Molina, Antonio Calderón in Spain. An uncle he'd had no knowledge of. Told of being duped into fetching an imposter king to Devon and about *Sea Witch* being wrecked, of losing his men and being arrested by the militia. Confessed his fears for 'Cesca and the child she had carried, and spoke of her other son and the promise he had made to find and protect the boy. Of his concern that Tiola would not understand why he had made such a promise. To his relieved surprise, and a necessity to swallow down more grief, she had reassured him he had done the right thing.

"No child," she had said, "should be left alone in the world without mother or father."

As the old longcase clock in the hall downstairs had struck its ponderous chime of eleven, Jesamiah had thoughts of all the things that were not lost. Prime above them, Tiola.

Their next lovemaking began slowly with tender kisses and light caresses, but their passion had demanded more. Hampered by her splinted ankle and bandaged wrist, their positioning had been awkward but had heightened arousal. Tiola sprawled across the bed, sheets and blankets thrust aside, hair tumbled, head back, uninjured leg twined around his hips. Ready and erect, Jesamiah had entered her with savage roughness, thrusting hard and fast, driving her to that crescendo of elation where nothing beyond the deep penetration of mutual desire mattered.

Neither had been aware of the door opening or the Night-Walker standing there, watching. Only when the door had closed as her pleasure had reached its pinnacle of exultation did Tiola catch that distinctive whiff of sandalwood and cigar smoke. When the sweat glistening on her body and breasts had dried, when Jesamiah slept, his arms curved around her—only then did she speak into Maha'dun's mind.

~ You must understand, I am Jesamiah's wife now. ~

* * *

Cara'mina watched Maha'dun enter the house. Like him, she required no light, beyond the natural reflection of stars and moon, the Night-Walkers' vision perfectly adapted to seeing through the mask of darkness. She did not know who she was more angry with, Maha'dun the imbecile, Tiola the witch, or Acorne the death-defier. None of them would escape her vengeance this time! But how to take that revenge, how to perform her retribution?

Maha'dun closed the door; a few moments later she saw his silhouette move behind one of the upstairs windows—one of the long thin ones that gave light onto the upper landing above the stairs. Was he going to the witch-woman then? Had she called him to service her? Cara'mina's only regret; the one thing Maha'dun was good at. Fucking. He never complained when she wanted sexual satisfaction through implementing pain. She had bound and beaten him to within an inch of his life on more than one occasion, but he had always finished by entering her and bringing her to climax. Was that why she despised him? Because, whatever she did to him, he never surrendered? Only once, once in many hundreds of years had he refused to pleasure her, and that was when he had pledged his loyalty to the witch. She had taken revenge by giving him to the humans, thinking they would have fun torturing him for a while, had not expected them to try to drown him.

Aside from the crude human obsession of beheading or

skewering through vital organs, there were only the four ritual ways to kill a Night-Walker: burying alive, suffocating, burning or drowning. Earth, Air, Fire, Water. She laughed; and these humans thought the elements were sacred because of their feeble gods and goddesses? How banal—they had so soon after developing from apes forgotten the true nature of the Four Deaths!

Her decision made, she set aside dwelling on the mistake she had made with that man in the tavern—the woman's death had been nothing to do with her. If the target had been Acorne, not the woman, then he would be dead—she never failed where killing was concerned. That man in the bed. He should have been Acorne. She had thought it was Acorne and had killed him. Like all Night-Walkers, she usually killed by ripping the throat open, but tonight she would use one of the other ritual ways. Sometimes alternatives were necessary, and more entertaining.

Chapter Nineteen

Maha'dun stood at the edge of the water where river became sea and sea became river. Fresh tears crawled down his cheeks, with none but the frosted stars and a low-hung moon to see his turmoil and his pain. He had loved Tiola for so, so long. And all he could see, all he could picture in his mind, was the man, Jesamiah Acorne, standing naked over her, his muscles rippling as he took her to that singularly most wonderful place of united delight. Love, for so long embraced, now replaced by bewildered confusion.

Desperate for a cheroot, he slumped, exhausted, down among the marram grass and sat there watching the moon rise higher and brighter, wondering, as sometimes he did, about the pinpoints of light that were the stars. Tiola had told him that some of them had names; Alnilam, Alnitak, Mintaka. Betelgeuse, Rigel, Sirius. Had said, too, that the stars were like the sun but were thousands upon thousands of miles away, and that the night sky was not a ceiling but an ocean of Space. He knew *that* was one of her stories. If they were like the sun, why did they not bake with heat and burn his skin?

He fell asleep—rare for him to sleep during the hours of

night—woke again with a start, desperate for the comfort of tobacco. He started wondering about the stars again, what made them glow, who had lit them in the first place—not the why, for that was obvious; to make a suitable light for the Night-Walkers. He stretched cramped muscles, realised he must have dozed for longer than he had thought for dawn was paling the sky. Odd, the few dawns he had seen had always been a purplish-blue that changed into pinks and golds. This one was sending an orange glow into the sky. Agitated, he plucked at some grass, undid the buttons on his waistcoat, did them up again. He so badly needed a cheroot. He could taste the tobacco smoke on his lips, smell it... He was on his feet, running, leaping mounds of grass, slithering down slopes of sand, running, running, arms pumping, head back, legs pounding. Dawn came from the east and did not bring with it a column of acrid black smoke and the crackle of flames!

He ran beneath Tawford Barton's walled arch into the cobbled courtyard, old Rob and his wife were there, she was standing with her hands clutching her night-time rag-bound hair, screaming; he was desperately trotting to and from the well with a single bucket trying to quench flames that filled one of the ground-floor rooms, the parlour. A hopeless attempt. The timber-panelled room with its brocade window drapes and cushions, the wall tapestries and wooden chairs, tables and cupboards, was well ablaze. Screams were coming from the gabled dormer window on the floor above; one of the maids, terrified, was leaning out as far as she could beneath the thatched roofing, the second maid, pale-faced and sobbing, behind her.

Rue appeared, breathless, dressed in boots, breeches and shirt—his small room was to the other end of the house, as yet unscathed. Maha'dun took it all in as he ran, kept running, stopped only as Jesamiah emerged from the front door carrying Tiola wrapped in a blanket. He wore only his shirt, half-buttoned breeches and boots.

Tiola pointed to the two maids, "Someone help them!"

Rue was bellowing for Pamela, "Where is Pamela? 'As anyone seen 'er? Pamela! Pamela! *Où es-tu? Où es-tu!*"

"I am here, Rue! I'm here!" Pamela ran, coughing, from the cloud of smoke now billowing from the kitchen. There was a crash from somewhere indoors, the sound of breaking glass. Her nightshift and bare feet were soot blackened, her two dogs, bundled in her arms, were wriggling and desperate to get down, frightened. Pamela collapsed to her knees onto the cobbles, coughing and retching, put her arm out to save herself and dropped both dogs. They fled beneath the arch towards the river and beach, Pamela scrabbled to her feet ready to run after them. "Lorna! Poppy! Come back!"

Rue grabbed hold of her. "We are needed 'ere!" he cried. "*Les chiens* can look after themselves, *ma chère*, they will not go far. They will be safer out the way!"

He was right, of course, except she could not dismiss the quick come-and-gone thought of relief that at least her old boy, Rum, buried beneath the lilac tree two weeks since, was no longer a worry.

"The maids!" Tiola cried again.

Jesamiah set her down on the bench outside the barn that formed the opposite side of the courtyard to the house, with the shippon, cow byre and small fox-proof chicken house linking the two. "Tuck that blanket round yourself and bloody do something! A spell to make it rain. Anything!"

"I can't bloody do spells like that!" she shouted back. "Don't you think I wish I bloody could?"

He was not listening, he was already pulling the barn doors

open. "Rue? Rue! Get a lantern, we need to find a ladder!"

Maha'dun was there beside him, as one door opened he hurried inside—with no need for a light in the interior darkness found what was needed instantly.

The two hurried across the courtyard carrying the ladder between them, Jesamiah set it against the stone wall and began to climb, even before Rue, elbowing Maha'dun aside, had ensured it was set secure.

Other people were hurrying from the cottages along the track, men mostly, pulling on jerkins over shirts and breeches, a few women running, clutching shawls and blankets over their shifts. Someone, alert to what was happening, had brought buckets. Within moments a water-chain had been set up across the yard. But there were too few people and too many flames.

The ladder was a foot too short, but from the top rung Jesamiah's head was level with the glass and he could see in. Black smoke was filling the interior, flames were visible licking beneath the wooden door.

"Climb out the window!" he ordered to the girl leaning out, as he moved down a couple of rungs to make space. "Come on! Squeeze through!"

"I cain't!" she shrilled. "'Tis too far down, I be afeared o' fallin'!"

"We'll catch you if you do!" Maha'dun shouted up, holding his hands out to grasp Rue's and form a cradle.

"Are you mad?" Rue snapped, snatching his hands away. "We will never be able to break 'er fall!"

"We can try, or at least give her the confidence to do as the captain is asking. She does not know we are unlikely to catch her."

"Come on," Jesamiah was urging, "come out backwards, I'll guide your feet. Close your eyes… that's it!" He moved down another rung, speaking slow and calm, his voice low and coaxing, even though he wanted to shout and scream and curse; to tell her to shift her fokken arse.

"That's it. I have your ankle—here, can you feel the rung? Good. Now the other foot. That's it. You're out. Now down, come on, come down with me. That's it."

Pamela was there at the bottom, enfolding the girl in her arms. "Susannah? Are you hurt? Oh, my dear, my dear!"

They held each other tightly, tears from the smoke and from fear streaming their sooty cheeks.

The other girl was at the window now, screaming for someone to help her. Jesamiah went back up the ladder. Mary was shorter than Susannah, plumper, broader abeam and abust. The casement window was small and narrow. Too small and narrow for her to climb out.

"A rope," Jesamiah yelled down, "we need a good sturdy one to pull this frame out!"

"I will get something!" Maha'dun answered and ran for the harness room, returned almost immediately with a set of leather reins from a carriage harness. He went up the ladder, gave one end to Jesamiah who passed it to the girl.

"Thread it round the centre frame, out the other window and back to me—come on girl, jump to it—that's it! Now find something heavy to hit the frame here in the centre from your side. Come on, girl! You've got to fight your way out!"

Mary was frantically looking round at the bare essentials; two truckle beds, a chair, a clothes press, nightstand with china laver and jug. The pisspot beneath the bed was pottery... her shoe! She had sturdy wooden clogs, would they be strong enough? She ran to get them, screamed again as flames caught at the door and within moments were crawling upwards.

"Tha door's a-vire!" she shrieked, "tha vire's comin' in!"

"All the more reason to get to work," Jesamiah urged with as much calm as he could muster. "Come on!" He slithered down the ladder and taking up the slack, coiled one length of the leather reins round both hands, Rue did the same with the other—and Maha'dun, behind Jesamiah followed their example. Old Rob grabbed hold behind Rue, other men following suit.

"All right, make taut!" Jesamiah said. "Ready? Two, six ... pull! Two, six ... *pull*."

Tiola had closed her eyes and had cleared her mind—difficult to shut out the noise and the fear, but she had to concentrate. She could not summon rain, not the sort of downpour that would be needed to put out this well-alight blaze without risking flooding and the damage that could cause. But she could summon physical help. She focused her mind on Instow church sitting like a broody hen with its chicks huddled around; concentrated on the bell tower and the bells within. The bell ropes. Grasped one within her hands.

"Two, six ... pull. Two, six ... pull!" Jesamiah's voice, in her mind; she hauled on the thick bell rope, dropping it down and letting it swing up again on its own momentum, dropping it down, letting it swing up. Gradually, slowly, with each plunge the bell high above began to move. A faint, hesitant *ding* of sound chimed. Again and again she pulled and let go, the bell in its cradle swaying back and forth, further and faster, the clanger knocking against the bell, light at first, then firmer, *ding... ding...* sounding out over the village, the bay, across the river. *Ding! Ding!* Villagers were hurrying from their houses, some naked, some scrabbling into clothes. The sky above Tawford Barton was lit with the glow of fire, and a plume of smoke. They came running, grabbed at tools—hoes, pitchforks, buckets, rope. Fire, the greatest fear for those who lived in

timber-frame cottages with reed-thatched roofs.

The first men to clatter into the courtyard joined on the line behind Jesamiah, Rue and Maha'dun. Another shinned up the ladder, deftly attached a length of stout cordage to the central window frame, before he had even climbed down again a chain of men were taking the end up, and heaving with their combined strength as if competing in a bizarre tug-o-war.

And still Tiola sat there, ringing and ringing the church bell.

"Curse these soddin' well-built houses!" someone gasped.

Inside, Mary had been hammering at the window frame, looking round nervously every few moments at the burning door. Her clog was useless, it had not even made a dent. What else could she use? Desperately she glanced around the room. What about the table beside the bed? It was square, solid, made of oak. Could she smash it against the frame hard enough? She could try!

She ran to fetch it, screeched in terror as the floorboards beneath her bare feet gave way. A roar, as if it were a cannon blast, erupted from the window. A ball of orange flame blew outward carrying shards of glass and burning splinters of wood across the courtyard to the thatched roof of the barn and stables opposite.

Tiola fell forward, her good arm raised protecting her face as she felt the scorching heat race past above her. People—men and women—were screaming, Pamela was darting across the cobbles to the byre—why had they not thought of the animals earlier? At least the horses were in the meadow, but what of the cows and chickens? Pigeons that had been roosting in the eaves took flight, one with its feathers caught by flames. It fell quickly, its neck mercifully broken. Little birds, sparrows mostly, were darting out—thank goodness it was yet too early for the swallows and house martins to have returned to their nests!

In silence, everyone was gaping up at the belching furnace billowing from the broken window and devouring the thatched roof of the house, the makeshift ropes falling slack and the bucket chain ceasing. Pamela was the only one not looking. Wisps of smoke were spiralling from the roofs of the outbuildings and barn, the fire was taking hold there too. She ran to the chicken shed shouting for help—flinging the door open, hurried in, flapping her arms and night shift to shoo the hens out. Fowl tumbled into the yard like a cackling waterfall, feathers flying into the air as the creatures flew or lurched and waddled with their odd-gaited step. Pamela ran, next, to the byre, looking over her shoulder to see Rue and a few other men checking that the stables were empty. The two cows were lowing, frantic, their large, liquid eyes rolling, feet kicking the partition walls as the crackle of flames overhead scurried along the roof beams and struck into the heart of the hayloft above. Pamela slid the gate to the first stall open, but Daisy-Bell was too frightened, would not move. Pamela tugged at her horns, got behind her, slapped her rump, shouted.

"It is no good like that!" Maha'dun said, taking off his coat and tossing it over the cow's head. "Look, she is coming now! Guide her outside, I will get the other one."

But he was nearer the door, easier for him to usher the animal to safety, grab his coat and go back in.

Pamela was at the other cow's rump, pushing at the protruding hip bones, pulling on her tail, yelling and yelling; "Go forward! Go forward!"

Maha'dun flung his coat over the animal, got her moving. "Come on!" he bellowed over his shoulder at Pamela. "Get out!" The cow was at the door, another man—Jesamiah—was there, slapping her rump, shooing her out. The hay overhead was ablaze, the entire roof and the supporting beams creaking and groaning. Maha'dun hurried back to the stall, reached forward to grasp Pamela, had her hand... She tripped, fell, taking Maha'dun to his knees with her. The roof groaned again.

Clawing his fingers into Maha'dun's shirt and hair, Jesamiah pulled. "Hold on to her! Hold on to her!"

Maha'dun had Pamela's hand, held tight, his nails digging into her flesh. He looked into her terrified eyes, tried to smile, to reassure, but her sweating hand was slipping...

The byre roof caved in with a roar of flame and burning hay, dust and debris.

Jesamiah flung himself clear—hearing Tiola's anguished scream in his mind. Others grabbed at him and Maha'dun, pulling them across the cobbles to the far side of the yard, out through the arch, everyone clearing the enclosed space, everyone coughing, wiping at streaming eyes. Someone guided Rue beneath the arch, someone else scooped Tiola up, bundled her into Jesamiah's arms barely before he had regained his feet.

They stood there on what passed for a lawn between the house and the river estuary, numb, silent. Husbands with arms around their wives, wives with faces buried in hands or a husband's chest. Stood numb and silent as the house roof also collapsed and the fire destroyed what was beyond saving.

* * *

At first light the villagers, with reverence and tear-filled eyes, had taken the two bodies to the church. Tiola, hobbling with a makeshift crutch. Her brother's wife, Pegget, had carefully wrapped the burnt remains in winding sheets, two coffins were on their way from Bideford. The morning was dull and grey, with a heavy river mist twining with the shroud of smoke like the breath of two monsters mating with each other. Not a single bird chirruped or tweeted, the only sound a harsh caw from a jackdaw and the mournful low of one of the cows from the meadow. All else was graveyard silent.

There was nothing left of the house, save for some of the solid-built stone walls, a pile of smouldering, black and charred rubble, and the two chimney stacks reaching, soot-blackened but otherwise unscathed, up into the dank mist. The villagers had returned home or gone about their daily business; cows still had to be milked, bread had to be baked, fields ploughed and early seed scattered; workers had to earn their meagre wages. The living could not stand still for the dead. Even so, those alive went about their business with heads bowed and tongues silent. No one had questioned who had rung the church bell; no one had thought to ask.

With a blanket around his shoulders, Rue sat on the low wall that kept the garden separate from the scrub grass. He sat there staring at the estuary but seeing nothing, feeling nothing.

Pegget had come across from Appledore several times since the fire had awoken the town, first bringing food and blankets, then clothing for Tiola and Jesamiah. Carter's clothes were a little on the small side, but not enough to matter. Pegget's shift and gown fitted Tiola well enough with the lacings pulled tight. Susannah had been taken in by the parson's wife and put to bed with a generous dose of brandy inside her, and Pamela's two dogs stretched on the bed as outside warmth and comfort.

"'Ave they any suspec' o' what started it?" Pegget quietly asked Tiola as she nodded towards where Jesamiah was talking to John Benson and Sir Ailie Doone. Benson had come soon after dawn when stunned word had spread to Knapp House. Doone had come by chance, intent on asking after progress on the repair of Captain Acorne's ship, had been horrified at what he had encountered.

Tiola shook her head. "It appears to have spread from the parlour, but that room has not been used since we laid out Pamela's aunt Beth after her passing. There were no candles in the sconces, no embers in the fireplace. No oil in the lamps, yet Master Benson says there is a strong smell of whale oil and pig tallow. There were pools of both on what remains of the stone floor beneath the window." She looked steadfastly at Pegget. "The parlour was one of the rare places where beeswax candles were used, and we store animal fat oil, not whale blubber."

Pegget frowned, cocked her head to one side. "Are you saying," she whispered, wary to speak too loud for fear of sounding to be a fool, "are you sayin' tha fire were started deliberate?"

Tiola nodded once. "I am."

She dared not say more. How could she tell of her suspicions? That the sooty, scorched earth beneath their feet stank? As a dog could pick up the scent of a prowling fox, then so could she smell the essence of a female Night-Walker.

You will pay for this, Tiola vowed as she looked at the forlorn, hunched shape of Rue, his face buried in his hands, his shoulders shaking as he wept for the loss of the woman he had loved.

You have killed once too often, Cara'mina. You will not kill again.

Chapter Twenty

"So, what are your plans now?" Doone asked Jesamiah. A simple question that did not have a simple answer. At least, Jesamiah could not immediately think of one.

Instead, he answered, "Master Benson here informs me that my ship will be completely restored by the morrow. A pity that various stores do not open on a Sunday as I will have to wait to provision her. As long as my crew turns up, I will expect to set sail as soon as I can."

Ailie Doone, hiding his doubt that any of the crew would appear, said tactfully, "But after the funeral I assume?"

"Aye. After the funeral on Tuesday."

Jesamiah was also concerned that his crew would not arrive; if they were not drunk, if they were not locked up, if they were not engrossed in whoring, had sufficient funds for travel; could get a ship or cart. What if they had not received the message? If they had, remembered it. That was a lot of ifs.

There was a long silence, all three men, hands in pockets, staring out across the estuary looking at everything, seeing nothing.

Doone cleared his throat. "I need a reliable and," he

emphasised the word, "*knowledgeable* captain to take care of the shipping of my wine. I have not been satisfied with the recent sailing masters. I have warehouses in France, Spain and Portugal. One in the Hebridian Islands as well."

Jesamiah raised an eyebrow. It was news to him that Scotland had a viable wine trade.

Seeing the expression, Doone explained further. "I am the fortunate owner of one of the six legal whisky distilleries. Scotch malt—the Water of Life—is most appetising to the palate."

"And how many illegal stills do you own?" Jesamiah asked casually, not expecting an answer.

To his surprise, Doone confessed, "Enough to employ a worthwhile sea captain or two. Whisky is taxed hard. Like many a merchant, I see no reason why all my profits should go to King George's Whig government."

As candid, Jesamiah also told the truth. "I'm flattered that you think me trustworthy, but I have no intention of sailing back and forth in Scottish waters. I do not know them, but I know enough to know they are not kind to sailors or ships."

Patting Jesamiah's shoulder, Doone laughed. "I said nought about trusting, Captain, nor about Scottish waters. I need my Scotch whisky, my Spanish wine and brandy, transporting to the colonies from, how shall I say, suitable-to-access storage places?"

"And the kegs and barrels that carry it brought back again at half the fee?"

Doone smiled, nodded. "As I said, I need a knowledgeable captain."

"I'll think about it."

Sea Witch was almost stranded in the low tidewater, not quite laying over as she was anchored in the deepest channel, but enough to give her a forlorn lopsided look. Jesamiah hated seeing her like that, a beached whale, a stranded fish. She needed to be back at sea, running before the wind, all sails set with the wind singing in her rigging. Dammit, he needed to be back at sea!

"Your sailing will perhaps be somewhat delayed, though, Captain," John Benson said. "Tawford Barton is—was—your property. As the only surviving grandson of Alexander Dynam you now have two houses to deal with. This sorry sight and the Dynam's old Marley Court, which has one derelict wing. Will ye be rebuilding, sir? Or maybe selling the land on?"

Jesamiah stared at him, taken aback. In all truth he had completely forgotten that legally the entire Dynam estate had passed to him through his father, Charles Mereno, whose birth name had been St Croix, and whose siring had been questionable; but acknowledged by both Alexander himself and subsequently granted as legitimate by King Charles II. As had the inherited title of Viscount Westley after the sudden fatal heart seizure that had taken the previous Viscount, Sir Cleve, two days after Lady Bethan's passing. A title and position which Jesamiah did not want.

"I will have to think about it," he repeated, guessed that perhaps this one he would have to.

He looked over his shoulder at the still smoking ruin that less than twenty-four hours ago had been a lively, full of warmth and love home, and now housed nothing but ghosts and the echoes of terrified screams. Tiola was hobbling on a crutch, poking through the debris with Pegget for anything worth salvaging. They had not found much. Some kitchen utensils, an iron bucket, a few pieces of soot-blackened jewellery. Nothing of value, nothing of practical use. They had no clothes or possessions, only what Pegget had given them.

Jesamiah only hoped Benson's reassurances that everything that had been aboard *Sea Witch* had been carefully salvaged. Benson had said that his cabin had not suffered much; from his inspection yesterday that was an accurate statement. When Finch arrived—if Finch arrived—he would get him to setting the cabin and his meagre wardrobe straight. Tiola would need new clothes, as would Rue. And the maid. And the cook and her husband. If he recalled correct, stored in the warehouse in Bideford were stacks of material among the items bequeathed to him from his father's estate.

"Has the inventory for the goods in the warehouse been completed?" he asked Benson.

"My good lady wife is, as we speak, copying the rough-made lists into a ledger for you. I will deliver it personally by six of the clock this evening."

"Is there a quick and clever seamstress hereabouts?" was Jesamiah's next question.

Benson was only too pleased to answer. "Susannah, that poor maid of Mistress Pamela's, sews very fine, or there is a woman in Appledore but she is not so quick with her fingers."

"Then I will engage Susannah as soon as may be." Jesamiah bowed slightly, hid a grimace; how long would it take to sew garments—outer and under—for himself, Tiola and Rue? Days probably; days that he did not have. There was going to be lots to do, lots to sort. Where to start? He made a decision, final and absolute.

"I will be selling Marley Court, I have no interest in the place. Tawford Barton I will give to Instow as common ground. The villagers can clear this rubble and use the land as they will. I have no interest in making money from the tragedy that has occurred here."

"Commendable," Doone retorted with a slight bow, "but

not sound business sense. You will never make a living from such rash thinking."

When first they had met, Jesamiah had admired Doone's sharp wit and bold confidence, but the wit had turned to sarcasm and the confidence to arrogance.

Covering the pause of embarrassing silence, Benson asked, "And what of the servants? The beasts? The cattle, sheep, horses, fowl?"

Puffing his cheeks and removing his hands from his pockets, Jesamiah started walking away. "Old Rob can have one of the empty estate cottages, a few acres of Tawford Barton land, the cows and the horses in return for his good service to the family. The hens will come aboard *Sea Witch*. Save me purchasing them. I have enough financial means to keep me going, Sir Ailie, and enough business sense to know what to do and what not to."

He stopped, turned back. "For instance, are you interested in Marley Court? From what I hear from m'wife, it would be a more fitting residence for the Earl of Exmoor than the tawdry shack you presently occupy."

Doone raised one eyebrow. "To be honest, sir, I do not think I have ever thought about it."

Jesamiah offered a small, courteous bow. "As one honest man to another then, Sir Ailie, it appears that neither of us has done much thinking of late."

Chapter Twenty-One

The smell of smoke lingered despite the rain that had been falling since noon. Maha'dun had sat hunched on his bed, then moved to a dry corner of the cellar beneath what was left of the house. The slate kitchen floor, laid over an intricate mesh of supporting rafters, was, more or less, still intact, although rain dripped through cracks and holes in the ceiling, where before there had been no cracks or holes. He had sat on the edge of the bed, chin in hand, elbow propped on his knee, staring at the drips of rain and the spreading puddles, terrified that the inferno had not been properly put out and would flare up again, reason not prevailing over an abject fear of burning to death. He usually slept during the day, had been too frightened to close his eyes. Above him, people had come and gone, sifting through the rubble, talking in hushed voices until the rain had ushered in an early dusk when all had fallen silent except for the scurry of a single surviving rat. No one had come down into the cellar, perhaps it had not occurred to them that there were unscathed bottles of wine, barrels of stores and preserves among the clutter that had accumulated over many years? Or had Tiola stopped them coming? He had heard her shuffling awkwardly with a crutch, sobs choking her voice whenever she spoke. She knew he was here, hiding from the daylight, for just the once he had heard her mind-words in his head.

~ *Are you alone, Maha'dun?* ~

A strange question; of course he was alone! Who else would be squatting amongst the ash and soot of a ruined house waiting for the night to come? There was only one other Night-Walker in the vicinity and she would not dare, surely, to show her face, not even to Maha'dun, after what she had done.

If they ever found out, if the people who had known those who had died ever discovered that it was a Night-Walker who had burnt a house to the ground... Maha'dun covered his head with his arms, drew his knees up to his chest and cowered further into the corner, the cold, damp, solid stone offering a slight comfort. Tiola knew. Her anger had been in that mind-speak voice. She knew what Cara'mina had done, but would she tell, or even if she did not and others guessed, would she save him from the mob if they found him hiding here? Others would not care that he had tried to help save lives. Others would not care that it was not he who had poured whale oil and pig tallow around a room and then tossed a lighted lamp through the window, the flames bursting into a rage within moments.

How had Cara'mina done that? Stood and watched the house burn beyond saving? How could she have disappeared and left him to face the consequences if anyone learnt the truth! How? That was easy to answer. Cara'mina gave not a curse for consequences, or for anyone else, save herself.

Another question bumbled into his brain. Why was she so obsessed with killing Captain Acorne and Tiola? He sighed, knew the answer. Cara'mina was possessive, she regarded everything and everyone as hers; when he had turned to Tiola, the enraged jealousy had erupted like a volcano. And now spite was taking its insidious toll, spite directed at him and Tiola. Add to that, Tiola had failed to rescue Cara'mina's partner from that awful death.

Maha'dun massaged his face and neck with his fingertips. He could not stay here. It was dark enough outside, safe to move. He stood, eased the stiffness from his joints and looked regretfully at the travelling chests stored to one side that were his. He would have to leave them behind for he had no coach now, nor even if he did, a coachman to drive it.

Time to leave, time to find new hunting grounds.

Using the trapdoor out into the courtyard, Maha'dun stepped into the deepening night and, scenting the air to ensure all was safe, set out with shoulders hunched against the rain. He would head for Dover. It would be a long walk, and there were, he knew, other, nearer ports—Plymouth, Exeter, Weymouth...but Dover would mean the shorter sea-crossing and he did so fear the sea. He did not walk with his habitual swinging stride, nor his usual fast pace. He walked for five miles, slowly, his body, his head, his soul, slumped into a pit of dark dejection, his hands thrust into pockets, his feet stumbling, the rain masking the drizzle of falling tears. Then he stopped and turned to look at the way he had come. His breath caught in his throat as he shuddered down a sob, resumed walking. He looked back as he topped each rise of hills, saw the track of his passing through a cascade of tears that would not cease flowing. Dawn was not far off. If only this despair would disappear with the dark of the night when daylight came.

* * *

Several hours later, Maha'dun hesitated, stood for a while beneath the archway into what had been a homely farm courtyard. He had gone twenty miles, skulked in someone's barn during daylight, then, an idea forming in his mind, had turned around and walked back to Instow. He could not leave. He knew it was a stupid decision, one he would probably regret, but what point in running away if you had nowhere worth running to?

The air was thick with a smell he had hoped not to encounter ever again. Cara'mina was here, gloating at her triumph. He walked with silent footsteps across the cobbles, bent and opened the trapdoor into the cellar and, closing it behind him, descended the stone steps. There were more steps on the other side of the cellar, leading up to the trapdoor in the kitchen, but that entrance was gone, buried beneath a heap of rubble and charred timber.

He splashed through a couple of puddles, clumps of soggy ash clinging to his boots as he walked across the stone floor to where he had made a bed for himself. That too was ash-strewn, but at least the tucked-away corner of the cellar was dry. Only Cara'mina, sprawled atop the blankets, looked unsullied and unspoilt.

"I knew you would come here eventually," she said stretching her arms behind her head, emphasising the perfect shape of her breasts beneath her silk chemise, "for where else is it safe for you to cower away from dawn till dusk?"

Resisting the temptation to feel his coat pocket for cheroots that he knew were not there, Maha'dun went to the wine rack instead, selected a bottle of port and, finding the bottle opener where he had left it atop a cask of pears in honey, opened it with a satisfying sound. He had an array of crystal glasses, gleaned from the parlour, wiped two free of dust with his kerchief and poured. He sipped from one before taking the other drink and holding it out to Cara'mina.

"You cower from the daylight as much as do I."

"Ah, but I have better taste for my lodgings than do you."

He refrained from answering that his lodgings had been perfectly tasteful until she had destroyed them. "If you have better quarters, madam, then why do you not make use of them? Why are you here instead?"

Cara'mina stood, her bare arms gleaming in the light of the single lamp hanging from one of the rafters. The Night-Walkers shied away from sunlight, but the soft glow of candle or lamp was pleasant and often sensuous. She slid the straps of her chemise from her shoulders, the garment sliding like water down her body to lay in a silken pile at her feet, revealing not a scar or blemish on her perfect skin. Even though he detested her, Maha'dun had to admit that she was exquisitely beautiful.

"Because," she went towards him, took the offered glass with one hand, trickled her fingers with their talon-like nails up his chest, stopping to unlace his shirt and stroke the smooth skin beneath, "I need satisfying. I find killing heightens my appetite." She placed her mouth over his, was annoyed when he did not kiss her back. "I would advise you to accommodate me, and accommodate me well, scut, else I might destroy more of your pathetic friends."

"Killing the innocent? You are adept at that."

She struck his face. "You dare insult me?" She struck him again, and once again.

Ignoring the stings, Maha'dun caressed her face. He wanted to get out, get away from here and there was only one way he would be able to do it. Play along.

"It is against our honour to kill the elderly, the innocent or women and children. But," he kissed her lightly on the lips, "but your disregard for our quaint traditions arouses me."

She drank the port with one gulp then sashayed to the bed, her hips swaying beneath the curtain of her thick black hair tumbling loose down her back to her buttocks.

"Tell me," she purred as she arranged herself alluringly atop the covers, "the names of those who died here. I would hear of my triumph from you."

If his hatred for her could increase, if it were not already at full capacity, how Maha'dun felt for this evil apparition would at that moment have been immeasurable. But he had to fight it down, could not antagonise her. Honour forbade it, and if he were to admit the truth, he was too frightened of her to even dare. Too frightened to lie also, yet he had no intention of telling her the truth in case she did not know it—which given her recent record and from her apparent triumphal gloating, she did not. Had she made a mistake yet again? How could he lie while telling the truth? By being evasive and letting her assume? As she often did because she considered her mind superior to his.

He had one other advantage he could play against her. Cara'mina enjoyed voracious sex and if sated to a high enough capacity would sleep at a depth where nothing would wake her for over four and twenty hours or more. That would give him the time he needed. He peeled off his coat, removed his shirt, his eyes partially closed, lips slightly open. His talent would be more than enough to make her sleep for several days and nights. Moving close to her he cupped her breasts in his hands, bent and flicked his tongue over the nipples. He looked up at her, smiled, oozing passion and desire. "There was a maid. I do not know her name, and the witch and her husband," he purred, "will be of no more trouble to you."

"Good. When you have finished pleasuring me, I will return to my task of finding the last two caskets."

"We, madam. When *we* have finished our pleasuring, we can return to our task."

* * *

With barely a sound, Maha'dun carried his clothes chests, one by one, from the cellar and piled them in the little summer house to the far side of the garden. It was a nuisance not having his carriage to load them straight into. He would leave his things, collect them when he could. The final chest removed, he looked one last time at Cara'mina sprawled face down on the bed, seemingly dead to the world. A pity she wasn't, but then his sexual prowess would not be of such acclaim if his clients expired from the exertion of his elaborate and intense skills. His eyes narrowed as he watched her sleep, not with false lust this time, but with venomous hatred. His fingers clenching and unclenching, every inch of him wanting to smother her, or cut her throat, or drive a blade through her heart, but he did not possess the courage.

He climbed the stone stairway, stepped out into the quiet darkness before dawn stirred and, closing the cellar doors, bolted them. For extra security, piled on stones that had once formed the house walls, along with debris and scorched timbers. He wiped his soiled hands on the wet grass and nodded, satisfied. She would not be getting out of there for a good while! He grinned to himself as he loped off into the night. By the time she woke and eventually burrowed her way out he would be long gone. It would take her several nights to do so. He chuckled as he jog-trotted along the lane. Stupid, was he? He was not educated, was slow with some things, but as did many others, Cara'mina always underestimated him. The grin broadened. His only regret, he would not be here to witness her fury at being so easily outmanoeuvred—nor at her discovery that she had not, as he had implied, killed her intended victims. His first goal was to find Tiola and put his idea to her. The second, to hope she was agreeable to it. He was being bold, daring, and he was not wholly sure that perhaps he wasn't being over-optimistic, but for once in his long life he felt sublimely elated.

Oh, Cara'mina, he thought as he hopped over a low wall to head off across the fields, *which one of us is the fool now?*

Chapter Twenty-Two

"Most fitting, I thought," John Benson said, twiddling his hat in his hands and masking the fact that he was struggling to find appropriate words to say. "The services were good, uplifting, most reassuring."

Helping the man out, Jesamiah acknowledged the remarks with a nod. By definition, were funeral services good? He preferred these rituals at sea, there was not so much protocol or adhering to what was acceptable, what was not. Aye, everyone wore their Sunday best for burials at sea—which basically meant a clean shirt and breeches—maybe washed, shaved, and a hat removed if one was worn, but that was about it. Land-based church services for funerals required sombre clothes and melancholy words. No simple, brief reading from the Bible, the speaking of the Lord's Prayer, maybe a psalm sung and then, whoosh, the body tipped over the side and committed to the deep. That was it, done, finished. Here, the official Mass had lasted more than two hours but had included services for both those departed, and burying the maid in the shade of an ancient hawthorn at the western end of Instow's small graveyard. Pamela's laying to rest in the Dynam family vault at Marley

Court had been a similarly sombre affair. It was a depressing enough place without the mournful overtones of a funeral. Pamela had been much loved by many in the area, and outside it. The church had been packed to overflowing, even a small tribe of gypsies had come down from the moors to pay their respects. How, in the space of only a few short days, they had known about the services Jesamiah had not a clue, but Jennet, Pamela's grandmother, and Alexander—his own grandfather—had held close connections with the proud nomadic people and had respected their ways. Out of the same respect, Jesamiah had invited them to Marley Court for the wake, a gesture that was warmly appreciated but politely declined.

The vault was an octagonal, somewhat opulent construction of marble and Portland stone, resembling a Roman temple in style and built by one of the family when he had been in favour with King Henry Tudor, eighth of that name. During the reign of which particular unfortunate Tudor wife had never been made clear. Windowless, the only light inside was by lantern or candle, or when the single door was propped open. Airless and cold, the interior smelt dank and musty, of decay and rot. Cobwebs hung like strands of dust-covered curtains from the high ceiling, draping over the individual tombs arrayed like spread fingers from the walls, with a grand tomb at the centre, the heart of the memorial. That original Viscount Westley lay there, accompanied by his wife and fifteen children, all of whom, save one, had died in infancy. Jesamiah could not help thinking what a burden it must have been for the remaining poor fellow to carry on the esteemed family name. Much as he, now, was apparently expected to do by certain people of the community if some of the overheard whispers were to be taken seriously.

Was Benson about to become one of them?

Only a few had been invited to witness Pamela's interment beside her mother and father, in their own modest family tomb—apparently a new resting place was added when the first male grandchild was born. Not a very fitting christening present in Jesamiah's opinion; on the other hand, knowing your resting place was taken care of perhaps made life a little more secure? He surreptitiously peered round. Was there an empty place set aside for his father, and therefore himself? He resisted the temptation to look closer. His father was mouldering in a grave in Virginia, in a picket-fenced cemetery plot. He knew that for certain; he had seen his father's ghost there. He puffed his cheeks, suddenly not so sure; perhaps ghosts could appear anywhere? Tiola would know, he must ask her, but to be interred here, where the walls appeared to be falling in on you, where there was no light or air could be—was—hell. Since childhood he had feared enclosed spaces. Thankfully, most of the invited party were already heading for the house, eager for the provided food and drink. He wiped away the sweat starting to dampen his forehead, and looked towards Tiola, seated on a chair to one side, her crutch propped beside her, her newly re-bandaged ankle resting on a footstool. He gestured with one hand towards the door, his expression conveying that he wished to leave.

~ I would stay a moment, ~ she said into his mind. *~ You go, John Benson seems to want to speak with you—but keep close watch on Rue, I am concerned for him. Come back for me in a little while? ~*

He nodded, clutching Benson's elbow, walking quickly, steered him out into the afternoon rain. "Let us join the others in the house; Rue is taking the loss badly," he said, "I would prefer to keep a discreet eye on him."

Benson nodded. "A bitter blow for him, he was most fond of Mistress Pamela."

"He was."

"As were we all, of course," Benson added, then after a pause, stopped walking and cleared his throat. "Might I have a quiet word, Captain, before we are within earshot of others?"

Cocking his head to one side, Jesamiah tucked his thumbs into his waistcoat pockets, ignored the rain trickling down his neck. He could see Rue ushering the last of the guests into the house, for all the world a polite and generous host. Was it only himself and Tiola who realised that Claude de la Rue had not been one minute sober these last few days?

"As long as it is a quick word; it is not exactly congenial out here, is it?"

As if surprised at the rain, Benson stared up at the grey sky. "I always think it is somehow wrong to hold a funeral on a sunny day. Drab skies are more in keeping with the mood, I think." He held out his hand, inspected the rain that pooled in his palm. Jesamiah waited.

Benson cleared his throat again. "It is like this, Captain Acorne. Sir Ailie Doone has offered to see my son apprenticed."

"Aye. I was in court when he offered, remember?"

"Doone is an influential man with various profitable businesses, but..."

"But you do not trust his morals or scruples."

Frowning, about to protest, Benson admitted, "You have hit the nail square with the hammer."

A moment's silence. "So?" Jesamiah prompted. "What is it you want of me?"

Putting his hands in his pockets, taking them out again, John Benson glanced at the house to reassure himself that no one would be overhearing the conversation. "It is like this,

Acorne. Thomas needs taking in hand. He runs wild here, spoilt by his mother as most last-born sons are. I want him to learn a trade, become somebody, be able to follow on from me in later years."

"Shipbuilding and merchandise?"

"Yes, but I want him to know what ships *are*, what they do, how they sail. I want him to know where the tobacco comes from, the rum, the spices, the fish the—well, whatever. It is not enough just to see vessels sail in and out of our small harbour, to see kegs and barrels and firkins piled on the quayside."

"I agree, to experience first-hand the other side of trade is a good thing."

Benson beamed, took hold of Jesamiah's hand and pumped it as if it were the handle of a waterspout in a courtyard. "So you will take him? I am that relieved!"

"Whoa, belay there, mate!" Jesamiah extracted his hand with difficulty. "How did you reach that conclusion?"

Puzzled, Benson spread his hands. "You are setting sail within the next few days, are you not? You require crew? My boy will make an excellent midshipman."

"No, wait," Jesamiah patted the air, unsure how to get out of this—even more uncertain how he had got into it. "I do not need or require a midshipman, and I do not know, yet, precisely where I am sailing to or how long I will be gone. Or even if I will be coming back."

As if he were talking to a confused child, Benson set one hand on Jesamiah's shoulder. "As I understood it, you are taking a lucrative cargo of Spanish wine and some English oak coffins to Virginia for Ailie Doone. Making a return trip with tobacco, sugar and rum. Have I misunderstood?"

When Jesamiah said nothing, Benson relaxed and smiled, "I will, naturally, pay you for my son's education. I reckon a fair trade, my son becoming a seaman in exchange for half the cost of repairing your ship?"

"I thought Doone were payin' that. He seems to be controlling everything else."

The sarcasm was lost on Benson who merely frowned, not understanding.

"Look, John, I have no intention of working for or with Doone. I have my own plantation, there's a warehouse full of what-not to trade, and m'own way o' doin' things. I am also perfectly able to pay for the repair of my own ship. I will expect the bill tomorrow and will settle before I sail."

Benson looked crestfallen, despite the prospect of a handsome financial gain. "I do urge you to reconsider, Captain. You would be a fitty tutor for my son. I respect you as a man and as a sailor. I would appreciate him growing up to be as you are."

Jesamiah almost laughed aloud; had he not been standing getting soaked to the bone dressed in ill-fitting borrowed funeral black, he would have done so. "Sir, I assure you that you would not. It were not so long ago I sailed as a pirate."

Patting Jesamiah's arm again, Benson smiled and, indicating they should enter the house, confided, "There are few of us here, lad, save perhaps the vicar, who have not seen our share of piracy, smuggling or something else as questionable. And I am not all that certain about the vicar. The difference between you and us is that you are a damned sight better at it than ever we were!"

* * *

Doone assailed Jesamiah the moment he stepped into the smoke-fugged room. The chimney in the front parlour had always been known to send more smoke outwards than upwards, this rain-wet afternoon it was doing itself proud.

"It is not wise to permit those Exmoor grubs to hang around, Captain. They are thieves and rogues. Not to be trusted."

"You mean you and I are not thieves, and we are to be trusted? If we were honest men, we would not be arranging deals that are not to King George's liking, or trying to put another king on his throne in his stead, now, would we?"

"Speak for yourself, Captain. I am as honest as an Irishman."

Jesamiah laughed. "Spoken like a true Scotsman!"

Doone acknowledged the comment with a bow and helped himself to another glass of wine from the table beside the door. "We have a deal then? You take my goods to where I need them to go, and you receive twenty-five per cent of the profit."

"I am not sure about these coffins of yours. It seems a bit, um," Jesamiah waved the hand holding his own glass towards the people filling the room, "disrespectful."

"I prefer the word practical. People die, people need to be buried. And there is a taboo around coffins." Doone sipped the wine, "A very useful one."

Jesamiah cocked his head to one side, frowned. What was he missing here? "Which is?"

"No one likes to snoop inside a coffin."

Light dawned. "Ah."

Raising his glass in a toast, Doone smiled. "You have my meaning. You can pack a fair few bottles of Scotch whisky into a straw-lined coffin."

Clinking his own glass against Doone's, Jesamiah acknowledged the smuggler's ruse. "The wine is legitimate. The rest is not. Sixty per cent. I am taking all the risks."

"The risk is as much mine. I could lose all were you to sink or get caught. Thirty per cent."

"Aye, but your head will not go into the noose. Mine will. Fifty."

Doone held out his hand. "Five-and-thirty and we are agreed?"

Finishing the wine, Jesamiah put the glass down, Rue was at the door beckoning him. "Forty. And I'll think about it." He walked away.

"Rue?"

"They 'ave arrived."

Puzzled, Jesamiah looked past Rue's shoulder into the dour entrance hall. Dark panelling, rusty, dusty suits of armour, one single window—two others had been bricked in to avoid paying the government's unpopular tax on light. "Who?"

Rue grinned, pointed towards the kitchen from where came the sound of something being dropped and broken followed by a torrent of verbal abuse from a woman.

His frown deepening, Jesamiah strode through the door, intent on chastising whoever was doing the shouting; his face altered to a broad grin.

"Skylark! Am I glad to be seeing you! Put that wench down, we've enough broken crocks as it is in this hovel of a house, and come with me to where we can talk freely. Are you on your own? Where are the others? You were supposed to be here Sunday, 'tis Tuesday today!" While delivering his torrent of questions he looked round the busy kitchen expecting to see more of his crew molesting the hired servants.

Correctly interpreting the glance, Skylark explained. "They're at Instow, Cap'n. I reckoned it only needed the one pair of feet t'come 'ere, I left 'em ferryin' across to *Sea Witch*. They, uh," Skylark—his real name Joe Meadows—grinned back at his captain's delighted face, "they took offence at landlubberly grouts crawlin' all over her. They reckon we know better t'put her shipshape as she should be."

Jesamiah's grin widened. Almost, he wanted to hug the man. Thought better of it when he saw one of the maids grinning back at him. He turned to Rue and, beckoning him and Skylark to follow, went into the library, an even gloomier and dustier room. Shut the door. Somewhat regretting his first essential question, fearing a poor answer, he asked Skylark how many men had come.

Scratching at his chin the man studied the cobwebbed ceiling. "I ain't so good at me numbers..."

"You're perfectly good. With numbers and letters alike. How many!"

"All of us who were in Bristol, sir. Two-and-thirty men."

Jesamiah puffed his cheeks and looked at Rue. "Any chance getting more?"

"*Cinquante, cinquante-cinq?*"

Rubbing at his cheeks—shaved close for the funeral—Jesamiah did some rapid calculations. "Five-and-fifty strangers, plus our own two-and-thirty. For a full complement I would prefer another forty at least, but we ain't goin' to find that number here, and I guess as we are no longer a fighting ship we'll not need more anyway. How much more is there to do?"

Rue pulled a non-committal face. "Guns are aboard, just need securing. Apart from food and water, provisions are taken care of and stowed."

"The stuff from the warehouse?"

"Aboard. Some of it in your cabin, the personal items, the linens, calicoes, wools and those bolts of silk. Some, the goods you wanted as cargo, is in the 'old as you ordered."

Jesamiah was pleased. "Shot? Muskets? Gunpowder? Sailcloth, cordage..."

"Some shot, some muskets. A few barrels of powder. Appledore, she is not the right place for such. Other items, *oui, finis.*"

Delighted, Jesamiah thumped Rue's shoulder, then Skylark's. "What we haven't got now we can get in Spain. Men and provisions. Let's get aboard, see what's what. If you would be so kind as to ask John Benson to join us, Rue, then fetch m'wife to send this rabble to their homes, I reckon we could make tomorrow's tide."

* * *

"They have all gone," Tiola said, pulling her shawl a little tighter. Even for her it was cold in this dank mausoleum. "You may come out now."

With an apologetic expression Maha'dun stepped from behind one of the furthest tombs, dusting cobwebs from his sleeve. "I will not insult you by asking how you knew I was here," he said as he offered a polite bow.

"Apart from the aroma of tobacco, sandalwood and brandy Maha'dun, your smell is as distinctive to me as a mine does to you."

Maha'dun acknowledged her observation with a nod of his head, wandered to where they had resealed the tomb now containing an additional occupant. "It has always seemed odd to me," he said, "that we Night-Walkers are so afeared of fire, yet we burn our dead."

"That is why you are afraid of it," Tiola answered pragmatically. "Where is Cara'mina?"

Maha'dun inspected the dust covering the stone lid of the adjoining tomb. Someone had drawn a collection of crude little naked figures in it showing explicit male genitalia. From the size of the fingerprints the artwork had been performed by young Thomas Benson. "The lad has a bit of learning to do regarding what goes where," he grinned. "This fellow appears to be putting his penis in this rather heavily endowed young lady's ear."

"He will discover the intricacies all in good time. Where is Cara'mina?"

Completing a drawing as equally explicit as Thomas Benson's crude figures, but more accurate, Maha'dun wiped the dust from his fingers onto his breeches. "Her mate was one of those horribly killed. His blackened bones form one of those bone-boxes, and until they are all destroyed, she cannot be certain that his soul rests in death, not in the eternal agony of Wandering."

"I know," Tiola said quietly. Did she ask her question yet again? Even if she did, would he answer?

"That is why she is so obsessed."

"I know that as well, Maha'dun. Why are you suddenly defending her?"

"I am not!" he protested, looking up sharply, then lowering his gaze again. "I am not defending her, I am just trying to explain, and, and... and I need safe passage to take me far from here. As soon as possible."

"Would this dire need have anything to do with the gossip that ghosts are already haunting Tawford Barton?"

"I know nothing of ghosts nor hauntings."

"They are saying that a woman's screams are coming from the rubble that was once the house. Would this have anything to do with you, Maha'dun?"

He shrugged. "How would it? I have no influence over the dead."

"But you do have influence over the living, and Cara'mina is still very much alive—and from what I deduce, very angry.

The cellar will not hold her for long, you know."

Looking glum, his shoulders sagging, head bowed, Maha'dun admitted the truth. "She has woken earlier than I anticipated. I thought to gain at least two nights' start." He gazed at her, pleading. "If she finds me, Lady, I am dead."

"I will see you safe, Maha'dun, if I can, but I sail with my husband soon. I will not be here to protect you."

Maha'dun strode to her side, knelt, bent his head, touching his forehead to her hands. "Take me with you, Lady. Take me onto this sea-ship and take me from here."

~ *You would brave the open ocean?* ~ Tiola spoke into his mind.

He looked up into her eyes. "Yes. If it is safe enough for you and Captain Acorne, then surely it is safe enough for me? And aside," his mouth formed one of his more alluring smiles, "I swore to protect your husband's life. I cannot do so if I am not there to protect it, can I?"

"And would this idea of yours," Tiola countered, determined not to show even a hint of amusement, "have any connection with my husband's intention to find the son of the English woman with the Spanish name? The son who, being male, if he has handled one of the caskets, may die by the vengeance of the Night-Walkers? That, I cannot permit, he is but a child."

Maha'dun stood, spread his hands, made a crude noise through his lips. "Sons? Your husband's intentions? I know nothing of these."

Abandoning stern pretence, Tiola smiled: "Maha'dun, you lie but rarely. When you do, you do it most poorly. My husband will need to give you tuition."

The responding grin had more meaning to it than just a laugh. "I would willingly learn from Captain Acorne. Maybe in return I can teach him a few of my own perfected skills?"

"I doubt there is much he does not know. Sailors learn quite a few of the tricks harbour-side whores keep beneath their skirts."

Maha'dun pretended to be wounded. "Madam, I am no harbour-side doxy to poke for a shilling against an alley wall! I am a professional artiste when it comes to making love!"

"As you made love to Cara'mina? Do you not think it poor taste to have done so where you did so?"

Like Tiola, Maha'dun lost that slight edge of humour. "It was more than poor taste, Lady, but Cara'mina thrives on the things that disgust others. It heightens her pleasure to fuck where she has killed."

Accepting that, Tiola reached the crux of her questioning. "You want to find the bone-box. Is it possible that the son of the woman with the Spanish name has it in his possession, or knows where it is? To find him you need to sail on my husband's ship."

Stretching out his finger he placed it against her lips. "Hush. Someone comes." He shrank back into the cobwebbed shadows, added in a whisper, "To find a bone-box will buy me high status among the Night-Walkers, but I would not kill a child to obtain one."

Tiola used her crutch to stand.

A small, tanned-skin, rough-dressed man entered, paused in the doorway to adjust his sight to the dark interior and remove his hat. He focused on Tiola, bowed with an elegance that belied his poor-man's apparel.

"M'lady, forgive tha intrusion, I need word with th' Night-Walker."

Curtseying—somewhat awkwardly because of the pretence of an unhealed ankle and arm—Tiola beckoned the man forward. "You are Jeb, grandson of Cobb, a dear friend to my husband's grandsire, I believe?"

Jeb smiled, nodded. "I so be. Our gypsy fam'lies been close fer many a year. 'Tis sadness at Mistress Pamela's death that sits in our 'earts, but it be with pleasure we welcome thy 'usband back t'Devon. Albeit fer a short while. I b'lieve 'e is to sail soon?"

Tiola nodded. "We are. Although where to, I am uncertain."

Maha'dun returned into the feeble light, offered Jeb a courteous nod of his head, and by way of small explanation said to Tiola, "I often took shelter within the gypsy-folks' wagons. They do not fear those of us who are different."

Again Tiola gave a small bob of a curtsey. "For protecting my friend, I thank you. But I trust your generosity does not, for your safety, extend to all who walk the night?"

Jeb's answer was nothing more than the slight hand movement. "There be bad'uns in those who walk b'day or b'night. There be also good'uns. Folk who lived by Tawford Barton, they were good to us. Your 'usband too 'as proven 'is worth t'day."

"My husband," Tiola answered, acknowledging the compliment, "judges folk by what they do, not by who they are."

"As 'tis proper." Jeb turned to Maha'dun, "We 'ave thy coach, would 'preciate sellin' 'er if thee 'as no further need of she?"

"By all means, dispose of it."

Jeb nodded, deal struck. "We burried them dead'uns on the moor. Best no one find 'em, 'specially since they 'as worked fer Doone."

He turned to go, pausing only to bow respectfully towards

the silent tombs. "Thy 'usban' ought t'know an' all, ma'am; tha one who ran, us'n did nay catch 'im but I know 'im as also one o' Doone's men. Be careful o' them Doones, they be bad'uns." He bowed, disappeared as unobtrusively as he had come.

A moment later, Rue entered, slapping his hat on his thigh to rid it of rain, looking behind him at the man disappearing into the gloom.

Maha'dun glided away, silent, to hide in the shadows.

"As well Jesamiah sent me," Rue said with a growl, "gypsies are not to be trusted, Miss Tiola."

"That one is, I assure you."

"*Oui*, maybe." Rue did not sound convinced. "Jesamiah sent me to fetch you. 'E is summoned to Instow, our errant crew 'as arrived. 'E asks for you to be 'ostess to those people *dans la maison* and to see them soon gone. 'E 'as the idea to set sail on tomorrow's tide; the next two are 'igh spring tides, *parfait pour nous*."

Exaggerating her limp—in fact her ankle barely hurt—Tiola walked up to him and gently laid her palm against his cheek. He had shaved, trimmed his hair and was neatly dressed in borrowed clothes, as all who had lost everything in the fire were.

"Perfect for us?" she queried. "You are sailing on *Sea Witch*?"

Rue nodded slowly. "There is nothing for me 'ere. Not now. At sea I might forget." He looked at the sealed tomb and then at Tiola, his face a mask of bereft despair. "What am I to do? I 'ave nothing to remind me of 'er, no trinket, no piece of lace, or glove or ribbon. No lock of 'er 'air. 'Ow do I keep 'er close if I 'ave nothing left of 'er?"

Tiola's heart broke at the enormity of his grief. How did anyone survive such sorrow? "At sea, a man's mind is on the wind and the tide. You are doing the right thing, my friend."

Tears flooded Rue's cheeks and he spread his hands in hopelessness. "'Ow am I to live after this? I loved 'er with all my 'eart, an' now... *Cassé en petits morceaux*, broken to pieces!"

Weeping also, Tiola set her arms around him, held him close, her hands stroking his back. She could have used her Craft to ease his pain, to help him forget, but no matter how deep the sorrow or how hard the pain, the last thing Rue needed was to forget, because to forget was to lose love completely.

"Pah, this is not good," he said pulling away from her. "My love, she is gone, I must forget 'er. Return to the sea, the one who 'as 'ad my 'eart all the years." He wiped at his face, tried a smile. They both knew his words were mere bravado, spoken to hide his pain.

"What of her dogs!" Tiola said suddenly. "Pamela's dogs? She loved those two, would be devastated to learn they have been abandoned."

Rue's own excited expression mirrored Tiola's. He had often jested that they were yappy little things fit for no purpose, but had secretly been fond of them and despite Pamela's protests had fed them titbits under the table at mealtimes. "*Oui!* They are only *petits chiens*, they would not be in the way aboard."

"And they would be company for me."

Rue nodded, pleased, "And excellent for warming the cold feet, though they are too pampered to be any use with keeping the rats at bay!" He placed his hands on Tiola's shoulders, kissed her on both cheeks. "*Merci, chérie,* I do not know what we would do without you."

"Bumble along like you always used to?"

As he turned to go, Tiola put her hand on his wrist. "I

would have you do something for me, Rue?"

"*Oui?*"

"There are some travelling chests in that little summer house. Would you see to it they are taken to the great cabin please?"

"*Bien sûr.*"

"*Merci.*"

Tiola walked—limped—with him to the door, had not failed to notice his hand lightly touch the tomb where Pamela lay in the darkness of death. They went out, Rue shut the door with the finality of parting and, offering his arm, escorted his captain's wife to the house.

She did not look back, but said in her mind, ~ *Meet me on the shore as dusk settles, Maha'dun. If you are not there, then you will need look to your own short future.* ~

CHAPTER TWENTY-THREE

~ Jesamiah? ~

~ Mm? ~

Pleased that he was somewhat distracted by overseeing cargo being brought aboard, Tiola pressed on. *~ Maha'dun needs a place of sanctuary. ~*

~ Don't we all. ~ He shouted something to a man who had let go of a rope and nearly dropped a valuable piece of furniture into the rising tide. Tiola caught the residue of her husband's uncomplimentary rebuke in her mind.

~ He may also be able to help find Francesca's son. ~

~ Oh, aye? ~

~ He would like to be a passenger aboard. ~

~ I don't take passengers, you know that. ~

~ Then he can be a companion for me, or crew? ~

Another burst of expletives as the item of furniture dangling from the hoist was knocked against the side of an open hatchway.

~ I'm your companion, and I can't see that dolt being much good as crew. ~

~ You said yourself he is good in a fight. Francesca was

in trouble, was she not? Might there not be fighting? ~

"For fok sake, be careful with that bloody rope!" ~ *I'm busy, Tiola. I've no more cabins. He will have to sleep with the men. ~*

Tiola smiled, Maha'dun was not averse to 'sleeping' with men. But perhaps best not mention that?

~ He can make a corner for himself in the hold. Screen a small part off with a sail? The dark will be most suitable. ~

~ Do what you like. As long as he don't get in my way. ~

That went well. Now all she had to do was ensure things stayed that way between Jesamiah and Maha'dun.

Almost immediately, Jesamiah forgot the conversation. "Ah, Benson, my thanks for coming aboard. An' good evening to you, young sir." Jesamiah nodded at Thomas, who stood stiff and straight in his best clothes, a waterproofed canvas bag slung over his shoulder. "You sure you want to come aboard an' sail with us, lad?"

Thomas Benson nodded. His father nudged his elbow. "Take your cap off, boy."

Hastily whipping the woollen cap from his head, revealing short-cropped hair that stood up in damp spikes, Thomas blushed.

"Skylark 'ere will show you where t'put your dunnage."

"Aye, Cap'n," Skylark acknowledged. "Come on then, Hedgepig, let's get you some clothes more suited for a foremast jack, eh?"

Jesamiah hid a smile as the boy trotted off at Skylark's heels.

"My name's Tom, not Hedgepig."

"Is it now. What happened to your hair? You look more like a hedgepig to me."

Thomas ran a hand through his short, spiky hair. "My

mother sheared it. She said she didn't want me getting lice."

"Lice'll be the least of your problems," Skylark chuckled.

"You will look after him, Acorne?" Benson asked nervously as he watched his son disappear down an open hatch, apparently not in the least bothered that he would be leaving home and family for several months. "His mother is weeping a flood in our kitchen, and I confess to a lump in my own throat. I will miss the boy, although my dear wife has threatened to never speak to me again because of this. Which may, if I am fortunate, be something of a welcome blessing as I am hoping that will include an end to her constant requests for a new gown, bonnet and shoes."

Jesamiah laughed. "Is that the bill for what I owe you?" He turned away from scrutinising who else was following in John Benson's wake through the entry port. The longboat seemed full of tars, so maybe they would set sail with an adequate compliment of men after all. He took the slip of paper Benson proffered, scrutinised it a moment, grimaced, and invited his guest to his cabin.

As he stepped through the door behind Benson, he apologised; "It is a bit of a mess. Finch has not got around to straightening things out yet." He frowned and swept a pile of maps off a chair and indicated Benson could sit. Ridding the chair beside his desk of several shirts and a pair of breeches, seated himself. The desk was a fine piece of oak wood carpentry fitted into the curve of the bulkhead, with oak leaves and acorns carved into the panels, drawers and cupboard doors. "If I knew where Finch was, it might help," he muttered, glowering at several chests stacked to one side. They looked familiar.

"I have detailed all the expenses," Benson said, pointing at the invoice, "Rue told me to use best quality, so that new main topmast and main t'gallant cost a penny or two. You could do with a completely new mainmast, you know, I weren't able to check it as thorough where it do go down through the deck quite as I would've liked, but I'll be wanting more time to do that."

Jesamiah nodded as he looked at the expense of the articles in question, raised one eyebrow. The total was somewhat more than pennies. He queried one or two items, but was basically satisfied. Benson had done a good job.

"The mast should be fine, she is not an elderly vessel, and I do not have the extra time a full investigation would need. We'll check next time we careen." Rummaging in his desk drawer, and mumbling that this too needed sorting, Jesamiah found what he was looking for, then had to search again for quill and ink.

"Gods but I will be pleased to see everything shipshape!" he confided as he signed a bank draft and, having flapped the paper for the ink to dry, handed it to Benson. "All paid to the last penny. And this," he gave Benson another document, "contains my instructions for you to act on my behalf as my estate manager."

Benson's expression was a mixture of puzzlement and delight. "Manager?"

"Aye. I want Marley Court, and everything of mine left in that warehouse, sold. You know well enough what a reasonable price is, and I don't care who you sell to, just get shot of it all. The money is to be paid into m'bank in Bideford." He pointed to the bank draft, "My lawyer tells me that Master Drummond of Charing Cross, London, is reliable, I believe this bank I've selected is in a suitable and trustworthy business relationship with him."

Benson nodded, impressed. Both the local and London banks were frequented by some of the top names. In London, it was rumoured, even some of the royals banked at

Drummond's. "Yes, but I still don't…"

"I want you to manage my affairs here in England, John. Rue was going to do it, but now, well, all that has changed. I need someone I can trust, and I think that someone is you."

"But, but…"

"Look, stop the burbling. You are a very good merchant trader—as good as you are a shipwright—and I know you will not cheat me. I will offer you an income of ten per cent per annum of whatever is in my account. The better the deals you make for sales, the higher your profit."

"But I… "

"Very well, fifteen per cent. That is my final bid."

"Fifteen will do nicely, but…"

"Good. That is settled then. Take this letter as well, it is your proof that you are working for me. I have already sent a copy to the bank and to my lawyer—you'll find his name writ there on that document an' all." Beaming a smile, Jesamiah crossed to the door and leaning out, shouted for Finch. He didn't appear. "I apologise for not offering refreshment, John, but there is a lot for me to do."

Taking the hint, Benson, still somewhat bewildered, rose, clutching the papers in his hand.

"You understand," Jesamiah said, "I may not return to Devon for some while, but I will, where possible, ensure young Tom writes."

"Thank you for that. My wife will appreciate it." They walked out through the narrow corridor onto the main deck, Jesamiah called for the longboat, now empty of men and preparing to go back for the last of the new crew, to hold a while.

"May I ask when you intend to set sail?" Benson asked, looking round at the scurried activity.

"I'm moving into the deeper channel nearer the Bar as soon as the tide is high, ready to leave tomorrow. Out there we can finish making ready with *Sea Witch* full afloat."

Benson nodded. A wise decision. "May I ask also," he said, pausing before the entry port and preparing to descend the ladder, "we have stowed a good deal in your hold from the warehouse; china, silver, cloth; expensive pieces of furniture. Where are you intending to put Sir Ailie's cargo?"

Evading the question, Jesamiah answered, "I noted everything had been stowed nice and secure, my thanks for that, John." He pointed to the boat. "The oarsmen are ready to fetch that last load of men waiting to come aboard and sign up."

Benson started to descend the ladder cleats, halfway down he paused, looked up at Jesamiah. "Why is it you seem so assured that you can trust me? I am flattered, of course, and as a God-fearing man I will do my best to serve you well, but..."

"Now there you go with those buts again, Master Benson. I know you will do a good job and you will not cheat me because I have your son as surety."

* * *

Reaching beneath his desk to retrieve a dropped quill, Jesamiah swore as he banged his head. Straightening up, swore again as someone rapped at the cabin door.

"Bugger it. Come in!"

Not looking round, he searched through a pile of charts. "Finch? Where's the chart for the Azores? And where's that coffee I asked for?"

"If Finch knows I am afraid he is not here to tell you; nor is there any coffee."

Jesamiah spun round, frowned. "Hello, Henry. What are

you doing here?"

Henry Jennings entered the cabin, took his hat off, then his boat cloak, giving it a vigorous shake to rid it of rain; indicated if he might sit.

Jesamiah nodded, waved his hand towards a chair.

"I will not beat about an offshore wind, lad," Jennings said as he eased himself down, wincing at the protest from aching knees and the residue of gout. "I am being sent back to Nassau. Trouble's brewing with the Spanish and pirates alike. It seems I am one of the few who might be able to sort out the latter. The king has extended the amnesty, we're hoping more will take it, and fight on our side against Spain. I also want to go back to where it is hot. I have had it up to here with rain and cold."

Jesamiah narrowed his eyes. "I recall you once said to me that you wanted to settle here in England. Your dream was to own an estate in some rich English shire."

"That would have been because I had forgotten what godawful weather England has, and I had assumed Catholic James would be on the throne, not Protestant Hanover. Aside, I have been awarded an estate in the Bahamas."

Putting the pile of charts away, Jesamiah perched on the edge of his desk. "And what if I am going nowhere near Nassau?"

"Spymaster Harley thinks I am already on my way, but I didn't much fancy any of those Bristol tubs. Too many of them have rotten hulls and even more rotten crews. And too many of them are slavers. The holds stink." Jennings pointed at a scrolled chart teetering on the edge of the box-bed in the side cabin. "Would that be the one you are looking for?"

Jesamiah went to fetch it, scowled on discovering it was indeed the right one.

"I would wager," Jennings added, "that you are considering

dropping anchor a few miles along the coast above Cádiz? To visit the Marqués de Molina? I quite fancy having a word with him before I head west."

The scowl deepened.

Jennings chuckled, "Oh, do not look so sour, I know you well enough to guess your intentions—by the waves, boy, you learnt most of what you know from me or Malachias Taylor, and who do you think *he* learnt from? Eh?"

Saying nothing, Jesamiah resumed his seat on the edge of the desk, folded his arms. "I ain't yet decided where I'm goin'." Even to his own ears the retort sounded churlishly false.

Jennings leant forward. "We both know you are intending to find Francesca Escudero's son." He held up one hand to stem the denial. "I was there when you promised the dear lady, if you recall. If you had not done so, I would have undertaken the same oath. 'Cesca meant a lot to me as well, Jesamiah. She and her husband and father-in-law were dear friends. We were very close."

Jesamiah wondered, how close? Friendly close or between-the-blankets close? He decided on a small test. "I guess you were close to Francis Chesham as well?"

"No one knew his real identity. Between you and me, I think the fellow was Francesca's father-in-law." Jennings sighed. "We will never know, now."

He seemed to be telling the truth, was unaware that Francesca and Francis were—had been—one and the same person. *Am I the only one to know?* Jesamiah wondered. "So what is your point?" he asked tersely.

"The Marqués also knew Francesca. He will be a good starting place to find the boy. And maybe he can shed light on that missing casket?"

Ignoring the casket reference, Jesamiah asked, "Is the boy

in danger?"

The cabin door opened, letting in a gust of wind and Finch bearing two cups of coffee.

"I reckoned Cap'n Jennings would 'preciate one an' all. If you want more, get it y'self, I'm busy sortin' out stowin' the vittles." He put the two cups on the desk, turned to go, then paused. "Rue wants you on deck, 'e says there's crew 'e wants you to approve. An' where am I s'posed t'put they trunks over there?"

"They are to do with my wife, ask her. Can't Rue handle crew?"

"Not these 'uns he cain't." Finch went out, almost immediately peered back round the door. "An' drink that coffee while it's hot, don't be takin' it up on deck. If you do, bring the soddin' cups back."

"Miserable old bugger," Jennings grumbled. "Why do you keep him on?"

Jesamiah sipped the steaming black coffee. "Because he is good at making coffee, even when we've run out of coffee, and he is one of the most trustworthy men I know. You were saying?"

Henry Jennings looked seriously at Jesamiah through the steam of his own cup. "There are a few people out there who want that casket. Badly enough to kill even a child to get it."

Looking up sharply, and remembering Maha'dun out on the moors, Jesamiah asked, "Is that why someone's attempted to kill me, twice?"

Jennings shook his head. "Do you possess the casket? Do you know where it is?"

"No to both."

"Then why kill you? It's the box that is valuable, not you."

"I did look after it in Hispaniola for a while. I had it in my coat pocket."

Jennings' turn to laugh. "I could very happily kill you myself, right now, for not keeping hold of the damned thing!" As an afterthought added, "I suppose she did not tell you where it is?"

"I just said, no. I didn't hear anything about any of this until after she got us acquitted. And I do not care a ripe fig for this casket, I only have an interest in finding the boy. He's an orphan now and I promised 'Cesca I would take care of him."

Grimacing, Jennings expressed his opinion; "Your dear lady wife might not approve of that sentiment."

"I have already discussed it with her. She is in entire agreement with me."

Henry Jennings doubted that. In his experience wives never took kindly to the sons of other women, especially if that other woman had been, even for a short time, a mistress.

Jesamiah could hear laughter up on deck, and Rue calling for him. "I do wonder, though," he said, getting up and fetching his new hat and coat—he missed his old favourites, but he would soon break these in. "If..."

"If?"

"If she left the box with the boy?"

"I wondered that too," Jennings said, hiding his disappointment. For a moment there he had thought Jesamiah was going to make an important revelation. "We will just have to find him and ask him, won't we?"

Jesamiah narrowed his eyes, was quiet a moment, thoughts tumbling into making sense. Jennings wanted the casket more than the boy. Was he behind all this? But no, 'Cesca had implied that Henry was not involved. Someone of a greater mind was pulling the strings, making the marionettes dance to a set tune. Who? Doone? That fellow Harley?

Whoever it was, Jesamiah was not going to hop to a manipulated jig. He had never liked to dance, and he had no intention of starting to do so now. He decided to ask a direct question.

"Who is behind all this, Henry? Who wants me dead? Who killed Francesca? Who would threaten a boy, and who else wants that box, and why? Doone? Harley?"

Drinking the coffee down, Jennings appreciating its warmth, and the generous addition of expensive sugar as it swept down his gullet into his belly. "Doone would dearly like to get his hands on the box, for his own reasons. It is my understanding that he has employed various people to get it for him. So far they have failed."

The men on Hispaniola and the moors? Maha'dun? Jesamiah thought.

Henry was still talking as he shrugged his coat on. "'Cesca was supposed to deliver it. I think she made several deals with several people, and had not the slightest intention of giving it to any one of them."

"And what about the diamonds that were in it?"

Jennings pulled at his earlobe. "They were in payment for the weapons supplied to the rebels on Hispaniola. Governor Rogers in Nassau is pretty cross with both myself and Francesca because he did not get paid for those guns. I don't suppose you have any knowledge of where those precious gems disappeared to?"

Jesamiah shook his head. "None at all."

Knowing that was very far from the truth, Jennings let the matter go. "Our aim was to fund getting James back on his throne."

Jesamiah laughed outright. "Well, that's the end of that scheme then! Your attempts to support the Catholic cause really is not going too well, is it?"

* * *

"What is it, Rue?" Jesamiah called as he ducked his head away from a squall of rain and pulled his hat lower. "As long as you think them fit for purpose, I've given you free rein to recruit a crew." He hauled himself up the ladder onto the quarterdeck, several men were standing there in a group. Their laughter died away at the sound of Jesamiah's voice.

"I thought you would prefer to decide over these yourself, Cap'n. They look a bunch of rogues to me, I'd as soon throw them over the side, personally."

Jesamiah grimaced, someone was playing damned fool silly games here and he was not much in the mood for it. Then one of the men turned around and the sourness fled as quickly as a mouse flees a cat.

"Jasper! Young Jasper? By God, boy, we thought you were dead!" He grabbed the lad's hand and began pumping it up and down, gave up, hugged him. Turned to the other men, "Ray Wheeler—Spokesy! Albert Moody, Nicholas Partridge, Daniel Woods; am I pleased to see you! Where've you all been hiding?" He pushed further into the clustered group of men, greeting another five-and-twenty by name, shaking their hands, slapping their shoulders.

"We ran off fast with the local folk, hid along with them," Ray Wheeler said.

"When we heard *Sea Witch* was looking for crew we thought it could be a trap," Moody added.

"Then your brother-in-law here sent word round that t'weren't."

Jesamiah looked towards the man loitering at the back.

Carter. "And what are you doing here? Should you not be tending customers in your tavern?"

"Pegget does well enough without me getting under her feet." Carter looked Jesamiah straight in the eye. "I heard you were going to Spain. I want to join you as far as there, fetch my brother back home."

Jesamiah cocked his head to one side. They had not got on well from the first instant of meeting. For one thing, Carter Trevithick thought Jesamiah Acorne was not a good enough husband for his sister. Every brother's initial suspicion, but in this instance the objectionable view was unlikely to change. The two men disliked each other. "I think Tiola is quite capable of seeing your brother sent home."

"Ah, so it is true, you are dragging her along with you? Even after the way she suffered at sea on the voyage here?"

"She is a grown woman, Carter, she makes her own mind."

"So you do not want her to accompany you? There, I knew it! First opportunity and you run out on her!"

Folding his arms, Jesamiah battened down the impulse to punch a fist straight into this muck-stirrer's belly. "You have a wonderful way of twisting everything I say and do, Carter. How your sweet sister came from the same mother as you is beyond me." And then he lit the fuse by adding, "I can only assume you have different fathers."

The fight was short and not very effective. A few traded blows, kicked shins; a bloody nose and a rapidly blackening eye. Rue, Jennings and a couple of the other men pulled them apart before the damage became more serious.

"In answer to your request," Jesamiah said, breathing heavily, aware his bruised eye was already closing, "get off my ship and don't, ever, get in my way again."

Spokesy and Bert Moody grasped an arm each and

marched Carter to the entry port.

Carter shouted a threat over his shoulder; "If my sister comes to any harm, Acorne, you will pay dearly for it. Mark my words!"

"Now, now, mister," Spokesy advised, "you speak nicely to our captain or you might be swimming for the shore, not taking advantage of that nice dry boat waitin' down there at the bottom of the ladder."

"Treat him with respect," Jesamiah called. "He is my wife's brother." Beneath his breath muttered, "For all he is as likeable as an overfull cesspit on a hot summer day."

~ *Jesamiah?* ~ Tiola's voice soothed into his mind. ~ *Is there anything amiss?* ~

~ *Nothing that weighing anchor and setting sail will not cure.* ~

~ *You have been arguing with my brother?* ~

Not bothering to ask how she knew, Jesamiah did not deny it. ~ *He irritates me.* ~

~ *He cares for me. For that you should be grateful.* ~

~ *He wants to sail with us.* ~

~ *Then let him. If you do not, it will only heighten his dislike of you.* ~

For a moment Jesamiah was not sure how to respond. Was she being serious?

~ *I thought you wanted to get away from the people here because you did not want them to realise how quickly you are healing? Or do you trust your brother to know what you are?* ~

The last was a slight challenge, a double-edged sword. Did Carter know she was a witch, knew her secret?

For her part, it was Tiola's turn to pause. Admitting the truth of it, she said into her husband's mind, ~ *You are right.*

Carter would be suspicious of my rapid recovery. Nor would he understand, or accept as you do, my gift of Craft were he to know of it, but... ~ she fumbled for the right thing to say. Jesamiah beat her to it.

~ *But you want me to be tactful and not hurt his feelings?* ~

He sensed Tiola smile. ~ *Exactly so, Captain Acorne! Could you send a boat for me in about half of an hour? I am making my farewells to the ghosts of Tawford Barton.* ~

~ *I can allow no longer than that. And mind your step, there might be flooding with an exceptionally high tide and all this rain.* ~

~ *I will take care. I need no longer. Is Susannah aboard and settling? Although I am still not certain I need a maid. What if she grows suspicious of my quick healing?* ~

~ *She is, you do, and we have already discussed this. You are to tell her it was not a fracture after all. I do not recall anything said about her bringing two yappy dogs with her, though.* ~

He was aware of Tiola's laughter and warmth surrounding and infusing within him.

~ *Do you not? Maybe your mind was on more carnal thoughts?* ~

He snorted, unaware it was an actual sound, not a thought.

"What was that, lad?" Jennings said, looking up from the binnacle box where he had been studying the compass, not that the needle lying passive here in harbour would give him any hint of an intended heading.

"Nothing, Henry, I want to make sail, that's all. I'm just waiting for high tide and my wife to come aboard." He sent Henry a swift smile, a reassurance that all was well, and walked to the rail. Cupping his hands round his mouth, he called out to the boat being rowed away.

"Carter! Carter Trevithick! We sail on the next high tide; up t'you if you're aboard or not."

"The morrow's tide?" Carter called back, uncertain. He did not receive an answer.

Jennings brought out his snuffbox from his waistcoat pocket, dabbed a fair amount of tobacco to his hand and sniffed it up his nostrils. Sneezed into a red kerchief. He walked to the side of the ship, glanced over at the river below, the water rippling and bubbling with the swell of the incoming sea. "Another half hour, I reckon." He glanced up at the pewter-grey, rain-sodden sky. Thunder was rumbling somewhere. "It'll be dark then, too." As if double-checking his calculations, Jennings looked at the rising water again. "I thought you were supposed to be taking a cargo to Virginia for Sir Ailie?"

"Thought wrong then, didn't you," Jesamiah answered, rubbing his hand in a gentle caress over the spokes of the helm. He could have sworn that his ship responded. Similar to Tiola's mind-speak, but this was more subtle; this was feelings, not words. A leap of excitement, the wonder of joy—an embrace of love. He responded with the same empathy: relief, pleasure. The reciprocation of love.

"Sir Ailie is under the impression—as I conclude is Master Carter Trevithick—that you are not sailing until tomorrow at the earliest."

"Is he now?"

"He is."

"What I do or do not do, Henry, is of no consequence to Sir Ailie Doone or Carter Trevithick. If you are not agreeable with sailing to where I intend to sail—in just over half of an hour, with a cargo of my choosing—then I suggest you call that boat back and commiserate with my brother-in-law when he wakes tomorrow and finds me gone."

Jennings sneezed again, sniffed loudly. "Have you engaged a pilot?"

"Nope." Jesamiah patted the helm as he would a favourite dog, walked over to where Skylark was coiling cordage with one of the new crew.

"Your name?" Jesamiah asked. He hated having to get to know new men.

"Tearle, Cap'n. Richie Tearle."

"Have you been to sea before, Tearle?"

"I sailed with Woodes Rogers and William Dampier on their last circumnavigation."

Impressed, Jesamiah's eyebrows rose. "Dampier was a good man, I was saddened to hear of his death a while back."

"A sorry thing, sir, he died nearly two thousand pounds in debt, I heard. All that achievement of discovery and all he gets is an unmarked pauper's grave."

"It should not have been so," Jesamiah agreed, "but it's a possibility we all face. So, what is your story? Why are you seeking a passage as lowly as *Sea Witch*?"

Tearle grinned; "Hardly lowly, sir, *Sea Witch* has a name for being a good ship under a good captain."

Skylark laughed. "He knows how to secure himself a decent berth, this one! It's more likely you're not so keen on being a guest of His Majesty, I'd say."

Scratching innocently at his chin, Tearle offered, "Let us just say that I thought the king's offered accommodation was not quite to my taste."

"Fair enough," Jesamiah acknowledged, understanding the meaning. "You're welcome aboard as long as you work hard and cause no trouble. Skylark?"

"Cap'n?"

"When that jolly boat of ours returns, take Jasper to fetch Mistress Acorne from Tawford Barton. Don't dawdle. We sail on the first of the ebb tide."

Skylark touched his forelock. "Aye, Cap'n."

"Do you think you should engage a pilot?" Jennings persisted, following in Jesamiah's wake as he descended the ladder to the main deck.

"Nope." Jesamiah halted abruptly, turned to face his friend. "As you once said, those who don't want to draw attention don't use pilots. Those who know what they are doing, probably more than the pilots, don't need pilots."

"I said that?"

"Aye, Henry, you did."

"Guess I cannot argue with you then, can I?"

"Nope."

Chapter Twenty-Four

The rain had not ceased. It was as if the sky wept for the dead, as Tiola, standing in the garden that the ladies of Tawford Barton had so loved, also wept.

The wall of the sturdy and intricately designed dyke was holding back the tide as the water rose to maximum height. Spindrift spilled over the top like a monster seeking potential prey, the occasional trickle of seepage finding a way through the stones as if the beast was ravenously salivating. The wall was holding, but had the house been whole everyone would have been out here, frantic to ensure no breach occurred, anxiously watching and waiting for the point of high water, willing for that moment when the incoming tide turned outward again. But not this time. There was no one to protect the house. No house to protect.

Tiola stood a while, bereft for the loss of her friends. Death happened, it was a part of life as much as breathing, eating or making love. There were only two sureties: birth and death, both inevitable and unstoppable, but it was the manner of these deaths causing the great grief and bitterness. A cold rage clumped like undigested porridge in Tiola's stomach. Innocents had perished through the malice of murder. This revenge killing had to stop.

The Law of Craft dictated that, unless to defend herself, she could harm no human; a law set in place millennia into the past to preserve integrity and honour. All too easy to use such a gift for self-purpose, for vengeance, greed or jealousy. Those who had broken the Law had suffered as they had perished. With Craft removed, life was shortened, threatened, or all too often taken by others. Many of those hanged or burnt as witches had defied the Law and paid the ultimate price. A few survived, corrupted and devoid of Craft, one day their betrayal would be punished, but there were other matters to dwell upon this night.

The fury within Tiola that this non-human creature, who sneered at any life other than her own, who bragged and boasted, tortured, belittled and betrayed—had attempted to destroy one of the White Craft—was too much to tolerate. Tiola was not permitted to do harm, but Cara'mina was not human, although even that could have saved her, for all life was precious, but her spite disqualified her from the privilege of protection. She had to be eliminated, and it was Tiola's responsibility to ensure it done.

Dusk was fading into night, the sky turning as dark as an angry bruise. Above the drumming of the rain and the keening of the wind Tiola could hear Cara'mina screeching. The villagers had already spread word, and made surreptitious signs of protection, about the pitiable cries coming from the tormented departed souls of Tawford Barton. Fortunate that no one dared linger near enough to hear the explicit curses and threats of all Cara'mina would do to Maha'dun when she caught up with him. No self-respecting ghost would dare to use such foul language. Tiola smiled wryly at a particularly rancid tirade of detailed cruelty, regretted being unable to speak into Cara'mina's mind as she could with Jesamiah and Maha'dun. It would have been satisfying to inform this malignant bitch that her curses were for nothing, that Maha'dun would be safe, and it was she, Cara'mina, who was about to perish. She would need to impart the information another way.

Walking across the rain-drenched grass, heedless of the spreading puddles, Tiola cleared her mind of all thought. Turning to face the sea, she concentrated on the stones in the wall, on the way each nested against the next, snug-fit and tight; shape matching shape. Concentrated on the rising sea, pushing and beating at the wall, demanding a way in...

~ Who seeks me? ~

~ I seek you, Tethys, Lady, Spirit, Life of the Sea. I, Tiola of the White Craft, seek you. ~

~ I am not your servant to be summoned. Be gone, your mind-tricks are not welcome, Witch-Woman. ~

~ I come to offer you a gift. ~

~ A gift? ~

~ I wish to return to you land which was once yours. ~

Tiola emptied her mind and envisioned the promontory of Tawford Barton encroached by sea, then focused on the sea swell heaving against the solidity of the wall, its weight pressing against the wet stones. She selected one at random; saw its shape, felt its texture, honoured its great age and how it had been formed beneath the seas, envisioned the remains of tiny creatures settling in the sand, layer upon layer, crushed and moulded into rock, millennia after millennia. Then the great surge of Gaia pushing and buckling, folding and heaving upward. The rise and fall of the ice over the land; the heating and cooling, wetting and drying—and that single stone within the wall moved. Tiola felt it give, felt the wall waver... and the sea rushed in through the breach, more stones caving in, tumbling down, one, two, three, four yards of wall disintegrating beneath the heaving, frothing inrush.

Within minutes the flood was up to Tiola's ankles, then her knees. Her gown, sodden, floated about her legs, her cloak spread out behind as if it were a thrashing mermaid's tail. The lawn became a lake of swirling water, the spring-budding trees in the orchard were stranded like beleaguered sentinels, the rubble of the ruined house hissing steam where some of the masonry retained that last vestige of heat. Tiola ignored it all; the incoming flotsam of seaweed and driftwood, a long-dead bird, a length of frayed cordage. Charred rafter beams floated by her; swirling in the torrent, a broken pot, a shoe, a tarnished pewter plate. A silver spoon, lodged between the prongs of a fork, caught the flare of a distant lightning flash. A nightgown, undamaged apart from its lace torn and blackened at neck and cuffs, drifted lazily, its long sleeves flapping slowly, spread as if arms encased within were paddling it forward. The last remaining section of the house wall crumbled, crashing and splashing into the water, sending waves rippling outward, the floating debris bobbing and rocking as they passed.

Only the chimney stack stood stark against the storm-drenched night sky. Thunder grumbled. Lightning cleaved the darkness. Rain hissed into the sea, and the water surged through the remains of the house, barn and outbuildings. Where the kitchen, the heart of the home, had been it poured through holes and cracks and rifts into the cellar below.

No longer shouting rage, Cara'mina screamed a cry of desperate fear.

Tiola closed her eyes and released her soul to drift, swirled and buffeted with the current, the roar of the sea and the spatter of the rain in her ears. The blackness of the night, the white of the foam; the purple glare of the lightning... Falling, tumbling with the torrent... Stood in the darkness of the cellar. Unheeding of the rising cold, black water, she stood, staring, unblinking, uncompassionate, at the bedraggled, frightened Night-Walker.

Teeth bared, Cara'mina snarled her fury, reached out with claw-like fingernails attempting to scratch at Tiola's eyes and face, but the witch-woman was an apparition, an ethereal figure, the talons made no mark.

"You cannot kill me, bitch-witch! These walls will not hold with the weight of this water, they will collapse and then I will be free to kill you and them, your bastard husband and that scut Maha'dun. You will regret this night! You will regret it!"

Tiola allowed her to rage, indifference closing her ears to the spite. "You tried once already to kill Maha'dun and failed."

Cara'mina snarled an answer. "I did not intend for him to die, only frighten him. Those men were responsible for trying to drown him, not I." She feigned bravado. "I am not afraid of you or this water. Let it rise, I will rise with it and be free of here!"

"You wanted to kill Maha'dun because he was my friend."

"He was your lover. He was not permitted other lovers, he was, is, my property."

"He is no one's property. He is a Night-Walker, not a slave. You punished him because you thought it would punish me because I was unable to save your partner."

"You left him to die!"

"I died. I could not save him, but I saved you."

"Do you think I wanted to live after the way he died? Do you?"

Tiola indicated the rising water. "Then die here and let us end it all. I promise I will find the last casket and release the last soul, and you will be with your lover again in the Beyond."

Cara'mina tilted her head higher. "And are you going to kill me? I think not! You are not permitted to harm or kill."

"There is a side to me few know; I have the ability to kill."

The laughter came again, mocking. "You? Kill? You are too weak of mind to take a life." Cara'mina touched her fingers to her head, "Too soft in the head. You save life, you do not spill it."

"You have forfeited your life, Cara'mina. Over and again you have played your vicious game with innocents as your prey. This is where the game ends."

Whatever she said, whatever she thought, Cara'mina did not want to die. "You will not kill me, Tiola Oldstagh. You cannot."

"I can, and I will, by the strength that flows from the air to the depth of the earth, by the force of water, and the cleansing of fire will I put an end to you."

Tiola lifted her arms, with one hand she made a small figure-of-eight movement and released a slow *'hieshhh'* of breath. Palm outstretched, fingers extended as if grasping the very storm clouds that loomed in the darkness above, she sang. Sang with notes of a pitch inaudible to the human ear, a song to put out the sun, to darken the stars, boil the seas and cause the sky itself to crumble and fall. A song of ending.

Lightning split the sky and thunder cracked directly overhead. Tiola stretched higher, her spirit reaching up and up to grasp the energy of the storm, to catch the lightning within her hand, twisting it around her fingers as if it were a coil of burning rope. She brought it down, the power searing through her, illuminating both her true and spirit body. Brought the lightning down and set it into the ruins of the house. The fire leapt upward as the rain and the sea, and all within, burned. She watched as the lightning fire consumed everything around her. Let it all burn as the grief tore at her heart.

Cara'mina's last screams were drowned by the roar of the thunder, the crackle of the flame, and the relentless drumming of the burning rain.

* * *

"Lady! What are you doing? What have you done?"

Tiola felt arms catch around her waist, dragging her earthly being backwards through the water, forcing her soul abruptly into her living body. She gasped as the coldness of the water hit her, shrieked for Maha'dun to let her go.

"Maha'dun, you are hurting me!"

The Night-Walker hastily released her and Tiola toppled forward, he grabbed her shoulders before she fell, the rising water swirling in waves around them both as they scrabbled together for a secure footing. Gasping for breath, each helping the other, they waded through the flood towards the rise of higher land where the house had been. Collapsed to the wet grass breathless, sodden.

The night sky was alight, the chimney stack, that last standing remnant of Tawford Barton, was afire—the lightning had struck as a direct hit. The once sturdy, four-foot-thick brickwork groaned, then toppled, hissing steam and smoke into the flood.

"What have you done?" Maha'dun said again, staring at where there was nothing but falling rain and frothing sea. "What have you done?" he repeated in a barely audible whisper.

"The flood breached the wall and lightning can be unpredictable," Tiola answered.

"But Cara'mina..."

"Is dead."

Maha'dun sat staring into the flames that made it seem as if the night itself was afire, his arms wrapped around his knees, his body rocking backwards and forwards, unsure whether to be relieved or saddened. For all he despised her, Cara'mina was one of his own, and there were so few of them left.

"She died through the four sacred elements, Maha'dun. The four invincible powers."

He looked at her, grief creasing his face. "I cannot mourn her," he admitted at last, "I despised her. Is it wrong to be glad that she is gone?"

Tiola touched her fingers to where the tears overspilled from his anguished sapphire eyes. "It is not wrong to be glad that her troubled soul is now at peace."

"Ahoy! Ahoy! Mistress Tiola?" Skylark's voice interrupted, shouting from the darkness, the shape of a boat bumping against the breached wall.

"Here! I am here—quite safe!" Tiola stood, waved her arms, watched as Skylark and Jasper rowed carefully towards her.

"We got a bit worried when that lightning struck," Skylark said, offering Tiola his hand to help her into the boat.

"Reckon the house be proper done fer now," Jasper observed as Maha'dun manoeuvred awkwardly over the thwarts, attempting not to show his stark fear at the prospect of having so much water beneath him.

As the two men rowed across the flooded orchard and garden and reached the river estuary, the strain on the oars suddenly eased, and the bubbles and ripples slackened.

"Tide's turned," Jasper said, "Cap'n'll be wantin' to make way."

"Best put our backs into it then," Skylark answered.

"I am relieved," Maha'dun said again to Tiola. "But other Night-Walkers will not forgive you when they hear of this. Do you know what you have done?"

~ I have done what should have been done long ago, Maha'dun. I have set you free. ~

* * *

Jesamiah paced to the far side of the quarterdeck, peered over the rail into the dark night, grunted, then paced to the other side to repeat the same process. He had paced, peered and grunted for some while.

Out of the corner of his eye, and from beneath his hat which was well tipped forward to discourage the rain from dripping onto his face, he watched the new crew members scurrying about the deck and rigging preparing to make sail. Darkness made no difference to them, all experienced sailors had good night vision. Most could do their job with precision even with their eyes closed. Or the wrong side of sober. He would have to learn all their names; he hated the thought of that. He had known the old crew as well as if they were brothers. He peered over the side again. Slack water. Where the bugger was that boat bringing Tiola aboard? He was kicking himself for letting her go ashore. What if they missed the tide? That would mess his plans up. Screwing his eyes half shut to see the better through the misted, heavy rain, he strove to focus more clearly on the shore where only a few days ago Tawford Barton had squatted comfortable and content. Now that place was abandoned, never to be rebuilt.

Thunder grumbled, then another louder rumble a mile or so away, followed immediately by a shattering crack almost overhead. The sky lit up with dazzling tendrils of lurid purple lightning illuminating the shore and rounded hills of Instow, throwing into stark silhouetted relief the remaining chimney stack of the ruined house. He cried out, instinctively put his arm up to shield his face as the sky burst into flame.

Alerted by the sound that had echoed across the estuary and the shouts that skittered through the ship, men ran up from below; crowded the starboard deck, leaning over the rail pointing and chattering excitedly.

"Pipe down!" Jesamiah shouted angrily. "Can anyone see Skylark and Jasper? Are they returning? Have they got my wife safe?"

Shaken heads, a few answers of "No," and "No, sir."

~ *Tiola!* ~ Jesamiah called in his mind, knowing it would be futile. ~ *Tiola!?* ~

He hurried down to the main deck, glancing every few paces towards the shore, stopped beside the longboat stowed and secured, neatly covered with oiled sailcloth. Should he order it made ready? Take a crew, see what was happening over there? That would delay their sailing. Could he afford the time? But what if Tiola had been injured by that lightning blast? Repeatedly she had assured him that there were only certain ways she could die. Burning was one of them.

"Gawd, that's some fire!" Finch announced, coming on deck with his usual cup of coffee for the captain. Henry Jennings and Rue were close behind; ahead of them, Thomas with Pamela's two dogs. The deck wet, the boy skidded to a halt beside Jesamiah, who put out a hand to steady the lad.

"Walk when you are on a wet deck, lad, unless you want to risk a swimming lesson. And keep a close eye on those dogs. I don't want no calling cards on my deck."

"What was that loud bang?" Tom responded, ignoring the rebuke and not very successfully masking the tremble of fear from his voice. "Was it cannon fire? Are we being shot at?"

"A lightning strike putting an end to what was left of Tawford Barton by the look of it," Jesamiah explained, sounding very unconcerned and matter-of-fact, even to his own ears.

With no reason to be scared, Tom's expression altered into that of awe. "Gawd, look at those fokken flames; they're lighting up the whole bleedin' sky!"

Jesamiah clipped the boy's ear. This short while aboard and already the lad was imitating his captain's crudities? Tom's mother would not thank Jesamiah for it.

Somewhat apart from the press of onlookers, Rue was leaning out over the rail, as if stretching his body would take him nearer the land. Tears were streaming down his face. Everyone pretended there was nothing amiss with him.

"There they are!" one of the new men shouted, pointing. "The boat's coming back!"

"You sure?" someone answered, "I can't see a bleedin' thing."

"Yes! There!" another man added. "There they are!"

Closing his eyes, releasing the breath he had not realised he was holding, Jesamiah sent a quick prayer of gratitude. He should have had more faith in Tiola, but he had lost enough friends these past weeks. Lost one lover too many. He looked at the last man who had called out, Richie Tearle. Had he seen him before? Ah, he had sailed with Dampier and Rogers... "Did I meet you in Cape Town a couple of years back?"

"Not as I recall, Cap'n, but then the Cape be a busy place."

A minute passed, two, three, the boat was pulling nearer. Jesamiah could clearly see Skylark and Jasper heaving at the oars, picked out Tiola, her black hair uncovered and coming loose from its restraining pins. Beside her a tall, slender man.

"Shite," someone leaning on the rail nearer the bow exclaimed, "what the beggar is he doing coming aboard?"

Frowning, Jesamiah switched his gaze away from the approaching boat. That voice was familiar. Recognition flooded Jesamiah's memory as he headed for the quarterdeck. Changing his mind, he turned back.

"Not that it is any of your business, Ascham Doone, but Maha'dun is to be a guest of my wife's. I would like an explanation, however, of why you are here?"

Doone straightened, matched Jesamiah's gaze stare for stare.

"Um," Jennings stepped forward, scratching at his cheek to hide a certain amount of embarrassment. "I am afraid he is with me. I invited him."

"Not that it is any business of yours, Acorne," Doone reciprocated the insult, "but I have family mercantile matters to attend with Señor Calderón. Do you have a problem with this?" His blunt stare remained challenging.

"Quite a few," Jesamiah snapped back. "For one I ain't a passenger ship, for two I don't carry people for free..."

"I have paid my way to your insolent steward."

"Have you now? And while aboard this ship you address me as Captain."

"Understood, Captain. Except things will not be agreeable with that blue-eyed devil spawn sharing the same deck."

"Well, the blue-eyed devil spawn probably has the same opinion about having to put up with you. And if you don't like *my* guest you still have time to leave." Jesamiah emphasised the '*my*' and elaborately indicated the entry port.

"I repeat that I have already paid my passage. Perhaps he and I can ensure we stay out of each other's way?"

Not bothering to hide his irritation, Jesamiah was curt. "As he is likely to be with me and my wife for most of the time, that sounds doable.”

So that was a tally of four he did not particularly want aboard. Maha’dun Nightm’n, Thomas Benson, Henry Jennings, and one of the Doones. Had Ascham spoken the truth or had Sir Ailie sent him to keep watch over things? Both, probably.

“I thought we were supposed to be taking our cargo on board?” Ascham Doone queried, looking around for his grandfather’s property.

Another curt reply; “Thought wrong then. Finch, take Rue below, will you? Find him a bottle of something strong.”

“I got things t’do.”

“Haven’t we all?” Jesamiah responded angrily, but, relenting, added, “take Tom with you then, he can do some fetchin’ an’ carryin’. And don’t you ever accept passengers again without clearing it with me first.”

Finch waved a hand as a vague acknowledgement, with every intention of ignoring the order, but he was gentle as he encouraged the distraught Rue below.

“Come along, old son. Got yersel’ into a right ol’ state, ain’t yer? Thomas Hedgepig—stop playin’ with them damn dogs an’ fetch me the Cap’n’s best brandy from ’is cabin.”

Jesamiah almost protested, but let it pass. Waiting beside the entry port for the boat to come alongside and the men to help Tiola and her companion aboard, he wondered who he would quite happily prefer to toss over the side. At least he did not have to concern himself with Crawford anymore. He smiled briefly. What was that saying about dark clouds and silver linings?

Jennings offered his hand to Tiola as she scrabbled through the entry port, her skirts, sodden and bedraggled, hitched and secured almost to above her knees. Breathless, she nodded her thanks, for modesty, released her gown and patted it smooth.

"Goodness," she panted, "that was a bit of a climb! Fortunately, my ankle is healing enough for such exercise, though it does ache abominably. Is Maha'dun managing all right?" She peered down the side of the ship, looked into Maha'dun's pale face tipped upward as he slowly climbed the cleats, hand over hand, each foot feeling for a firm, secure step before moving to the next one. Fear hammered behind his eyes, not for the climb or the drop below, but for the tossing water beneath him. He smiled at Tiola as he reached the top and jumped down onto the deck, pleased with his achievement.

"I will grow used to it," he said, hoping he sounded more convincing than he felt, "but there must be a more civilised way to come aboard?" The few small merchant ships he had made use of to cross the Channel had always been moored alongside a wharf with a convenient gangplank to use.

"We'll rig a bosun's chair for you next time," Jesamiah said. Thought, *If there is a next time.*

Not knowing what a bosun's chair was or what it did, although sensing it was something derogatory, Maha'dun made light of the situation; "I am sure I can manage."

"Jasper will show you to your quarters," Jesamiah said as the boy came aboard. "Our carpenter has rigged you a private corner in the hold where it is always dark."

"Thank you," Maha'dun responded, giving a slight bow, "but may I wait until I need to make use of it?" He did not want to admit that he had a mixture of fear and excitement coursing through him, nor that he did not fancy being shut away unnecessarily.

"I am going to our cabin to change into something less,"

Tiola shook her sodden garments and laughed, "… less wet!"

Jesamiah cocked one eyebrow at her.

~ You all right? ~

She touched his arm, reached up to kiss his cheek, her relief intense. Cara'mina was no longer a worry, and no longer did her past rival, Tethys, Goddess of the Sea, pose a threat for that dead-born son of Jesamiah's had served a purpose of appeasement. The free-given gift of a soul for a soul. Tiola kissed Jesamiah again, a more intimate gesture on the lips, smiled, said;

~ I am now, that I am safe aboard with you. Can we leave here please? I would be gone from this sorrowful place. ~

Chapter Twenty-Five
At Sea

With night descended and the darkness seeming heavier with the falling rain, Jesamiah watched Tiola disappear through the sparsely lit narrow corridor which led to their great cabin and indicated for Jennings to precede him onto the quarterdeck, paused as he considered what to do with Maha'dun. The last thing anyone needed was a landlubber dolt getting in the way.

"You are welcome to join us," he said, indicating the ladder companionway which Henry was ascending. "It will be wet and blowy out here, though."

"A drop of rain and a puff of wind has never before done me much harm, Captain," Maha'dun answered cheerfully as he copied how Jesamiah easily went up the ladder steps. "Aside, the rain seems to be easing."

Even with the downpour slackening into a heavy drizzle, the wind was howling through the rigging, making a discordant sound like an out-of-tune chorus of wailing banshees. Maha'dun tucked himself into a corner between the rail that looked down onto the main deck and the right-hand, waist-high wooden wall round the deck. He pulled his cloak tighter and watched the proceedings. Still that thump of fear coursed through him—he was on a boat which was on the water—but not one of these fellows seemed bothered or anxious about the fact. Not even those who, when Jesamiah, cupping a hand round his mouth, shouted, "Make ready! Hands aloft!" scurried up the tall masts, apparently quite able to see in the dark, and went out along the poles that stuck out sideways. *'Yards'*, he heard someone call them. He watched the men ship and pin the capstan bars then, putting all their weight to them, began to walk round and around. The boats that he had been on before—much smaller than this one—had all been secured by ropes trailing to bollards ashore. When making way these had merely been unhitched and reeled in. This was something quite different, more active, more powerful. More fascinating and exciting. The capstan pawls were going *clunk, clunk*, as the metal and wood machinery turned, the men working it singing a rhythmical chant, their feet stamping in unison. He could see the wet, seaweed-slimed cable jerking slowly through a hole in the side of the ship, could almost feel the boat quivering beneath his boots.

"Hove short!" someone called.

"Loose main and fore!" Jesamiah shouted from where he stood, legs apart, his hands on the spokes of the helm—and suddenly everything seemed to happen at once.

The anchor was dragging free of its tethering shackle to land, the cable coming in quicker now.

"Anchor aweigh!" That was the man they called Skylark, the one who had rowed them here from the shore.

The men, strung out along the yards high above the wooden deck, were working quickly—and without warning the great folds of canvas fell, cracking and rattling and billowing with an immediate and startling effect.

"Sheet home hard!" Jesamiah called, spinning the wheel between his firm hands.

The wind filled the canvas, and with nothing now to restrain her, *Sea Witch* leapt forward as if she were a hound let free of the leash and set to chasing a hare. The entire ship leaned over, the deck canting steeply. Maha'dun clung to the rail in front of him as if his very life depended on it. The boat was going to topple over! Was going to sink! Yet, no one else seemed bothered that it was tilting at an absurd angle and white foam was rushing and spewing up the sides and spilling over the deck.

Then she righted a little and the dark shore was slipping past, the blaze of fire at Tawford Barton which had died down— there had not been much left to burn—and was now behind them. The wind was sharper, stinging his face as if someone were shooting tiny needles at him. Sounds had changed too, the wind was higher in pitch, the rigging sang, more coordinated, a sweeter voice. Foam was boiling past as *Sea Witch* moved faster, and then a horrendous lurching and tossing. Maha'dun stared, transfixed, at the surge of swirling, churning, white bubbling water hurtling past and beneath them, certain they were all going to die. He gripped tighter, closed his eyes. The Night-Walkers had no religion or deities, but at this moment he understood the human need for both.

"Jib and tops'ls!" Jesamiah yelled, his voice barely carrying over the scream of the wind, but the men seemed to know what he said for more scurried about, their bare feet slapping on the wet decking, their hands coiled around ropes, hauling hard as more sail spread and billowed.

"Man the braces! Shift your arses there!" Jesamiah boomed, with a hint of impatient anger. Men scurried to haul at the yards, heaving at them until they began to squeal and squeak round. *Sea Witch* went about and as the great expanse of canvas sails filled out completely, hard and firm, she gathered way, thundering over and through the waves, lifting, dipping, diving and soaring, spindrift spraying and spewing as she thrust the sea aside. Men were securing the anchor; everything was creaking, banging and rattling, drumming and whining. In wonder, Maha'dun turned around to look at Instow and the smoking ruins where Cara'mina's body had burned, found nothing there to see through the murky mist except a vague outline of land a long way off.

They had crossed that turbulent white-capped sandbar, were away, out at sea. Flying, it seemed. Even on a well-bred horse Maha'dun had never travelled so fast. He let go of the rail with one hand, adjusted his balance, finding he could stand quite firm with one leg bent at the knee, the other slightly ahead—as Jesamiah was standing. He let his body sway with the rhythm of the ship, tossed his head back and howled in utter enthralled, exultant, pleasure.

* * *

"This is exciting, is it not, sir?"

Maha'dun turned away from staring at the men scampering about the rigging to smile at the boy who appeared beside him. "Should not all children—and their dogs—be abed at this late hour?"

"Probably," Thomas Benson admitted with a grin. He had voluntarily taken on the role of kennel master and, pushing Lorna away from licking his face, put her down so that she could run off after Poppy. "But no one has noticed that I am not, and besides, I am a midshipman now, midshipmen go to bed when they please."

"I do not think you have that quite right, young man," Tiola interjected as she came up behind both of them. "Captain Acorne will be most concerned if his midshipman were to nod off, sound asleep, during his next turn on watch. And are you not looking forward to spending your first night in a sailor's hammock? If you do not claim yours soon, someone else will occupy it."

Thomas looked askance. "But I have my things stowed beneath!"

"You had best get to bed then," Tiola advised, "but sluice the deck where Poppy has relieved herself first."

The boy hastily touched a finger to his forehead by way of salute, and trotted off to find a bucket, gather the dogs up and head below. He was sharing quarters with Rue; no one else would dare take his assigned berth, but until he discovered that fact it was a good enough ploy to entice him to bed.

"He is a good lad," Maha'dun observed, "Captain Acorne made a wise choice to bring him aboard."

"He did not actually make that choice. John Benson backed him into a corner."

Maha'dun stared up the great height of the mainmast, wondering what it would be like to climb up to the top and look down. One night soon he might find the courage to do it. "The same corner as you backed him into regarding myself?" he asked.

The white lie of, 'Of course not,' hovered on Tiola's tongue, but she guessed he would hear the platitude for what it was. "He expects you to find this missing boy, for the lad most probably knows where the casket is hidden, and my husband knows you want to find that casket."

"As do several others. Ailie Doone among them. Why is his grandson here?"

Tiola leant her arms on the rail and gazed down at the mesmerising surf creaming away along the ship's side. She had been wondering the same while changing into warmer, plainer garments. "I think at the moment that is a question without an answer. Maybe he is, like you, hoping to find his freedom? He is but a young man and his grandfather is somewhat..." she hesitated, uncertain of the right word.

"Domineering?" Maha'dun offered. "I could add arrogant, bullying, rude and unbearable."

Dragging her attention from the foam, Tiola turned to face him. "If you do so not like the man, why did you work for him?"

"Because Cara'mina ordered it, and because we assumed he was to be acquiring a bone-box. The English woman with the Spanish name was supposed to have delivered it to him. She did not do so."

Tiola snorted disdain. "That might well be because your Cara'mina murdered her!"

Maha'dun was watching the men climbing up the ropes that supported the middle pole—mast? When they reached the cross-pole yard thingies they ran out along them as agile as cats. Were they not afeared of falling? How could they see so clearly in the dark, they did not possess a Night-Walker's vision, surely? His thoughts trailed away as he finally answered Tiola. "I am not sure Cara'mina did kill the English lady."

"Then who did?"

That he could not answer so he said nothing, turned his attention, fascinated, to the canvas tumbled from the yards, watched with awe as the sail billowed and wallowed like an untamed wild animal for a moment, then filled with wind and became docile. *Sea Witch* put on a discernible spurt of speed.

"How fast can this boat go?" he said.

"You will have to ask Jesamiah, but I suspect he will say

something useless like, 'as fast as I want her to'," Tiola answered with a laugh.

Settling his arms beside her along the rail, Maha'dun studied the surrounding darkness. Nothing to see for miles except sea and a black, clouded sky that had a faint tinge behind it where the moon glided. He thought he would have been terrified out here in this vast emptiness but his feelings were quite the opposite. "Why did I think I would be so frightened of the open sea?" he wondered aloud. "It is most beautiful."

"You were frightened because Cara'mina said you would be. She had much to answer for."

Maha'dun sighed, turned around so his elbows and back were against the rail. He could see Jesamiah at the helm talking to Henry Jennings. Jennings was pointing up at one of the sails, Jesamiah adjusted the wheel. Maha'dun felt the boat shift slightly, as if she were making herself more comfortable.

"She is a lovely boat," he said.

"Ship. *Sea Witch* is a ship, not a boat."

"There is a difference?"

Tiola laughed at his incredulity. "Oh yes, a very big difference. And that is another thing to ask Jesamiah to explain."

"So, these men can see well in the dark?" he asked. "I always understood that humans slept at night because they could not see without their little burning lights to guide their movements."

"As long as there are no lights to dazzle their vision, sailors can see well, although not as far or as clearly as you and I," Tiola answered.

Wishing he'd had the foresight to acquire some cheroots, Maha'dun nodded his understanding and stood chewing his lip. Many of the men, he had noticed, sucked at clay pipes—not all of them filled with tobacco, he assumed because it was too expensive for them to purchase. Maybe he could make friends with some of them if he managed to buy a hogshead or two and shared it out? There again, most sailors liked their rum. Perhaps that would go down better as a gift?

"I do not think your husband will be too forthcoming with answering my questions. I have the impression he does not much like me." Conversation was helping to ease the craving.

"That is because he does not know you. He will talk to you about *Sea Witch*, he is too proud of her not to. And make him laugh, make him trust you. Both will make a big difference."

Maha'dun capered a little jig. "I do not think playing the fool will impress him."

"No, but courage and honesty will."

"Is it true that he was a pirate? This was a pirate ship?"

"It is."

Maha'dun raised a surprised eyebrow. "I imagined all pirates to be dastardly rogues, drunk all the time, unwashed, uncouth. Renegade slobs fit for only the hangman's noose. Their ships I took to be leaking wrecks."

"Many pirates are ruffians—they have little except the hope of acquiring enough wealth to drink themselves into oblivion. They are thieves and scoundrels, though a few are monsters to be avoided for they are dangerous men." She tossed a wry smile at Maha'dun, "Pirates are, for the most part, though, more shout and threat than actual deed. They intimidate by pretending to be fierce and will only attack a ship that is incapable of defending itself. You have killed more men than most pirates."

"And is your husband one of the most or one of the few?"

"In between. He would defend a woman or child, a horse or

a dog if they were being ill-treated. But danger lurks behind his smile. Threaten him, or me, and you are likely to find yourself on the wrong end of his cutlass or pistol."

"Will he ever go back to piracy?"

Tiola laughed. "Goodness, what a lot of questions! I hope not, but I cannot see him following the sedate life of a merchant trader, for all he has a hold-full of goods to sell for a fat profit. He has wealth enough already, so it is not about the financial gain; it is the excitement of the Chase, the thrill of the hunt and the unpredictability of the fight." She looked towards Jesamiah, could slap his face and yell at him for so many stupid things, but she loved him with a love that went beyond reason. He would go back on the account when boredom called. She laid a hand on her womb. Unless, perhaps, he had a greater need not to?

Unaware of his companion's thoughts, Maha'dun had his own: I *would like to be a pirate. To rule the sea, to pick and choose where to go at no one's behest. To be free. But would Acorne ever accept me? Trust me? And, anyway, what use would I be during daylight hours?* Breaking the silence he admitted, "I have not been worthy of your trust, my lady, so I stand little chance of gaining his. I have not protected him well from threatened dangers thus far."

Tiola touched his arm. "That is not what I have heard. You fought well with those men in Bristol, and the previous attempts on my husband's life were made before you arrived there. Add to that, Cara'mina will trouble us no more."

"She was not the only problem," Maha'dun replied. "Your husband is certain that someone is trying to kill him. And I am certain the Doones are behind a lot of things. I am not sure why Ascham is here."

Tiola was sceptical. "What experience of killing would he

have? He barely has a beard!"

Giving a half-hearted smile, Maha'dun took her hand and held her palm to the smooth skin on his face. "The presence of whiskers, dear lady, has nothing to do with the ability to cut a man's throat."

* * *

"At least the rain has eased," Jennings observed, tucking his cold hands under his armpits. "Let's hope it holds, eh?"

He received nothing more than a grunt from Jesamiah.

"You did well to bring us safely over the Bar."

Grunt.

"You are like your father as far as handling a ship is concerned. Do something once and you remember it forever." Jennings chuckled and nudged Jesamiah with his elbow. "Same goes for women, I reckon. Both you and your pa knew how to sweet-talk the beauties." He had expected a laugh, or at least a grin. Got another, gruffer, grunt.

Giving up trying for congenial banter, Jennings indicated the mainsail. "We need to come up a point, that'n's flapping a bit."

Jesamiah adjusted the wheel. He was barely listening to Jennings' prattle. Half his attention was on his ship, the other half on watching Tiola and that Nightman. They both seemed very familiar with each other.

"You there!" he called to Perkiss, "see to that line, it shouldn't be dangling like that!"

As if he were not certain it was himself being addressed, Perkiss looked about, realised he was on his own, scowled.

"Do as you're bloody told, and hop to it!" Jesamiah yelled, "or I'll have you flogged."

The scowl deepened as Perkiss touched his forehead and

286

did as he was bid; muttered, "Like bugger you will, you bastard."

"Is that how you talk to all your men?" Ascham Doone remarked from where he was smoking a pipe on the far side of the quarterdeck.

"Only to the bloody useless ones." Jesamiah answered with a growl in his voice. "They're getting paid to do a job. I expect them to do it."

"You do not include that devil spawn who is so enamoured by your wife then?"

Fingering the blue ribbons laced into his hair, Jesamiah turned to glare at Ascham. "She can look after herself, and he is not standing, uninvited, on my quarterdeck."

Doone shrugged, knocked his pipe ash out over the side and sauntered towards the ladder, made his way into the waist.

"Go easy on Doone," Jennings advised. "He has the look of a green-behind-the-ears boy, but he is sharp-minded and there is more to him than meets the eye. His grandfather, and most people, see only the boy and undervalues him—as did his own father, there was no love lost between them—but they are a dangerous family to cross and likely to unite together against common enemies. Add to that, Doone is believed to be hand-in-pocket with Spymaster Harley. There's even rumour that he intends to step into Harley's boots if he can raise enough capital—and the gratitude of Fat George—to do so."

"Which Doone are you talking about? Ailie or Ascham? That boy would not make a peeping Tom, even if you stuffed him behind a lace curtain in a whorehouse." Jesamiah said as a squall of wind and rain suddenly swept over the deck, taking his words with it as it howled away landward.

"What? Eh? You will have to speak up lad, too many years of guns ain't done my hearing no good. Don't underestimate

Ascham. As I said, he looks like a greenstick boy, but he's only a year younger than you, you know."

Jesamiah was not listening. What was that Nightm'n fellow doing? He appeared to be dancing a jig. His frown of disapproval deepened as Tiola put her hand on Maha'dun's arm. To Jennings, said; "Did 'Cesca know about it?"

"Mm? About what? 'Cesca in a whorehouse? Nay, nay, she was far too well bred for that. Granddaughter to Charles, you know. Wrong side of the blanket, of course, but weren't they all where our Merry Monarch was concerned?"

Was Jennings aware that 'Cesca had done her share of whoring? Jesamiah decided not to enlighten him. If he did know, what was the point of raising it, if he didn't—same answer. Tiola was taking the nightman's hand in her own, caressing his face. Old friends? Aye, like Old Harry they were!

He raised his voice, clarified his question. "I meant, Henry, did Francesca know about Doone's scheming?"

"Of course she did. And there's no need to shout, I am not that deaf. She it were who told me about him when we met at Ponta Delgada. *'Don't trust Doone,'* she said. Not that I ever did."

That did make Jesamiah laugh, although with more than a hint of sarcasm. "I thought you and Ailie Doone were best pals? You gossip together like a pair of rickety old grandfathers often enough—and you brought Ascham aboard!" Did Tiola have to sway her hips like that? Was she deliberately enticing that interloper?

"Like it or no, you occasionally have to get into bed with a pox-ridden doxy. The Doones carry a lot of influence—and pay well," Jennings admitted with a sour expression. "I always felt you could never be quite sure if Doone was for the Cause or not, though."

Ah, so Henry had lined his pocket by agreeing to bring Doone aboard. Crafty old bugger. "The Cause? And what do you mean, 'when you met at Ponta Delgada'?"

Exasperated, Jennings shook his head. "Have you not listened to anything? I told you, days ago. I bumped into Francesca," Jennings chuckled, "almost literally, soon after I arrived in the Azores. She was waiting for passage on a ship to Cádiz—both of us heading east for the same reason of setting King James on his rightful throne."

Not him again, Jesamiah thought, thoroughly bored with this whole Jacobite nonsense.

"I commandeered a navy vessel to catch up with you, remember?"

Jesamiah grunted again. Yes, he remembered; that frigate had given him much to worry about, considering he'd had a hold full of contraband at the time. Why hadn't 'Cesca tried to catch up with him as well? Presumably, at that point, she had not wanted him to know about the child. If he hadn't, in turn, gone to Spain, would he have ever known?

"You never mentioned 'Cesca before. Did she have her son with her? Or this bloody box that everyone is on about?"

Jennings shook his head. "She was with several Spanish families returning home from Hispaniola. The place is in a state of chaos since the governor drowned in that terrible accident."

"It was no accident," Jesamiah corrected. "I blew his ship up."

"Aye, well, I'd not boast of that too often, if I were you. The bastard should have been killed years ago but the Spaniards take exception to their vessels being wilfully destroyed, and their governors along with them."

"The box?"

"We talked of more important things—though I did mention that she was supposed to have delivered some diamonds to me." Jennings frowned at Jesamiah. "She said someone had stolen them."

Conveniently at that moment another squall flurried in and all Jesamiah's concentration was taken with keeping his ship on a steady course. When satisfied that he had her settled aright, he called to Skylark down on the main deck; "Where's Rue? I could do with his assistance up here."

"Dead to the world, Cap'n. He's not been away from a bottle since we weighed anchor."

"He has cause, I reckon," Jesamiah responded. "I'll give him two days. If he hasn't surfaced of his own accord by then, we'll do something about it."

Skylark agreed, nodded.

"I'm going below," Jennings announced, hugging his boat-cloak tighter around his chest, then put a hand on Jesamiah's shoulder. "Despite all I said, watch young Doone. I had no choice in inviting him aboard, lad. I apologise for it, but, well, I owe Sir Ailie and he has a habit of calling in debts at inconvenient moments. And he offered me a small financial incentive, which I would have been daft to have refused. I disliked Ascham's father, he was a traitor, Ailie I am uncertain of, and the boy himself, well, who knows how he will turn out?"

"If he gets in my way, he will turn out drowned," Jesamiah answered.

"I repeat, be careful. If they get their hands on that box, the Doones could become the most influential men in England. As well as a necessity to take messages to Calderón, young Ascham is undoubtedly here to see if you find it." Jennings walked a few yards, turned, came back. He tapped the side of his nose with his finger. "Give him enough rope to hang himself would be my advice. But do it tactfully, Jesamiah, we do not want the powder blowing on too short a fuse do we? Goodnight to you. Like your father before you, I trust you. Remember that."

"Remember that when I find that bloody box, you mean?"

Jennings laughed as he started down the ladder to the main deck. "Aye, well, you do owe me for those missing diamonds!"

Halfway down, he paused, looked up, said, "Francesca worked with your father. He trained her from when she was no more than a girl, fifteen, sixteen years old? I doubt you knew that? And he in turn worked for Harley. When your father died, she moved into Harley's patronage; became his best spy. If she had been a man, she would have become king's spymaster after Harley, and there are more than a few, myself included, who thought even the impediment of being a woman would not have stopped her. It is very likely she had exactly the same intention for using that box as has Doone—and Harley."

Jesamiah stared at him, a lump catching in his throat, several niggling puzzles partly unravelling in his mind. "She was with my father?"

"She was working with him up until he died. He and the Marqués de Molina—Calderón, your uncle—found her a Spanish husband. A marriage of convenience, for both parties." Realising he might have divulged too much, Jennings touched his wet hat. "I am to my bed."

A dozen questions flooded Jesamiah's mind, followed rapidly by the disconcertion that he was not brave enough to ask Jennings a single one of them. Especially the two that were shouting at him: was any of that why 'Cesca was murdered? Was the Spanish husband the boy's father or not? If not, who was? His father, Charles Mereno? If so, that meant Francesca had been the whore to father *and* son. Jesamiah felt sick. He took several deep breaths, needed a drink. A big one.

He called for Skylark to take the helm. "Keep her on this course, I'm going below."

"Aye, Cap'n."

"And send word for my wife to put that over-egged pudding down and to join me."

"Aye, Cap'n."

* * *

"You summoned me?" Tiola entered the great cabin and stood just inside the door with her arms folded, head cocked to one side. Rain was dripping from her hair, the hem of her gown was stained with saltwater and rain.

About half an hour ago, Jesamiah thought. Said: "No, I merely wanted you to join me. We've been up most of the night, I thought it time we went a'bed." Jesamiah was sitting on the edge of their box-bed which hung on stout ropes from the ceiling beams in the small bedchamber side cabin. He had undressed down to shirt and breeches, was busy tugging at the remaining left boot. Most of his clothes, stored in sturdy chests, had been salvaged; maybe they smelt a little musty, were damp at the edges—but then, that applied to almost everything aboard ship.

Tiola unfastened her cloak, shook off the rain and hung it from its peg, sat on a chair to remove her own boots—easier to do than his, for they were fastened down the front with laces. She frowned at the linen bandage strapped around her ankle beneath her stocking. Did she need to pretend now? Very few of the men aboard were aware of her accident on the moors.

"Maha'dun likes the area Chippy has rigged for him in the hold," she said as she removed her stocking and the redundant strapping.

"Oh?"

"It is somewhat cramped with a bed, table, and all his cumbersome clothes' chests, but Chippy has fashioned some hanger poles, and Finch has donated a few warm blankets. It is quite cosy and will be dark for him during daylight hours." She unlaced her overgown, stepped out of it and placed it carefully on the clothes pole on the far side of the bedchamber. Thank goodness for her sister-in-law's few wardrobe donations, it had been a lot easier and quicker to alter garments rather than make them, although once Susannah had found her sea legs, sewing would start in earnest.

"Good." Jesamiah got the boot off.

Tiola did not wear the conventional corsets while aboard *Sea Witch*—she even abandoned the tight-laced garment when ashore, particularly if she was attending a birth which could involve many long hours. Comfort was always her priority. She finished undressing and, wearing only a short lace-edged chemise, climbed into bed.

Jesamiah removed his stockings, breeches and drawers. Pulled his shirt over his head, blew out the lantern and, naked, scurried beneath the linen sheet, hauling the top layer of blankets and quilted counterpane over them both.

Tiola had turned her back to him. "The over-egged pudding asked me to bid you goodnight," she said into the darkness.

Something told Jesamiah he was not about to enjoy the pleasure of sex. He lay still, listening to the sound of *Sea Witch* creaking, her timbers groaning and complaining. Skylark's voice called out, shouting for a sail to be trimmed. Tempted to get dressed again, Jesamiah thought better of it. Churlishness would only compound the trouble he was apparently in. He turned over, his back to his wife. Went to sleep.

The mahogany dining table, which could be extended to cover almost the width of Jesamiah's great cabin when required, was laid for six people. Finch had sorted out the best white linen tablecloth and napkins, the silver cutlery, crystal glasses and decanters, and the expensive china with the delicate blue floral pattern. Two plates were chipped, but he folded linen napkins to hide the blemishes. At the centre of the table stood an elaborate crystal candelabra; with the eight candles lit, rainbow colours danced and sparkled on the reflective glass. To match the formality, the aroma of roasting venison and all its accompaniments was filling the ship. The opulent effect ruined by two large charts spread over the table with Jesamiah and Henry Jennings examining one chart, young Thomas Benson scrutinising the other.

"Is that Falmouth?" Thomas asked, pointing to the southern coast of Cornwall. "Father has always promised to take me there one day. I would dearly like to see the navy ships harboured there."

"If this bloody wind doesn't stop assaulting us," Jesamiah remarked, "you might well have your wish." He stabbed a finger at the group of islands off the French coast. "We'll head for Jersey. Drop anchor there, wait things out for a few days."

Jennings sucked his cheeks, shook his head. "Somewhere in France would be a better option."

"I'm no more welcomed by the French than I am the Spanish," Jesamiah pointed out. "At least Jersey is British."

Jennings laughed. "Not that the French are happy with that!"

"What is this bit?" Maha'dun asked, pointing at the Moroccan coast.

"Africa," Jesamiah answered, barely paying attention. "A long way off."

"Africa?" Maha'dun repeated. "Is that not where the slavers are?"

"Which ones?" Henry Jennings said, looking at him. "Black or white?"

Maha'dun hesitated. "Both?"

"The Barbary pirates are from Morocco," Thomas announced, pointing to where Maha'dun had indicated. "They often raid as far as the Cornish and Devon coasts seizing slaves and ransacking villages. They got as far as Lynmouth not long ago. Bad luck for them, Sir Ailie Doone's men happened to be there unloading a contraband cargo. There was quite a spectacular fight, so I've heard tell, with Moorish prisoners taken and executed."

Jesamiah ruffled the lad's hair. "They ain't the same sort of pirates that I know. Our lot in the Caribbean can usually be bought off if enough gold is offered. Them Arabs are driven by bloodlust and the sex trade for young innocents. Nasty pieces of work, the lot of 'em."

Maha'dun held his silence. He had heard the same tale, but from the Doone side. Not all the prisoners had been murdered

—a few had been bought off and persuaded to become useful informants. "So, where do black slaves come from then?" he asked.

Thomas indicated a location well off the map. "Way down there."

To Maha'dun the distance on this map-thing did not look that far. He had no comprehension of maps and charts, had never seen or needed them. And what were the indecipherable ink marks and squiggles littered all over them? He abandoned trying to understand and traced a meandering line with his finger. "What is this?"

"What it says. The River Loire. Where the wine comes from," Jesamiah retorted with a hint of irritation as he stabbed a finger at the neat handwriting. "We do not need Morocco, Africa or France. We're heading—albeit reluctantly, to the island of Jersey."

Tiola touched Maha'dun's arm, drawing him away from the table. "This strong wind, my dear, is blowing us eastward. We cannot sail against it, so it would be sensible to find shelter for a few days and wait for it to blow itself out."

Finch, pushing his way backwards through the door bearing a large silver tray of various dishes, caused everyone at the table to look up. "I couldn't give a bleedin' nun's virginity for whether you want to eat or not," he grumbled, "even tho' I've been all soddin' day in the galley preparin' this. But I ain't bloody standin' 'ere like a whore's fanny 'oldin' this soddin' 'eavy tray all bleedin' night. Get them things orf my table and sit your arses down." He nodded at Tiola. "Beggin' y'pardon, ma'am, fer m'language."

In haste, Jesamiah and Jennings rolled up the charts and straightened some of the askew cutlery. Maha'dun offered to take the tray, but Finch merely grunted and set the dishes along the centre of the table. "Dinner," he announced, "is served. Up t'you whether you bloody want it or not."

Giving a small gracious bow, Jesamiah smiled. "Thank you, Finch, we are most appreciative." He ruffled Thomas's hair again. "Especially this young lad? I doubt you expected such a treat to celebrate the day you were born, eh?"

Thomas grinned up at him, not daring to admit that even at home he was unlikely to celebrate much of his special occasion. Oh aye, his mother would be giving him hugs and exclaiming how tall he was getting, but beyond cooking a tasty supper and perhaps a small surprise package containing a pair of gloves— last year's gift—or, the year before that, a leather satchel for his schoolbooks, his birthing days were like any other. This, a splendid feast especially in his honour, was very much an exception to a rule.

"Where's Rue?" Jesamiah whispered to Finch. "No, do not bother formulating excuses. Get him here, now. He has had enough days to himself while we have been beating backwards and forwards in this wind. It is time he sobered himself."

As if rehearsed, the cabin door opened and Rue ducked in, smartly attired, clean-shaven, hair combed and tied back in a queue. "Pardon me if I am a little late," he grinned at Thomas, "but these two demanded a stroll around the deck." He held Pamela's two dogs beneath his arms, set them on the floor their tails wagging, their delight at being reunited with Thomas marked by both of them scrabbling at him to be made a fuss of.

"I was as about to tell you," Finch remarked to Jesamiah, "that Rue was on 'is way. You never gives a chap a chance to bleedin' say as what 'e wants t'say, you don't."

"That's because you never tell me what I want to know when I want to know it," came Jesamiah's response. "Do we need these dogs in here?"

"Of course we do!" Tiola interrupted, bending down to retrieve the smaller of the two terriers, Poppy. "They are a part of our family."

Jesamiah muttered something facetious under his breath.

"I have taken them down into the hold, several times, sir," Thomas anxiously defended the dogs. "They are proving to be excellent ratters."

Rue grinned at Jesamiah. "Better than that mangy ship's cat you pretend to despise." Earned himself a scowl as Jesamiah went towards Tiola's seat at the end of the table to pull it out for her. Maha'dun had got there first. Another scowl, which deepened when the elegantly dressed nightman seated himself to Tiola's right.

"Thomas, you sit next to me in the place of honour," Jesamiah said, taking his own seat at the opposite end of the table and indicating the chair immediately to his right. "Henry, you are opposite Thomas."

Tiola smiled at Rue. "That leaves you, dear man, to also sit next to me."

Gallantly, Rue bowed. "The 'onour is all mine."

Finch was bringing in a large silver tureen, steam emanating from the top. "Soup," he said. "Leek and potato, my best recipe."

The wine flowed, conversation became more laughter than talk. Finch replaced used plates and empty dishes with clean china, a variety of fish, more meat. No one noticed that Thomas and Jesamiah surreptitiously fed titbits to the dogs, or that Maha'dun partook of only the fish, soup and wine.

"How does he cook all that?" he asked Tiola soon after Finch had placed a haunch of venison before Jesamiah to carve.

"There is an efficient, brick-built stove in the galley," she said, "have you not noticed the smoking chimney while on deck?"

He had, but he'd assumed it led to a fireplace here in Jesamiah's cabin. Looking around he saw that was not the case. "Is it alight all the time?" he queried.

"Unless there is a storm, or Jesamiah needs to prepare for a fight, then yes." Added, "But do not concern yourself, it is never left unattended and there is no fear of the fire spreading to the rest of the ship. It is well contained within brick and metal."

Maha'dun looked alarmed, had not considered there was a possibility of the flames spreading, but asked; "Would it be possible to burn some things on it?"

Tiola took the plate passed to her, reached for a dish of vegetables. "I should think so. What sort of things?"

As Finch brought in a jug of rich, thick gravy, Maha'dun became vague. "Oh, just a few items that I have no use for. Trinkets that no longer have any meaning and it is pointless to continue to keep. My quarters are somewhat cramped; I thought I would make it as spacious as I can. Would there be anywhere else to put the trunk that belonged to the English woman with the Spanish name? It has been put in my quarters, I assume by mistake with my own things."

Tiola's turn to frown. "Have you looked to see what is in it?"

Maha'dun sipped his wine. "It is a very large trunk with very few contents of interest. Feminine things; gowns, undergowns, stockings and such. There are some wooden boxes."

Tiola raised an eyebrow.

"They seem to contain fripperies," Maha'dun continued, ignoring her unspoken question. "One has lace kerchiefs, another lawn scarves, another has pins and clips for the hair. There are also a few bottles of perfumes, and another box containing an array of face paints. Why do women so spoil their natural features by applying lead and cochineal? It damages the skin—or do they not realise this?"

"Even if they did, I doubt many a vain woman would pay heed." Tiola was very tempted to instruct him to hoist everything overboard, but on reflection, maybe Susannah could make use of the clothes and trinkets? Certainly the material, if not the garments themselves, would be welcome. Poor Susannah had not shown her worth as a maid for she had been closeted in her small cupboard-like cabin since leaving harbour, suffering from the discomfiture of seasickness. Perhaps a few days ashore on Jersey and some finery to wear would cheer her? Tiola well knew the misery of seasickness, for she had suffered greatly on the voyage from America to England a little over two months past—was it really only two months? But then her malady had been caused by the malevolence of the supernatural, not the queasiness of adjusting to an unfamiliar motion.

"I will sort out what is usable," she said. "For the rest, and the trunk itself, do what you please. I expect Finch will be delighted with the additional firewood."

* * *

The celebrations continued on deck. Extra rum had been sent around and the men were carousing, singing increasingly bawdy songs, and dancing jigs on the main deck. Old Toby Turner had been the one who had scraped reasonable tunes from a worn fiddle; Spokesy had the most talent to replace him, although when the captain and his birthing-day party of guests came up to join the men, it transpired that Maha'dun was even better. The songs became louder and bawdier, and the jigs livelier as he expertly wielded the bow, energetically coaxing popular tunes from the catgut strings.

Several men offered to dance with Tiola, Thomas included, although he admitted he had no instruction in the art of dancing. Susannah had managed to rouse herself enough to join them on deck. She sat with the two dogs, hugging them to her, pleased to share their company.

Jesamiah took the helm, his hands gentling the spokes as *Sea Witch* bowled along, seemingly enjoying the light-hearted festivities as much as the men.

The mood changed slightly as Maha'dun eased from the jigs and produced a melancholy air of exquisite beauty. The men sat, listening, nodding or tapping feet or fingers slowly to the graceful beat; someone started to hum, others joined in. The lament was for home, for wives, sweethearts and lovers left behind. A gentle tune that caught at the throat and the depths of the soul.

~ Play something else, ~ Tiola said into his head, glancing at Rue. *~ That tune was one of Pamela's favourites. ~*

Maha'dun's nod was almost imperceptible. "That is too sad," he declared, "this is supposed to be a joyful celebration. Come, let us produce some genteel dances for our ladies! *Well Hall!*" As he announced the dance, he raised the fiddle again and began to play. Skylark joined in with a tin whistle and several of the men la-la'd. Thomas bowed to Tiola and led her to the dance floor—the cleared space on the main deck. Ascham Doone stepped towards Susannah and, bowing, offered his hand. "My lady?"

A little flustered, Susannah glanced at Tiola; was it permissible for a maid to dance alongside her mistress?

Tiola, smiled, nodded; "We are but the two of us, my dear,

let us stand up for the fair sex amidst this bawdy house of ne'er-do-wells, who do not know their left foot from their right elbow!"

That brought laughter and several of the men draped bits of cloth around their waists to form crude skirts. With their chortling partners they formed two lines, and Maha'dun began the music again.

Well Hall was a romantic dance, starting with a right-hand turn, the arm extended to the partner with right hands lightly clasped, before casting to second place. Thomas, poor lad, had never seen the dance, let alone performed it, and within moments he and Tiola—and everyone else—were in guffaws of laughter as he tripped over his own feet, then Ascham Doone's.

"No, no, no!" Maha'dun declared as he ceased playing and passed the fiddle back to Spokesy. "Stand aside, boy, go sit with your pampered dogs, let me show you how 'tis done."

The two lines formed up, the men dressed as women fluttering their eyelashes and plumping up false bosoms made of rags stuffed down their shirts.

As the music began, Maha'dun gently pulled Tiola towards him as they pivoted around each other, bringing her in close, her hand held lightly in his, brushing against his chest. The cast aside at a graceful walk, pause a moment before exchanging positions across the dance with the next couple in line. Leading the next crossover they passed face-to-face, Maha'dun's intense gaze never leaving hers. Coming close again, their bodies briefly touched—then they were apart to rejoin the line. The second couple, Ascham and Susannah, exchanged places, then Maha'dun and Tiola again, their arms brushing as they passed each other, their gaze locked, the movement finishing with a half-circle, wait a moment, then the pattern repeated. For each crossing, each turn and pass they met in the centre, intimate moments where Tiola demurely dipped her gaze, before looking up, her eyes sensuously meeting his, their bodies touching whenever they were close.

The music played on, the men posing as women gradually dropped by the wayside, standing back to watch the two couples of Doone and Susannah, Maha'dun and Tiola dance. Ascham ensured he did not embarrass Susannah by passing too close, holding her hand that fraction too long, or catching her demure glance as she walked gracefully through the steps. But no one was watching Ascham Doone and the maid. All attention was on Maha'dun and Tiola. It almost seemed that the very deck itself would catch afire with the sensuous intimacy of their dancing.

Jesamiah watched every step, every movement, every barely concealed touch and caress. He growled at Jennings, leaning on the quarterdeck rail, to take the helm.

"I am going below," he snapped.

Agreeably, Jennings took his place, but he gave a verbal caution. "It is but a dance, lad. He is an exotic fellow, and they have known each other a while, so I believe. Read nothing more into it."

Jesamiah brushed him aside. "Not that long ago I could not understand why my wife had not visited me in Bristol gaol. I know why now."

He headed for the ladder leading from the quarterdeck. Rue was near the bottom sitting beside Thomas with Jasper, Chippy and several other men, their faces turned to the flowing symmetry of the dance, mesmerised by the music and the picture of exquisite, erotic beauty that Tiola and Maha'dun were creating together.

Jesamiah broke the spell. "'Tis time this carousing ended. See the men returned to their work, Rue. I want to drop anchor in Jersey harbour soon after dawn."

The music stopped, the dancers momentarily confused and disorientated parted. Ascham returned Susannah to her seat upon a pile of canvas sails. Maha'dun's hand lingered on Tiola's a moment before she withdrew it.

Jesamiah had gone below, went straight to bed. Was asleep when Tiola slid in beside him.

Or at least, he pretended to be.

CHAPTER TWENTY-SEVEN

Jersey—The Channel Islands

Apart from the assigned watches, the crew had been enjoying several days ashore. Most had made straight for the St Helier taverns and brothels that stretched along the sand dunes to either side of the old Norman church, and mingled with the string of houses, shops and warehouses bordering the market square. The courthouse stood imposingly to one side, while a prison gatehouse at the western edge of the straggling town reminded the more boisterous to not overstep the mark. Jesamiah had warned each and every one of his crew that he was not prepared to bail any drunken sot out of gaol, even for trivial misdemeanours.

He and Jennings had been ensconced with the rector, François le Couteur, for most of the day. Of an old and established local family, the rector's father had known the princes Charles and James during their exile from England, with the islanders' hospitality rewarded by land in the colonies being named New Jersey. Over the years trade had flourished, a fact that le Couteur took good advantage of, despite the English Whig government taking most of his profit in taxes. His cider trade was doing well; almost as well as his apple-brandy smuggling business. It was this, for the most part, which formed the topic of conversation, the good rector recognising a potential for expanding his covert routes northward into Virginia.

Ascham Doone had held no interest in carousing with men he was not particularly fond of, nor did he wish to waste his time with the whores—even if they were clean, French and experienced. He had a different fish to catch. Susannah. And the baited hook had been swallowed as easily as throwing worms into a tankful of eels.

"You look particularly becoming this evening, Mistress Susannah." He swept the young lady a low bow, then took her hand and placed a light kiss across her knuckles, before turning it over to offer another kiss to her palm.

She blushed. The gown she wore was of the finest quality, both in material, design and sewing. Of pale blue silk with a darker blue stomacher decorated with exquisite embroidery, the dress had fitted her almost perfectly, with only a few minor alterations to the hem and bodice. The previous owner had been taller and of a fuller bosom. The delicate lace at cuff and neck was French, and had one small tear in it, soon mended by Susannah's skill with a needle. In her dark hair, piled as high as she could get it, she had threaded a pale blue ribbon, the one Ascham had presented to her the previous afternoon as they had strolled together through the Jersey market stalls. "To match your eyes," he had said as he gave it to her with an elegant flourish.

Evening had settled and the lanterns and torches were illuminating the market square, now empty of stalls and produce.

"I am in love with you, Susannah," Ascham suddenly

declared. "I would ask the good rector, but I fear he would counsel against haste, and so when we return aboard I will plead for Captain Acorne to unite us as man and wife."

She opened her mouth to speak, but he placed a finger over her lips. "No, do not answer me now. Let us walk to the beach, away from this noisome bustle. A slow pace, undertaken in silence, will give you time to consider a response." He stroked her cheek. "I will only ask you this once, and will accept your answer whatever it may be."

Susannah did not know what to say. Those first days aboard the ship had been, she was certain, her last. She had survived fire, now she was to die at sea, so bad had been her sickness. And then it had stopped, she had ceased spewing her stomach into a bucket. Tiola had given her an armful of sumptuous gowns, and then the young and handsome Ascham Doone, grandson of the Earl of Exmoor, had sought her out and personally escorted her ashore to savour the delights of this small but pleasant island. He had treated her like a high-born lady; had wined and dined her in the more respectable establishments, and had been courteous and charming. Their conversation had become fluent and friendly—he had asked her several times about the captain and Tiola, questions which Susannah had seen no reason not to answer. Yes, they both seemed out of sorts with each other; yes, Mistress Tiola spent many hours below deck with that peculiar fellow, Maha'dun.

"In privacy," Ascham had remarked. "When I have been nearby, the door has always been closed." He had stroked Susannah's hand, coaxing her answers. "What is it, do you suppose, they do down there together?" He had taken the liberty to kiss her cheek, "I wonder, are they lovers?"

That Susannah had not answered, but she had blushed and remarked that her mistress did always emerge with a contented smile on her face.

Linking her arm through his, Ascham strolled away from the noise and bawdy laughter of the town, walked with her along the dunes and down onto the beach. *Sea Witch* was anchored in the bay, her riding lights reflecting in the sea. A boat was pulling away, some half a dozen men left aboard to cover the watch.

Ascham removed his coat and spread it on the sand, assisted Susannah to sit; sat beside her. "Did you ever," he said by way of opening conversation, "manage to find that wooden box I asked you to look for?"

Susannah bit her lip and stared out at the ocean. His attention and flattery was exciting, but the nature of his questions embarrassed her. She did not like talking about Captain Acorne or Mistress Tiola in the fashion he was forcing her into, telling tales, imparting secrets. But then, what was he asking that differed from the gossip that buzzed throughout the ship, and these questions about this box were not, really, all that intrusive.

"There was a wooden box such as you described at Tawford Barton," she said, turning to look at him, elation flooding her face. "I had forgotten all about it. Old Mistress Jennet had kept it beside her bed, until Mistress Tiola arrived in Devon and took possession of it. I did not see the box after that." Her mouth sagged, and she bit her lip to stop it quivering. "It must have been destroyed in the fire."

Ascham stroked her cheek. "Alas you are probably right, but I seek a second box, another one of similar description. The lady who used to own those clothes you are wearing possessed it—and I must add, if you will permit me, that you are far more beautiful wearing them than ever was she. I just wondered if the box had been with the garments?"

She shook her head. "I do not understand why this box is so important to you."

He stared at the sea a while, watched the boatload of men pull up against the church wall and tie up to the rings there for them to disembark.

"Apart from the fortune of being alongside you," he said at last, "I have no desire to be aboard this ship. I miss London, the politics, the Inns of Court. I am studying to become a lawyer, you know, my grandfather being my patron." He took her hand, held it within his own. "I want to enter politics. I want to become a respected High Court judge. I want a grand house in Pall Mall with carriages and servants." He squeezed her hand, "And a perfect wife to be my companion and run the household for me."

Susannah could see several flaws in this schedule, but on the other hand, Ascham Doone was the only surviving grandson of the Earl of Exmoor. He would take the title, and no doubt the wealth, when Sir Ailie passed to God. That Ascham should be requesting the hand of a serving maid as his wife, not the daughter of a wealthy gentleman, was the puzzle, but she set that one aside.

"My grandfather," Ascham continued, "is, alas, not as wealthy as he asserts himself to be. He desires that box as to sell it will regenerate his—our—fortune." He sighed heavily. "The box is rightfully ours, for grandfather paid a substantial amount to possess it. Not least of which was the cost of bringing the lady who owned that gown of yours to England." There was a hint of spite in that statement, but Susannah failed to notice it. "The lady was supposed to deliver the box to my grandfather. She failed to do so. The last person she was with was Acorne."

"And you think she gave it to him?"

"I do." Ascham turned to face her, thrust his arms around her and held her close as if his very life depended on her. "Oh, my dear, I need to remove myself from this nightmare voyage! If I had that box, I could return home with you as my wife, and live my life without the incessant unreasonable commands of my grandfather! He treats me as his lackey, as a servant, as a..." he stammered the words, "as a slave to do his bidding! I can stomach it no longer!" He buried his face in her bosom, heaved a few sobs of despair.

"Hush, my dear man, shush!" Susannah stroked his hair, rubbed his back. "Can you not just go home? We could take a ship from here..."

"No! No!" He sat back, his words sharp. Had the fool girl not listened to a word he had said? "I must gain possession of that box. If I do not stay, and if Acorne does have it, then at all cost I must not allow that devil spawn Maha'dun to find it first!"

Susannah was askance. "He also seeks it?"

"He does, and this is why he is making love to your mistress. He hopes to find it through her."

It did briefly occur to Susannah that this was exactly as Ascham was doing to herself, but it was a brief, mean, thought and she brushed it aside.

"Maha'dun," he was explaining, "works for Grandfather. Oh, he would soon report back if I were to dare to put a foot out of place! He spies on me, have you not noticed?"

She had not, but then she had been curled on her bed alternating between spewing into a bucket and groaning in misery these past days and nights, and, now that she was recovered, spent all the daylight hours sewing and stitching.

"He is a vile man, Susannah. Be wary of him, keep your distance."

Flattered at his concern for her safety, she felt she had to be truthful, however. "I see him but rarely. He is only abroad at night, and I am not fond of the darkness."

Ascham laughed, his head back, a loud guffaw.

"That is all a play-act, my dear. He is no more a night creature than are any of us. That was a story he invented to account for his never appearing before mid-afternoon. And why was he so often absent? I will tell you, because he would crawl into bed at dawn as drunk as a man about to hang. When he is sober he is out on the moors waylaying innocents who travel there. He is nothing more than a highwayman, a common thief. I am afraid he has very much duped you all."

So much of what Ascham had said made sense that Susannah had no reason to doubt him. When he asked her again if she would become his wife she accepted. Delighted, he kissed her, encouraged her to lay back on the sand.

She tried to say no to what followed, but he did not seem to heed her pleas to let her be.

* * *

Although dark, enclosed spaces disturbed him, Jesamiah rarely felt any disquiet in his own hold, whether in storm-tossed conditions or as now, at anchor in Jersey's sheltered bay where *Sea Witch* only gently rocked. This afternoon, however, he was in too foul a mood to notice the elongated shadows cast ahead by his lantern, or the pressing darkness beyond as he stepped down off the ladder and made his way past the stowed kegs, crates, boxes and barrels. He could hear Maha'dun's low voice and Tiola laughing; smell the unmistakable whiff of tobacco. The private chamber rigged at the far end was makeshift, with cargo piled close against the temporary wooden walls. Jesamiah strode to the flimsy door, kicked it open. Tiola, sitting on the gay-covered bed, squeaked alarm; Maha'dun sprang to his feet, crouched, ready to fight. He dropped the cheroot that he held between his fingers.

Emitting a cry of rage, Jesamiah strode forward, stamped his boot on the glowing end and ground it into the wooden floor. There was a tankard of ale on the side table; he picked it up, dashed its contents over the crushed ash. Throwing the empty tankard aside, he had Maha'dun by the neckband of his linen shirt and was shoving him up against the outer bulkhead.

"You... do not... smoke... below... deck!" he raged as he slammed Maha'dun's head back against the wood, the shirt collar ripping. Grasping Maha'dun's hair, Jesamiah half pulled, half kicked him outside and trundled him along the narrow walkway as if he were a barrel of fish. "Over there," he yelled, pointing, and forcing Maha'dun to look, "is where we store the gunpowder. I don't give a monkey's pink arse if you blow yourself to bits, but I do fucking care about losing my ship!"

"Leave him alone!" Tiola demanded, clawing at Jesamiah's arm.

He released Maha'dun and swung round to push her away, his rebuke harsh. "You should know better! You know the dangers! Or are you so besotted with him that you don't care about anything else anymore?"

"And just what," she yelled back, "do you mean by that?"

Nostrils flaring, fists bunched, Jesamiah took several deep breaths. His instinct was to hit first, talk later, but Tiola was standing in front of him, hands on hips, her extreme anger matching his. He knew many a harlot who could fight as dirty as hell and would expect to receive as good as they gave, but Tiola was not among their sort. He would never hit her. Never.

"You know bloody well what I mean," he said lamely as he pushed past and snatched up the lantern which he had left on the top of a barrel, stamped off up the ladder, venting his fury by bellowing at a group of sailors who were fooling around on the foredeck.

* * *

"I hear there was a bit of a disagreement below deck this afternoon," Henry Jennings said as he hooked a stool forward and, sitting, lit his pipe.

Swallowing a mouthful of rum, Jesamiah topped up his glass from the bottle on the table.

"Getting drunk will not solve anything, you know," Henry added, clicking his fingers for the pot-boy to bring another glass and another bottle.

Jesamiah did not bother to answer.

"So, what was it about? Anything important?"

"None of your business."

The glass and the bottle arrived. "According to word buzzing like hornets around your ship, and in almost every tavern here ashore, you caught that Maha'dun fellow swiving your wife."

No answer.

"The speculation—and, I might add, generous wagers—are on how long it will take you to kill him. And how you are going to do it. The popular bets are on a knife in the back; my guess is garrotting with one of your ribbons."

Again, Jesamiah topped his drink up. Remained silent.

"Of course, all that is hearsay. I have a feeling you caught them doing nothing of the sort which is why both he, and she, are still alive." Henry filled his own glass. "If I were you, I would do away with Ascham Doone, he is the real troublemaker."

"Oh, you'd like that, wouldn't you?" Jesamiah jeered, his

speech slightly slurred from the drink. "The Doones are your rivals, let Acorne do the dirty work for you."

"Ailie Doone is nothing of the sort. We disagree about a few things, and I do not trust him, but we are not rivals."

"Bollocks."

"Well, I am not sitting here arguing with you. Ailie Doone is a business colleague, his grandson is a different matter entirely. Why Ailie trusts the boy to do things in his stead is beyond me. I assume he is attempting to make a man of the conniving little sod. However, I came to tell you that the good reverend here on Jersey has received some news and it has changed my plans. You are to be rid of me. There is a ship sailing direct for the Bahamas. I have sorted my passage aboard."

Raising one eyebrow served good enough as a question for Jesamiah.

"It seems I need to do as Harley instructed me and get to Nassau as quickly as I can, after all. That threat of Spanish trouble in the colonies? Remember I mentioned it?"

A single nod from Jesamiah who was only partially listening.

"We are soon to be at war with Spain again."

Jesamiah was not overly concerned. "War's been off and on for months, years; the peace status changes with the seasons."

"Skirmishes, squabbles, aye, but that armada against England? Even though it spectacularly failed, it was an open attack and has upset King George and his Whig government. Add to that, so the good reverend tells me, the Duc d'Orléans recently ordered a French army to invade the western Basque area. So now both England and France are waggling their cocks at Spain, and you can bet your last bottle of rum that the

Dutch will poke their butterball arses into the argument before long. When they do..." He spread his hands, the gesture enough to convey his meaning.

Resting his arm on the table, Jesamiah leant forward. "You know what, Henry? I don't give a crusted shit."

Henry stood, tired of arguing. "Fair enough, but maybe you ought to think on this; you have just made a most lucrative trade agreement with our good Jersey reverend. He will make a tidy profit on that fancy furniture you've sold him, and those cider brandy casks now in your hold instead will equally make you a handsome excess when you eventually reach Virginia. You also intend to visit Calderón and bargain a future in trade with him—a future for you and your wife and a possible family. You need to decide that future, my boy—else you'll find yourself tempted to go back on the account, then where will your good lady be? Are you to sail with her, leave her behind? We could be facing a bitter and brutal war. Spain will soon be out in force patrolling her coast and harassing French harbours. I would hate for you to be blockaded here in Jersey, as pleasant as it is, especially as, while you have been here drowning yourself in liquor, the wind appears to be turning in your favour. That ship I've secured a passage on? She sails within the hour. I suggest you consider doing the same."

He paused at the door, one hand poised over the handle. "Oh, and the good reverend has told me that Barbary pirates are roaming the area. Kidnapping young virgins of both sexes is highly profitable, so I'm told, worth the risk of raiding coastal villages, killing, burning and plundering."

"So, what's that got to do with me?"

"Nothing at all. Just thought I'd warn you. These furriner heathens can be a nasty lot to meet up with."

"I can be just as nasty."

"So you can, my boy. So you can."

* * *

By evening, the wind had swung right around. Despite a head that had thrummed as if an entire army of clog-footed giants were stamping about inside it, Jesamiah had ordered all sail set, and once out into the open ocean, had pushed *Sea Witch* into a speed that matched the pod of dolphins which accompanied them for two whole days. He heard his ship complain a few times, her hull, masts, and rigging creaking and whingeing as she thrust her bow through the surf, but she was of a sturdy build and could take the pressure. Twice, he was not quite certain whether some of those grinding squeaks and creaks were not grumbles but delighted conversation with their silver-backed escort. It also occurred to him that he was becoming ridiculously fanciful, or perhaps the influence of rum had lingered longer than he thought.

Two reasons were pushing him onward. One was to make up lost time. He desperately wanted to get to Spain and quiz Calderón about 'Cesca before the present fracas between squabbling countries escalated; and he wanted to lose a frigate which had been dogging their wake since leaving Jersey. The dilemma: what nationality was she and what colours should he fly to prevent attack? English, Spanish? French? Dutch?

He had elected to steer well clear of Ushant's perilous rocks —he did not care to risk another possible calamity with running aground. Taking a wider arc to avoid the area, though, meant going further west—a matter which would not normally have concerned him, but that trailing frigate was becoming a damned nuisance. He had wondered if maybe this ship was the Barbary pirate Jennings had mentioned, but very early on discounted that. Those African coast troublemakers usually sailed small, fast ships and rarely attacked anything bigger than themselves. *Sea Witch*, under fighting sail, would be no match for them.

He had then hoped that the vessel would sheer off on her own course, but when she stayed there, he tried convincing himself that she was English navy and he had nothing to hide—which he hadn't. For once, his entire cargo was legitimate, even the cider brandy was logged as cargo. All that would change when he neared the colonies, but for now he was quite safe. If they were a British patrol, let them come up, board!

Except old habits died hard; his instinct was to either run or fight, and a naval ship—of whatever country of origin—never stayed so solidly on a following course unless it had reason to. And not knowing the reason was beginning to feel unwelcome.

"If I had my way," he remarked to Tiola one evening in the great cabin as the sun had slipped beneath the horizon and the sky had bloomed into a patchwork of vibrant colour, "I would let him catch up and then blast the guts out of him."

"That is your answer to everything," Tiola retorted, not looking up from finishing the last few stitches in the cuff of a linen shirt. "Kill it or blow it up."

She had been in a petulant mood since leaving Jersey, or if she was honest with herself, the irritability had been expanding since Francesca had given birth to that baby. The death of the child had not been preventable, his little underdeveloped lungs had been unable to breathe in air; the lie had come when she had told Francesca that he had been born dead, although the truth that he had lived a few minutes would not have made much difference to the outcome. The guilt came with her momentary lapse of being pleased when he had not survived. That was unforgiveable, but the jealous streak of knowing that

Jesamiah had made love to another woman continued to tick away in her mind, fuelling her petulance. She should not care so much about his infidelities—sex for the sake of a passing fancy was not the same as sharing the mutual pleasure of making love, but she could not shake off the mental image of Jesamiah and Francesca together. And now this additional stupidity of his aggressiveness towards Maha'dun, jumping to wrong conclusions, not having the trust in her or sense to talk openly and calmly—it was all becoming exasperating.

As for Cara'mina, was there any regret for her death? How could there be when the lives of others had been in such danger? And Maha'dun was so blissfully happy now that she was gone, although the happiness was adding to the problem. Jesamiah was completely misinterpreting Maha'dun's joy.

* * *

With the sun set and night descended, Maha'dun emerged from his private sanctuary to lean, contented, on the quarterdeck rail looking down at the ocean racing past. The sky was clear, scattered with stars as if someone had tossed handfuls of precious jewels up into the void: diamonds, sapphires, rubies... The sea itself was sparkling with the reflected light. His fear had completely vanished, replaced by an almost obsessive passion for the ship and the water she sailed on. The dolphins had created an extra magical pleasure for him; he had watched them, mesmerised, through all the hours of darkness, returning to his secluded privacy at dawn with a grin that Tiola had said was wider than the ocean. It was disappointing that the splendid creatures were no longer with them, but other entertainments were proving to be as intriguing. The exchanges between Tiola and her husband, one of them, although non-exchanges was more accurate. Jesamiah had taken to rolling himself in a blanket at night and sleeping beneath the little boat that was secured to the deck, and had been steadfastly ignoring Maha'dun.

"Why is it," Maha'dun asked, "that humans who have a great deal of affection for each other spend such an inordinate amount of time bickering? Is it some form of foreplay or a mating ritual?"

Tiola, leaning on the rail next to him, laughed. She could see the amusing side of the comment for he was right; it was a bizarre form of arousal. The spats she and Jesamiah had exchanged in the past had always ended with them in bed—or elsewhere—enjoying themselves.

But, overhearing, Jesamiah failed to catch the tongue-in-cheek side of the remark. "I do not see you two squabbling," he growled as he strode to the other side of the quarterdeck.

The atmosphere changed as if a sudden freeze had turned everything to ice.

"And what," Tiola called after him, hands on hips, "is that supposed to mean?"

Maha'dun threw the butt of his cheroot over the side—having established that it was perfectly acceptable to smoke on the open deck. "He is unsettled about our friendship, Lady." He nodded towards Ascham Doone who was sitting with a group of foremast jacks playing dice on the main deck. "That one is very free with spreading gossip. He has made sure everyone aboard thinks we are lovers. Your husband included."

Resisting the urge to respond that perhaps this was a good thing, Tiola found a spark of common sense to override what was nothing more than pettiness. She glanced at the sailors, some working, some resting, caught the surreptitious looks, the veiled eyes, the barely concealed interest in the exchange going on up here on the quarterdeck, and knew that Maha'dun was right—she had known it herself these past days but had shrugged it aside. *Let him stew*, she had thought, *let him discover what it is like to have someone you cherish make love to another!*

Her gaze fixed on Ascham Doone. Very briefly his eyes met hers but he looked quickly away, a slight flare dilating his nostrils, a mild smile curving at the corner of his lips.

Why are you here, Doone? she thought, resisting the temptation to use her Craft to gain an answer. A sudden fear chilled through her. Was that, perhaps, what he wanted? For her to give herself away? No, there would be no reason for any of them to guess what she was beyond the outward appearance of healer and midwife, although even that could be fraught with danger. She lost few patients, far fewer than many physicians or other midwives. So far, her premise of gentle hands and soft words had guided her through any untoward speculation, but there was always the chance that one person, one malevolent soul, could compromise her safety. And there was Maha'dun to consider. He would never consciously betray her, but what if he had let something slip within Ailie Doone's hearing?

She looked again at Doone's grandson; he had glanced up —and away again when he saw her watching him. No, she was not under suspicion for witchcraft, that lascivious smirk, that quick come-and-gone glance told the real tale. He was convinced that she and Maha'dun were engaged in a torrid affair and was bent on making mischief out of it. Well, it had to stop, and stop now.

"Something," Maha'dun said, echoing her thoughts, "has to be done here. And soon." He looked over the rail, down at the churning foam of water. "I love you very much," he added, "but not, I am afraid, enough to throw myself overboard."

Tiola laughed. "I do not think that will be necessary. Nor do I think our especial friendship should be tarnished because of the lascivious minds of ignorant men."

Maha'dun grinned. "Ah, you want me to toss Doone overboard? That I will do with pleasure."

Askance—it was not a jest—Tiola hastily answered that no, that was not what she wanted. "All I need is for my husband to see sense. It would help if we could find a reason for him to trust, not mistrust, you."

Maha'dun gazed again at the sea that was blacker than the star-pocked sky. With his night vision he could see further and clearer than any human. The ocean was vast—frightening but exciting at the same time. He could see the undulating rollers, white-edged, magnificent with their power and strength. He could see the stars closer, brighter, than could the human eye. Those wisps of cloud gathering to the eastern sky; and the distant ship.

"Would it help," he suggested, "if I were to inform your husband of the nationality of that ship which is so concerning him?"

"It would help very much," Tiola answered, "but first I must heal this rift between him and myself, and show him that he has got things wrong."

"Out of interest, I would be delighted to discover exactly how you intend to do so," he said as he lit another cheroot, "but I suspect the manoeuvres will be private?"

Tiola nodded. "They will. Very private."

Eyebrows were raised throughout the ship when Tiola stood before Jesamiah and ordered, "Our cabin. Now!"

* * *

Susannah had been relieved that beyond an hour or so of feeling mildly queasy, the seasickness had not returned. She amused and enjoyed herself by day sewing with Tiola, sitting on the new velvet-cushioned seats atop the locker that ran across the length of Captain Acorne's cabin where the light streamed in through the five rear windows. The great cabin had been refurbished; the new cushions and matching drapes, the chairs re-covered in fine brocade, the woodwork scrubbed and re-varnished. The floorboards replaced, an exquisite Turkish carpet partially covering them. There was still a faint aroma of damp, a little mould, but then the cabin had been awash with seawater for some days when *Sea Witch* had foundered.

Susannah was a neat and quick seamstress, and the pile of completed clothing was growing with the passing of each day. Undergarments mostly, for they were the easiest and most urgently needed: cambric and flannel to fashion chemise, bodice and under-petticoats for Tiola and herself, shirts and linings—men's drawers—for the captain and Rue. Tiola would be easily pleased when it came to the overgowns, for she cared little for fashion or convention. No hooped petticoats or whalebone corseting, preferring simple calicoes and dimity for her everyday gowns. Secretly though, Susannah was looking forward to working with the bolts of silk and brocade, had in mind several ideas for a few sumptuous gowns for Mistress Acorne.

Come the evenings, there was not enough steady light to sew by. The lanterns tossed and swung, and the shadows streamed across the bulkhead walls, so with the dark came leisure, unless she was required by Tiola for other reasons, to assist with bathing or washing hair, but since she was more often than not with the one they called Maha'dun, Susannah had most of the hours before bed to herself. She had hoped to spend some of them with Ascham, but since they had set sail from Jersey he had been avoiding her. At first, she thought this was because of the men; he would be teased unmercifully were he to announce their attachment, but as one day became two, then two became three she began to realise that he was not merely avoiding, but entirely ignoring her. There were no stolen glances, no shy smiles or quick winks. No words, no gestures, it was as if she were as invisible as the wind.

Sitting alone tucked behind the stowed longboat, she sat, arms clutched around her knees, watching the stars and listening to the wind soughing through the canvas and rigging. Had she been braver she might have asked if it were possible for her to climb a little way up one of the masts, just to see what the deck looked like from above, but that would involve losing her decorum and dignity—she could hardly climb even a few yards in her gown! What if the wind should blow it out like the sails? Every man below would be able to not only see her stockings and legs, but her thighs—and beyond! And to wear male apparel for the purpose... out of the question!

What if she were with child? The thought kept coming back to her, despite every effort to think upon other things. She knew, now, that it had all been false, all those sweet words, the charming smiles, the tender caresses. All he had wanted was to fu..., she could not bring herself to think the word, let alone say it.

Tears trickled. It was because she had not been able to find that box. But she had looked! She had! Whenever alone in the great cabin she had set aside her sewing and searched, in, under, on, behind. Finch had caught her once, going through the drawers of Captain Acorne's desk. "I am looking for scissors," she had hastily lied. Had blushed scarlet when he had pointed to them on the seat beside her sewing basket.

"Mistress? Are you unwell?"

Susannah started, stifled a gasp, looked up to see Maha'dun standing over her.

"Thank you, I am quite well," she stammered, brushing away the wetness from her cheeks. "It is this spray!"

Maha'dun refrained from mentioning that the wind was blowing the spindrift entirely the other way. He indicated a bundle of canvas nearby, asked if he may sit, keep her company.

She rather wanted to be alone, but was too polite, and in awe of this strange man, to refuse.

"Forgive me for saying," he said after he had lit and enjoyed the first few puffs of his cheroot—thank goodness for the two tobacconist stores in Jersey's market square. He had bought almost their entire stock. "But you seem discomforted? I have known women to weep when they are delighted by something, when they are angry, in pain, or sad. You do not appear to fit the first three."

"Truly, there is nothing amiss, sir." Susannah wished he would go away, for all he was intending to be kind.

"I would wager," he continued blowing smoke into the air, "that Ascham Doone has distressed you. He is very accomplished at doing that."

She stared at him, how had he known? And then she did weep. She leant against Maha'dun, burying her face in his shoulder to cry silently, her body shaking, her fist stuffed into her mouth to stem any untoward noise.

Maha'dun set his arm around her, pulled her close and gently rocked, letting her grief and fears flow unchecked, unremarked upon. Because of his silence, his gentle compassion, it then all came out, every fear, hurt and embarrassment, although she could not bring herself to admit the dreadful truth that she had been violated. She could not bear to talk of it, Maha'dun guessed.

"What if I am with child?" she whispered through gulps for breath. "What shall I do now that he has reneged on a declaration to take me as his wife?"

"I would hazard that Mistress Tiola would be the better to advise you there, but I am willing to stand up and ensure he does not go back on his intentions."

She hiccupped several times, brushed at her cheeks, his words allowing her to see the clear truth. "I do not wish to be his wife. I am afraid of him, I do not even, really, like him. He swept me away with honey words and sugared promises. All he wants is for me to find that bloody box!" She gasped, clapped a hand over her mouth. "Forgive me, sir! I did not mean to speak so profane!"

Maha'dun laughed. "There is nothing to forgive, it is indeed a bloody box, and you are right, he wishes for it to be found. But I can assure you his wish will never be granted."

Someone called out that the dolphins had reappeared. Maha'dun leapt to his feet, held out his hand to help Susannah up. "Forget your fears, my dear, let us enjoy the splendour of these charming sea-animals!"

They watched together for a while, the starlight and phosphorescence sparkling along the wet, grey skins of the leaping and chattering escort. Then Maha'dun noticed that Susannah was shivering. "I will fetch your cloak," he said, as he pulled her back from leaning too far over the rail. "Be careful, the deck is slippery, if the ship bucks, as she regularly does, you may fall, then it will be a waste of my time fetching your cloak, will it not?"

She smiled at him. "They say, the men, that you are strange; that you are a hobgoblin. That you are to be feared.

But I think that you are the kindest man I have ever met."

He bowed, hurried away to fetch the cloak. Chivalry was all very well, but he wanted to get back to watching the dolphins.

Chapter Twenty-Eight

"You," Tiola stated, as she firmly closed the cabin door against Finch's prying, "are behaving like a brainless jackass."

"I," Jesamiah tossed back as he poured a more than generous measure of cider brandy and sat in his favourite chair, "am behaving like a brainless drunkard. And I have no complaints about it."

"A brainless drunk jackass then, and I have several complaints!" Tiola strode over to him, removed both bottle and glass from his hand and, setting them on the table out of his reach, knelt before him. She put her hands on his knees and looked up at him.

"Why are you doing this?" she asked. "Destroying our marriage because of the untrue things that your men are gossiping about? Gossip that is sent skittering across the deck by Ascham Doone?"

He reached for the glass, could not quite touch it but found, when he tried to move, that her hands were pressing on his thighs, effectively restraining him. "You are the one destroying everything, madam, not me."

Sliding her hands a little higher, Tiola leant forward and

kissed him, her breath melting into his mouth.

After a moment he pushed her away, said gruffly, "I've told you never to use your magic tricks on me."

"I am not using magic." Tiola's hands went another inch higher. She started unbuttoning his breeches. "*This* is magic," she added, desperately trying not to laugh, "when something small and flaccid becomes big and hard at one delicate touch. Like this."

Summoning a strength of resolve, Jesamiah succeeded in pushing her aside. He rebuttoned himself, grasped the drink and swallowed it down in one gulp. "I saw you with my own eyes," he snapped, "sitting on his bed, making up to him, your head on his shoulder, tangled in each other."

Remaining kneeling on the floor, but unlacing and removing her bodice, Tiola thought it time she put his misconceptions right.

"You saw what you expected to see, not what you actually did see. Ascham Doone is mischief-making. He is very good at it. He has ensured that the seeds of doubt were planted in your mind and has very carefully nurtured them into bloom. You expected to see Maha'dun and me making love. You were too angry to see anything else." She stood, unfastened her skirt and let it slide to the floor, stood there in her undergown petticoat. "I grant," she continued as she also removed that, "you were justified to get cross about the cheroot. I apologise for not taking heed and reprimanding Maha'dun myself, but as for the rest..."

She sat in his chair, removed her garters and stockings. "You failed to see the book that we were holding. My head was not on his shoulder, I was leaning forward to point out the words to him. Maha'dun," she stood, discarded her chemise, and stood there naked, "cannot read. He was embarrassed not to be able to decipher the markings on those charts. I offered, in secret, and therefore with no chaperone present, to teach him what they all mean. At the very least, to show him how to read and write his own name."

Jesamiah had been standing with his back to her, he turned round, stared stoically over her right shoulder to avoid looking at her body. "Am I expected to believe that?"

"You are not expected to disbelieve it." She reached up and slowly unpinned her hair, letting the midnight blackness cascade sensuously across her breasts and down her back to below her waist. "I am expected to not notice your indiscretions. To not mind that you lay with a woman and gave her a child. That because you have an itch to scratch you can scratch it wherever and whenever you please. Yet when I meet, after many years, a very dear friend I am the one accused of adultery? Why is that, Jesamiah?" She moved two steps closer to him, the swinging lanterns overhead casting shadows that rippled erotically over her flawless skin.

He stood, silent, struggling with an assault of conflicting emotions.

~ *Have you ever known me to lie to you, Jesamiah?* ~ she said into his mind. ~ *I never have, and I never will. I love Maha'dun as a friend, a brother, but I love you as my husband, my lover and my soulmate.* ~

He uttered a low moan, gave in. Sweeping her up into his arms he strode to the side cabin and the bed, laid her down, cupped her breast. As he bent to kiss her, a cry reverberated through the entire ship that struck a chill through every soul.

"Men overboard! Men overboard!"

Jesamiah was out of the door, along the narrow corridor and heading up the ladder to the quarterdeck. Tiola, bare foot, wearing only a hastily pulled on chemise and a shawl, not far behind him.

Men were leaning over the side, pointing, shouting, Rue was at the taffrail with more men who were also pointing and shouting.

"Mizzen braces! Back the mizzen topsail! Boat away!" Jesamiah bellowed as he ran to the rear of the ship, glad that most of his crew were capable men and did not query orders; followed with, "What silly bugger is it?"

"The maid—Susannah," Rue answered, his face drawn and pale, memories of that terrible night of the fire flooding back into his mind. "And Maha'dun. She fell. he dived in after her."

"I tossed a couple of the barrel buoys over," Tearle said, peering anxiously into the darkness, hoping to see heads bobbing against the white brightness of their wake, two people clutching the empty barrels set aside for the purpose of floats in this situation.

For maybe a heartbeat, Jesamiah hesitated, but already the men had braced aback and *Sea Witch* was flying up into the wind, her way instantly checked. The jolly boat was being swung out... but he could cancel his order...

"We have no hope of finding either of them in this darkness," he said. "The best we can do is hope they broke their necks as they fell."

Tiola stared at him, incredulous. "Are you telling me you are not going to even attempt to rescue them?" Outrage blazed in her eyes. "You would leave Maha'dun and Susannah to drown?"

That moment of indecision—heave to and give that following ship time to close distance, heave to for a wasted reason. The cold of the sea, the darkness... they did not have much hope of finding even a corpse, let alone a living person. And he would then be rid of Maha'dun...

"Of course I ain't bloody saying that!" Jesamiah yelled back, the shout louder for his guilt. He would have happily left Maha'dun, but his crew would not forgive leaving the young lass, and the surly mood against a captain who did not value the life of anyone who pitched over the side could be difficult to counteract.

He headed for the entry port, pointed to four men, "You, you, you and you. Oars." To Tiola, at his heels, "No, you are not coming with us."

"Try to stop me!" As with Jesamiah, she took a quick moment after shouting, to think clearly, said into his mind, *~ I can see far better than can you in the dark, and might be able to find them by other means. I must come. ~*

He nodded as he stepped down the ladder cleats. "Find my wife a cloak! And I need a shielded signal lantern!"

Someone handed him a lantern, its light dimmed by a cover, while Finch scooped up Susannah's cloak that Maha'dun had flung aside and, setting it quickly around her shoulders, tied the laces. "Mind yer step, ma'am, as y'go down."

Tiola thanked him, followed Jesamiah downward, too sick in the stomach with fear for the two in the sea to concern herself with the descent, the slippery rungs, or the froth of the sea beneath.

"Keep *Sea Witch* hove to!" Jesamiah called up to Rue as the boat, the four men pulling with all their strength, shot out from beneath *Sea Witch*'s stern. To Tiola, squatting in the bow, peering ahead, he whispered, "We haven't much hope. The seas here are bitter cold, and the currents are treacherous."

~ Maha'dun is like me, he will not feel the cold, ~ she answered, *~ and he will be able to see Susannah. ~* That last she was not so certain of. She turned to face Jesamiah, fear crinkling her face. "Maha'dun is terrified of the sea; fear of

drowning is for him like dark enclosed spaces are for you."

"But he can swim?"

Tiola was quite pale, her eyes wide. "No, he cannot."

"Then why the bloody hell did he jump in after her?" A string of eloquently descriptive words followed.

"Because she is my handmaid, because Maha'dun is devoted to me and mine, and," a little rueful smile formed at the side of her mouth, "and Maha'dun tends to act first, think after, as often do you."

"Well, he has either learnt to swim very quickly, or we are wasting our time and effort." Seeing her bottom lip tremble, he pulled the draped cloak tighter around her shoulders, then cupping his hand around his mouth began to shout. "Nightman! Nightm'n, Nightm'n!"

~ Maha'dun? Maha'dun? Can you hear me? ~ Tiola called in her own way; there would be no answer, for he did not have the ability to respond, but if he could hear then he would know they were searching for him.

"Bloody dolphins!" one of the men, Perkiss, pulling at the oars cursed, "they keep getting tangled in m'bloody stroke!"

Tiola leant over the side, there indeed were the dolphins, all of them to larboard, several nosing their blunt snouts at the oars—and one, as she watched, began nudging at the hull.

"Damn things will have us over in a minute!" another oarsman snarled. "Get away, bugger you! Get away!"

"No!" Tiola cried, suddenly aware. "They are trying to direct us... Over there, go that way!" Frantically she waved her right arm, ignored the twinge of complaint from the new-healed wrist, almost laughed with delight as the school immediately shot ahead, leaping and chattering with excitement.

"Put your backs into it!" Jesamiah encouraged as the four men struggled to keep up. And then a shout!

"I am here! I am here!" The words turned into a splutter, then coughing. "Help! I am here!" Against the dark sea, a white face and a silver dolphin, Maha'dun clinging desperately to its dorsal fin.

They manoeuvred the boat and hauled him inboard. He half lay, half sat, breathing heavily, trembling, resisting the urge to spew his innards up. "Seawater," he said after a moment, "tastes bloody foul."

Leaning over the side, Tiola ran her fingers lightly along the nearest dolphin's back; ~ *Thank you, my friends, thank you.* ~ She was unsure whether they understood, but they peeled away and disappeared into the night.

"Susannah?" Jesamiah asked, head cocked to one side, the one word an adequate question.

Maha'dun shook his head. "I managed to grasp hold of her, but not firm enough. I lost her."

~ *She is gone,* ~ Tiola said, hoping that Jesamiah would not realise that Maha'dun could also hear her words, just in case, she spoke aloud. "She is gone. Let her soul rest."

Two of the men crossed themselves, then, as Jesamiah uncovered the lantern and swung it to and fro to signal *Sea Witch* that they were returning, they took up the oars, dipped them into the water and began to row.

"I am trying to decide, Nightm'n, whether you are the bravest or the stupidest person I have ever met," Jesamiah announced, his expression quite bland.

His teeth chattering from the release of fear, more than cold, Maha'dun attempted a grin. "It is not brave for a brave man to be brave, but it is brave for a man who is not."

Jesamiah laughed. "Very profound, but I will stick with stupid."

* * *

At the insistence of the majority of the men they held an immediate short service for the departed soul. Not especially believing in a faith or a god, Jesamiah was irritated by the further delay, but superstition meant a great deal aboard a ship and if the right things were not done when the wrong things happened, trouble could follow in the form of unrest or even mutiny. For the sake of spending a couple of moments saying a prayer and reading a few appropriate words, long term confrontation was avoidable. Except the trouble came anyway, as soon as Jesamiah had finished reading and closed the ship's Bible with what he had intended as a signal of finality.

Ascham Doone stepped forward, pointed at Maha'dun, his hand shaking in fury.

"That man—that *thing*—murdered the young lady. He pushed her over the side!"

Agreement and disagreement buzzed through the ship. *Aye* and *shame* vying with *untrue* and *not so!*

More voices, some agreeing, some not, but the ayes had the louder shouts and when someone cried *'Hang him'* the majority followed the escalating chant; a hanging—however gruesome, was exciting.

Maha'dun shuffled closer to Jesamiah, alarmed at the sudden rise of hostility. The Night-Walkers, by way of their lifestyle, were used to being accused of despicable crimes—some justified, some not, but superstition and dislike of things that were different drove many a sensible mind beyond the line of reason. Because of it, many of the Night-Walkers, and those of Tiola's kind, had died terrible deaths.

"We will investigate further later," Jesamiah barked. "Now is not the time."

"With respect, Captain," Ascham protested, "how can we be certain he will not push someone else over the side? He is a known murderer, that was why my grandfather employed him."

"Your grandfather employed Maha'dun because he wanted to get his hands on a certain box," Tiola countered, angry beyond further words.

Jesamiah eased her to one side, giving her a warning look to stay quiet. "Most of us aboard this ship, with one or two exceptions, can be classed as murderers, Master Doone. We have all killed, but that don't mean we are about to attack our shipmates."

"Aye, but he ain't no shipmate, is he!" Perkiss jeered.

Maha'dun was scared. He told himself that he was shivering because he was wet and cold, and the sea had frightened him; he was all those things, but above them, he was scared. Memories of the lake where he had almost drowned, of seeing friends and lovers burned, skinned, buried alive, or chained to stakes and left to die in the scorching sun; horrible deaths whirled in his mind. At least hanging, a death of twenty minutes or so, would be preferable to one that lasted days. He knelt before Jesamiah, bowed his head and placed his hands together as if he were at prayer.

"I submit to you, Captain, that it is true I have committed murder in the past, from my own doing and at the orders of others, most recently by word of Sir Ailie Doone and his son, this man's grandfather and father. They employed me to keep unwanted prying eyes off the moors on certain nights when the little boats slid into the hidden bays laden with contraband. There are more than one or two militiamen decaying in Exmoor bogs, but I doubt many aboard this ship will weep over that fact. Sir Ailie also employed me because of that box your wife mentioned. He wanted it, and so did the Night-Walkers; we had an agreement of sorts to find it. But I say to you now that it cannot be found. To all this I own, but I did not harm the young lady." He looked up at Jesamiah, pleading to be believed. "You called me stupid, and to this I also own when it comes to things I know little of. I cannot read or write, I do not understand numbers or complicated things—but I am not so stupid as to push a young maid into the sea for no reason when others are nearby watching, and then jump in after her."

Ascham laughed. "Oh, he had a reason! He was making up to her, wanted his way! I saw him sitting there with his arm around her, making her weep with his persistence. It is obvious that when she refused his advances he lost his temper!"

More jeers and shouts of outrage supporting both sides of the argument.

Tiola needed to ask: ~ *Is this true, Maha'dun? Is any of it true?* ~

He turned to face her. "None of it is true, Lady, by the dark of the night I swear it. The lass was distraught, yes, but not of my doing. I was attempting to comfort her."

"What 'e says is all true," Finch strode forward, folded his arms, giving a stance of authority before the men. He had no particular fondness for this peculiar fellow, but Maha'dun had silver coin and did not stint on rewarding favours which Finch enthusiastically supplied. Strong coffee, brandy, lavers of hot water of a morning and evening. Broths, fish, cheese, bread, no meat, and a safe, dry, place to store baccy—which he also shared exclusively with the Nightm'n.

Finch dipped his head once to confirm his sincerity. "Maharden 'ere came below to fetch 'er cloak, the one Miss Tiola is presently wearing; an' if you don't mind me sayin', Cap'n, it ain't keepin' 'er very warm. I 'elped 'im find it, I came up on deck wiv 'im—the young miss were standin' on the rail over there. An' she didn't fall, she jumped. Me an' 'im were nowhere near 'er."

The chatter rose and fell with nods of agreement, although one or two diehards, Ascham Doone's friends, insisted this was not how it was.

"I too saw 'er weeping, long before Maha'dun 'ere tried to 'elp 'er," Rue added, putting his hand out to assist Maha'dun to his feet, his French accent all the stronger for the emotion that was ripping through him. "This man tried to save the life of the woman I loved, it was not 'is fault that 'e could not do so. Tonight 'e risked 'is life again to try to save a young lady who 'as seen the sort of terrible things that no *petite fille* should see. We should be 'onouring 'im, not condemning 'im!"

"Three cheers for our Nightm'n!" Skylark carolled, and the crew waved hats in the air, declared huzzah, clapped their hands and stamped their feet.

"Very well! Very well!" Jesamiah shouted. "Now can we please get under way? Rue, lay the ship on the starboard tack, a good full; get about your duties, you scabrous dogs, or I'll be tossing the lot o' you over the bleedin' side!"

As *Sea Witch* gathered way the yards creaked and squealed their protest, and the canvas filled with a crack and a roar, Jesamiah sidled up to Ascham Doone. He clamped one hand on his shoulder, said, very quietly, "If you ever try to undermine my authority in front of my men again, mate, you'll wish to bloody God that I'd order Maha'dun to do away with you, for what I'll do to you instead don't bear thinkin' about. Savvy?"

* * *

In bed, cuddled together for his warmth and her comfort, Tiola had shed some tears for a soul which had parted life for a reason beyond reason. Maha'dun had told her the truth as they had headed below to get warm and dry, and to please Finch who had insisted on getting hot broth down the both of them—although Maha'dun had opted for fortifying brandy instead.

"She was raped," Tiola told Jesamiah. "By Ascham Doone."

He was silent a while, staring up at the ceiling beams. "Can you prove it?" he asked at last.

"Not without resorting to my Craft, no."

"How do you know then?"

"She told Maha'dun. He told me. She feared she might be with child—foolish girl, she as much might not have been, but she was deeply ashamed at being violated. And too much has happened to her these last days for her mind to think with clarity."

Another long silence. "You do love me, not him, don't you?" Jesamiah asked.

Tiola was not sure whether to treat the question with the contempt it deserved. She decided to say something else instead. "Did Maha'dun get a chance to tell you that the ship following us, the one you are so worried about, is Spanish?"

Jesamiah sat up, alarmed but mystified. "And how does our Master Nightm'n know this?"

Trickling her fingers through the black hair on his chest, Tiola stated the obvious. "He is like me, he sees things that others cannot." She leant forward, kissed him, while her hand strayed lower. "And as for your other question, if you make love to me, I will show you my answer."

On The Account

* * *

Come morning, as Jesamiah had suspected, the Spaniard had gained on them because of the night-time delay. As she closed to within cannon range he had to decide what to do; attack or continue his bluff and hope it worked. He chose bluff, and a ruse he had used successfully on other such disconcerting occasions.

Several hours before dawn he had ordered gun practice and created some deliberate damage to the rails, oversaw a couple of ragged sails bent to the yards. As the sky lightened, he had Spanish colours run out, and sent three of the crew to perch on boards slung over the taffrail to appear to be repairing damage to the stern, effectively hiding the ship's name. Everything ready, he brought *Sea Witch* to such a slow speed that she could be overtaken by a rowboat.

The shout from the Spaniard came quicker than he had expected; there was now nothing he could do, for her guns would blast *Sea Witch* out of the water, unable to fire a single shot in retaliation.

"*¿Quién es usted?*"

In perfect Spanish, Jesamiah called back, "I am Captain Ramón Ramírez Escudero."

"*¿Cuál es su barco?*"

Again in flawless Spanish: "She is the *Sea Queen*. I captured her from the English some months ago during the last bout of this crazy war. We met with two bastard English frigates last night, one bloody opened fire on us—look at the sodding damage! Did you not hear? Could you not have come to our assistance? What the fok is the Spanish navy for, if not to protect our trade, for fok sake!"

"*¿Usted es un comerciante? Con quién tiene negocios?*"

"*Sí*, I am a merchant. I trade with el Marqués de Molina." Jesamiah took his hat off, wiped his brow with his sleeve. "I lost four men last night and had the shit torn out of my stern! Where were you?"

A moment later, Skylark called down from the masthead—also in Spanish, "Sail ho! Those bloody English frigates are coming back, Captain!"

"*¡Mierda!*" Jesamiah shouted orders to get to the cannons; then to the Spaniard, "Why are you not beating to quarters? I have three working guns, the rest are all out of use. I sodding expect you to protect me against these English bastards!"

The Spanish captain called something derogatory back, ordered all sail set and hastily altering course, headed for the horizon as if there was to be no tomorrow. As Jesamiah had estimated he would.

"What was that 'e said?" Finch asked, handing Jesamiah a cup of coffee. "Rub your own cock?"

"Something similar, same meaning," Rue said, accepting his own coffee, then grinning, added, "That was a *très jolie* piece of work, Jesamiah, you 'ave not forgotten the tricks we used as pirates. I take my 'at off to you!"

"One Spanish ship that size, leaking like a holed bucket and with only half the crew she's supposed to muster, would never dare tangle with the English," Jesamiah answered modestly, "but we have to get out of here quick and hope those degos don't realise they've been duped. And shifting our arse is another thing I ain't forgotten how to do!"

CHAPTER TWENTY-NINE

News of impending war had not reached the little town of San Vicento along the coast north of Cádiz. The harbour below the small, scantily-manned fortress and Calderón's lavish castle-like home made no resistance when *Sea Witch* dropped anchor, although Jesamiah had taken the precaution of extravagantly flying Calderón's own colours—an accoutrement obtained from his last visit when he had been made less than welcome at the outset. Only one other ship was in harbour, a Moroccan, the *Safeena Hamra*. The formalities of greeting completed, the Marqués de Molina, Antonio Luis Calderón, invited Jesamiah into his study to talk business.

Tiola remained with the Marqués' wife, Catriona, a lady some several years younger than her husband and who, in less than two months, was expecting her ninth child. In addition to Calderón's own gaggle of seven girls and one four-year-old son, there was a substantial flock of excited nieces and nephews running around, all come, so the Marqués had explained, for the annual visit to his wife's grandmamma.

"Her estate is a few miles along the coast, at seven-and-eighty she does not left her bed now, but she enjoy much seeing the children." He had gone on to explain, in reasonably good English, that on the morrow he and his wife, and the children, would travel there in a convoy of coaches.

"The events is become something of a tradition these past years," Calderón had laughed, putting his hands over his ears at the shrieking caused by a particularly exuberant game of tag. "The fortunate parents send their little goblins into our care for all of seven days and enjoys the peace and quiets while they are gone. I cannot recall why we start it, nor how to stop it! I confess, I have no idea of who all these childrens are, they could be village urchins for all I know!"

To Tiola's disappointment, her brother Ben was not at Calderón's house. He, it seemed, was intensely enjoying himself in Spain and, ever willing to help Señora Calderón where he could, had gone ahead to her grandmother's house only that morning with the baggage to see to various accommodation arrangements. Although Tiola suspected, when Catriona let it slip, that he had other motives in the form of Catriona's maid, who had also gone ahead.

Catriona herself was healthy in her advanced stage of pregnancy, although her swollen ankles had caused Tiola some minor concern, the diversion of medical matters had eased the disappointment about Ben. When Catriona had suggested that Tiola could accompany the party, she had eagerly agreed—she could meet Ben the sooner, keep a subtle eye on the pregnancy and enjoy the children. Their combined noise did not seem to bother her as much as it did the Marqués. In turn, he had been as pleased as Jesamiah to retreat into the quiet privacy of his study. Pleased, also, to avoid Ascham Doone who had been seeking an audience. Diplomatically, Calderón had managed to postpone an immediate meeting, conveniently forgetting to mention that he would soon be gone for a day or two.

"I have not much liking for any of the Doones," he confided to Jesamiah as they settled themselves into comfortable chairs, the brandy decanter close at hand. "Sir Ailie he is become greedy. He offers less, wants more."

"It's a wonder they do any trade," Jesamiah remarked drily.

"Ah, but what they sell is exceptional qualities. And there is no more successful a contraband runner than the Doones. The profits are worth the risk. But forget them, I have other businesses I wishes to discuss."

Jesamiah listened thoughtfully as the Spaniard explained his need for someone who had a fast ship to transport his wine to the colonies and would not cheat him. Unsure whether he really wanted to spend the rest of his life sailing back and forth across the Atlantic nannying a hold-full of wine casks, Jesamiah said he'd think about it. Agreed to think about it harder when Calderón offered to make him an equal partner in the business. It was a tempting offer. Transporting your own wine was a more lucrative prospect than merely ferrying the stuff.

Leaning back on the couch, Jesamiah said openly, "I want to know about Francesca Escudero."

"Francesca? I know littles of her. She married the brother of the wife of the eldest brother of my wife—so she is my, *dios mio*, I cannot work such a kinship out!"

"The husband? That would be Ramon Ramírez Escudero?"

"Indeed. A tragical accident, his death."

It was no accident, Francesca's husband had been murdered, but Jesamiah held his counsel. "And their son? Leandro?" he asked instead. "Did he come with her here to Spain?"

Calderón frowned. "The son? Ah, there is the tale!" He leaned forward, glanced over his shoulder as if expecting someone else to be in the room, eavesdropping. "There was the... how you say? Scindel?"

"Scandal."

"*Sí*, scandil. She met and marries with Ramon in a matter of weeks. Love at first sighting. Huh, if you believe such nonsense! Ramon's family, despite their status, were as poor as the church mouses—then suddenly, *poof!* As rich as bankers! Seven months after the wedding the son appears. Early-born, she says. A cuckoos, we all think."

Interesting, Henry Jennings had implied the same 'scandil'. Unsure whether he actually wanted to ask, Jesamiah took the plunge. "I wonder, do you know if Francesca knew my father?"

Calderón raised his arms upward, palms outward, then slapped them down on his thighs as he leant back, laughing. "*Mi ah mi! Sí!* I was not supposed to be knowing, of course, our family they would have nothing to do with your papa, but it is he who brought Francesca to España; he who has known Ramon. She was young, very young. Very pretty, but in the big troubles with her mama in England." He made a rounded motion over his belly, indicating a pregnancy.

So that was that confirmed. Very probably this son of Francesca's was also the son of Charles Mereno, Jesamiah's own father. Which made the boy his half-brother. Jesamiah suppressed a groan. Not another one! So far, supposed half-brothers had not turned out to be very brotherly.

He tried a tactful question. "Do you know the name of the father, by chance?"

"No. Your father, he smuggle her aboard his boat, brought her here to his friends." Calderón frowned, "I was not supposed to be knowing all this, my family and your father being estrenged. Is that the word?"

"Estranged. Don't you think it odd that Escudero did not want to know her background?"

Calderón laughed heartily. "With much gold paid for a marriage? He would have takes her not even knowings her name!"

He probably didn't, Jesamiah thought. *Not her real name, anyway.* It occurred to him that possibly he did not either. 'Francesca' could be as false as all the rest of her background. "So, the boy is not here? Francesca was concerned because his name is on a list of people to be murdered. Know anything of this?"

"A list of deaths?" Calderón pursed his lips, shook his head, "No, I know nothing of this. Nothing. Why is it you not ask the lady? Can she not answer?" Calderón queried as he rose to refill Jesamiah's brandy glass.

"She is dead. I need to find a box she had, and her missing son. Not necessarily in that order."

His face paling with shock, Calderón sat down heavily, then gulped at his own glass. "This is sad, bad news indeed. Francesca, she was a beautiful woman. How had she dies?"

"Someone stabbed her. They were aiming for me."

"Are you sure?"

"Sure that she is dead? *Sí.* Aiming for me, maybe."

"But why? Why?"

Jesamiah sighed, finished the brandy and held the glass out for a refill. He savoured the taste before replying quietly, "That's the reason I am here. I was hoping you could have told me."

* * *

The ship had fallen very quiet once all the hubbub of dropping anchor had ceased. Maha'dun had sat on the edge of his bed, aching to smoke a cheroot, his hands clasped together between his knees, listening intently to all the noise. Shouts of command, bare feet pattering on the deck, boots clumping. And all that was without the sounds of the ship itself—herself, they all called it 'her'.

"A ship is a she," Jesamiah had explained when Maha'dun had taken Tiola's advice to talk about the vessel whenever he could, "because she has stays and a waist, can be capricious, has a mind of her own but relies on a man to guide her. She needs paint to look beautiful, and becomes uncooperative when things go wrong." Some of which Maha'dun did not understand, but he got the gist of the meaning.

The sound of the anchor cable running out through the hawsehole had alarmed him for it echoed and boomed through the hold as if the entire ship were being wrenched apart. The splash of the anchor itself had convinced him that a major catastrophe was about to happen, but as no one else seemed alarmed—and the ship did not, after all, appear to be sinking— he sat patiently and waited for nightfall.

Tiola had called in to inform him that she and Jesamiah were going ashore, that most of the men would be as well, but a few would remain to stay on watch. All he need do was ask one of them to row him to the nearest wharf once night fell.

"Spokesy or Jasper will oblige you. Particularly if you offer a silver coin or two for their trouble."

And she had been right. The one called Spokesy had cheerfully helped him down the ladder into the boat bobbing at the bottom, had rowed him across the bay and seen him safe up the steps at the harbour wall.

"How do I get back?" Maha'dun had asked.

"Stand here and whistle, one of us will see and hear you. Or summon one of those bumboats; they're always pleased of a few extra coins." He had pointed at some of the small boats toing and froing between the harbour and the other ship resting at anchor, then hopped into his own boat and rowed back to *Sea Witch*.

Maha'dun stood watching him for a while, in his mind practising the movement of rowing. It looked easy enough... He pursed his lips, blew; only air came out. Could he learn to whistle before dawn? He pulled a wry expression. Probably not.

The town was small but busy; Maha'dun had hoped they would drop anchor in Cádiz harbour, but as Spanish towns went this one was good enough. It would suit his purpose. Putting exploring temporarily aside, he stood, concealed by shadows, watching Ascham Doone sitting outside a dockside tavern, a terracotta cup of wine in hand, legs crossed in confident comfort. He was with another man who sat opposite, his back to Maha'dun, his Arab garb obscuring any way to identify him.

Doone handed over a folded piece of paper and a heavy pouch of coin. The man hastily concealed both beneath his garments but as he did so he turned slightly. Maha'dun bristled but he caught a glimpse only, for a crowd of drunken men surged past, blocking the view. Tempted to wait and watch, Maha'dun decided against. He had probably been wrong, and there were more pressing things to do than spy on that pimp, Doone. Finding a good taverna, downing a bottle of something nice and taking the opportunity to sate his preferred appetite high among them.

As always when visiting somewhere new, he methodically quartered the place, strolling along side streets and subtly peering into prospective shelters from sunlight. He visited three taverns, eyeing up the young men, sailors mostly, but two further taverns interested him, both with slim, young pot-boys, dark-skinned, dark-eyed and shapely-bottomed. Deciding which one of the establishments he should grace with his presence, he leant against a wall in a cobbled alley, enjoying a cheroot and blowing smoke rings into the air. A woman was screeching somewhere, berating a lazy husband, another was singing—badly and out of tune. It was an hour past dusk and with the easing of the April heat the town was coming alive. The smells were evocative: pine logs and charcoal smoke from cooking fires, the aroma of coffee, herbs and spices. Baking bread, sizzling sardines and fresh-caught fish. Beer and wines. Lemons. New, spring-blooming jasmine; orange blossom and honeysuckle. Perfume, as strong on the men as it was on the ladies. The warm, dry air mingled with the ozone of the sea and the stench of human and animal waste. Maha'dun inhaled, glorying in it all. He loved Spain, the country and the people. Was that why he was drawn to Jesamiah Acorne? Because of his rich, Spanish blood?

He finished the cheroot, tossed the butt aside and walked away, smiled to himself as he retraced his steps to grind the discarded, still glowing cheroot end into the cobbles. Shipboard life was beginning to have an effect.

The unlit alley ran almost at a right angle into another, he turned the corner, hastily ducked back out of sight, his heartbeat suddenly racing. He peered cautiously, withdrew again, leant against the wall, head back, eyes closed. It took several minutes to ease his pounding blood-anger. Maybe he had been mistaken? Maybe he had not seen what he had just seen? No! Despite what Cara'mina had often insinuated, he was rarely mistaken, aside—he sniffed the air—he could smell them. Quite distinctly.

Ber'ell, a Night-Walker, and that traitorous low-life half-breed bastard, Yakub Pasha; The Carver who had killed so many so cruelly. What in all the names of everything sane was Ber'ell doing talking to him of all creatures? So Maha'dun had been right—he *had* seen this scumbag sitting with Doone back there on the dockside!

He peeped again, saw Yakub Pasha give Ber'ell a slip of paper, take in exchange a coin pouch. Maha'dun ducked back out of sight again. Remaining hidden, he strained to hear what they were saying, but a Night-Walker had a softer cadence than a human voice and it was hard to make out the words. He caught only the occasional one: *pirate, wise-woman...* Captain Acorne and Tiola? More words; *children, profit...*

Yakub Pasha. Half Night-Walker, half witch. Yakub Pasha. Barbary pirate. Slaver. A bastard who made his money out of human misery and selling children for sex. Why was Yakub Pasha known to the Doones and Ber'ell? What was a Night-Walker doing talking to this outcast traitor who carried the death sentence? Five-and-ten years ago Maha'dun had almost fulfilled that sentence, but had been ordered to stand aside. He closed his eyes, not wanting to believe the realisation. Who had done that ordering?

Ber'ell!

Wanting another cheroot, Maha'dun forced himself to decline the urge. Looked up at the night sky and counted stars instead. Got to fifty and taking a deep breath, feigning innocence, he sauntered around the corner. The alley was empty... No, maybe not.

Removing his plumed hat, Maha'dun gave a brief but courteous bow to the apparent empty space ahead of him. "I smelt you long ago, Lord Ber'ell, there is no need for you to linger in the shadows."

Ber'ell, tall, slim, handsome, a Night-Walker like Maha'dun but of superior rank, stepped out from a wall recess, did not return the bow. "I sensed you come ashore, Maha'dun. I was expecting Cara'mina. Is she not here with you?"

No sign of Yakub Pasha.

Maha'dun returned the harsh, accusing stare eye to eye. Ber'ell's eyes were of a deep lavender hue, extremely beautiful like the rest of him.

"Cara'mina is dead. She was caught by lightning, her death was by fire; she rests at peace." It was near enough the truth.

Ber'ell dropped the slight air of hostility, accepted Maha'dun's explanation—had no reason not to. "Did she obtain the caskets?"

No mention of Yakub Pasha.

"She did not." Maha'dun felt quite pleased at being able to report Cara'mina's failures.

Ber'ell's hostility returned. "Señora Escudero was to have delivered the one she possessed. I personally gave her the bone-stone pendant to ensure she was recognised in England."

"She is dead also."

Ber'ell inhaled a sharp hiss of irritation. "You were supposed to protect her. I sent word via my informer."

Yakub Pasha?

"I received the wrong word."

"Why does that not surprise me? Cara'mina always said you were an imbecile."

Being with Tiola, and to a certain extent, Jesamiah, had given Maha'dun an edge of courage and self-respect that he had been without for many years. He was wary of Ber'ell but had never been afraid of him. And the suspicion of why he had been talking to that slime-turd added confidence. "It is possible that

Cara'mina killed the English woman. I am the one alive, Cara'mina is the one dead, and it was not my fault the message was incorrect."

"Was it her fault then?" The tone was sarcastic.

Cara'mina was dead, Maha'dun had no one to gainsay his view of things. He answered simply. "Yes. Her mind has never been stable since she lost her partner in that barbarity. Surely you realised this?" To say such was a daring move on Maha'dun's part and he tensed, expecting retribution, but to his surprise Ber'ell merely nodded and touched Maha'dun's arm.

"You have grown bold since we were last together. I find this new Maha'dun somewhat exciting." Still no mention of Yakub Pasha.

Maha'dun bowed, although he kept his gaze fixed onto Ber'ell's eyes. Such beautiful eyes... Except his own sapphire blue were far more beautiful and of a deeper, more intense, penetrating colour, heightened and darkened by his blazing inner anger. Yakub Pasha, the traitor and torturer every Night-Walker had vowed to slay if ever opportunity arose. Every Night-Walker bar one, it seemed!

Rewarded with a smile, Maha'dun was playing Ber'ell as smoothly as a fiddle. From the instant he had been aware of Ber'ell's presence he had known he would have to be the attentive lover again, for there was—atop of Yakub Pasha's presence—another worrying problem. Ber'ell would sense Jesamiah. And kill him. Maha'dun could not allow that, although it would be difficult, and dangerous, to prevent it. Possibly as dangerous as acknowledging that he had seen Ber'ell talking to a traitor. Their honour ordained that no Night-Walker could slaughter or maim another of their own kind, but to Maha'dun's mind, Ber'ell could, unfortunately, do as he pleased, when he pleased. And then—piled on top of all this—there was the matter of finding the missing boy, but at least *that* subject might distract attention away from Captain Acorne.

"There is a possibility that the bone-box is with the son of the English woman with the Spanish name. Is he here?" Maha'dun asked.

Ber'ell's air of ease shifted slightly to irritation. "If he is, I know nothing of it. Why was I not informed? If he has the box, then we must find him, but there has been no boy with the scent of a box about him here. Mayhap he is in Cádiz? I believe the lady went there first."

"Then it seems my quest to find him will take me to Cádiz," Maha'dun used one of his most seductive smiles. "But there is no hurry."

The smile, and the boy, failed to offer a diversion, for Ber'ell said, "However, I would know why there is another who has come ashore with the scent of a casket about him. Why have you not dispatched him?"

Bugger, Maha'dun thought, said, "He is important to the ship, the one who knows how to navigate it. Aside, I assumed you would prefer the pleasure of taking his blood-life?"

Ber'ell touched his palm to Maha'dun's cheek, relishing the soft, smooth feel. "I like this new confident you, my friend, it is arousing. But where is he now, this important navigator?"

"He is with the Marqués, he will be a guest for a few days." *A pity this unexpected praise will soon be suspended*, Maha'dun thought, aware that he was going to be in trouble when Ber'ell discovered he was hiding the truth.

Unaware of Maha'dun's subterfuge, Ber'ell was satisfied with the explanation, relieved that the agitation oozing from Maha'dun was for this bone-box carrier, not Yakub Pasha.

"Then we shall visit this seafarer when we are ready. But first, shall we celebrate our reunion by feasting on the best in all Spain at a taverna I know where we can partake of our fill and then retire for the sharing of more intimate pleasures." A command, not a suggestion. He placed his mouth over Maha'dun's, when he drew back, purred, "I take it, now you have found the guts to speak out, that you have no objection to my proposal? Or have you also ceased using your lover's skills?"

Maha'dun returned the sensuous kiss. "No objection whatsoever."

As with Cara'mina, if he could give pleasure for the next few hours Ber'ell would sleep afterwards for many, many more. Enough, Maha'dun hoped, to slip away, find Tiola, and warn her. How she was going to persuade Jesamiah to set sail again was beyond him. Even more concerning, how was he going to get himself aboard if he could not do so before daylight came? Stupidly he had left his sun-protective garments aboard *Sea Witch*. The only comfort, Ber'ell would not be emerging into the bright Spanish sunlight either.

* * *

Feigning intoxication, Maha'dun swayed into Ber'ell's underground chambers, impressed. Formed within natural caves beneath the fortress, the walls were marble-clad with tall pillars and even a bubbling subterranean spring forming a focal point to the luxurious living room. Beyond, through an open door, an equally resplendent bedchamber, bedecked with silks and sumptuous velvets. Most Night-Walkers were rich and Ber'ell, one of the high-ranking nobles, was exceptionally wealthy. The only detriment was the pervading aroma of Yakub Pasha. He had been here then. And for some while, for his scent did not merely hang in the air but clung to the furniture as well. If it was on the bed...? Maha'dun shuddered. Surely Ber'ell would not have lowered himself that far into such an obnoxious relationship?

"Come, pour yourself wine, then sit!" Ber'ell, sprawled on a leather couch, smiled an invitation, provocatively patted the cushion next to him. "Or is something troubling you? I assure you, we are quite safe from sunlight and prying humans."

Maha'dun poured two generous crystal glasses of Spanish wine, then glided across the floor, his body rippling with potent sexuality. He set his own glass down on a side table, handed the other to Ber'ell. His hand wobbled and several drops of the blood-red wine dripped over Ber'ell's thigh and white linen breeches. Aghast, Maha'dun apologised, went swiftly to his knees, his hand dabbing at the spreading stains.

"How clumsy of me! Please, let me remedy this!" His long, slender fingers brushed against Ber'ell's genitals as he began to undo the breeches' intricate lacings, then piece by slow piece, every item of his lord's clothing. He made love, caressing and smoothing and stroking, bringing his master to ultimate satisfaction—for every minute, concealing that he was gagging at the stench of Yakub Pasha clinging to the leather, and, when they moved to the bedchamber, the smell of his foul, spilt seed was even stronger.

I should have killed The Carver when I had chance, Maha'dun thought, forcing himself to retain a seductive smile, to appear relaxed and at ease. *I should have ripped his heart out, not his eye. He is a half-breed traitor, a torturer, a killer of women and children. A rapist, a slaver, a...* He thought of more descriptive words, but not once as he lay with Ber'ell did he lose his skilful touch. If anything, his anger heightened it.

Chapter Thirty

"You do not mind me disappearing for two days, then?"

Tiola was packing a few personal items into a valise, Jesamiah, his arms folded behind his head, lay stretched out between the fresh-smelling linen sheets of an enormous bed. At least, they had been fresh-smelling when he and Tiola had crawled into bed at about eleven last evening. This morning, while not exactly soiled, the sheets were crumpled and dishevelled; a result of several energetic bouts of lovemaking.

He yawned, stretched. "I will be busy reprovisioning *Sea Witch* and making ready for the voyage across the Atlantic. Calderón's to supply me with the extra ammunition I need; it all has to be stowed this morning, along with the wine casks that are to be sent aboard—hah, I am apparently now a signed and sealed, legally documented partner to the wine trade! I reckon I can manage on my own until tomorrow night. The young man," he pointed at his crotch, "is taking his ease at the moment."

Tiola closed the valise, buckled the straps then, walking to the bed, pulled the sheets back and stood, arms folded, looking down at Jesamiah's naked body.

"From where I stand," she said, her expression completely bland, "he looks somewhat old, wrinkled and spent."

Sitting up, Jesamiah threw a pillow at her, then swung his legs over the side, got out of bed and stood scratching his left buttock. "If you hadn't decided to get yourself dressed, I reckon I could have sufficiently roused the fellow." He inspected his floppy penis, waggled it about a bit, grinned. "Or perhaps not."

"So, you do not mind?"

Looking over his shoulder at her while he pissed into the chamber pot, Jesamiah shook his head. "You want to see Ben. Understandable. Though for some equally non-understandable reason you want to spend time with about eighty very noisy, all under the age of twelve, ankle-biters. You are either pursuing sainthood or have gone mad."

Tiola lightly slapped his buttocks as she passed by. "There are fifteen children and they are all sweethearts."

"So sweet their darling mamas are eager to be rid of them for several days?"

"I think," she responded, "it is the grandmamma that the mamas wish to avoid. Apparently the old lady is highly disapproving of her several daughters—all except her youngest, Catriona, but she dotes on the children, although the doting wears off once they become young adults."

"Can't see the point of that. Most children only become interesting once they grow up."

"That depends on how interesting the grown-up is!" Tiola laughed, peering out of the window into the courtyard below as the rumbling sound of several carriages drew her attention. "There's our transportation. I must go."

"Rue and young Thomas are going with you?" Jesamiah, breeches halfway over his backside, looked up at her.

"Thomas, yes, it will do him good to mix with others of his own age, he has already made friends with a boy a little younger than himself but very much more mature in mind. Donréal, one of the cousins. Rue, I cannot see why you insisted he accompany me. I shall be perfectly safe, I do not require a bodyguard or chaperone."

"I asked him to escort you because it will give him something useful and important to do. Otherwise he will sit in a tavern drinking himself into oblivion."

"And you will not?"

Jesamiah responded with a rude gesture.

Tiola grinned back at him, said, "Susannah's suicide was very hard on him, atop everything else. You are right, the distraction will do him good."

From outside, Thomas, shrieking laughter with Donréal and some other boys, accompanied by frenzied yapping from Pamela's two dogs, drifted up through the open window.

"Thomas is taking those damned dogs with him?" Jesamiah asked, joining her at the window, his arms encircling her waist. The Moroccan ship, he noticed, was preparing to set sail. "I thought they were supposed to be Rue's dogs? Thomas seems to have adopted them."

"Yes, they are coming. And don't pull that relieved face, I've seen you rubbing their bellies and feeding them scraps!"

Laughing, Jesamiah helped her on with her cloak. "Are we talking about the dogs or my crew?" He tied the cloak's lacing into a bow. "What about the nightman?"

Attempting to look unconcerned, Tiola merely answered, "What about him?"

"Do you know where he is, what he is up to, whether he's going to come aboard again when we sail? Does he know that will be as soon as you get back from this jolly jaunt?"

"No. No. Yes. I hope so."

* * *

Maha'dun stretched lazily, then quietly left the bed. Ber'ell was on his stomach sound asleep and dead to the world, but Maha'dun did not want to take any chance of inadvertently waking him. He reached for a silk robe, winced as bruises and scratches made their presence known. The sex had been intense, violent, although not to the degree of Cara'mina's outrageous demands. Maha'dun's gift of sexual ability enabled his energy to be almost limitless; he could pleasure a partner—or several at once—for hours without tiring. A talent he appreciated when his clients were enjoyable company, but was equally useful when he wanted to ensure after-sex solitude.

Wanting a smoke, he went into the main room and rummaged in his longcoat pocket, then thought better of the idea. The smell could wake Ber'ell. He settled for a large glass of Scotch whisky instead. Ruefully he looked at his clothes scattered over the marble floor. They had been ripped off. Literally in the case of his shirt, it was in shreds. Even the buttons were torn from his breeches. On inspection, the only items intact were his boots, waistcoat, and the longcoat which he had removed himself as they had entered Ber'ell's underground chambers.

With a heavy sigh he wandered back to the bedchamber and into Ber'ell's extensive closet, a small anteroom to one side. One dim lamp was burning. He found a taper, lit several of the beeswax candles in their sconces. The clothes, folded neatly on shelves or draped carefully over poles, were all quality, made by the most expensive tailors. He looked inside the first two drawers of a Queen Anne-style cherrywood highboy, found silk stockings in one and silk underdrawers in the other. He helped

358

himself to both and put them on, then pulled on a pair of soft knee-length chamois breeches—Ber'ell was of similar shape and height as were all Night-Walkers, the only major variations being gender and hair and eye colour.

For a shirt he chose a soft cambric with a froth of lace at the cuffs and a matching cravat. Wearing his own delicately embroidered waistcoat, he stood back to admire himself in the mirrors adorning one wall. The picture only slightly marred by a vivid bruise on his right cheek. It would heal.

All well and good, but daylight burned outside, what else could he wear to make his escape? He looked around: shoes, boots, coats, hats, cloaks, gloves, all of it designed for the night. It seemed Ber'ell never ventured outside until after dark. And then Maha'dun smiled: if that, draped over a pole in the corner, was what he thought it was... He grinned, delighted as, after selecting a pair of exquisitely soft leather boots, he shrugged on the traditional thobe, the outer garment of a desert Arab, made for Ber'ell in layers of soft Turkish angora wool, with wide sleeves that fell to the fingertips. To cover his head he draped an elegant *keffiyeh*—or was it a *ghutra* or *shemagh*? Different areas had different names; he never could remember which belonged to which. Securing it in place with its accompanying cord, he experimented with folding one end across his face. Only his eyes were visible. He looked again in the mirror, the garment was perfect, but he added a light-brown woollen *bisht*, the flowing cloak worn for prestige and special occasions, or by the nobility. He grinned. Adequate payment for services rendered. Taking up a large leather bag, he selected several more pairs of the silk drawers and stockings, added three cravats, four shirts and a bundle of kerchiefs. Could not decide which gloves to take, chamois or kid?

Returning to the main room, his attention was drawn to a

rack of swords and rapiers with their accompanying scabbards and hangers. He studied them, chose a rapier, gave it several experimental flicks then secured its hanger around his waist over his protective Arab garment. It was probably Ber'ell's best weapon, but Night-Walker honour stated that a lover, if he or she had performed to satisfaction, could claim their own reward. Despite the tradition, he had a suspicion that Ber'ell would regard the appropriation of his clothes and weapon as excessive, and would not be pleased about it. Too bad, he should not have been so violent, should he? Nor should he have been consorting with half-breed scum. The thought reminded Maha'dun, and he felt in Ber'ell's coat pocket—the garment left atop Maha'dun's own over the back of a chair. He found the slip of paper, the one he had seen Ascham Doone give Yakub Pasha, who had then passed it to Ber'ell. He stared at the incomprehensible squiggles:

Winnard Doone—eliminated
Robert Harley—dying
Francesca Escudero—eliminated
Leandro Escudero—missing: unimportant?
Captain Jesamiah Acorne—to be eliminated
Calderón—to be eliminated
Henry Jennings—unimportant

The scribbles meant nothing. He put the paper onto a side table, weighted it with the whisky decanter. When Ber'ell found it he would know that Maha'dun knew about Yakub Pasha. Without further thought he picked up the luggage bag—decided to leave his old, scuffed boots, folded his coat over his arm and, on his way out, plucked an ebony walking cane with a silver knob from a rack beside the door.

Now all he had to do was navigate his way through the labyrinth of tunnels to find his way out, get to the *Sea Witch*, and persuade Tiola to convince her husband to set sail before nightfall.

* * *

Finding a boat to ferry him across the bay to the anchored *Sea Witch* was the easy part—fortunately, with no whistling involved. There was a flotilla of boats plying back and forth, many of them on the outward journey looking, to Maha'dun, as if they were about to sink, so heavy-laden were they. He spotted Skylark, asked what was happening.

"Hello there, mate, you had a good time ashore last night?" Skylark acknowledged, while heaving a wooden crate down to a man standing apparently not at all bothered by the bobbing and swaying of one of the larger boats. "We're reprovisioning, water, vittles. Enough to see us across the Atlantic."

"That's the big sea?" Maha'dun queried.

"Not as big as the Pacific, so I 'ear tell."

"But bigger than the one we've already sailed across?" Maha'dun was beginning to wonder if perhaps it would be better to find himself a horse and simply ride away.

"Much bigger, but also more exciting, more beautiful, more invigorating. I love the Atlantic, it's almost as if it were a living thing beneath the hull. You ready to go aboard with these crewmen here then, or wait till later?"

Through squinting eyes Maha'dun stared at the activity on the water and aboard *Sea Witch*. He could see Jesamiah standing on the quarterdeck waving his arms about in the direction of a large barrel being winched aboard. He thought of the ocean; he had grasped the concept that it was bigger than a sea and it terrified him, but then, didn't most things that brought excitement ride on the back of fear and danger?

"Yes," he said, smiling beneath the headdress covering head, neck, shoulders and face, "I wish to go aboard."

He hesitated at the bottom of the ladder cleats, watching as Skylark scrabbled up the side of the ship with ease. He was scared—what if he fell—but he took a deep breath, hitched his robe to secure the ends through the rope belt and grasped the first cleat, went up as quickly as he could, looking upward, not down and not thinking about where to put his feet, just doing it. The end of his headdress, tucked across his face, slipped, became undone and flapped about in the wind. His cheeks and chin were exposed, the pain from the sunlight burning into his skin was agonising, but he dared not let go the cleats to refasten it.

Jesamiah was standing at the top. He put his hand out to help Maha'dun over the entry port, frowned at the vivid red blistering. "You all right, Nightm'n?"

"I am perfectly all right, I thank you," Maha'dun responded, hastily tucking the ends of the headdress across his face, masking both burns and winced. "When do we leave here?"

"When all provisions are aboard and stowed, those last few wine casks safely stored, the last of the crew deign to join us, and when Tiola, Rue and Thomas get back."

Maha'dun digested the information. "And when will that be?"

Jesamiah laughed. "You're getting keen, aren't you? Tiola will be back later this evening. We'll probably sail soon after dawn. There's no especial rush."

"Um..."

Jesamiah cocked his head to one side, stared at Maha'dun. "Or is there?"

"Well, it is a little awkward, I..."

"You've made yourself unwelcome ashore and wish to avoid any unpleasantness?"

Maha'dun beamed with delight. Captain Acorne was very quick at picking up things! "Yes."

Turning away, Jesamiah shouted at Perkiss, "You will have that in the bloody sea if you don't put your back into it!"

Perkiss scowled, the other man with him, Richie Tearle, said something and they both laughed.

"Best get yourself below then," Jesamiah said, ignoring the guffaws. "If anyone asks, I'll tell 'em I don't know where you are."

That would not quite help if Ber'ell was the one asking, but Maha'dun could not very well say so, instead, he offered, "I asked about the son of the English woman with the Spanish name. He is not here."

"Can you be sure of that?"

"I can."

Ber'ell knew everything, although it occurred to Maha'dun as he hurried to the darkness of the below-deck world that perhaps he did not? Mayhap this English lady had been more clever than they had all given her credit for?

* * *

Having woken from a deep sleep, Maha'dun sat on the edge of his bed and held his fingers to the side of his head as pain seared through his brain as if he had been hit from behind with a hammer blow. Nausea rose into his gullet, he swallowed hard, concentrated on not passing out. Perhaps this was the effect of that feast he had partaken of with Ber'ell? He had said at the time that he thought the taste was slightly off, tainted with something unpalatable. Ber'ell had dismissed the suggestion and gorged himself; Maha'dun just hoped he was now feeling as sick as this as well. But that did not explain the scream he had heard before the pain had shot into his head, did it?

He sat a while, the dizziness easing. He needed air. That was the next thought, fresh air, for he felt as if he were being suffocated, as if something were covering his face making it hard to breathe. Was it dark out yet? Could he go on deck? He got up, paced the small room that was his; four paces by three. Would he feel better walking up and down outside in the hold? Opening the door, he ducked through, was surprised to find a few of the men there stowing some of the new cargo. Why had he not heard them? He must have slept sounder than he had realised. Perhaps the cause of this headache had been nothing more than a bad dream? Then he noticed Jesamiah over to the far side near a stacked pile of badly balanced crates. He too was bending over, holding his head and looking green-sick about the gills. Maha'dun made his way to him.

"Captain Acorne? Is anything amiss?" he asked quietly, his back to the other men—he had enough sense not to draw attention to Jesamiah if there were something wrong.

"No, no, I'm fine, came over a bit dizzy, that's all. Felt as if someone had hit me over the head." He puffed his cheeks, added, "Not much air down here. I'm not keen on enclosed spaces."

Out of the corner of his eye Maha'dun noticed someone sidling along in the shadows on the far side of the crates, lowered his voice even more. "I felt the same, Captain. I have a bad feeling. Is Mistress Tiola arrived back? Is she well?"

Jesamiah straightened, flexed his shoulders, rubbed at his neck. "No, she sent word that Calderón's wife was slightly unwell so they are staying another night. I intend to sail along the coast to collect her, Rue and Thomas tomorrow morning, assuming my lady wife wants to...”

He did not finish the sentence; Maha'dun slammed into his side, pushing him over as the stacked crates toppled, crashing down. There was a grunt of surprise from Jesamiah, a cry of pain from Maha'dun. Skylark, Spokesy and two others rushed from the far side of the hold and began clawing at the scattered crates crushing the two men.

“I'm all right!” Jesamiah said, brushing Richie Tearle off as he tried to help his captain to his feet. “Nightm'n? Are you hurt?” Squatting down, Jesamiah ran his hands quickly over Maha'dun's prone body; there was no blood, nothing appeared to be broken; there would be bruises, though, for he had taken the full force of the falling boxes.

Maha'dun groaned, sat up, wincing. “You can save yourself next time,” he complained, climbing gingerly to his feet and carefully testing protesting muscles. “This is becoming too painful an occupation.”

The men laughed heartily, all except Jesamiah who was staring coldly through accusing eyes at Perkiss and Tearle. “Was that deliberate? Who were you aiming for, me or the Nightm'n?”

Tearle blanched and profusely denied it, protesting that it had been an accident. “...Hardly my fault,” he finished, righteous anger starting to take hold, “if Perkiss cannot stow things properly in the first place!”

Jesamiah could not argue with that: the crates had been badly stacked, but without a shove at an appropriate moment, would they have fallen? Or was he seeing trouble where there was none? He stared at both men for a moment longer then dropped the matter, giving orders that everything was to be set straight, and, heading for the ladder, invited Maha'dun to his cabin. It was dusk, dark enough; and he had a bottle of Spanish Cogniack he wanted to sample.

"He is trouble, that chap Perkiss," Jesamiah announced as he handed Maha'dun a large glass of amber liquid. "I think I'll get shot of him before we sail."

"Do you not need him?" Maha'dun asked, sipping at the proffered drink and nodding approval; excellent quality. The best.

Sighing, Jesamiah sat in his favourite chair, crossed his legs at the ankles. His left boot, he noticed, had a wide scuff mark from where one of the crates had caught it. Finch would grumble. "Either that or I wait for a dark night to tip him into the sea."

"Like Doone did to Susannah," Maha'dun muttered.

"She jumped, she wasn't pushed."

"Depends on what you mean by 'pushed', does it not? Pushed physically or pushed mentally."

Jesamiah raised his glass to concede the point, then sat silent for a few minutes.

Noticing a crammed longboat pulling away, Maha'dun asked if Jesamiah was certain his men would be back by dawn to set sail.

"Most of them will; their money is running low so they'll be wanting more." He laughed. "Not that many of them will be sober, but they know the ropes well enough to do everything in their sleep or drunk."

"And you do not wish to be ashore carousing?" Maha'dun hoped he had worded it tactfully. He had two meanings, one to ascertain whether Jesamiah was also wanting to spend silver on women and liquor—women in particular given that Tiola was not here—and whether he could relax and stop worrying about Ber'ell. On board ship they were safe, well, safe-ish.

"Me? I would have done once, and not that long ago at that, but when you've got a good woman to share your bed with, the street doxies don't seem so appealing, do they?"

Maha'dun stared thoughtfully into his glass. Jesamiah was a lucky man: for himself he wouldn't know, he'd had no experience of either a good woman or street doxies.

Another companionable silence, punctuated by a rumbling noise and raucous laughter on deck.

"I was going to go to bed early, it's been a busy day, but shall we join them?" Jesamiah said, pointing overhead.

Following him out onto the deck—refilled glass in hand—Maha'dun could not help thinking that the cabin was by far a safer place to be. On the other hand, Ber'ell was unlikely to be ferried across the bay to board *Sea Witch*. Like himself, the Night-Walker had an inbred fear of water, but unlike himself, had not had opportunity to realise that it was a false fear. Thankfully, once on deck there did not seem to be any boats carrying extremely irate passengers in their direction.

There were about twenty men aboard, amusing themselves by playing a vigorous game of boules using small cannonballs, a game which appeared to be going well despite *Sea Witch* shifting slightly at her anchor, giving a minor tilt to the deck. Another great guffaw of laughter as one man made a careful shot by rolling the ball gently, only to have it swerve to one side and stick fast in a scupper hole.

"You damage my ship, you'll know all about it!" Jesamiah chuckled as he refused the offer of having a go at knocking the jack off its marker pot.

Maha'dun was leaning on the rail, staring at the night sky. It was a clear, calm night, the heavens littered with stars. Something was bothering him, nagging at him. When Jesamiah joined him, he plucked up courage. Spoke out.

"You can hear Tiola in your head," he asked, tapping at his right temple. "Hear her words and her voice as if they are your own thoughts?"

Jesamiah tossed back the last of his drink. Made no response.

"I hear her too," Maha'dun admitted, knowing he was taking a risk. He turned to face Jesamiah, looked at him eye to eye. "About an hour ago I heard her scream. I am anxious to know whether it was nothing of concern, or you heard it too."

Still Jesamiah said nothing. If this night creature was hoping to lure him into the trap of giving Tiola away, then he was going to be bitterly disappointed. But his fingers tightened around the glass and he recalled that disturbing bout of dizziness, the feeling of a blow to the head.

~ *Tiola?* ~ he tried. ~ *Tiola?* ~

He stared into the darkness. There was nothing unusual about not getting an answer, but something *was* wrong. He could feel it in his bones.

"Something has happened," Maha'dun whispered. "You feel it as well as do I."

The glass in Jesamiah's hand shattered, cutting his hand; shards and blood dripped onto the deck. He barely noticed. A small gust of wind flurried through the rigging, bringing a waft of the smells of the town towards them. Cooking, effluence, spices. It shifted around, bringing the scent of the hills, trees, damp earth, aromatic plants and flowers. A faint, very faint, trace of smoke. Maha'dun's sensitive olfactory nerve detected it immediately.

"What is that glow over there, behind the low hill?" he asked, pointing.

Winding a kerchief around his hand, Jesamiah peered to where Maha'dun pointed. Sniffed the air. The wind had died, he smelt, could see, nothing.

"I smell smoke," Maha'dun said firmly. "There is a fire somewhere near that hill."

Jesamiah stared, straining his senses. The glow was not particularly obvious but the dark night sky along the coast to the north-east was lighter.

~ *Tiola? Tiola, there's a fire. Are you in danger, are you hurt?* ~

He glowered at Maha'dun. "Do you hear her?"

Maha'dun shook his head.

Jesamiah spun on his heel, shouted, "Sound the alarm. We're leaving. Now. Anyone ashore not paying attention falls behind."

Without question or falter, the men aboard had loaded the cannons and fired three enormous booms that spat and echoed across the bay towards the town. Within minutes Maha'dun could see men ashore running for the boats, hurling themselves into those that already had oars manned and dipping into the water.

"Three bangs?" he asked.

"The men of my original crew know the sound of the guns, they are as distinctive as voices. Three shots, quick succession: shift your arse, we're leaving in a hurry. Anyone not aboard within fifteen minutes gets left behind. A lot of them don't make it, although a good man always stays close to his ship when in harbour." He grinned, the stern lantern light glinting on his two gold-capped teeth. "It's always handy having the brothels and taverns built along the shore. I've had to scuttle aboard without m'breeches many a time during my pirate days!"

Maha'dun smiled at the image conjured. "And most of the men respond to this emergency signal?"

"Most, aye. Usually it means their life is dependent on it, when the press gang's raidin' for crew for instance." He chuckled again. "Or there's a few irate husbands on the rampage."

Within ten minutes men were scrambling aboard and running to their posts. The only sour note, Ascham Doone also scrabbled aboard. His expression gruff.

"What is it?" Spokesy queried, heading for the capstan to join the men already starting to haul in the anchor.

"My exact question," Doone echoed. "I do not much care for being torn away from a good bottle of wine."

"You could have stayed nursing it," Jesamiah retorted, "no one would have noticed."

"And risk possible danger? Your crew said it might be hostile warships on the prowl. I figured I would be safer here than ashore while Calderón is gone."

Despite the annoyance of having him aboard, Jesamiah had to concede there was logic in that. "Something's on fire over there," he pointed vaguely at the dark line of coast silhouetted along the edge of the starry sky. "Calderón told me there is only one residence along that stretch of marsh, it used to be a hunting retreat for the nobility. His wife's grandmother is its present occupant—and that's where they've all gone."

Chapter Thirty-One

Jesamiah had seen some terrible things during his life. Some of them he had inflicted on others himself—pirates were not known to be sensitive, gentle souls when they boarded a Prize, especially if the opposing crew had put up a fight. He stood inside the shattered doorway of a large, grand house, his boots crunching on the debris of splintered wood and broken glass, most of his crew arrayed behind him, all of them with pistols and cutlasses drawn, several also holding flaring torches. All of them as equally stunned into silence. Only the bleating of sheep and the lonely neigh of a horse could be heard on the starlit salt marshes outside. Their boots had carried in blood from slaughtered livestock which was slicked everywhere on the earthen courtyard, pooled in ruts and puddles, trickling in runnels towards the high tide of the cove, colouring the languid waves a lurid pink. Not a single carcass. Not one cow or pig, the livestock had been butchered and carried off. The barn was a smoking pile of charred timber, the last of the previous summer's hay gone up in smoke, along with several small servants' cottages and half a dozen fishing boats moored beside the wharf—all quick to burn. Everything stank of tar, smoke and roasted fish.

The house—more a palace in size and splendour than the hunting lodge Jesamiah had expected—had not been torched, but had been torn apart as if a hurricane had hurled through from one side to the other. Furniture and furnishings, ornaments, windows, doors, shelves, cupboards. All smashed, broken or torn.

"Find some candles and lamps. Get some more light in here," Jesamiah snapped.

What made the skin crawl and the hairs on the back of the neck prickle was the silence inside the house. Nothing moved or stirred. Not a clock ticked or a floorboard creaked. The place had become a charnel house. Bodies were strewn, horribly mutilated, over the blood-soaked tiled floor. Most of them servants by the look of their clothes, all men. They had put up a fight to defend the house and its occupants, and lost.

Jesamiah took a deep breath, slowly sheathed his cutlass and took a torch from the man next to him, stepped towards the nearest corpse. Squatting beside it he wiped a hand over his face, hoped none of his men noticed he was shaking. He reached out, closed the dead man's staring eyes, then clamped his hand over his mouth swallowing the vomit that rose to his throat.

Rue. His best friend. The man he had thought of more as a father than he had his own real one. Claude de la Rue. His body ripped open from throat to crotch, his innards scattered over the floor. The same as several of the others, equally as brutally murdered. Impossible to know which dismembered bit or organ belonged to which body. This had not been an attack, it had been a vicious bloodbath.

Beside Rue, a young lad was barely recognisable. Half his face had been hacked away, but there was enough left to identify him. Ben. Tiola's brother. They had hacked off his hands and feet as well. Gorge rose again in Jesamiah's throat. They had done so while he had still been alive.

No women. Not one female lying among the dead. No children, either. Where were they all?

"You men, search through there," Jesamiah stood, pointed to the left. "You lot take that side. You others, search outside. Maha'dun, Skylark, Spokesy, come with me, we'll look upstairs. Jasper, Finch, Tearle, cover these poor sods with something, give them some dignity."

"What if they are still here?" That was Ascham Doone, he had vomited twice, was as pale and shaken as all of them, and like several of the others was peering carefully into the shadows.

"If any of them are," Jesamiah spoke with rigid iron, "you bring them to me. Alive. There's to be no quick deaths." He glared at his men. "Savvy?"

"Aye, Cap'n."

"Aye."

They understood all right.

"If I had known..." Doone muttered, then gulped and, clamping a hand over his mouth, fled outside.

Maha'dun stared after him. *Did you know*, he thought. *Did your friend Yakub Pasha do this?* He could smell him, a lingering stench, but Maha'dun stayed his counsel for he could be wrong.

~ *Tiola? Tiola?* ~ All the while Jesamiah had been calling in his head. As he went up the stairs he shouted aloud. "Tiola? Tiola! Are you here? Tiola!" All the while ignoring the blood dribbling down the white marble, stepping over butchered bodies draped grotesquely over the bannisters. Twice Jesamiah stooped to ensure a corpse was a corpse; flickering shadows created the illusion of movement.

At the top, two women—older servants, ladies' maids by their finer clothing. Both dead, both raped and mutilated. The doors to several rooms were wide open, all had been smashed in with axes, the bolts on the inside of the distorted frames still slid home. The occupants had tried in vain to protect themselves. Jesamiah swallowed anger; he could imagine the screams of fear that had been in these rooms, the sound almost lingered with the smell of blood and urine—the bastards who had done this had peed and defecated wherever they fancied. In the first room, four women, all stripped naked, all used, abused and killed. The next: the old woman, the grandmother, was on her bed, head lolling, sightless eyes staring. Her frail, aged, wrinkled body also exposed to the obscenity of nakedness. She had also been raped.

Maha'dun stepped forward and with a low growl more animal than anything else, wrenched one of the ripped curtain drapes from the overhead tester frame and placed it reverently over her.

"What kind of lowlife does this sort of thing?" he asked, turning to Jesamiah, questioning anger in his blazing sapphire eyes.

Jesamiah did not answer, there wasn't one he could give. Had Tiola been here in this room? Had she been forced to watch what they did to the old lady, had she been... He shut his mind to that next thought. Firmly, decisively, shut his mind to it.

"Where's Calderón?" he said. "We'd better check these other rooms."

"If they've done the same as they did here to his wife," Skylark began, "with her in her condition..."

Spinning around, his clenched fist raised, Jesamiah's face puckered into a snarl. "Don't go there, mate. Don't bloody, fucking go there!"

They peered in the next room—empty, as was the next, both debris strewn, everything smashed, torn or turned upside down. Spokesy went into the next. There were broken children's toys scattered around, boys' toys; hoops, toy boats, carved wooden soldiers. He investigated something bloody concealed behind one of the overturned chairs, poking with the tip of his cutlass. Walked away, out of the room, grim-faced.

"It's the dogs," he growled, hiding his disgust and anger. "The little dogs." No one said anything as they descended a short flight of steps into another wing of the house. Words were not adequate.

"There must have been a good few of them," Maha'dun observed as he swung open another partially closed door, "to do this amount of damage."

"A whole shipload, I would guess," Jesamiah answered. "One hundred, a hundred and twenty men? Oh God! Calderón!" He pushed past Maha'dun into the room; a man was tied to the bedpost, double-secured by a pitchfork piercing his stomach, skewering him. On the bed a pile of blood-soaked covers. A woman's clenched hand poked from beneath. Jesamiah did not look closer; the blood told story enough.

She was dead, but Calderón was alive. Just. He slowly raised his head, blood dribbling from his contorted mouth, his jaw clearly broken.

Instinctively Jesamiah grasped the shaft of the pitchfork, but Maha'dun jerked his hand away.

"Don't! He is already a dead man, pull that out, you will cause him more pain than you could ever imagine. And I would imagine that could be quite a lot?"

Nodding, Jesamiah picked up a stained linen cloth from the floor, dabbed it at Calderón's face.

"I would have the water?" the man rasped. "Please. Water?"

Skylark was out the door, relieved at the excuse to leave.

"Who did this?" Jesamiah asked in Spanish. "Who was here?"

"They raped her," Calderón whispered, also in his own tongue, "before my eyes, and there was nothing I could do to stop them. Nothing I could do to help her."

"Who?" Jesamiah persisted. "Who were they?"

Tears streaming from Calderón's eyes mingled with the blood.

"Who?" Jesamiah repeated, still speaking in Spanish out of respect for his dying friend.

"Barbary pirates. They raid for slaves. Children make the most money." Calderón lifted his head a little higher, his gaze pleading. "I will not be able to go and find my beloved children. You are my sister's son, you are of my kin, my blood. I charge you on your mother's soul to find them and take revenge. Promise me. Promise me you will find and kill that bastard who calls himself Yakub Pasha."

Maha'dun stepped nearer, his brows furrowing into a deep frown. He had been right then. "How do you know his name?" He also put his question in Spanish.

"His men spoke it and he boasted of it himself."

"Where would he be heading?" Jesamiah hated asking these questions, hated hearing the breath and seeping blood gurgling in Calderón's throat as he struggled to reply. But he needed the answers. "Where do they sail from? To?"

"I do not know," Calderón stammered. "Algiers? Tangier? Salé?"

"And how do I recognise this Yakub Pasha?"

Maha'dun's face puckered into disgust and answered in

English for Calderon.

"He has one eye, with a scar that runs from here to here." He drew his finger from the bridge of his nose, across his left eye, and down his cheek to the tip of his chin.

"You are sure?" Jesamiah asked, also in English. "How would you be knowing him?"

"I am quite sure. I removed the eye and gave him the scar at the same time. I was not permitted to complete the score I was trying to settle, but the tally for revenge runs higher now and I will not be prevented again."

Jesamiah nodded, once, briefly. There were no more questions he could ask. No more answers he could be given. He pulled his dagger from the sheath that nestled in the small of his back, drew the sharp blade across Calderón's throat and ended his pain. For Jesamiah, it was just beginning.

* * *

Urgent shouting from downstairs. Skylark ran in, the task of fetching water forgotten. "They've found the women down in the kitchens, they're all dead, violated, and someone else, one of the scum. He was sampling what was left of the brandy in the cellars; claims he's a servant, but he don't look or sound much like one."

"Does he speak English? French? Spanish?"

"No, just the jib-jab nonsense of those A-rab infidel Muslim Jews."

"He cannot be a Muslim *and* a Jew, Skylark. He's one or the other."

Skylark did not care for the pedantics. "Whatever, Cap'n. He speaks only jib-jab."

Jesamiah hesitated, a captive was important, but so was seeing to the dead here. "Give me a moment; I'm coming.

Truss the bastard up, get him back to the ship and secure him in the bilge. I'll get answers from him once we've set sail. And fetch me back four kegs of gunpowder and fuses. We haven't time to bury these poor sods but I have no intention of leaving them like this."

Fully understanding, Skylark nodded.

Maha'dun flapped a hand vaguely towards the door. "I will go with him. May I question our prisoner?" He suppressed a grim smile. "I speak Arabic 'jib-jab', and it will unnerve him that I will be able to sit in the dark, yet be at ease and able to see as clearly as in daylight. And it is rare for a human to not give answers to the questions Night-Walkers ask."

That all made sense, but remembering his annoyance on the moors, Jesamiah answered with a caveat. "As long as you don't cut his throat before he has chance to answer."

Affronted, Maha'dun stood straight and proud. "I had no reason to question that robber. He clearly had no knowledge of where the missing bone-box was, and I knew who he was, who had sent him, and why."

Jesamiah raised an eyebrow, refrained from asking why the fokken hell Maha'dun had not divulged this before now. Instead, he retorted, "Then maybe you would be good enough to tell me—but not now. I have more pressing things on my mind."

Left alone, he wondered whether to try to free Calderón's body, decided against. To what point? He pulled a ring from Calderón's left hand and slipped it onto his own finger, on his right hand. It nestled there as if that was where it belonged. A gold signet ring bearing the Calderón family crest: an oak leaf and an acorn. His mother had possessed one just like it, had given it to him once, long ago. It was at the bottom of the sea somewhere now. He figured that as the eldest male member of the family, he should take this one and give it to Calderón's son when he found him.

The irony that he was now looking for two missing boys—no three, there was Thomas as well—did not escape him.

* * *

It did not take long for a few of the crew to return to *Sea Witch*, fetch what was needed, row back, then set the kegs in strategic places and fix lengths of fuses. Finch and young Jasper had stayed behind to wrap Rue's remains and had carried him to one of their other boats. For him alone would there be a burial at sea, the one comfort, he was now reunited for eternity with his beloved Pamela.

Sick to his stomach for the loss of his dearest friend and helpmeet, Jesamiah swallowed hard. Now was not the time to grieve; his anxiety for Tiola overstepped all other emotion, his fear for her making it hard to breathe. The dead were dead, there was nothing he could do about that, but Tiola, and the children—for there was not one child's body among the scattered corpses—may still be alive. That, he could do something about.

Jesamiah took another glance around the bloodied entrance lobby, the opulent grandeur marred by the carnage.

"Right, that's it," Jesamiah declared as he blew a slow match into life. "Off to the boats and *Sea Witch*. We will be sailing hard and sailing fast. I am going after this Yakub Pasha. He has got my wife and young Thomas, a member of my crew. I want them back." Grim, added, "And there is a debt to be paid for the dead."

He looked carefully at every man present. "I am going to hunt the bastard down, and I am going to kill him and every last one of the scum who sail with him."

A few nods; words of agreement.

Jesamiah looked again, one by one, at the assembled, sombre-faced crew. "To catch a pirate, you need to think like a pirate. I am going back on the account; nothing, no one, is going to get in my way. We've enough ammunition for what we need; and if not sufficient, we'll get it from whatever ship we meet."

"We're at war. Taking from the Spanish will be of no consequence to anyone—except the Spanish—but what," Richie Tearle queried, "do we do if we meet with English, or French?"

Walking up to him, Jesamiah stared at him eye to eye. "I ain't fightin' that war. I'm fightin' a war of my own. We take what we need if we need it, and I don't care who we take it from." He stepped back, surveyed his men. "If you don't want to join me, you're free to walk back to town. Your choice."

There were a few murmurs, a couple of waverers, but only seven elected to stay behind, Perkiss among them, and Ascham Doone.

Before he bent to touch the slow match to the length of splayed fuse lines, Jesamiah said to Doone, "So you don't fancy a fight? And you have given up trying to kill me?"

"I did not envision this fight, no, and believe me, Acorne, if I had been trying to kill you, I would have succeeded. I was sent to do business here, business that is now of no consequence. I was, I admit, ordered to keep eye on you, for there are those of us who want that casket. Alas, the Maha'dun creature informs me the wretched thing is not here in Spain. I am not sure whether to believe him, but no, I will not sail further with you under a black flag. I have too much to lose and not enough to gain, I therefore regard my assignment as fulfilled. I make no secret that I would rather have you dead because I despise you for what you are and for the threat you pose, but Sir Harley wants you to work for him, so you are to remain alive. Until you are of no use, that is, or I take his place as King's Spymaster."

Jesamiah laughed, derisive. "You? You are naught but a boy!"

"I have the advantage of a youthful face which leads others to believe me to be so; it is a most useful distraction on occasion, but I am barely younger than you in months and several years older in intelligence. I have studied law and I intend to inherit Harley's position now the other possible contender is no longer a threat to me."

"And who might that have been? Your rotten-to-the-core father? No, don't answer, I don't want to know." Jesamiah lit the fuse, started walking to the door. They had ten minutes before the whole place blew up. "You would be advised to leave Spain as soon as you can. I don't know how long it will be before word of this war will spread."

"I am no fool, Acorne. I have the money to take safe passage to Gibraltar. The Royal Navy will be there in force now it is our territory—the Dutch were damned stupid to cede it to us in 'thirteen. I shall be in England as soon as may be."

"When you get there, tell Harley he can stuff the offer of a job up his arse. I ain't interested."

"It will be my pleasure, Acorne," Doone removed his hat, gave a mocking bow, and beckoning the opted-out men to follow, walked briskly away.

* * *

"You are one of Yakub Pasha's men?" Maha'dun sat squatting on his heels, lazily smoking a cheroot, figuring there was no risk as there was no gunpowder down here and this lowliest place of the ship where the anchor cable was stowed was dark,

381

dank, stank, and had water aplenty sloshing about. He got no answer from the man bound by ropes and tied to a cable ring. He hadn't expected one.

Inhaling the tobacco deeply into his lungs and slowly releasing the smoke, Maha'dun mulled over a few things. The other ship that had been anchored in Calderón's harbour had been Yakub Pasha's. A pity they had not realised it then. Yakub Pasha had been talking to Ascham Doone. Did he work for Doone? Were the Doones involved in this slave trade of children? Was that how they made their money?

'If I had known...' Doone had said. Known what? Known what Yakub Pasha really was? What he was capable of doing?

On the reverse side of the coin, Ber'ell also knew Yakub Pasha very well, and he had stopped Maha'dun from killing him. Were they in this sordid business together? Were all three of them enmeshed in this spider's web of human misery?

Grinding out the cheroot stub, Maha'dun moved the single, somewhat feeble cow's horn lantern to one side, casting elongated eerie shadows across the confined space. Then he moved fast, leaping forward, his hand reaching out, grabbing at something that had attempted to scuttle away. Without even looking at the rat he broke its neck, tossed its twitching body onto the prisoner's lap.

"Your death will not be so quick," Maha'dun stated in Arabic, lighting another cheroot. "First I will break each of your toes and ankles. Then your legs and knees. After that I will twist your balls and cock off. By then you might have told me what I want to know. If you have not, I will prise out your eyes. None of this will kill you, and it will take me several hours, but I am going nowhere and neither are you, so we have plenty of time together, have we not?"

He smoked the cheroot without another word, then took a

sip of brandy from the bottle by his side. "Now," he leant forward to stub the butt out on the man's cheek, "it is my guess that you have no particular loyalty to your leader. I know Yakub Pasha. It was I who took his eye out and gave him that scar. You will, therefore, realise that I am the better and stronger of the two."

The man glowered back at Maha'dun, said nothing.

"I would guess," Maha'dun said, "that he has never endeared himself to you. I would say that he is a harsh taskmaster, there is no love between him and his crew. You all fear him for he is of the Devil's seed, is he not?

"So, shall we get started with some answers? Where is your ship sailing to?"

* * *

Maha'dun ambled up the ladder onto the quarterdeck, leant against the rail and lit a cheroot. There were a few early stars, the sky had clouded over; there would be rain before dawn. He blew a long stream of blue smoke into the air, watched it curl up and away and then watched Jesamiah standing, legs slightly spread, at the helm, his hands firm around the spokes, gentling his ship into keeping a steady course, his face grim, lips fixed into a taut, straight line. The pose, the stance, to one such as Maha'dun, was erotic.

A sail flapped slightly and Jesamiah nudged *Sea Witch* to starboard, glanced at the compass in the dimly lit binnacle box, readjusted the helm slightly. The wake frothing behind them was as straight as an arrow flight.

"Well?" he asked, unaware of Maha'dun's private thoughts and not taking his gaze from his line of sight straight ahead.

Maha'dun tossed the half-smoked cheroot into the water. "Have you heard any word from Tiola?"

Jesamiah shook his head, dared not make a verbal answer for Maha'dun would hear the choke of desperation.

"Neither have I."

Tempted to retort that if he himself had not heard, then why would Maha'dun, Jesamiah bit the sarcasm back. He had enough things on his mind without picking a fight with this night creature.

A minute dragged by. Another. Maha'dun moved to stand beside Jesamiah, tentatively put his left hand on one of the helm's spokes. "It looks easy to steer, but I would hazard that, like making love well, perhaps it is not?"

With a slight nod of his head Jesamiah stepped aside, indicated that Maha'dun was to take the helm. "Be my guest, Nightm'n."

Astonished that he was being permitted this privilege, Maha'dun grasped the spokes with both hands and the ship began to turn to the right, causing the sails to flap and the few men on deck to stare in confused astonishment towards the quarterdeck.

Calmly, Jesamiah reached out and placing a hand over Maha'dun's right, brought *Sea Witch* back under control. "Go gently," he said, "treat her with the same respect you would a beautiful woman. Treat her harsh and she'll kick and buck like an unbroken filly."

Maha'dun relaxed his grip, the sensation of Jesamiah's hand on top of his tingling up his arm, down his spine and into his loins. The close presence, the pulsing throb of blood and his smell was almost overpowering—male sweat, tar, rum, sex...

"So?" Jesamiah asked. "You have been with him the entire day. How fares our guest?" His hand still on Maha'dun's, he brought the helm up a little.

"He was reluctant to talk, and I cannot be certain that he

eventually told me the truth."

"But he told you something?"

"The ship is the *Safeena Hamra*."

"The one that was in harbour."

"Yes. It is an Arabic name."

"I guessed that."

"But you do not speak Arabic?"

He was starting to try Jesamiah's patience. "I did not need to know her name to know she was a Moroccan vessel, and if I could speak Arabic, I would have asked the questions myself, not left it to an irritating clodpoll like you."

Did he mean that as an insult or was he being sarcastic? Maha'dun often found these human quirks hard to distinguish. "It means *Red Ship*; and Yakub Pasha is indeed the captain." Should he mention Doone and Ber'ell? Decided on not quite the truth. "I think I saw him, Yakub Pasha, talking to Doone. Maybe that stinking turd was telling the Arab about the children?"

Jesamiah compressed his lips, biting back anger. "According to young Benson, there was trouble along the Exmoor coast a while back," he said, mulling thoughts aloud. "Trouble with raiding Barbary slavers—the Doones intervened, executed prisoners. I wonder if they decided to employ this Yakub Pasha instead of hanging him?"

"My same conclusion."

"*Safeena Hamra. Saf...eena Ham...ra...* How would that be written in Arabic squiggle-words then? It would have been across her stern. I never bothered looking."

Maha'dun's turn to look blank.

Poking at the inside of his cheek with his tongue, Jesamiah regretted the question. He'd forgotten that this nightman could neither read nor write, although Arabic was not the same as civilised writing, was it? To hide embarrassment, said, "Bring the helm down a little: see how that mains'l is shivering along its edge? It should not do that. What else did he jib-jab then?"

Not seeing what the captain meant by the sail 'shivering', Maha'dun adjusted the helm slightly, which seemed to be the correct thing for Jesamiah grunted approval.

"He told me they had raided along the English coast, but when the weather changed, they headed back to Portugal and Spain instead."

"The wind's shifting. Keep it brushing your left cheek, not the back of your head—no that's your right, that's your left, and bend your knees a little. That's better. What else? I need to know where they are heading, Nightm'n. The ocean's a big place. Finding a needle in a haystack would be easier."

"He was reluctant, but when most of him was in bits he saw the wisdom of speaking up. He said Salé. They have an arrangement with a trader there. They provide the children, he provides the gold."

"You are sure?"

Maha'dun nodded. "If he spoke the truth, then I am sure."

Ruminating on the information, Jesamiah studied the sails, concentrated on the rising wind, the roll of the sea beneath *Sea Witch*'s keel; the rise and fall of the deck. Salé was on the western coast of Morocco, a long way off, and in waters he did not know too well. He had been to *ad-Dār al-Bayḍā*, the 'Place of the White House'—Casablanca. But that had been as a raw boy of fifteen, a foremast jack with a pirate crew under Malachias Taylor. Immaterial, if they were to catch this *Safeena Hamra* it had to be at sea. That was where Jesamiah's skills lay. Chasing a Prize and capturing it. All they had to do was find the ship. She could be anywhere. Heading straight for her home port, or maybe cruising the coast for opportunity of more easy-come trade? It all depended on how full her hold already was—no trader of this sort would finish a cruise half-empty.

Where was Tiola? Why in all the oceans wasn't she communicating with him? She could so easily tell him what he needed to know—unless she was... Jesamiah refused to think on that tack. There were other explanations! Weren't there?

He indicated that Maha'dun was to step away from the helm. As he took hold himself, he fancied he felt his ship ease a sigh of relief at being returned to his safekeeping.

"Yakub Pasha is a half-breed," Maha'dun said.

Jesamiah looked at him, one eyebrow raised in question. "Half-bred from what race? Spanish, Moroccan? Moorish, Turkish?"

"Man-witchish, Night-Walker. He is like both myself and your wife in breed, but not in deed or honour."

Sea Witch's bow rose and fell; a slight roll added into her movement, almost as if she were trying to impart a warning. Still uncertain how much Maha'dun knew about Tiola—and determined not to inadvertently fall into a possible trap and betray her—Jesamiah did not answer. He switched the subject back to their prisoner.

"Is our guest still alive?"

"No." Maha'dun licked his tongue across his lips. "I finished him off."

For the first time Jesamiah noticed the stains of fresh blood on the front of the nightman's white shirt and splashed onto his cheek and chin. "As soon as dawn gives us light, we'll make full sail. We've delayed long enough, but now we know where they are heading, we will find them."

"We do not need the dawn," Maha'dun said. "I can see perfectly clearly at night."

Jesamiah gazed at him, thoughtful, assessing.

"Tell me what I need to look out for?" Maha'dun waved vaguely at the ocean. "All I see is sea. What else is there?"

"The sea changing; bigger rollers, getting choppier—wilder. The weather shifting, clouds massing." Jesamiah pointed landward. "A few miles over there is the coast of Spain. If it can be seen I need to know. Are there any islands ahead—not everything is marked on my charts. Or another ship. If you see another ship I need to know."

"The *Safeena Hamra*?"

"Of course the *Safeena Hamra*, but anything else as well. We are at war, I don't want to tangle with anyone unless I have to."

Maha'dun looked doubtful. "How will I know the difference?"

"We'll worry about that if we come to it. Just shout if you see a ship."

"And from where is it best for me to observe?" The question was made on a half-breath—part excitement, part fear.

Jesamiah pointed upward to the top of the mainmast. "Up there."

A lurch of blood-rush. It looked very high up there. Did he want to go? "I am not sure how I get there?"

"I'll take you up. And fetch you down again come dawn."

To sail fast at night, although in the open ocean, was chancy. But there were times when chance, for a pirate, had to be risked.

Climbing the mast nearly caused Maha'dun to empty his bowels and stomach simultaneously—yet with each step up the rigging, going slowly hand over hand, higher and higher, his sense of achievement and exultation soared. Jesamiah was right behind him, his firm grip guiding where he was to put his feet on the weather shrouds—he was not overly impressed by that term; a shroud reminded him too much of funeral garb—and then the ratlines. Less than halfway up he found himself breathing heavily. Jesamiah, by contrast, was barely puffed. Unaware of the effect of tobacco on his lungs, Maha'dun put the breathlessness down to exhilaration and excitement.

At a difficult bit, where they had to swing out and round the futtock shrouds—why did they have such odd names for these things?—Jesamiah said there was an easier way if Maha'dun preferred.

"Is that where you would go?" Maha'dun asked.

Jesamiah shook his head.

"Then we go the proper way." Bravado was sometimes a stupid companion, Maha'dun realised as he felt the full weight of his body on his clinging fingers, and dared not—dared not—look down at the men way, way, below.

Jesamiah made the manoeuvre with ease, apparently oblivious to the sails billowing, filling and emptying as the wind changed its mind whether to blow or not. The noise up here was incredible! The cracking of the canvas, the groaning stays, the creaking and squeaking yards, the wind howling in Maha'dun's ears and the rigging sounding like several dozen scalded cats all yowling at once. When they reached the wooden platform near the top, he slumped against the solid mast, silently reciting a catechism to *not look down, don't look down.* It was a long, long, way to fall...

The corkscrew motion made him dizzy, sweeping him up, round, down, but again it did not seem to affect Jesamiah who had calmly straddled one of the poles—yards—not even bothering to hold on.

"Hook your arm and leg round that stay," Jesamiah

suggested, "it'll hold you firm and support your balance: that's it, aye, like that."

The darkness was all enveloping up here, apart from the few stars which peeped occasionally through rents in the clouds, and a luminescent bank of cloud-covered sky low down where a crescent moon was hiding.

Satisfied that Maha'dun knew what to look out for, Jesamiah left him to stand watch on his own. "I'm for some shut-eye," he said, starting his downward descent, "from tomorrow I might not get much chance."

Maha'dun dared, just once, to look down. Figured it was safer to watch the sky.

Alone, the inner feelings almost burst like an erupting volcano. He wanted to sing, dance, prance and jiggle; to shout and shout to the world. Happiness in his life had been a rare and treasured thing. He had known it with Tiola long ago, but this... this unequivocal freedom was elation beyond his wildest hopes and dreams. He settled himself and practised his whistling. He thought someone had said it was bad luck to whistle on deck, but then he wasn't on deck, was he? And his whistling was not very good anyway.

* * *

When Jesamiah climbed all the way up again, just before dawn pranced over the horizon, Maha'dun concealed a growing unease that had wiped away the earlier good feelings. How long would it take to get down again? Would he be quick enough to avoid the sunrise—the glare would be bad up here. He would fry, it had not occurred to him to bring his day-shelter clothing. But as Jesamiah's head had appeared, followed by the rest of his body, the fears evaporated.

"See anything?"

"Nothing," Maha'dun admitted, not mentioning that three times he had forgotten to look. "Sea, stars, the moon and clouds. Something startled a flock of gulls over that way." He pointed eastward.

"That's the Spanish coast, did you not see it?"

Maha'dun squinted, studied the white-capped expanse of sea. Lied. "Of course I did."

"No ships?"

Maha'dun shook his head. No ships. Well, not that he recalled. There had been lights, tiny ones bobbing against the black sea, but they were behind them, not ahead, so it wouldn't be this red ship, would it? Should he mention them, though?

Jesamiah was scanning the brightening horizon to the north. Was that the glimpse of a topsail? He couldn't be certain, cursed beneath his breath for not fetching up his telescope. "Can you see anything over there?"

"What am I looking for?"

"A ship."

Studying the shades of light and dark, the moving shapes, the shifting greys and blacks, Maha'dun shook his head. "I cannot see a ship."

Satisfied that the brief glimpse had been nothing more than imagination, Jesamiah said, "You were going to tell me about those men."

Maha'dun frowned. "What men?"

"On the moor."

"Oh. Those men."

"Well?"

"There is nothing to tell."

"I think there is."

Maha'dun scratched his nose. "They were looking for the bone-box. They thought you had it."

"That much I have worked out for myself. Who were they working for?"

"How should I know?" Maha'dun's lie did not sound very convincing, even to his own ears.

"You seem to know everything else."

"I do not!"

Maha'dun, Jesamiah had discovered, could be stubbornly obtuse when he wanted to be. He carried on scanning the sweep of the horizon. Peering through the rising grey of an incoming fog, looking for any telltale sign of a sail.

"Why don't you ask him yourself, if you are so desperate to know?"

Jesamiah stared at Maha'dun. Finally, very slowly, very patiently; "Would you mind enlightening me?"

Maha'dun's turn to look up and stare, uncomprehending. "The man who galloped away, he is one of your crew."

Silence while Jesamiah tried to decide whether to stay calm or lose his temper and hurl this irritating imbecile into the sea. "What?"

"The third man on the moor. He is one of your crew. I thought you knew."

The temper won. Jesamiah grabbed Maha'dun's coat lapels and shook him. "How the fok could I have known? Why the bloody hell did you not tell me this earlier? I've been ignorant of a man who sodding tried to kill me, who probably knows who killed 'Cesca—who possibly killed her himself... is aboard *my* ship and you say bloody fok all?"

"He didn't."

"Didn't bloody what!" Jesamiah's voice had risen to full, furious bellow.

"Did not kill the English woman with the Spanish name. His orders were—are—to find the bone-box she had. He will not, of course, because Tiola and I found it long ago hidden in a secret compartment in the lady's travelling chest. I burnt it in Finch's cooking fire."

"So," the words came slow, clear, precise; "who is this man?"

"Richie Tearle. And would you mind if we finish this conversation later? The dawn's dawning..."

The responding frown conveyed much, but to Maha'dun's relief, going down proved much easier. Jesamiah showed him how to swing out, grab hold of the taut, sloping backstay and, hand over hand, slither to the deck. When their feet touched down the crew gave a cheer. Maha'dun bowed regally, enjoying the acknowledgement of his prowess, then hastily scuttled below to his quarters. Almost, he had forgotten the reason why they were here, what their mission was. And he was aware that Captain Acorne was cross with him, though why was beyond him.

He stretched out on his bed, mused on how fond he had become of this small, and somewhat cramped below deck world of his. He listened to the sounds of the sea gurgling past the hull, the overhead tramp of feet, the shouts, the laughter of the men. Heard Jesamiah's voice calling a command. Maha'dun pulled a blanket over himself, slept with a smile wrinkling the corners of his mouth. Despite the seriousness of the situation and his worry for Tiola, he could not but feel contentment for this new, exhilarating, life.

Chapter Thirty-Two

She was on a ship, that much Tiola realised for the motion and the sounds—the rush of water beyond the bulkhead, the timbers creaking, the constant mithering of the wind through overhead rigging—were unmistakable. She gathered the courage to open her eyes, as well that she was lying down for the ache whirling around her head would have toppled her. She hastily shut her eyes again. The dizziness did not cease but at least it was more bearable. She was aware that it was pitch dark, and with people packed in like herrings, guessed this was the hold of a slave ship. How many were crammed in and to where they sailed was a different matter.

A hand squeezed hers. She tightened her fingers a little, acknowledging the attempt at communication.

"Mistress Tiola? Please, wake up!"

Thomas, young Thomas Benson, his voice strained, taut with fear.

She tightened her fingers again to let him know she had heard, but she could not open her eyes. Her head where something had struck her pounded too much, ached too much. Easier, much easier, to sleep...

The dreams came. Mixed-up nonsense dreams, crowing and crowding with the headache which pounded and pounded, even in her sleep. Cackling laughter and leering faces. Behind and beneath, almost buried, a persistent voice calling her name but it was quieter, hard to be heard.

"Please? Please wake up!"

Tiola lay still, not daring to move, for even to open her eyes caused nausea to churn into her throat, but by mid-afternoon at least the headache was easing. If she were to lay quiet, breathe slow and calm, it would pass, although there was something important to do. If only she could remember what it was.

"Please wake up! Please!"

The scared boy had been pleading for many hours. Tiola had heard him from far off, the clouding fog invading her mind, drowning it out. But she could not sleep forever, no matter how much she wanted to. She opened her eyes to see his face bending close, listening for her breathing. Startled, he jerked backwards, his shed tears glistening in the faint grey-dim shafts of light filtering down from above.

"Thomas?"

"Aye, it be me! Oh, Mistress Tiola, please, wake up now; you are needed. We're all so frightened and I do not know what to do."

She took a short while to work out exactly where she was and what had happened... Dark. Stinking. Moving. They were aboard a ship. She sat up, Thomas and another younger boy on her other side helping her. Donréal, the lad who had become firm friends with Thomas. Tears were streaking his cheeks too. She was confined in a ship's hold with many others and it stank of vomit, urine and faeces. The atmosphere was as taut as a wire, with no sound beyond the squeak and scrabble of rats, the scurry of water pouring past the outer side of the hull, the creak of the ship, the thudding of feet overhead and the silent scream of suppressed terror.

"How did we get here?" she asked, brushing the back of her hand across her forehead. She scratched at something crusty, realised it was dried blood. She had taken quite a blow—when? Where? How?

"It's a ship," Thomas answered, his quiet voice quavering. "A slave ship. We are prisoners."

"Kidnapped," Donréal corrected, speaking in very good English, but in a muted whisper.

Tiola's mind was clearing, the memory hurtled back. She had been with the old lady, a crotchety besom because of her many aches, pains and fear of death. Tiola had been pleased that she had actually made the old lady laugh. And then there had been shouting with shooting and fighting downstairs. The screaming had followed and the wicked cries of death. She remembered running to the door, on the threshold meeting a big, one-eyed man with a scarred face and a snarled expression. Remembered her horror and frozen fear at their mutual, startled, recognition. Remembered his raised arm and, vaguely, the crumping sound as the butt of his pistol had slammed into her temple.

Thomas threw his arms around her in a desperate hug, burying his face in her neck and hair, most of which was hanging loose and straggled, escaped from its pins and clips.

"I am so frightened," he sobbed, the sound muffled against her shoulder. "They killed them, I saw them kill them!" His voice was rising, there came agitated movement in the hold, whispers and shuffling.

She stroked his hair, held him as closely to her, secure, comforting, suppressing her own rising fear. "Who, darling?

Who did they kill?" Did she really want to hear an answer?

"Rue. Your brother. All the men. And my dogs, they killed my dogs!" The sobs increased.

A few frightened cries in various languages—English, Spanish, Portuguese, Spanish—of "Sssh!" and "Be quiet!" rippled through the hold.

No, she did not want to hear, but hear she must. Nor could she weep or show distress; these children needed the solidity of confident strength.

It was hard, but she said, "They are all safe now. Gone to where there are sun-filled skies. Rue is with Pamela; they are walking, hand in hand together, the dogs running at their side through a green meadow."

Cuffing his nose, Thomas looked up at her and wiped his eyes. "You see them?"

Tiola nodded. "As clearly as I see you. They are happy, do not grieve for them."

Biting his lip, Donréal looked doubtful. "The nuns who teach me say it is blasphemy to talk of such things."

"Is it blasphemy to give comfort?" Tiola rebuked gently.

Donréal shook his head, supposed not. "I am not sure about the dogs in Heaven."

"They are God's creatures," Thomas stated with firm finality. "I don't suppose your nuns had dogs as pets so they perhaps would not know?"

That made sense. Donréal nodded acceptance.

Despite her words, grief was almost bursting Tiola's heart. Rue, dear, dear, Rue. Her brother... What of Calderón and his wife? The old lady? She closed her eyes, beyond hearing the fighting and opening that door could not remember anything. They were all bound to be dead, but she hoped, prayed, they had not suffered bad deaths.

The pale light was filtering down through the criss-cross wood of the overhead hatch, Tiola looked around, aghast that the hold was crammed with children. "How many of you are here?" she exclaimed, her words eliciting a ripple of movement, a few more subdued admonishments of, "Ssh!"

"What? What is this!" she demanded, her anger growing, she could see pale, frightened, tear-streaked faces turned towards her, girls, boys; bedraggled, dishevelled, more than a few nearer the hatch shivering, their clothes damp. Water sloshed about on the floor. More than sixty or seventy scared little faces.

"We must be quiet," Donréal explained. "If we make any noise, they"—he pointed upward—"dowse us with buckets of seawater."

"This is disgraceful!" she hissed.

"I want to go home," a girl of about nine years of age murmured, choking back her sobs. "I think they killed my ma and pa." She spoke in English, a distinct Cornish accent.

"Where are you all from?" Tiola demanded, her expression as fierce as her words.

"All over," Thomas answered when no one else spoke. "Dorsetshire, Devon, Cornwall and Spain." He gulped his own tears, looked up, visibly trembling as the hatch above opened, the silhouette of a man appearing against the greyness beyond, and Tiola's fear returned shuddering like creeping ice through her body to her very soul. Her breathing quickened, her head swam, nausea choked into her mouth. She reached for Donréal's hand, clasped it, her other arm tightening around Thomas as if their lives depended on it. With determined effort she slowed her breath, relaxed her muscles and limbs as she forced herself to look up at the man peering down at them. You could not fight fear with fear, you had to face it. And face it she would have to, for her own sake and that of these poor children.

The children cowered away as the hatch lifted and grey light seeped downward. Covering their faces and heads, a few uttered muffled screams. Girls mostly, a few boys. All here for one reason. Tiola was the only adult, but then, she was here for a completely different reason. One girl, less afraid, pushed forward and held her arms up to the man. Spoke in Portuguese. "Please! We want food. I will trade you what I can offer for food!"

The man leant into the open hatchway, leered at her. In Arabic, answered crudely with a derisive laugh, "Your pimple tits and un-bushed cunny have no worth for us if your slit is used!" Perhaps it was fortunate that the girl did not understand his crudity.

He peered further in, pointed directly at Tiola and beckoned. "You. The captain orders you to come."

Thomas, not understanding the words but interpreting the gestures, moved immediately in front of her, fists bunched, his friend Donréal at his side equally as defensive. "You leave her alone, you bloomin' pudding pie, lard-stuffed, offal meat turnip!"

In other circumstances, Tiola would have smiled. As cuss words went, Thomas's repertoire was somewhat tame. Donréal added something more elaborately rude in Spanish; she appreciated the sentiment, but not their willingness to put themselves in danger on her account.

"Thank you, boys, but I will be all right." She winked at Thomas as she stepped past, whispered, "If we are to get out of here, someone needs to be up there." She rolled her eyes, indicating the deck above. "Your task, my young and gallant friend, is to keep these frightened souls calm. It is unpleasant down here, but you are only of value to the men who captured us if you are alive and unharmed. Remember that." She grasped Thomas's arm, "Whatever happens, remember it."

The guilt at getting out of that stinking, fear-clogged hold weighed heavy on Tiola's conscience as she walked slowly, with dignity and grace across the fog-shrouded open deck towards the quarterdeck where she could see a man standing, legs straddled, arms folded. His black cloak over the white ankle-length thobe, billowing about him, adding to the impression of size and importance. A red-and-white headscarf pulled close about his face hid all but his eye—one eye and an empty eye socket alongside the tip of a livid scar. The last time she had seen him... She shoved aside the memory, took a deep breath and placed her foot on the first step of the companionway ladder. She looked straight ahead, but had been able to glimpse the distant coast occasionally visible through banks of rolling fog. The ship was too far out for her to make sense of any landmarks, and she had to be careful for if he saw or encroached into her mind, all hope of rescue would be lost. The thought that he had not already blocked her mind was a puzzle. Perhaps he was testing her? A baited trap? She had to ensure he had no inkling whatsoever of Jesamiah or *Sea Witch*. While he considered himself not to be under threat, there was every chance of a rescue. One doubt, one suspicion, and lifelong slavery would be the fate for those children below. Not for Tiola. She would be dead or dying. He would not let her live— he had already slain her once because she had defied him, and this time there was no granddaughter's soul for her to transpose into. This thickening fog-shrouded spring afternoon could be her last. She was halfway up the ladder. A few more steps and she would be standing before him. Sickness churned in her stomach, she wanted to scream, to turn around, run...

She put her foot on the next step up. ~ *Maha'dun? Maha'dun! I am aboard a ship with red sails. We are following the coast south.* ~

She stepped onto the quarterdeck, looked direct into the man's single eye. Did he expect her to fall to her knees? Grovel at his feet? Built as strong as a bull, as dangerous as a snake and as cold and cruel as an unmarked grave, the only man in all her many reincarnated lives whom Tiola feared stared back at her.

Yakub Pasha. The Carver.

~ *Maha'dun. He is here. Find a boat; find me.* ~

"So, the slave who faked the enjoyment of pleasuring me managed to survive the fire?"

Yakub Pasha's insult fell on closed ears. Tiola had heard it all before, and words only hurt if the hearer let them.

"You know full well I did not. There are many ways you and I can cheat death, Yakub, but burning is not one of them. Because of you I suffered, I died. But you miscalculated; my daughter was with child—you did not know I had a daughter? I was a slave within your harem for eighteen years, yet you knew nothing of me, except what I was—am—a healer of the White Craft. When you raided our village and captured me, she was but a babe in arms; her father's mother raised her to become a fine woman. I transposed and lived again within the new life of my granddaughter, and have lived on through other daughters of daughters."

"Of course I knew," he snapped, but she could tell he was lying.

Her confidence grew. Despite his size and arrogance, he was not the powerful man she had once known, the man who for all those years had controlled her through fear. Fear, not for herself but for his threat of punishment to others. Only once had she used her Craft against him, back then in that dark time. To punish her he had thrown a living six-month-old girl-child to his hunting dogs. His power, fuelled by the malevolence of the Dark, had overruled hers and she had never dared use her Craft against him again, not even as the flames had licked around her feet and spread up her naked body.

"Time has not been good to you, Yakub," she said. "I can see you are shrivelling inside. You are dying." She bit back an urge to laugh. "Your seed is dead, you have not sired sons for many, many years, and because you have no male line, your gift of reincarnation has deserted you. All you have left is your Night-Walker half-breeding. Which also appears to be failing you."

Her eyes widened with sudden-come realisation, contempt and disgust rising within her. "The women of your harem? The ones I tended in childbirth? Your loathsome counsellors and officers sired all their children!" She covered her mouth with her hand, momentarily stunned, the past rushing back into her memory. "You watched as they repeatedly raped us, week after week, month after month, believing your foul story that violation strengthened the womb, that your generosity was a reward for their loyalty."

Another realisation, Tiola's face crumpled into horrified disbelief. "You thought I knew that not one of those children was of your own siring! Back then, you thought I knew; that is why you had me killed!"

One of his men had been sidling nearer, lust crimsoning his face. He came closer to Tiola, reached out to touch her black hair. Yakub Pasha roared anger and with great bear-paws grasped the man by the scruff of the neck and, ignoring the rapid apologetic plea, hauled him to the rail and with no effort, no concern or compassion, tipped him over the side into the fog. The scream ended with a splash, and other men nearby hurriedly moved away to set about their work.

"Was that necessary?" Tiola challenged.

"You condemned him. Your presence provoked him."

"You brought me aboard, and all of your men are condemned. There is nothing but a noose awaiting them. The firepit for you. Let the children go. Selling innocents into slavery is beneath even your depravations."

He sneered a contemptuous answer. "But I send those dear children to loving homes where they are cherished and valued."

Tiola snorted disdain. "Until their bellies swell with pregnancy, they develop the pox, or lose the charm of childhood."

"What is that to me?" Yakub Pasha grasped her chin between his fingers, gave her face an aggressive shake. "You always were insolent. I recall having to beat you senseless, both before and after I had done with you. As I will beat you again if you use your Craft against me, madam, and I advise you to recall the punishment for when you attempted to use it once before." With his other hand he stroked a bone-thin finger down her cheek, his touch like that of an eviscerated corpse. "For every time you attempt to use your witchcraft, bitch, one of those children in my hold will feed the fishes. Do you understand me?"

Tiola stared back at him, nodded, unable to speak. His words were no idle threat. Her only viable defence was to not show fear, for he pounced on weakness as a cat would on an injured bird.

She found the courage to speak: "If you harm me, you will be the one to regret, Yakub. Your power was once great, but it is fading." She indicated the scar and the empty eye socket. "Maha'dun Night-Walker gave you that disfigurement, yet it has not healed. The Night-Walkers, you and I, and those few left of our kind, can repair wounds and injuries within a few days, weeks at the most. You cannot regrow the eye, but your skin and the scar should have healed. There is a greater power than you possess at work here, Yakub. Maybe your nemesis is just beyond that horizon?" She risked a smile, an expression of superiority. "Or maybe you are looking at her?"

Releasing her chin Yakub Pasha roared laughter. "You always did amuse me, that was why I kept you alive so long."

"Maha'dun is out there, ready to finish what he started," she said. He had kept her alive for her healing and midwifery skills, no other reason.

Yakub laughed the louder. "He failed before, and he has to find me first." He indicated the ship, the fog and the daylight. "In case you have not noticed, we are at sea and it is not night, both of which the Night-Walkers—unless half-bred like myself —do not tolerate."

"There are many," she retorted, "who make the mistake of underestimating Maha'dun."

Tired of her insolence, Yakub struck out, catching a blow to Tiola's face that hurled her to the ground and brought immediate bruising to her cheek.

Grasping her arm, he dragged her to her feet, thrust her towards two of the men, his face, whole being, a corruption of malicious spite. "Take her to my cabin and do what you will— pass word to the others; but there is to be no squabbling and I do not want her dead. That doing will be my prerogative."

* * *

Maha'dun stretched out on his bed, legs crossed at the ankles, arms folded behind his head. Padded with blankets and several luxurious furs he had acquired in Jersey, it was an acceptable bed, if somewhat narrow. Lovemaking, he had often thought during the secluded hours alone, would be quite challenging. Another reverie: how did Jesamiah make love to Tiola in that box-bed of theirs? How would you get purchase enough when you needed to, with it swinging and bumping about? Perhaps they did it on the floor, or that long bench that ran along under the rear windows... stern. *Stern*, not rear.

The day had been long—he guessed it must be mid-afternoon—desperately wanted to smoke, dared not, so reached for the brandy bottle instead. He had slept well from the instant his head had touched the pillow, and elation was still coursing through every fibre of his being. He hated this having to hide away once dawn came, especially when there were exciting things happening. The feeling of being left out felt as cumbersome as that Greek fellow in the stories carrying the world on his shoulders. What was his name? Hecalese? Itlas? Zorba? But sleep was essential, and surely if the captain had sighted the red ship, he would have called him? Wouldn't he?

Fully rested, he sat up, tried reading the book Tiola had given him. Despite the enticement of its somewhat erotic content, he found the squiggly words on the pages to be irritatingly uncooperative. They danced about so! If only they would stay still, he might be able to figure their meaning. Exasperated, he flung the book aside, lay back and dozed.

He could hear calls and shouts from above. They were furring sails. No, 'furling in the bunt', Jesamiah had said, which, if he had understood right, meant scrunching and tying up the great canvas sails beneath the poles—the yards. Why they could not just say 'fold the sails up' he had not dared ask.

He almost missed the other voice because he was listening to what was happening on deck.

~ Maha'dun? Maha'dun! I am aboard a ship with red

sails… ~

"Tiola? Tiola is that you?"

~ …find a boat, find me! ~

Her voice; shot through with abject fear. He had never known her to be frightened before, not of anything or anyone—except for *him*. Yakub Pasha. Half Night-Walker, half witch, he had transposed through the male line—grandfather to grandson—but long, long ago, embraced the dark side of Craft for his own gain of power and greed, and had survived through the millennia by lies, deceit, cunning and betrayal. Yakub Pasha; the one solely responsible for the deaths of ten Night-Walkers, despite his own kinship, but then he had procured the execution of many witches too—any of those who had attempted to stop him.

Is that, Maha'dun wondered, *why Ber'ell is in league with him? To protect his own skin?* He puffed his cheeks, expelled a slow breath. He could not see Ber'ell bowing so low to anyone, especially not a half-breed.

What did Tiola mean, *"Find a boat, find me"*? Surely she knew Jesamiah would be giving chase in *Sea Witch*? Loitering was not going to achieve anything beyond puzzling more unanswerable questions and fuelling rising anger. Was not going to help find her. Maha'dun got up, dressed himself in the Arab regalia—it was proving its worth and did not look out of place, apart from the leather gloves and a kerchief bound across his face. Hurrying from the below-deck gloom, he made his way to Jesamiah's cabin, found him partially dressed, standing before a mirror, shaving.

Waiting just inside the door, Maha'dun studied Jesamiah's upper torso. He could see why Tiola was attracted to him: tall, dark-haired; lean, muscular. Handsome.

"If you are coming in, then come in and shut the door. If

not, shut the door and bugger off," Jesamiah said to the reflection in the mirror.

Maha'dun smiled, entered the cabin, flourished his hand. "I could give you a closer shave. My knives are pristine sharp."

"If you think I'm letting you anywhere near my throat with a razor, you can think again."

"Suit yourself." Sniffing, feigning effrontery, Maha'dun sat in the nearest chair.

"Pass me that towel, will you?"

Rising again, Maha'dun complied, indicating the lines of puckered skin across Jesamiah's bare back, a bullet wound to his shoulder and another, vicious-looking white-streaked scar along the soft flesh of his inner arm, asked; "Where did you get those?"

"A flogging and a fall through a window. These," Jesamiah indicated two more wounds, "I found myself on the wrong end of a pistol barrel."

"Any more that are not on show?" Maha'dun added with a grin.

"That's for me to know and you not to find out," Jesamiah answered as he wiped the residue of Tiola's best Castile soap from his face and reached for a shirt that lay over the back of a chair. The nightman's remarks unnerved him. He had never had any interest in bumboy mollies—and yet, there was something magnetically attractive about Maha'dun's flawless beauty... Jesamiah cleared his throat. "So, what can I do for you?"

Suddenly, Maha'dun was reluctant to mention that Tiola had contacted him. What if Jesamiah took it wrong? Instead he queried: "Any sign of our prey? The *Safeena Hamra*?"

Jesamiah shook his head. "No, and with this fog that's rolled in we'll be lucky to see even the other end of our own ship." He pointed to the stern windows, Maha'dun only now noticing that there was nothing to see beyond them except blanketing greyness.

"Is that why we're not moving very fast?" It suddenly occurred to him, also, that there was no pitch, toss or roll, no crack or thunder of the sails.

"It is. Unless we get out and push."

Looking doubtful, Maha'dun frowned. "Can we do that?"

"What?"

"Push?"

Jesamiah laughed as he put on his waistcoat. "No, I'm pulling your leg. We could tow her, but it is not worth the effort, we'd not get far. We wait for it to thin or lift."

"But we have to find Tiola and those children."

"That we do, but assuming they are not too far away, we could easily sail right past them."

A deep breath. Out with it. "They are following the coast south-west."

Jesamiah regarded him solemnly. "And you know this... how?"

Biting his lip, Maha'dun dared not look Jesamiah in the eye. He knew he would get angry again. "Tiola's just told me."

Jesamiah crossed the cabin, put his coat on. Picked up his hat. "She told you?"

Maha'dun nodded.

"She told you. Not me?"

Raising his gaze to meet Jesamiah's, all Maha'dun could do was explain as best he could. "Yakub Pasha is half like me, half like Tiola, only he does not follow the laws of her White Craft. He is known to us as The Carver because he had the Night-Walkers tortured and killed, then made the bone-boxes we seek from their remains." Maha'dun paused. How much did

Jesamiah Acorne know about Tiola and her past?

"Spit it out," Jesamiah snapped. There were too many secrets, too many untolds and withhelds.

"Many, many years ago, Tiola had a different life, a different existence." Maha'dun lowered his voice, reluctant to say the next too loud as if speaking it quietly would make the telling easier, "Belonged to another man."

Jesamiah's fists clenched.

Hastily, louder, Maha'dun blurted: "I know what you are thinking! No, not me; she was Yakub Pasha's slave. She was with him many years, serving as midwife to his harem. Something happened and he denounced her as a witch to the Inquisition." Tears filled Maha'dun's eyes. "She had tried to save those of my kind from that wicked death. She freed one only, a female called Cara'mina." He spread his hands in a gesture of hopelessness. "Cara'mina went mad. She never forgave Tiola for rescuing her but not her partner, she had been attempting revenge ever since."

"What happened to her?" Jesamiah asked quietly.

Did he answer with the truth? "I thought it was Cara'mina who killed the English woman with the Spanish name, but it was not. I think Ascham Doone was behind that. He had the scent of her blood on him, although if he had touched her body the blood could have stained him. He was there, after all."

The fists clenched tighter. "And you only think to tell me this now?"

Maha'dun raised his chin, defiant. "Tiola ordered me to remain silent. She wanted no risk of you hanging for murder, and it is only a thought." He hurried on before Jesamiah could make a scathing retort. "Tiola killed Cara'mina with that lightning strike, the night we left Devon."

That did rile Jesamiah; through gritted teeth he snarled,

"Tiola cannot, does not, kill."

"She does. She can. She killed her because Cara'mina killed that man Crawford thinking he was you, and then set Tawford Barton ablaze. Tiola could not permit her to endanger more innocents. Or you."

Digesting it all, questions buzzing, Jesamiah set them aside to say, "I will not believe Tiola is capable of killing, but that aside, I meant what happened to her, to Tiola?"

Another awkwardness to answer. Best to spit it out, as Jesamiah had said to do?

"The Spanish were not kind to witches. She burnt. Bound to a stake with no mercy of garrotting before the fire was lit. She burnt because that bastard, Yakub Pasha, ordered it."

* * *

From where Jesamiah stood, leaning against the taffrail, only the lower part of the mizzen and main rigging was visible; everything forward was shrouded in the wraith-binding of fog. He could almost fancy that the topmasts and spars had disappeared, spirited away by some mischievous demon. Not wanting to hear more from Maha'dun, feeling sick to his stomach at what he had already learned, Jesamiah had come up on deck. *Sea Witch* was moving, slowly, but the fog was moving with her, clinging like a form of ethereal weed to the spars, masts and rigging. Sounds were disorientated and distorted. They were hemmed in, as if a huge translucent net had been tossed over them. It was cold, wet and dreary, the one hope, that the *Safeena Hamra* was similarly fog-bound.

Jesamiah looked down at their wake, not much to see, they were not moving fast enough to create one, and the white froth that was there disappeared after a few yards into the yawning mouth of the greyness as if a monster were following, gobbling the sea up, inch by slow inch.

A man was walking towards him, the fog writhing about his feet making it look as if he were wading through something solid. Richie Tearle stopped, made a form of a salute by raising his right hand in the direction of his forehead, not quite making the actual connection.

"You wanted to see me, sir?"

"I did." Jesamiah shifted slightly, leant back with both elbows along the top of the rail. "I want to know why you and your friends tried to kill me."

To the man's credit the look of stark surprise appeared to be genuine.

"It's no good lookin' innocent. You did not run away quick enough. Maha'dun recognised you."

Tearle spread his hands wide. "I... I... I protest strongly, Captain!"

"Protest all you like, it will not make any difference. Of the two of you I believe Maha'dun and the evidence of my own experience. You and two others ambushed our coach. The driver was shot dead, I was threatened. Fortunate for me, your companions made piss-poor highwaymen."

"I did not run away, sir. Not in the sense you mean. I wanted nothing more to do with those two imbeciles. Our orders were to follow you and keep watch. If able, obtain a berth aboard your ship—which I managed to do. Waving pistols about and shooting people were not our orders. The other two grew bored and greedy. They were convinced you had gold aboard the coach within the box we were supposed to be looking for. They decided to turn robber and take any spoils for themselves. None, they assumed, would be the wiser as Exmoor is notorious for thieves. Even if the main thieving family also works for the man who hired us."

"The Doones. And the man they work for might be…?"

"Aye, Doones," Tearle admitted. "Sir Ailie and Ascham. At least Winnard is now dead, one less of the buggers. I do not want to fall foul of that lot, though. Turn traitor to the Doones and you are a dead man. I wanted no part in robbery, neither. Admitted, I hung around for a while but when that first shot was fired, I hightailed it out of there."

"Quite the hero then, are you not?" Maha'dun interjected from a few yards away. "I do not believe a word of what this scum-butt is saying, Captain. Toss him into the sea for the liar he is."

Jesamiah scowled at Maha'dun. "Nightm'n, you have the most annoying habit of wanting to kill people before I have finished asking them questions!"

Maha'dun grinned beneath his protective scarf, then bowed respectfully. "Ask away, Captain, if you think this thieving liar will condescend to answer you with anything remotely near the truth."

"The man they work for?" Jesamiah repeated. "And your orders were…?"

Tearle answered readily enough. He was either very good at lying, with answers tailor-made, or was telling the truth. "I work for Harley, Earl of Oxford and Earl Mortimer. My orders were to find the box and watch your back, Captain. A task made easier now Doone and his lackey are no longer with us."

"Lackey?"

"Perkiss. He has served the Doones for many a year. Lousy little sod."

Jesamiah raised an eyebrow. He should have seen that one for himself.

"And you are not a lackey?" Maha'dun queried.

Defiant, his chin tilted upward, Tearle regarded Maha'dun, dressed in his Arab garb, eye to eye. "Have you ever seen me on the moors? Was I at Badgeworthy? I do not serve Doone, I serve Harley." He looked at Jesamiah. "If you have a mind to recollect, Captain, you would have seen me standing close to Perkiss in that court room. He was dressed in a monk's cowl—a pathetic amateur's disguise. The best way to hide yourself is dress plain, be natural and normal. No one notices the usual, only the unusual. Ascham Doone does not know I work for Harley, or that Harley has no intention of passing his especial status on to him."

He paused, could read the doubt on Jesamiah's face. "If it helps plead my case for the truth, it was Perkiss who murdered Señora Escudero, probably on Ascham Doone's orders. Doone had no intention of standing aside for a woman to take power from him. I was tailing Perkiss, I saw everything. The lady mistakenly thought he was aiming for you, Captain. She took the blade herself."

A little put out that his belief of the murderer being Doone himself was wrong, Maha'dun's nostrils were flaring, inhaling vague scents. "I think that is another lie. You killed her. You smell of her blood. It is faint, but you do smell of it."

Jesamiah looked at him sharply. Was this so?

Tearle shook his head, his face puckering into a frown. "I do not know how you make that out, it was a while ago now and I bathe, if infrequently, but I do. All the same, aye, I would. I helped put her into the cart that took her to Harley's residence. We had hopes she might have lived." He spread his hands again. "Alas…"

"We?"

"Captain Jennings and myself."

To believe him or not? Jesamiah glanced upward at the

suddenly revealed maintop, it was drawing quite well, the moisture-wet canvas shining in the grey, drab light, a faint yellowish hue playing over its expanse. The sun was shining somewhere above, and the fog was, in patches, lifting.

"Deck there," young Jasper's voice floated down from the hidden-again masthead, ghostly, as if coming from nowhere. "Sir! Ship to starboard!"

The *Safeena Hamra*, the *Red Ship*? Could they be that lucky?

Jesamiah squinted into the dense mist, sight, touch, smell, hearing alert. He could sense nothing except fog. The smell of damp tar, wet wood, rope and canvas; the cold, clammy touch of the mist on his face and a faint breeze stroking his cheek— but not enough to flutter the bedraggled ribbons in his dew-glistening hair, or stir the sails. The creak of the ship, the squeak of rope rubbing against rope. Aware that somewhere to leeward the Spanish coast with its jagged rocks lurked unseen, he listened harder, expecting to hear the sound of the sea slapping against the shore. But all he could hear was the ocean gurgling past the hull, nothing else. Except—except his skin was crawling, the hairs standing up along his arms and at the back of his neck. There was *something* out there...

~ Tiola? Are you near? ~ His mind met the nothingness of blank, empty space. The nothingness of a coffin in a grave. No! He could not, would not, believe she was dead!

He wasn't sure if he heard or saw it first. A flashed glow of light, the *whoomph* of sound!

"Down! Get down!" He leapt towards Maha'dun and brought him down to the deck as a few pounds' weight of a lead shot ball ripped through the taffrail, splintering the wood and sending shards fountaining into the damp air. The ball hurtled forward, smashed through the quarterdeck rail, then, badly made, disintegrated into lumps of shrapnel—a miracle that not a soul had been injured.

"Run out the guns! Alter course three points! Steer sou'east!" Jesamiah roared his orders, hastily patting Maha'dun's shoulder to ascertain he was all right, then running to the rail to bellow more orders. Not that his regular men needed them—these were old-hand pirates, well used to quick action, to do, not to stand and think. A man's life depended on not questioning. Run out the guns meant just that.

The braces were already being hauled round as Skylark put the helm over. The effect was immediate. *Sea Witch* tilted as if she were a child's toy... A ball ripped in low, scudding across the waves where a moment before she had been, spray hurling upward in a spouted plume. No one on board noticed, all attention was on a ship looming out of the fog not more than four hundred yards away. The only comfort, from the shouting and bellowing coming from her, *Sea Witch*'s sudden appearance was causing as much alarm.

"Starboard guns run out!" Jesamiah was shouting as he launched himself down the companion ladder to the deck. "Run out my personal colours! Let 'em know who they are dealing with!"

A sound like squealing pigs as the gun trucks protested. Men were hurtling from the larboard side to assist the starboard gunners. Jesamiah's black pirate flag with its leering white skull atop a pair of crossed bones flew up the mast, hung there, motionless a moment, then the wind blew, filling the sails, making them crack and rattle, sweeping the flag outward, rippling and fluttering. The fog disappeared as if a magician had waved a wand. The sun shone, bright and apparently carefree, oblivious that two ships were near enough to blast the other out of the water—depending on which one fired a broadside first.

Maha'dun cowered into his robes, gathering them tight and, eyes narrowed to slits, squirmed away, like a beetle, into a dense patch of shadow. Sense was shouting as loud as Jesamiah to get below—but he had never experienced anything as exciting as this before! Danger awaiting around the corner was always a possibility but this time it had come trumpeting over the threshold with all guns blazing. Literally! No way was he going to miss this! The exhilaration, the pounding blood-rush through the veins; the feeling of being so, so alive because at any moment he might be dead!

Jesamiah stood, one leg slightly forward, knee bent, his left hand on the hilt of his cutlass, his right fiddling with the ribbons in his hair—both unconscious actions. Unheeding of the demented sails, the grunts of the men slipping on the wet deck, of *Sea Witch*'s protest at the sudden change of tack, all his attention was focused on that frigate looming closer, most of her deck in shade, none of her sails—as with *Sea Witch*—clewed up for action.

As calm as if he were ordering coffee, Jesamiah called his next order. "On the down roll—and make every shot count. FIRE!"

Maha'dun slammed his hands over his ears as the first gun roared, then a second, a third; each one blowing columns of flame and billows of acrid smoke across the water before hurtling inboard on their tackles from the force of rebound. The gun crews leapt in, working with sponges to clear the barrel of smouldering debris, reloading for a next shot.

Six shots struck below the waterline of the enemy ship as *Sea Witch* rolled downward and the frigate upward, exposing a length of her water-sodden, poorly maintained, worm-riddled hull at the height of her rise. A cheer went up, spread rapidly along *Sea Witch*'s deck. No need to reload, the frigate's crew were running about, leaving their guns, shouting and cursing. The frantic sound of pumps coming into play—she was holed, and rapidly sinking.

"Do we heave to, sir? Give them quarter?" Tearle was at Jesamiah's side, watching the frenzy on the other ship; men hurrying to launch the boats, throwing anything that would float into the sea before jumping in themselves. The Spanish coast was not far away, with help they would live. Without, they would drown.

Jesamiah stared at Tearle as if he had just been awoken from a trance. "Do you think they would stop for us?" he asked as he pointed upward to his flag contorting in the freshening wind. "Maintain previous course. Set all sail, we need to make way."

Skylark, as Jesamiah's second in command, cocked his head on one side, brows furrowed. "To bring the poor sods aboard would give us more crew."

"Which will take up a lot of time, and who would not want to fight for but against us."

"It ain't right to leave 'em t'drown," Finch piped up. "Don't think Miss Tiola would approve if'n she knew."

"They are the losers, death is expected," Maha'dun interjected, his eyes glittering for the blood-rush of excitement.

Finch, Skylark and Tearle were right, but so was the nightman, and Jesamiah was desperate to find Tiola. Unless luck was with them it could take days, weeks. He decided on compromise; as he went towards his cabin, ordered, "Lower the longboat for them, that'll have to suffice."

"And what," someone called with more than a hint of sarcasm, "are we supposed to do if *we* sink?"

Jesamiah glared at the sailor. "I suggest," he drawled, "you make bloody sure we don't."

A little under a quarter of an hour later, from the stern windows, Jesamiah watched, impassive, as the British ship went down. Perhaps he should have organised a rescue. Perhaps he should never have returned fire—but it was unlikely that the British captain, whoever he was, would have been so considerate. Those first shots had been well aimed with intention behind them, only Jesamiah's seamanship had saved *Sea Witch* from irreparable damage. War had been declared, that made men nervous and inclined to attack first, question later. Perhaps if he had hoisted a British flag, not his one of piracy...?

Jesamiah poured himself a large brandy. Who cared about *perhaps*? Perhaps, if he had not permitted Tiola to go to this blasted party, perhaps if he had gone with her, perhaps he would now be as dead as Rue.

Piracy was in his blood, it was how he thought and fought and no, that captain would not have stopped to pick them out the water. He would have left them all to drown, unless he'd possessed a merciful streak and ordered his marines to shoot them, or hang them.

Perhaps he should have brought the survivors aboard, but, beyond all else, Jesamiah wanted to find the *Safeena Hamra*, reach Tiola and set her safe. Or failing that, know she was dead and beyond his help.

Chapter Thirty-Three

The two men manhandled Tiola through the narrow door and shoved her towards the box-bed built into one corner. The cabin was small, smelling of damp and urine, was unkempt and unclean. Grime clung to the inside of the three stern windows, thick layers of salt stained the outside. The blankets were worn, patched and none too clean, with the single pillow sprouting feathers and fleas. Useless to resist, Tiola was thrown face down, her nose wrinkling at the noisome stains on the crumpled grey linen. She wriggled and managed to sit up, concealing her exasperation and anger. The men were arguing about who was to use her first.

I can look after myself, was something she had always maintained; against the vagaries of human nature, yes she could. Against these two dolts, also yes, but dare she? What if Yakub Pasha had not been bluffing? The men decided to violate her together, began unlacing their breeches. Use her Craft or endure rape?

The familiar hand gesture; *"Hieshh... You look tired; you need to sleep. Come, use the bed...sleep..."* The surprise that both men immediately stopped talking, submissively lay down and went straight to sleep was disconcerting: Tiola had not expected the command to succeed, and had been physically and mentally ready to fight her way out of the situation. So Yakub Pasha was not blocking her? Why not?

"I would have told them to jump out the window had I known," she grumbled as she stared, hopelessly now she no longer had to display a false bravado, around the squalid cabin. At the back of her mind; *Has Yakub lost the use of his abilities?* What was it he had said? *'Do not dare attempt to use your Craft' She* had contacted Maha'dun—at least, hoped she had; had sent these two lowlifes to sleep, and while with the children had watched Rue and Pamela walk in the Beyond. Yet Yakub appeared unaware? Was he testing her, permitting her to do these small things, waiting for her to attempt something more powerful?

From habit she put a shell of protection around the cabin, effectively ensuring that the door could not be opened, then stared forlornly through the grimed stern windows. Was *Sea Witch* out there, not far behind? On the other side of that fog-bank perhaps? Maybe she could contact Jesamiah. What if he still did not know anything about this? Each minute, each yard, this cursed red ship was taking her further away from him. What if Yakub *was* playing with her? If he knew about Jesamiah, about *Sea Witch*... She could not risk it, had to trust that Maha'dun had received her message, that Jesamiah was not far behind. If she inadvertently gave Yakub cause to suspect danger was following...

More thoughts flooded her mind. Yakub was frail, ill, dying —no, *disintegrating* would be more fitting. She snorted contempt; his death could not come quick enough in her opinion, although a voice of conscience whispered that it was her duty to care, even for a monster. Should she test him? Use her Craft for something that would attract his attention? Damage the rudder? Snap a stay? Cause a mast to topple? She walked away from the window, paced backwards and forwards. What if he was bluffing? Waiting for her to do something stupid?

She stood in the centre of the cabin, belatedly aware that her skin was tingling as if she had fallen into a mass of nettles. Had she been so blindly distracted? A casket was here, the last remaining bone-box, here in this cabin! No wonder the Night-Walkers had not been able to find it!

The throbbing sensation was coming from beneath the bed; she knelt down, peered under and gagged at the stench of soiled clothes, putrefying food and an unemptied pisspot full of mouldering faeces. Empty bottles. Three long-dead rats. Using the tips of her fingers she moved aside a pile of repugnant underwear and pushed her hand through a thin shield of protection around a small metal chest. Did Yakub not realise that his power was now so fragile he could no longer hide things from her? She grasped a handle, pulled, revealed a small, rusted trunk. She lifted it—slightly heavier than she had expected it to be—and set it down on a table on the far side of the cabin, sweeping the clutter off first; papers, more empty bottles, a few curled and torn charts, rotting apple cores... The lock was secure, no key. Not wasting time, she moved her fingers, breathed an incantation, and the mechanism clicked open.

Hesitating, she looked towards the cabin door expecting Yakub to burst through. Nothing except the sound of laughter; someone rapped on the door and she suppressed a squeal of fear. Were they queueing up out there? A fist banged again, the door shuddered, but her protective spell held.

A man's voice, the words spoken in gruff Turkish—Tiola

could speak and understand any language. "Come on! Remove your cock from wherever you've got it poked, and let us have our turn!"

"Almost done!" Tiola called, mimicking one of the sleeping men. "Rub yourself to keep it warm while you wait!"

Some more laughter, some growls of frustration. Quickly, she opened the trunk. Inside, a black-as-ebony bone-box bearing the mask of a Night-Walker with vivid amethyst eyes. It was exquisitely made and more elaborate than the others; each fragment of bone cut and fitted together as if the material had been wooden marquetry.

"Soon," she murmured with a mixture of relief and great sadness for the suffering caused, "soon I will set your soul free."

Taking up a grubby cloth she lifted it from the metal trunk —she avoided touching the caskets as much as possible for the carbon residue irritated her skin, causing soreness and blisters. The casket rattled, there was something inside. She flicked the lid open. Another box. Much smaller, square. No face engraved on the lid, just a plain box but one also fashioned from burnt bone.

Tiola turned away; her arms clutching her stomach as she sank to her knees and vomited. Her bone. Her burnt and blackened bone. The remains of herself as the woman who had been alive those many years ago. The woman he had repeatedly and brutally raped; the woman he had watched, with laughter in his eyes and wide on his lips, burn to death at the stake.

* * *

Her fear quite gone, replaced by an anger which burnt as fiercely as those pitch-fuelled flames that had devoured her living body, Tiola swept up onto the *Safeena Hamra*'s quarterdeck, shoving aside with the force that emanated from her upheld right hand any who dared try to stop her. She had used Craft to dress herself: a sumptuous red silk gown, shot through with strands of gold thread; the cuffs and neckband trimmed with exquisite embroidery, emeralds and rubies. From her shoulders a green velvet cloak edged in ermine. Red and green; the esteemed colours of her healer and midwifery status. Her black hair was piled high and crowned with a tiered diadem that tinkled and glistened from a thousand gold and silver half-moon shapes. Her slippers were soft wool spattered with more gems; at her waist, a gold chain from which dangled the caduceus, the ancient symbol of wisdom and healing: two snakes winding around a winged staff. Concealed within a linen cloth, she carried something in her left hand.

Tiola stopped a yard before Yakub Pasha who was leaning over the taffrail, listening intently. At first, he did not see her; turned with startled surprise. She sang one single high note, purposefully moved her fingers—and time stopped. The sea ceased its restless surge, the wind paused its strengthening bluster, and the billowing sails became immobile. The crew were as stone statues.

"You dare disobey me?" Yakub shouted, his voice like thunder, his rage as red as Tiola's gown. "You dare use your Craft wearing this, this..." he waved a hand contemptuously, "... whore's display of opulence!"

"I dare. And I wear the garments and carry the symbols of my high rank. As is my right to so do."

"You will pay for defying me, madam. I will not be mocked."

"Yet I see you doing nothing to counter me? Your ability of Craft began to fade many years ago, did it not? To replace it you sought a different path to prolong your life." She paused, pulled the cloth from the Night-Walker casket.

"All these years, these many, many years," she said, her rage bubbling as a volcano boils before it spews out its hot fury, "you have been drawing life from the bone fragments of ten Night-Walkers. The energy within the other caskets was nothing compared to this one." She lifted the box higher. "You created the false stories of longevity to add value to those worthless things, but this is the one with the power of life. This one has kept you alive. It was for this that you had them all killed. No wonder you had to stop me! I tried without using my Craft to help those poor unfortunates; had I known what your sick, evil mind was plotting, I would have risked every living child at your court to stop you, you loathsome, depraved creature!"

Yakub Pasha backed away as she took a step nearer, the casket outstretched in her hand.

"What you did not anticipate," she continued, spitting contempt, "was that as each casket was destroyed the life force within this one—and therefore you—faded."

"You talk nonsense. I need attend greater things—did you not hear the guns? Somewhere in that fog behind us ships are fighting. I want no possibility of the victor coming after me."

Tiola paused, listened, but could not hear while time stood still. Was Jesamiah in trouble? Were they his guns? Ah, concentrate on the one thing! She flipped the casket lid open, withdrew the second, smaller, box.

"And what," she asked with loathing, "did you plan for this? Were you hoping that my bones would bring you the health you needed? Well, I am sorry to inform you but my power is within my living soul, not the Beyond or the charred remains of a previous life." With satisfied contempt she tossed the box made from her own mortal, charred, bones over the rail, heard it splash into the sea, gone. Noted, from the corner of her eye, that the fog outside of the suspended bubble of time was lifting.

Yakub folded his arms, equally as contemptuous. "You cannot contain this inertia for long, it will disintegrate soon enough—as, yes, is the energy that has been keeping me alive. But until that black box is destroyed, I will live, and you can only destroy it by the flames of fire. Why not burn it now, here, on this quarterdeck?" He leered, leant towards her. "A difficult one to solve, is it not? Burn the casket, burn the ship, burn the children."

He waved his hand, breathed a hush of breath: time began again, and Tiola's illusioned robes faded into the gown she had been wearing when they took her, soiled and torn and ragged. Calmly he took the casket from her hand and, waving two crew forward, gave orders for her to be secured to the foremast.

"You see, not all my Craft has yet failed me." To the men, ordered, "Strip her and bind her tight. Gag her mouth. She can shrill like a fishwife and I do not want my ears torn."

He joined in with the crew's laughter, then added an abrupt order: "Bend all sail, I want maximum speed. We are being followed and I have no wish to be entertaining an uninvited guest." He glanced towards the horizon. If that Maha'dun creature was out there...? He shrugged. This was absurdity! Night-Walkers hated the sea. Aside from which, if he had heard those guns aright maybe any following ship was now crippled or sunk. He touched his empty eye socket, ran his fingers down the raised, rough edges of the scar snaking across his face On the starb'd side of looking at it, he had a score to settle.

CHAPTER THIRTY-FOUR

With Chippy, the carpenter, overseeing the repair of damage sustained, and the last few fog banks drifting into skeins of evaporating mist, everyone aboard *Sea Witch* was intent on scanning the horizon. That red ship was out there somewhere— and Jesamiah had promised twenty-five gold pieces to the man who first spotted her.

The day passed with slow frustration. Cloud gathered, obscuring the horizon. Rain began to fall. The wind swung one way, then the other. Again and again *Sea Witch* had to tack, slowing her passage. As evening approached, at last, the shout they had been waiting for.

"Deck there, sail on lar'bd bow. Long way off, mind." Jasper's voice from up in the crosstrees wafted down to the deck.

Lifting his telescope, Jesamiah peered into the distance but could see nothing against the grey swell of the sea and the pewter sky. Was it her? It had to be! *Had* to be!

"I'm going aloft," he said to Skylark who stood at the helm. Skylark nodded, from up the mast the view would be clearer.

Maha'dun appeared, stretching and yawning. "You do not get much sleep aboard a ship, do you?" he observed.

"Not when we're on a Chase, no," Skylark responded as he watched Jesamiah nimbly climb up the shrouds.

Maha'dun glanced towards where everyone was peering. "What is it we are looking at?"

"A ship," Skylark said.

A lurch of blood-lust scuttled through Maha'dun. "Are we going to have another fight? I enjoyed that last one!"

Skylark had been polite and helpful, saw no reason to be hostile, but the fellow did, on occasion, rub the cloth up the wrong way. "It'll not be so enjoyable when broadsides hit us, when full action is joined. That back there was a skirmish, nothing more. You'll see a difference when blood starts running out the scuppers, and men start getting killed."

Maha'dun's eyes were glittering, he smiled, showing perfect white teeth. "I have faced more fights than you've had tots of rum: I have crossed blades with Huns and Vandals; witnessed the fall of Antioch and Jerusalem, and watched the archers in that bloody, muddy, field at Agincourt. I was with Timur when he entered Delhi and sacked the city, leaving it in ruins. The army killed and plundered for three days and nights. One hundred thousand prisoners were put to death in one day."

Not having any knowledge of history, the boasting meant nothing to Skylark. "A pretty story. We all have tales of blood and gore to share. Different matter when the blood's real and your own. The story changes somewhat then."

"True enough," Maha'dun conceded, then thought it best not to elaborate further. The spilling of blood was as much a part of his life as was drinking and copulating. But then, he was not human, these men were.

Heads turned to watch Jesamiah descend rapidly down the backstay. He went straight to the newly repaired rail, steadied his elbows and peered again through his telescope. At last, satisfied, he folded the instrument with a sharp click and put it safe in his longcoat pocket. He leant out over the rail, studying the cream of foam along the hull, the froth of the wake streaming behind. Spray wet his face, his blue ribbons fluttered in the wind. He assessed the sails: they were drawing well, but he reckoned he could get another knot or two out of his ship.

Jasper had scurried down from the crosstrees, his face abeam with a broad grin.

The *Safeena Hamra* was smaller and lighter than *Sea Witch*. With a flatter keel she could sail into shallow creeks, turn on a farthing and make use of every puff of wind. But then, she did not have Jesamiah Acorne as her captain.

"Is Jasper getting the gold, then?" Tearle called, a tad peevish at missing the opportunity to get it himself.

"Not yet, he ain't," Jesamiah answered, ruffling the grinning lad's hair. "But he has mast-high hopes."

* * *

Half of an hour later, still at a distance of several miles—way beyond the reach of any cannon shot—*Sea Witch*'s quarry had, at last, been confirmed, her red sails distinctive in the fading light to Maha'dun's far-sighted eyes. None aboard were concerned that they would lose her during the encroaching night—Jesamiah had tailed ships before, often overhauling and being there, ahead of the prey as the sun rose, ready to claim the Prize. This Chase, however, was to be different.

"We cannot leave those children to suffer another night," Jesamiah had explained. "But taking them without doing damage and risking the lives of those we care for will not be an easy task."

"Will they be expecting pursuit?" Tearle asked. "They might not realise we know who—what—they are."

"That's what I'm counting on," Jesamiah confirmed. "Along with the assumption that even were we hostile, we'd not be idiots enough to attack at night." He stood on the quarterdeck, oblivious to the rain squall that raced in, the sting of the wind and the spatter of spindrift. He was fiddling with his blue ribbons, twirling them around his fingers. Always a sign that someone was about to have their life expectancy shortened.

As abruptly as it had come, the rain scurried off across the sea, and the wind blew the clouds into ragged shreds. The first stars glimmered in the fading twilight. Night, not far behind.

* * *

The evening star shone bright through the scudding banks of low, black cloud. Venus. Tiola recalled walking on a beach in Cape Town—how many years ago now? Three? Four?—and talking to Master William Dampier. She remembered his exact words:

"Is Venus not a glorious sight? My hope," he had sighed wistfully, *"is that one day man shall construct a telescope fine enough to see the six planets in all their full and wondrous detail. Alas, this poor apology of a specimen is all I possess."*

She had not been able to tell him there were more than six planets. He had been a kind man—she had been saddened to hear that he had died soon after their meeting. He had given her his small telescope to watch a ship sailing away—the *Mermaid.* Jesamiah had been at the helm, steering into the waves as her canvas had spread to catch the wind. He had not possessed *Sea Witch* back then, nor had he known Tiola for what she was, had not known their paths would cross, and their love would burn as bright as that planet. Tiola felt a tear trickle down her cheek, blinked away more, annoyed that her bound hands could not brush them aside.

Tied, naked, to the foremast she was saturated by spray and shivering from the cold. She did not mind the embarrassment of being unclothed, the humiliation was of no concern, but the filthy rag they had forced into her mouth tasted foul. She was cold, wet, hungry and tired—and dared not use her Craft to remedy any one of her discomforts for she needed all her concentration to protect the children. Before they had restrained her, she had managed to set a thin, protective shield around the hold—the best she could do to keep the children safe. The drain on her energy left her vulnerable, but she could endure, the children could not.

The binding ropes cut into her wrists, arms, legs, neck and waist—they had made certain she would not be able to escape— she could turn her head to either side. Enough to watch Yakub moving about the quarterdeck, enough to be aware that her presence was making him uneasy. A while since, he had scooped up the casket and disappeared into his cabin, leaving the ship, and her, to the mercy of the men. He was a fool to do so; his crew were a slovenly, lazy lot, not clever, not astute. They had no awareness of the nature of the ship coming up fast in their wake. Had no comprehension of their nemesis being but a few miles behind.

To be fair to the poor fools, she could see clearer in the gathering dusk than could they, and she held the advantage of knowing that Jesamiah was coming for her. They did not.

On The Account

* * *

Sea Witch was sailing faster than the *Safeena Hamra*; with a mile of water between them she was gaining with every wave she plunged over, her bow lifting and tossing through the spray as if she were a racehorse hurtling towards the winner's post at full gallop.

"She's weathering on us, Cap'n."

Maha'dun, standing a few yards behind Jesamiah, squinted at the rapidly darkening sky, then stared blankly at Skylark who stood at the helm. "May I ask what 'weathering' is?" he asked.

Jesamiah pointed to the sails. "He means that the *Safeena Hamra* is not yielding to the thrust of the wind down to leeward to the same extent as are we."

Maha'dun didn't like to respond that he still did not understand. He could see with his own eyes, however, that *Sea Witch* was moving faster than the ship ahead with its brazen red sails. They were coming closer, and it looked like no one aboard the Chase had yet seen them; at least there was no scurry of alarm or action on the other ship.

For that matter, though, there appeared to be few men aboard *Sea Witch* either. Only a quarter of her crew were on deck, and all her gun ports were firmly closed with bow and stern chasers carefully covered beneath drapes of canvas. She flew a Dutch flag and for all the world looked like an ordinary merchant ship heading out on a long haul to the East Indies. The dilemma: was the *Safeena Hamra* also playing a hand of bluff by pretending to be unconcerned?

"She's luffing," Skylark announced unnecessarily, for they could all see the other ship's topsails shiver, thereby losing some headway and gaining a few yards to windward. All except Maha'dun, who thought they could be talking gibberish for all

431

he knew.

"When giving chase," Jesamiah explained, leaning casually on the quarterdeck rail, "the best action to follow is to close to windward. If we can keep her in the eye of the wind, we'll have the advantage. The more weatherly ship closes the gap quicker, and can open fire with greater advantage."

Absorbing the information, Maha'dun remained quiet for several minutes. "But we're not going to open fire, are we?" he finally said, puzzled.

Jesamiah pushed away from the rail and took the helm from Skylark. "Nope," he said. "Not yet."

It was some while before anything else was said, each man, Skylark, Jasper, Tearle, Spokesy, Finch, others of the crew, intent on what they were doing—attempting to not look like they were swooping down upon their prey. Not quite dark, visibility was fading—another five minutes would see the night fully closed in.

"Dip our colours in friendly recognition if you please, Jasper. Let's see if we get a response."

"They're showing Moroccan colours, I see," Tearle said. "Neutral in this pending war. Same as with the Dutch at the moment?"

Jesamiah nodded. "They're probably unaware that anyone would be giving chase after their last raid. Like us, they're counting on not drawing attention, making their own way and minding their own business."

To his surprise, an acknowledgement signal was made—a similar lowering and raising of the flag, a sign of friendly exchange offering intention of no harm. A typical pirate trick.

"They might be thinking the same as us, of course," Jesamiah said aloud, "pretend an air of innocence then break out all hell when we draw alongside."

With the distance between the ships shortening, almost within cannon range now, night clamped in like a shutter being abruptly closed. No moon, just blackness and sparkling stars, broken only by the creaming froth of the two ships' wakes and the whitecaps of the scurrying sea. At night, sounds were different, louder, more pronounced. Every squeak, creak and rattle; every flap of the sail, every voice, everything sounding twice as loud. At night, shadows changed; dark places became darker, broader, wider, deeper. Distances became further away or disappeared completely. Only the familiar stayed the same, while the unfamiliar became a potential threat or hazard. No lights, save for the stars and the faint glow from the binnacle box illuminating the compass bearing, for lights affected eyes accustomed to the dark.

Except for Maha'dun whose vision became clearer—for him sunlight, even on grey cloudy days, all but blinded his sight, creating a misty impression as if peering through a dense fog, the brightness dazzling on his retinas, blocking his peripheral awareness. After sundown, things changed.

"What's that?" he said, suddenly anxious. "There against that front mast?"

As he spoke, frightened words thudded into his and Jesamiah's mind.

~ *You cannot fire into the hull! The children—they are below!* ~

~ *Tiola?* ~ Jesamiah screamed her name in his mind. ~ *Are you all right? Tiola! Have they harmed you? I intend to cripple them quickly. Our guns are aimed at the masts.* ~

Maha'dun clutched Jesamiah's arm, his fingers digging in deep and tight. He pointed. "No, Captain! Look—Tiola! They have her tied to the mast!"

Starlight glistened on the tears streaming down Tiola's

face, mingling with the salt spray, the sob torturing in her throat because she could not release it through her mouth. Jesamiah's scream had thundered into her mind, she could see him running the length of the deck to lean over the bow to see clearly. Could see and feel his anger.

~ How bloody dare he! ~

~ Stick to your plan, Jesamiah! The children are important, I am not! ~

~ Fuck that! ~

~ Jesamiah—please! Save the children! ~

He went quiet. She craned her neck to watch him running back to the quarterdeck. Could not hear, but guessed he was bellowing orders because there was sudden movement aboard *Sea Witch*, men appearing from nowhere.

~ I can protect myself! ~ she lied. *~ Tell him to fire at the masts, falling splinters and debris will not harm me. ~*

She sent the words to Maha'dun. Unlike Jesamiah, the Night-Walker did not know he could block her thoughts, even if he wanted to.

* * *

Sea Witch had been ready for action this past three-quarters of an hour, muffled thuds and bumps had resonated from below as screens and bulkheads were knocked out, the stern windows swung up and bolted to the cabin ceiling, Jesamiah's furniture and belongings hastily crammed below to give fighting room to the two guns situated aft in his cabin. Tiola, when aboard, draped linen tablecloths over them to hide their ugly presence.

Lashings had been cast off from the guns on deck, sand spread around their wooden transoms for a surer grip underfoot. Pistols primed, cutlasses, knives and cudgels to hand. The intention had been to slide past the *Safeena Hamra* as ships passing in the night, turn quickly—a speciality of both Jesamiah and *Sea Witch*—and blast the hell out of the masts, effectively disabling the red ship with the one swift, unexpected broadside. Jesamiah abandoned the plan as swiftly as a kestrel swoops on its prey. The wind was stronger, had shifted round slightly to Jesamiah's advantage, the last remnants of ragged cloud being swept aside. He stepped away from the helm, passing control of the ship to Skylark.

"Concentrate your fire on the mainmast and quarterdeck!" Jesamiah roared at his men. "You hear me? I only want everything aft of the foremast destroyed. Gunners? Aim high, fire at will and fire straight! Ten gold pieces to all of you who strike true, and another ten for every soddin' one of you who joins me on that deck over there! Ready?"

A shouted chorus of *'Aye, Cap'n.'*

They were within cannon shot, the other ship, on a more southerly course, was abuzz with men—as with *Sea Witch,* this red ship had suddenly come to scurrying life. Hauling on the yards, the panicked men were attempting to show the smallest target by turning the *Safeena Hamra*'s transom to her pursuer, but Jesamiah's orders, his men and his ship were quicker. *Sea Witch* was closing in.

"Open ports! Out guns!" Jesamiah bellowed—his concentration as taut as a stretched rope; with a clatter the guns were run out, appearing against *Sea Witch*'s blue hull like a row of gaping teeth.

Two minutes and *Sea Witch*'s jib was parallel with the *Safeena Hamra*'s stern; another minute and they were racing alongside with barely a good stone's throw between them. Men aboard the *Safeena Hamra* were hauling to fighting sail. *Sea Witch* was already there, her lower sails up and out of the way in a matter of moments—with the great expanse of canvas furled, the view along the length of the deck was clear from stem to stern—as clear as it could be in the starlit dark.

Someone was running along the *Safeena Hamra*'s deck, his arms waving ferociously. Maha'dun stiffened, his eyes narrowed, teeth bared. "That's him!" he snarled. "Yakub Pasha! He is shouting for the guns to be run out!"

"He should have shouted earlier and quicker then," Jesamiah stated as he drew his cutlass and raised it above his head, starlight glinting on the exposed blade.

"Jasper? We'll have our true colours, if you please," he called. "My flag, not that butterball Dutch nonsense."

"Aye, Cap'n!"

Jesamiah concentrated on the jib boom, pointing straight ahead like a sharp, deadly tusk, waited for it to come level with the other ship's foremast. "Easy does it..." he muttered to himself, "easy..." He must not waver his gaze towards Tiola captured there, naked and helpless. *Must not think of her, must concentrate!* At any moment the enemy would get themselves in order, have their guns out and blasting first... His salt-tasting lips and throat were dry, his heart drummed against his chest. If he got this wrong...

"On the up roll! Fire as you bear!" He brought the cutlass blade down swift and sharp.

The broadside roared as if it were a smoke- and flame-belching monster, the bright flame dazzling, the black smoke blotting out the stars. *Sea Witch* rocked as the recoil tore through her decks. Iron shot and langrage hurtled across the narrow gap of water and bore into the *Safeena Hamra*, smashing through rail, bulwarks, deadeyes and cordage; ripping through wood, canvas and men alike in the one deadly, devastating, strake.

Not expecting the great noise and the shuddering

sensations, Maha'dun fell, his feet going from under him. He grabbed the rail to haul himself upward, coughed as if he would spew up his lungs as acrid smoke rolled over him, choking his throat. Anguished cries were coming from the other ship, men wounded, men dying horribly. And he could hear Tiola screaming inside his head.

The red sails, when he could see clear enough through smoke-stinging eyes, were holed and torn, the fore topmast dangling at a forlorn angle; cordage, shrouds, and severed rigging flailing like angry, hissing, snakes. The damaged mast creaked, groaned then fell into the sea, dragging sail and rigging and several men with it.

A sound like a giant's bullwhip being cracked heralded the mainmast backstay giving way, the whiplash force so severe it decapitated a man as it swished crazily through the air. The mast tottered, lurched to one side, its supportive hold gone. Rails were smashed, the jolly boat resting keel-up on the deck was nothing more than a pile of splintered wood. Half the ladder up to the quarterdeck was missing, the quarterdeck rail, binnacle box, stern lantern and taffrail in pieces. Three men were staggering, one on his knees spewing blood, dagger-like shafts of wood protruding from their bodies like thrust-in spears. Men were on the deck, the dead, the dying. Heavy cannon fire and a man's body were not compatible.

All happening at once, but the *Safeena Hamra* was still ploughing forward through the churning sea under the thrust of her momentum; crippled, though, her gallantry would be short-lived.

"Reload?" someone called from *Sea Witch*'s gun deck.

"Aye!" Jesamiah shouted, knowing his guns would be ready to fire again in a few moments over the minute. He whistled for Skylark at the helm to put the wheel hard over, and in response, *Sea Witch*'s mighty bowsprit swung towards her prey. Men along the foredeck began to pound rhythmically on the rail with anything to hand—belaying pins, pistol butts, cutlass hilts; bare fists. Then the chanting began.

"Death to the buggers! Death to the buggers! Death! Death! Death!"

The Safeena Hamras responded with the *pop-pop-pop* of pistol and musket fire, some bullets finding sure targets, most missing or gouging into the wooden deck, rails or masts.

His cutlass sheathed, a pistol in his hand, Jesamiah was racing towards the bow. In his head he could hear Tiola screaming and screaming, no other sound, not the pounding, the chanting, the gunfire—just Tiola.

Maha'dun, recovering himself, ran after him. He jerked one of his own three pistols from his crossbelt as *Sea Witch* slammed into the *Safeena Hamra*. Her bowsprit, longer and higher than the red ship's squat beakhead, soared over the lower deck like a cat's paw clamping down on a caught mouse. Then her stern swung in, men were tossing grappling irons, hauling the two ships to close together. Jesamiah was up onto the rail, leaping across the slender, ominously black gap, not hearing the all but crazed carolling of his men, and apparently immune to the small arms' fire. He was on the deck, running to meet a man, open-mouthed, shouting defiance, coming at him with a raised cudgel.

Jesamiah shot him clean through the forehead, swiftly reversed his empty pistol and used the butt as a club to knock aside another assailant, breaking the man's collarbone with the force of the blow. The next man... ducking a cutlass swinging at him. Jesamiah retaliated by moving in under the blade and ramming the pistol into his attacker's groin. Barely pausing, he thumped his fist into someone's jaw, vaguely aware that

Maha'dun was at his side tackling his own share of opponents. The spit and flare of a primed, fired pistol... the ball seared past Jesamiah's face sounding like a rampant bumblebee, only on the periphery of consciousness did he realise it was not aimed at him, but a shot Maha'dun had fired at a man coming straight at them with a raised axe. The only thing in focus, the only thing he was aware of in this night-dark maelstrom of fighting madness, was Tiola tied to that foremast. Everything else a blur, everything else unimportant. The only goal, to get to her no matter who or what was in the way.

Jesamiah tossed the pistol to the deck, drew his cutlass—slash, kick, punch—anyone blocking his path dealt with, killed or maimed without thought or decision, just done. Pain across his upper left arm unfelt, dripping blood unnoticed. The weight of his cutlass unheeded as blade clashed against blade or ground through flesh, sinew and bone.

He was there! He'd made it! He yanked the gag out of Tiola's mouth, heard her gasp for breath then stifle the scream that was near to hysteria. He shoved his cutlass under his arm, whipped his dagger from the sheath in the hollow of his back and started sawing through the ropes binding her. Behind him, legs spread, teeth bared, Maha'dun was fending off men attempting to stop the rescue, a blade in each hand, swiping left and right, jabbing, thrusting, he held his ground. Jesamiah's dagger was sharp, but the rope was wet, he sawed more ferociously, heard Maha'dun's breath rasping, the shouts, the yells, the groans of the wounded and dying. Heard Tiola choking back frightened sobs. The last binding pinged apart and he grabbed her as she fell to her knees, holding her close, stroking her soaked hair. He let go briefly, thrust off his coat, wrapped it around her, held her close again.

"Are you all right? Did they hurt you?"

"No," she gasped, "no, my limbs are stiff, that is all. What of the children? Jesamiah! The children!"

Chapter Thirty-Five

For himself Jesamiah could not care less about the children, Tiola was his priority, but then there was Thomas Benson to consider. The fighting was easing, the Sea Witches vastly outnumbering the Safeena Hamras; men were surrendering, dropping weapons, raising hands or cowering down to their knees, but the screaming went on, an ululation of sound—children's terrified screams. Tiola ran to the closed hatch, began scrabbling at it, the tears flowing now, the sobs rasping in her throat: she could hear gurgling water and violent splashing coming from below. She pleaded for help—Maha'dun was beside her, lifting the heavy hatch, Jesamiah on the other side. The stench as it opened belched out like a ripe boar's fart, children's petrified faces peering up, a foot of water swirling around their feet. Beside the bulkhead two boys—Thomas and the other one, whose name Jesamiah could not recall—frantically attempting in the confined darkness to stop water pouring in through a hole by stuffing their shirts into it.

A sail was alight, someone ripped it down, began stamping out the flame—Spokesy grabbed a lantern from the askew mast, lit the wick, flaring it to life. He gestured at the nearby hatch ladder and Skylark thrust it into the hole, took the lantern, slid more than climbed down with Richie Tearle close at heel—all were dishevelled and blood-spattered, sporting various cuts to face and arms. Hooking the lantern onto a nail, Skylark grabbed the nearest child—a girl of about three, the water up to her thighs—and passed her to Tearle. He lifted her up to Spokesy who took her arms and, setting the crying mite on the deck, reached for the next child. Tiola ran to the little girl, enfolding her tight in her arms, crooning soothing words. The second child... then another. Tiola drew them all as near as she could.

"Smallest first!" Skylark shouted. "Thomas—forget plugging that hole, see the smallest kids out first!"

Jesamiah squatted down next to Tiola, touched his hand to her cheek. "Sweetheart, get the children aboard *Sea Witch*. They'll feel safer and not have to witness all this." He swept his hand towards the slaughterhouse of the deck, hiding his incredulity at the number of children appearing from the hold. How many had been stuffed down there?

Tiola nodded, and organising Finch and several men to help, made her way with the children across to the safety of the *Sea Witch*. Was that a little bob of movement from the ship? A welcome nod of concern for the children? Tiola snorted inwardly at her absurd imagination. The strain of these last few days was taking effect.

Fighting had dwindled to a halt, the ragged crew and the damaged *Safeena Hamra* a forlorn sight. The Sea Witches were rounding up the losers, herding them towards the bow— Jesamiah called out to avast the idea. "Keep them where they are. Once the hold is empty send them down there."

A pause, someone answered, "But it's floodin', Cap'n."

Jesamiah's response was terse. "So? They've a choice of

drownin' or 'anging. Those children were not going to have a choice of anythin', were they?"

Maha'dun stepped up to Jesamiah's side. "Where's Yakub Pasha?" he hissed. "I do not see him."

Jesamiah frowned, glanced along the deck. About to issue orders to search the *Safeena Hamra*, the shout of *'Sail ho!'* distracted him.

"Where away?" He squinted up *Sea Witch*'s mainmast to where Jasper—always the best lookout—was perched in the crosstrees.

"Starb'd. About half an hour away perhaps? I'm only guessin'. I just caught a glimpse of her tops'ls against the skyline—but I think she's putting on more sail and heading right for us. Prob'ly drawn by the sound and flare of our guns."

An explicit rude word escaped Jesamiah's lips.

"Hurry up with those kids! Tiola!" he shouted across the deck to her. "Get them below, we're leaving as soon as we can." The last thing he wanted was another tangle with another ship.

~ Where is Yakub? ~ Tiola's voice in Jesamiah's head. *~ I am not leaving here until I know he is dead. ~*

~ I'm about to look for him. ~ "You men—help get the children out of here."

Thomas and Donréal appeared from the hold, sodden and bedraggled, Skylark right behind them, lantern to hand. He walked up to speak quietly into Jesamiah's ear.

"Hold's empty, Captain, save for ten bodies. Poor little bairns. Couple of them have been dead several days, their bodies chewed by rats."

"Any way of identifying them?"

Skylark shook his head. "I recognised two. Calderón's youngest daughter," he hesitated, fighting anger and tears. "And his little boy. The son."

Jesamiah stared up at the night sky. The stars, so bright, so beautiful. He wiped a hand across his face, felt Calderón's ring on his finger. He bit his lip, closed his eyes. Calderón had only the one son. The rest were daughters. That left him as the last male in the line, but this was not the time or place to think on such things.

"Fetch their bodies up, we'll give them proper burial later. Then throw that lot into the hold like I ordered."

Skylark touched his hand to his forehead. "My pleasure, Cap'n."

Acknowledging with a curt nod, Jesamiah barked further orders as the *whoomph* of a cannon shot tore out from the darkness, and a flurry of bright light lit the not-so-distant approaching ship. There was a splash about a quarter of a mile away.

"You men—search the ship for stragglers. I want every man who served aboard this ship secured in that hold. Look sharp now!"

He looked around for Maha'dun, couldn't see him. Headed for the great cabin situated beneath what was left of the quarterdeck. Time was short, they had, at most, ten minutes to be done here.

* * *

Maha'dun could hear, and smell, a bone-box. All other sound, all thought evaporated as he followed the call that drew him. Rapier in one hand, reloaded pistol in the other, he kicked open the cabin door, not needing light to see, although silver starlight filtered in through a gaping hole in the cabin wall. Incongruously, the word 'bulkhead' popped into his mind. His mouth twisted into a grin. He was learning.

"So, the bitch spoke the truth. You have come after me." Yakub Pasha stood, half-hidden by the deep shadow of the far corner. He had a raised pistol in one hand, the bone-box in the other.

"I came after you, yes. But there is no point shooting me, for I am not alone. Lady Tiola's husband will hear the shot, and he is the one I would advise you to be afraid of."

That shook Yakub slightly. Tiola had a seafaring husband? Why had he no knowledge of this? Why had neither Ber'ell nor Doone told him?

"And Captain Acorne, when riled, is a dangerous, formidable man to fall foul of," Maha'dun added.

His eyes narrowing, Yakub Pasha snarled. Acorne! That name he knew—why had he not realised the connection!

Maha'dun was sniffing the air, his nostrils wide-flared. "You are dying, old man. I can smell the putrid rot in your flesh and innards. That bone-box has not given you the longevity you expected it to then? How unfortunate."

"I will live long enough to see you dead, Maha'dun."

"I wouldn't count on it." Jesamiah's voice directly behind Maha'dun. The cabin lit with a flash, the acrid smell of gunpowder, a puff of smoke, the *whizz* of a bullet. Maha'dun leapt forward as Jesamiah fired—was there as Yakub pitched to his knees, letting go of the casket, Jesamiah's well-aimed shot slamming direct into the Moroccan's chest, piercing a lung.

Snatching up the bone-box, Maha'dun cradled it to his body.

"We have to leave, Nightm'n," Jesamiah said. "Get yourself and that bloody box aboard *Sea Witch*. I'll finish off here."

Maha'dun hesitated. Jesamiah turned his head and his attention to repeat the order. Yakub lifted another pistol... Knocked the hammer home with the side of his hand, aimed.

The powder flared in the pan. The bang loud, so loud, in the confines of the cabin...

Night-Walkers were fast, their reactions honed to a sharpness far quicker than any human. Dropping the bone-box, Maha'dun threw himself at Jesamiah, his outstretched arms knocking him aside, his contorting body squirming between the bullet and Jesamiah.

The shot ripped in through flesh, sinew, bone and organ; a small hole in, a torn, jagged, bloody, gaping hole out, felling Maha'dun as efficiently as a leather swat destroys a fly.

* * *

It was dark, night, but the moon, full and round, sailed serene against the soot-black sky. Her glow so bright, so dazzling she outshone every single one of the stars. He stood watching, looking down—was he on a cliff edge?

There were rocks, great flat rocks below, and the wide sweep of sea. A calm, waveless sea, reflecting everything as if it were a silver-backed crystal mirror. The moonlight shone her radiant path direct towards him, beckoning.

~ Come, step out upon my path.... Join me... ~

He hesitated. The moon was beautiful, the water so still, so calm... but he did not want to go. He did not want to leave all this, all of everything, behind.

There was something else, something shadowed, something darker against the darkness. He squinted, held his hand across his brow to defuse the shining moonlight...

A ship! Silhouetted against the brightness, under full sail yet she did not appear to be moving. How could she, there was no trace of wind, not a ripple, not a breeze. Was she coming nearer or sailing away?

And then he saw himself, standing on that big, flat rock. Dressed as a pirate, ready for a life on the account. Boots, longcoat; cutlass at his side.

Was she coming nearer, or sailing away?

~ Come, join me... ~

He did not want to. He wanted to be with the ship, with the people and the life he had come to love. This was his life now, and he was not ready to give it up, nor the one he had fallen in love with that very first time their eyes had met.

Maha'dun was not ready to die.

But was that ship coming for him, or leaving him behind?

* * *

"Tiola! Tiola!" Jesamiah bellowed her name as he stumbled across from the *Safeena Hamra*'s deck to the security of his own. His men were pouring after him. In his arms, a bloody body.

"Tiola! Tiola!"

She was there, at his side, a gasp leaving her throat as she knelt beside the burden he laid down.

"He took the shot meant for me!" Jesamiah was distraught. "The silly bugger got in the way!"

Ripping Maha'dun's blood-soaked shirt open, Tiola inspected the wound. Was there anything she could do with this? Anything at all?

She cradled Maha'dun to her, her arms about him, her head against his, rocking him, tears raining down her face.

A *whoomph* of sound. A cannon ball spurred into the sea a few yards from *Sea Witch*'s stern.

"All hands! Cut us free!" Jesamiah cried, leaping to his feet with just one backward glance at Tiola tending Maha'dun's body. "Loose those sails—let's get out of here!"

No one queried him, no one hesitated. Within moments canvas tumbled from the yards, the wind filling them the instant they spread; like a great bird taking flight *Sea Witch* soared forward, racing away from the British frigate looming down on them. A ball sped through the air, landed where less than a moment before, *Sea Witch* had been.

"Out guns! Fire at will!"

Tiola glanced up, realised Jesamiah was ordering retaliation against the approaching ship.

~ No! Destroy the Safeena Hamra! ~

~ She's sinking; this frigate will not be able to save her or any of those bastards. If I don't fire back, we'll be sinking as well! ~

~ You do not understand... ~ Abandoning arguing, Tiola gently laid Maha'dun's body on the deck and ran to the rail, leaned out, staring back at the wreckage of the red ship. She was tilting, going down. In the confines of that sealed hold her crew were screaming and scrabbling, trying to get out as water poured in, their last moments of life a nightmare of living terror —as had their victims suffered at their merciless hands. Tiola felt no sorrow for them.

~ I cannot drown! ~ Yakub Pasha's voice sneered into her head. *~ And I still have the Night-Walker casket! Your human is a fool! ~*

~ No, you cannot drown, but you and the casket can, and will, burn. ~

Tiola brought a shield of immunity around herself so none of the crew would see or be aware of what she was about to do, the over-large coat covering her nakedness disappeared and in its place her gown of red silk, a green cloak, and a glistening diadem of precious jewels. She raised her arm and made the figure-of-eight shape with her hand, released a single high-pitched note of song on her breath. Palm outward, she leant across the rail, felt no remorse, no guilt or doubt as she hurled a ball of white fire direct at the *Safeena Hamra*, seeing in her mind Yakub Pasha curled on his knees, clutching for his very life at the casket made of the Night-Walker's bones. Outrage and despair keened from deep within his throat as death by fire engulfed him, his desperate cry drowned by the exultant ululation of the released soul within the casket, imprisoned there for so many years.

The dazzle of white, yellow and red flame from quarterdeck to stern engulfed the wrecked ship, the heat belching out and up as the gunpowder cache exploded. The British frigate instantly veered off, afraid to come close for sparks and flares threatened her safety. *Sea Witch* was already well away, the frigate let her go, her captain too lazy to give chase.

* * *

Standing beside the helm, the silvereen glow of the moon casting pale shadows, Tiola laid her hand over Jesamiah's hand, curled around a spoke, and stroked her thumb over where the scars and missing fingers disfigured the skin. She tilted his face towards hers with her other hand, her palm cool and gentle on his rough, whiskered chin.

"Thank you," she said.

"For what?"

"For coming for me."

"I came for young Benson, not you."

Tiola tucked her arm through his and buried her hand deep into his pocket. The moon was bright, but the air was cold. "Liar."

They were heading for Gibraltar, the nearest harbour, the

safest, or so Jesamiah hoped. He laughed, kissed her. "As if I would not have come for you. Stupid woman."

The wind flurried a sail. He adjusted the helm, felt *Sea Witch* smile, her pleasure seeping up and into his tight-gripping hands.

"Are the children settled?" he asked.

Tiola nodded. "They are, though Finch is cursing and mumbling about every available inch of space being taken up by a snivelling ankle-biter."

"And I would wager he is ensuring every one of them is covered by a warm blanket and is sleeping soundly. The curmudgeonly old sod is as soft as sun-melted butter."

"Sir? Captain, sir?"

Jesamiah looked around to see young Benson and his friend Donréal coming onto the quarterdeck, Benson carefully carrying a steaming cup of coffee.

"Mister Finch told me to bring you this, Cap'n," Benson said, "and he bade me remind you, Miss Tiola, that it be cold out here and you ought to be below."

"Quite right," Jesamiah confirmed, motioning for young Thomas to give him the cup and for Richie Tearle to take the helm. "The three of you, get yourselves below and get some sleep. We'll be busy when we drop anchor as I don't want to linger in Gibraltar harbour. We'll offload the children, send them ashore then sail away. I've no fancy to be explaining things to the Royal Navy—Tearle?"

"Cap'n?"

"Pick a few men and you go with them. You're as near as I've got to a government official."

"Aye, sir, though I was hoping to stay aboard."

Jesamiah made no answer. That may be so, but he did not want one of Harley's spies hanging around.

"Sir? Captain?" The boy, Donréal, pulled tentatively at Jesamiah's sleeve. "Sir?"

"Aye, lad?"

"Sir, am I to go with them?"

Putting out his hand, Jesamiah patted the lad's shoulder. "Your mother and father must be worried sick about you. Master Tearle here will ensure you are reunited with them."

The boy bit his lip, trying not to weep.

"His father's dead," Tom Benson explained in a low voice. "His mother too."

Tiola held out her arms to the boy, enfolded him in an embrace.

He looked up at Jesamiah, his small, pale face tear-streaked. "I would stay with you, sir," he said very quietly, "for I think you intend to find the man who killed my mama, and I wish also to find him, and kill him."

There was a long pause of silence, with only the wind sighing through the rigging and the slap of water tearing past the hull.

"And who," Jesamiah asked, although he suspected that he already knew the answer, "was your mama?"

"She called me Donréal when she could not use my given name. We often had to hide, for she was important and there were those who wanted her dead. My name is Leandro, and she hid me among the Marqués' children. She told me to wait for you, Captain, said that I could trust you." He wiped away the tears with the back of his hand. "Can I? Can I trust you to kill the man who killed my mama?"

Lost for words, not relying on his voice for his throat was choked with a mixture of regret, sadness and a brewing anger for Francesca's wasted life, and for lie upon lie, all Jesamiah could do was nod.

* * *

"Did you know about the boy?" Jesamiah asked Tiola as the children were handed down to into the bumboats that had swarmed out to *Sea Witch* before she had even settled at her anchor cable. Eager to gain money where they could, Gibraltar's poor folk ferried supplies to and from ships without question or comment. These goods—children—raised an eyebrow or two, but a few handfuls of silver coin soon stemmed any inquisitiveness.

"I guessed, yes," she admitted, fighting her grief as Maha'dun's coffin was lowered into the last boat. Tearle was under strict orders to take it to the nearest church and pay for the priests to set candles and say their prayers for one day and one night before committing the body to burial. Jesamiah had wanted to give the nightman a seaman's burial wrapped in a canvas shroud and offered to the deep, but she had dissuaded him. "Maha'dun was afraid of drowning," she had said, "let us not prolong his fear."

"The boy?" Jesamiah said again, wrapping his arms around her, stoically masking his own grief. He had liked Maha'dun, for all his faults. He wished there was something more he could do. The nightman had given his life to save Jesamiah's—it seemed callous just to send him off in a wooden box for someone else to bury, but Tiola had insisted, and he had to bow to her wisdom.

"The boy?" Tiola said. "He has recognisable eyes."

Taking a small step away from her Jesamiah answered sharply. "My eyes? I hope you do not think he is *my* son!"

She smiled, smoothed his alarm. "No, he is your father's son. He has his eyes."

He thought on that a moment, her words not coming as a

surprise.

The last boat was away; tempted to watch the children and the coffin taken safely ashore, Jesamiah resigned himself to his original plan. He shouted orders to weigh anchor, set sail. He had no wish to linger, had a cargo to get to Virginia.

"You do not mind?" he said to his wife as his men started stamping around and around the capstan.

"About what?"

"That the boy is 'Cesca's son?"

"Why would I mind? He is her son, not yours."

Tiola curled her fingers around his, brought his palm down to her belly.

"But this little one in here is."

Chapter Thirty-Six

The night was cool, no sound, save for the cicadas chirruping and a night bird singing somewhere. Maha'dun walked slowly along the shore, his hands thrust deep into his pockets, the light wind tugging and toying with his hair. It had been a long walk, leaving the lights of Gibraltar behind and slipping into Spanish territory. He had always felt at home here in Spain, where hot days gave way to sultry nights. The handsome young Spanish men.

His head down, shoulders slumped, he walked on along the beach, ignoring the sharp twisting pull in his chest where the wound was almost healed.

Did Jesamiah realise that, like Tiola, he had the ability to heal himself of certain injuries? Probably not. Jesamiah had never, really, understood what he was, had he?

They all thought him dead. All except Tiola who had insisted the coffin they had lain him in was to be taken to a church, the lid unsealed, candles to be lit and prayers made. That he was to lie in a state of reverence for four-and-twenty hours. What those priests had thought or done when they found the coffin empty after the passing of that first night,

Maha'dun did not care.

He bent, picked up a shell, put it to his ear. *'You can hear the sea in a shell'*, young Benson had told him. He would miss Thomas Hedgepig.

He listened. Nothing. Frustrated, he threw it away, watched as it plopped into the outgoing tide and disappeared. He did not want to look at the sea or listen to the sea, he wanted to be *on* the sea, aboard *Sea Witch*, feeling her lift and dip beneath his feet, watching the spray toss over her bow, hear the wind in her rigging. Wanted to stand beside Jesamiah at the helm.

As much as he wanted it, he could not. They all thought him dead. Jesamiah—Captain Acorne—Finch, Spokesy, Skylark, Thomas Hedgepig. They had seen him killed, had seen the blood, seen his body. All of them except Tiola *knew* he was dead. He would compromise himself, and, more importantly, Tiola, if he were to be seen alive, unharmed, unscathed.

What was he going to do now? What was there after these weeks of excitement and adventure? He had adored every moment—especially the ones fraught with danger, for he thrived on the blood-rush of fear, and even those moments when he ached to make love he cherished, despite knowing it could never, would never, happen.

The freedom to do what he pleased had released something inside of him and opened his eyes and heart to so much, much more than he had ever experienced before. But how was he to face the next week, month, year, without the joy of living that freedom?

But first, before anything, he had to find Ber'ell the Traitor and make him pay. Dearly.

He stepped out onto a flat rock, into the silver-shimmering path of moonlight, and stood, staring at the emptiness ahead of him. In his mind he saw *Sea Witch* gliding silhouetted against the moon-bright sky, her sails full, foam creaming along her hull. Realised that this had been his dream, his vision: seeing her sail away without him.

"Do you love her?" Jesamiah had asked him, that glorious night when they had sat together atop the mast, feeling the lift and sway of the ship, the touch of the wind on their faces. For Maha'dun, extreme joy in his heart.

"Of course I love her," he had said with an edge of reprimand. "Tiola saved my life, she cares for me and thus she is a dear friend. I love all my dear friends."

But I was never a lover to her. He had not added that.

In his mind's eye, Maha'dun saw him, Jesamiah, standing legs apart, hands caressing the spokes of the helm, black hair and blue ribbons tangling about his face, fussed by the wind.

It is you I love. He had not said that either, but he said it now. Said it again and again and again, louder and louder until he was shouting it at the uncaring, unlistening silver moon.

"It is you I love! I love you, Jesamiah!"

What was he to do now, now that Jesamiah had gone?

The sea lapped at the rock and at his boots, ran up onto the shore behind him, grating on the shingle. He could hear its voice, the same word repeated over and over as bereft tears choked in his throat.

"*Jesssh...amiah*," the sea seemed to say. "*Jesssh...amiah, Jesssh...amiah*."

THE END
DROP ANCHOR

On The Account

AUTHOR'S NOTE

A mention of matters historical:

Drummonds Bank was opened in London in 1717 when such establishments were popping up all over the place. It is highly unlikely that Master Drummond had a 'branch' in Bideford at that time (or even subsequently!) but having been invited to this delightful old bank at the edge of Trafalgar Square for lunch one day in 2012, I couldn't resist using it. We spent a wonderful few hours there. From the advantageous view of the first floor window overlooking Admiralty Arch and The Mall, we watched Her Majesty the Queen pass by in her Rolls Royce accompanied by several police cars and motorbikes, plus, because my arthritic knee does not indulge in stairs, I used the Queen Mother's lift, which had been installed for her use some years before she passed away. It was tiny— more like a cupboard. I do hope that sticklers for historical facts will forgive the use of this bank and my little bit of personal indulgence.

The Llandoger Trow is a real pub; a fine old hostelry in Bristol, part of which has been converted to a well-known hotel chain. Legend states that Stevenson used it as a template for *Treasure Island*'s Admiral Benbow public house. If it was good enough for Long John Silver, it would certainly suit my Jesamiah. The St Mary Redcliffe church is as I describe and I have had the great pleasure of voyaging along some of Bristol's waterways on the present-day replica of the *Matthew*.

Sea Witch herself should be dated a good few years later

than this story is set, for copper keels and such were not yet in use, but the Voyages are sailor's yarns, and all sailors, like fishermen, exaggerate.

I had intended to bring back Jansy, Isiah and a few others from previous stories, but as I started this tale I discovered that they had taken themselves off somewhere and did not return into my mind, whereas new characters sauntered in and wanted a part to play. And for Rue's fans; he just couldn't be parted from his beloved Pamela—his demise was unplanned and unintentional on my part. It just happened.

Tawford Barton is fictional, but Instow is not. I imagine the house to be located in the vicinity of the present-day Cricket Pavilion.

John and Thomas Benson were real people who lived at Appledore in North Devon. Thomas became a notorious smuggler when he grew up. I wonder who taught him the trade? Castle Rock, on Exmoor, located in the Valley Of The Rocks is a place well worth visiting. Watch out for the wild goats. The locations in Spain are entirely fictitious.

For lovers of dance, *Well Hall* is a traditional English Country Dance from the late seventeenth century. My thanks to John and Cathy Millar of Newport House, Williamsburg, Virginia for their advice concerning this dance. I wanted something that could have an element of risqué, (but discreet) contact in it and *Well Hall* was their suggestion. With eye contact, the gentleman bringing the lady in towards him, their bodies passing a little closer than necessary, he kissing her hand maybe—the result can become extremely sensuous. There are a few versions on You Tube.

As for Maha'dun, the Night-Walker, or 'Nightm'n' as Jesamiah calls him, eagle-eyed readers who remember his brief appearance in the original SilverWood Books Ltd edition of

Ripples In The Sand may notice a small discrepancy in the spelling of his name—*Mahadun*. Back then, he could not read or write and had not noticed the missing apostrophe; this error has subsequently been rectified. Maha'dun is a vain, predatory night-creature with some bad anti-social habits, and although his character was initially inspired by stories of vampires, (popular back in the mid-2000s, when the idea of the *Sea Witch Voyages* first came to me), by the time I actually got to writing about him, ten years later, he had very much discovered his own identity. He is, therefore, *not* a vampire in any garlic-hating, fang-sharpened, skin-glowing, coffin-sleeping, dark, or otherwise shape or form. He does not have fangs, and does not drink blood, so my (not very sincere) apologies to anyone who expected this occupation to be on his C.V. I concede he cannot function in daylight, but porphyria ('Poor Fairy Ear') is a very real condition aggravated by sunlight reacting on the skin. Exactly *what* he is, however, neither Tiola, Jesamiah, nor I will be revealing. Not yet, anyway.

I assure you that he will not be left wandering on that Spanish shore for long. He will be back in Voyage Six, *Gallows Wake*, and maybe, if he behaves himself, in subsequent Voyages.

Helen Hollick

2020

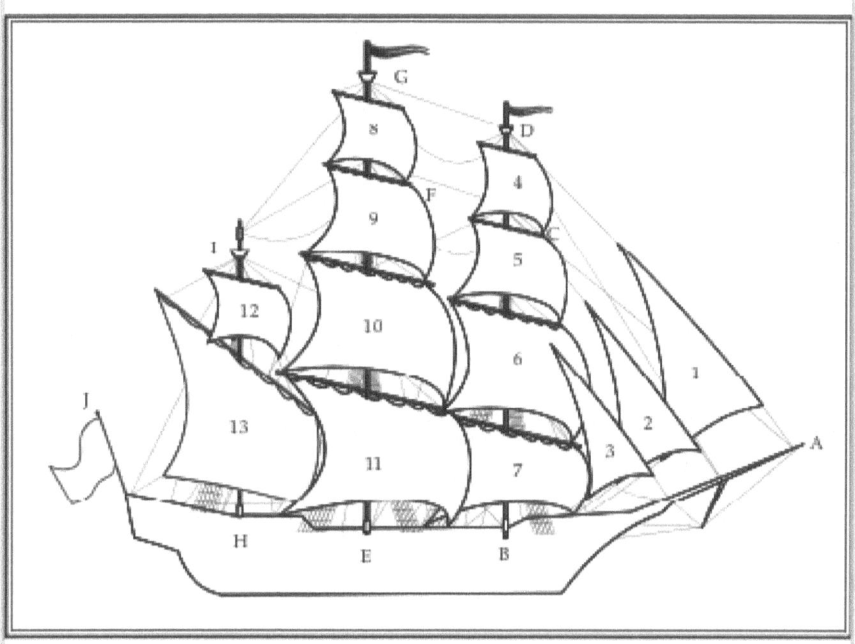

Sails

1	Flying Jib	8	Main Topgallant Royal
2	Jib	9	Main Topgallant
3	Fore Staysail	10	Main Topsail
4	Fore Topgallant Royal	11	Mainsail or Main Course
5	Fore Topgallant Sail (pronounced *t'gan's'l*)	12	Mizzen Topsail
6	Fore Topsail (pronounced *tops'l*)	13	Mizzen Sail
7	Foresail or Fore Course		

Masts

A	Bowsprit/Jib-boom	F	Main Topmast
B	Foremast	G	Main Topgallant Mast
C	Fore Topmast	H	Mizzenmast
D	Fore Topgallant Mast	I	Mizzen Topmast
E	Main Mast	J	Ensign and Ensign Staff

GLOSSARY

Various sailing terms used throughout the
Sea Witch Voyages

Aback—a sail when its forward surface is pressed upon by the wind. Used to 'stop' a ship.

A-cockbill—having the tapered ends turned upward. Said of the anchor when it is hanging ready from the cathead.

Aloft—up in the tops, at the masthead or anywhere about the yards or the rigging.

Articles—Each man when coming aboard 'agreed the Articles'. Some pirate ships were run on very democratic lines. The crew elected their captain, agreed where to sail, divided the 'spoils' fairly etc. Most rules were sensible things like no naked flame below deck, each man to keep his weapon clean and ready for use, and no fighting aboard ship.

Bar—a shoal running across the mouth of a harbour or a river.

Bare poles—having no sail up, the bare mast.

Belay—to make fast or secure. Also: 'Stop that', 'Belay that talk!' would mean 'Shut up!'

Belaying pin—a short wooden rod to which a ship's rigging is secured. A common improvised weapon aboard a sailing ship because they are everywhere, are easily picked up, and are the right size and weight to be used as a club.

Bell (ship's bell)—used as a clock, essential for navigation as the measurement of the angle of the sun had to be made at noon. The bell was struck each time the half-hour glass was turned.

Best bower—the larboard (or port) side anchor. There are usually two identical anchors on the bows of a vessel, the second one is the small-bower.

Bilge—the lowest part of the ship inside the hull along the keel. They fill with stinking bilge water or 'bilge'. Can also mean nonsense or foolish talk.

Binnacle—the frame or box that houses the compass.

Bosun—short for boatswain, usually a competent sailor who is in charge of all deck duties.

Bosun's chair—a platform on ropes made to form a chair-like structure, and hauled aboard.

Bow—the front or 'pointed' end of the ship.

Bowsprit—the heavy slanted spar pointing forward from the ship's bow.

Brace—rope used to control the horizontal movement of a square-rigged yard.

Brig—a two-masted vessel square-rigged on both masts.

Brimstone—formerly the common name for sulphur.

Bring It Close—the telescope.

Broadside—the simultaneous firing of all guns on one side of a ship.

Bulkheads—vertical partitions in a ship.

Bulwark—the raised wooden 'walls' running along the sides of a ship above the level of the deck.

Cable—1) a long, thick and heavy rope by which a ship is secured to the anchor. 2) A measurement of length = 120 fathoms or 240 yards.

Capstan—a drum-like winch turned by the crew to raise or lower the anchors or other heavy gear.

Careen—the process of beaching a ship, heeling her over to her side and cleaning the underside of weed, barnacles and worm; making essential repairs to the part of a ship which is usually below the waterline. A careened ship will go faster and last longer than one that is not.

Cathead—vertical beam of timber protruding near the bow, used for hoisting the anchor.

Cat o'nine tails, or 'cat'—a whip with many lashes, used for flogging.

Caulk—to seal the gaps between planks of wood with caulking (see Oakum).

Chain shot—two balls of iron joined together by a length of chain, chiefly used to destroy masts, rigging and sails.

Chandler—a merchant selling the various things a ship needs for supplies and repairs.

Chanty/shanty—a sailor's work song. Often lewd and derogatory about the officers.

Chase / Prize—the ship being pursued.

Cleat—wooden or metal fastening to which ropes can be secured. Can also be used as a ladder.

Clew—the lower corners of a sail, therefore 'Clew up'—to haul a square sail up to a yard.

Close-hauled—sailing as close to the direction of the wind as possible with the sails turned almost ninety degrees.

Cordage—rope is called cordage on board a ship.

Colours—the vessel's identification flag, also called an ensign. For a pirate, the Jolly Roger!

Courses—lowest sails on the mast.

Crosstrees—horizontal cross-timbers partway up a mast to keep the shrouds spread apart.

Deadeyes—a round, flat, wooden block with three holes through which a lanyard, or rope, can be thread to tighten the shrouds.

Dolphin striker—a short perpendicular gaff spar under the cap of the bowsprit for guying down the jib-boom. Also called a martingale.

Doubloon—a Spanish gold coin.

Drang—a narrow passageway between buildings.

Drashed—Devonshire word for thrashed, a beating.

Fathom—a depth of six feet of water.

Flukes—the broad parts, or palms, of the anchor.

Fore or for'ard—toward the front end of the ship, the bow.

Forecastle—pronounced 'fo'c'sle'; raised deck at the front of a ship.

Fore-and-aft—the length of a ship.

Forestay—the rope leading from the mast to the bow.

Fother—to seal a leak by lowering a sail over the side of the ship and positioning it so that it seals the hole by the weight of the sea.

Futtocks—'foot hooks'.

Futtock shroud—short pieces of rope which secure lower deadeyes and futtock plates to the top mast rigging.

Galleon—a large three-masted square-rigged ship used chiefly by the Spanish.

Galley—ship's kitchen.

Gaol / gaoler—pronounced 'jail' and 'jailer'.

Gasket—a piece of rope to fasten the sails to the yards.

Grenados—early form of hand grenade.

Grapeshot or grape—small cast iron balls bound together in a canvas bag that scatter like shotgun pellets when fired.

Gunwale—pronounced 'gun'l'; upper planking along the sides of a vessel. 'Up to the gunwales'—full up or overloaded.

Halliard or halyard—pronounced 'haly'd'. The rope used to hoist a sail.

Hard tack—ship's biscuit. Opposite is soft tack—bread.

Hatch—an opening in the deck for entering below.

Hawser—cable.

Heave to—to check the forward motion of a vessel and bring her to a standstill by heading her into the wind and backing some of her sails.

Heel—to lean over due to action of the wind, waves or greater weight on one side. The angle at which the vessel tips when sailing.

Helm—the tiller (a long steering arm) or a wheel which controls the rudder and enables the vessel to be steered.

Hold—the lower space below the decks for cargo.

Hull—the sides of a ship which sit in and above the water.

Hull cleats—the 'ladder' or steps attached to the hull via which entry is gained to the entry port.

Hull down—a vessel when it is so far away from the observer the hull is invisible owing to the shape of the earth's surface. Opposite to hull up.

Jack Ketch—the hangman. To dance with Jack Ketch is to hang.

Jolly boat—a small boat, a dinghy.

Jolly Roger—the pirates' flag, called the jolie rouge, although its original meaning is unknown. The hoisted flag was an invitation to surrender, with the implication that those who did so would be treated well and no quarter given to those who did not.

Jury-rigged—makeshift repairs.

Kedge—a small anchor used for mooring to keep the vessel secure and clear of her mooring ropes while she rides in a tidal harbour or river. Also used to warp (haul) a ship from one part of the harbour to another by dropping the kedge anchor, securing a hawser to its wooden or iron stock and hauling the line in.

Keel—the lowest part of the hull below the water.

Keelhaul—an unpleasant punishment: the victim is dragged through the water passing under the keel, either from side to side or bow to stern.

Knot—one nautical mile per hour.

Landlubber—(or lubber) a non-sailor.

Langrage—jagged pieces of sharp metal used as shot. Especially useful for damaging rigging and killing men.

Larboard—pronounced 'larb'd'; the left side of a ship when facing the bow (front). Changed in the nineteenth century to 'port'.

Lead line—(pronounced 'led') a length of rope used to determine the depth of water.

Lee—the side or direction away from the wind i.e downwind.

Lee shore—the shore on to which the wind is blowing, a hazardous shore for a sailing vessel particularly in strong winds.

Leeches—the vertical edges of a square sail.

Letter of Marque—Papers issued by a government during wartime entitling a privately owned ship to raid enemy commerce or attack enemy ships.

Lubberly—in an amateur way, as a landlubber would do.

Luff—the order to the helmsman to put the tiller towards the lee side of the ship in order to make it sail nearer to the direction of the wind.

Marlinspike—a pointed iron tool used to part strands of rope so that they can be spliced.

Maroon—a punishment for breaking a pirate ship's Articles or rules. The victim was left on a deserted coast (or an island) with little in the way of supplies. Therefore, no one could say the unlucky pirate had been killed by his former brethren.

Mast—vertical spar supporting the sails.

Molly boy—a homosexual prostitute.

Oakum—a material used to waterproof seams between planks on deck etc. Made of strong, pliable, tarred fibres obtained from scrap rope or rags which swell when wet.

On the Account—or the 'sweet trade'; a man who went 'on the account' was turning pirate.

Ope—an opening or passageway between buildings.

Painter—a rope attached to a boat's bow for securing or towing.

Piece of Eight—a Spanish silver coin worth one peso or eight reales. It was sometimes literally cut into eight pieces, each worth one real. In the 1700s a piece of eight was worth a little under a modern five shillings sterling, or 25p—this would be about £15 - £20 today. One side usually had the Spanish coat of arms, the other two lines symbolising the limits of the old world at the Straits of Gibraltar, the exit into the Atlantic Ocean from the Mediterranean. In later designs two hemispheres were added between the lines representing the Old and New Worlds. Pieces of eight were so widely used that eventually this sign was turned into the dollar sign—$.

Privateer—an armed vessel bearing letters of marque, or one of her crew, or her captain. A 'privateer' is theoretically a law-abiding combatant.

Quarterdeck—a deck at the rear of a ship where the officers stood and where the helm is usually situated.

Quartermaster—usually the second in command aboard a pirate ship. In the Royal Navy, the man in charge of the provisions.

Rail—timber plank along the top of the gunwale above the sides of the vessel.

Rake—when a ship strikes another with a broadside of cannon.

Ratlines—pronounced 'ratlins'; horizontal lines tied across the shrouds to form a rope ladder for climbing aloft.

Reef—1) an underwater obstruction of rock or coral. 2) to reduce the size of the sails by tying them partially up, either to slow the ship or to keep a strong wind from putting too much strain on the masts.

Rigging—the ropes which support the spars (standing rigging) and allow the sails to be controlled (running rigging).

Round shot—iron cannon balls.

Rudder—blade at the stern which is angled to steer the vessel.

Run—to sail directly away from the wind.

Sails—in general each mast had three sails. (See diagram).

Sail ho!—'I see a ship!' The sail is the first part visible over the horizon.

Scuppers—openings along the edges of a ship's deck to allow water to drain back to the sea rather than collecting in the bilges.

Scuttle—1) a porthole or small hatch in the deck for lighting and ventilation, covered by the 'scuttle hatch'. Can be used as a narrow entrance to the deck below. 2) To deliberately sink or wreck a ship.

Shank-painter—the stopper (a short rope) that secures the shank and fluke of the anchor to the cathead.

Sheet—a rope made fast to the lower corners of a sail to control its position.

Sheet home—to haul on a sheet until the foot of the sail is as straight and taut as possible.

Ship of the Line—a Royal Navy ship carrying at least fifty guns.

Ship's biscuit—hard bread. Very dry, can be eaten a year after baked. Also called hard tack.

Shrouds—ropes forming part of the standing rigging and supporting the mast or topmast.

Sloop—a small, single-masted vessel, ideal for shallow water.

Spar—a stout wooden pole used as a mast or yard of a sailing vessel.

Spritsail—pronounced 'sprit'sl'; a sail attached to a yard which hangs under the bowsprit.

Square-rigged—the principal sails set at right angles to the length of a ship and extended by horizontal yards slung to the mast.

Starboard—originally 'steerboard', pronounced 'starb'd'. The right side of a vessel when you are facing toward the bow.

Stay—strong, very thick ropes supporting the masts.

Stem—timber at the very front of the bow.

Stern—the back end of a ship.

Swab—a disrespectful term for a seaman, or to clean the decks.

Sweeps—long oars used by large vessels, especially galleys.

Tack/tacking—to change the direction of a vessel's course by turning her bows into the wind until the wind blows on her other side. When a ship is sailing into an oncoming wind she will have to tack, make a zigzag line, in order to make progress forward against the oncoming wind.

Tackle—pronounced 'taykle'. An arrangement of one or more ropes and pulley blocks used to increase the power for raising or lowering heavy objects.

Taffrail—upper rail along the ship's stern.

Tompions—muzzle-plugs to protect the bore of cannons from salt corrosion etc.

Transom—planking forming the stern.

Trim—a term used for adjusting the sails as the wind changes.

Waist—the middle part of the ship.

Wake—the line of passage directly behind as marked by a track of white foam.

Warp—to move a ship by hauling or pulling her along on warps (ropes); also the name of the ropes which secure a ship when moored (tied up) to a jetty or dock.

Weigh anchor—to haul the anchor up; more generally, to leave port.

Widowmaker—term for the bowsprit.

Windward—the side towards the wind as opposed to leeward.

Yard—a long spar suspended from the mast of a vessel to extend the sails.

Yardarm—either end of the yard.

ABOUT THE AUTHOR

HELLEN HOLLICK

After an exciting Lottery win on the opening night of the 2012 London Olympic Games, Helen Hollick moved from a North-East London suburb to an eighteenth-century farmhouse in North Devon, where she lives with her husband, daughter and son-in-law, and a variety of pets and animals, which include several moorland-bred Exmoor ponies, her daughter's showjumpers, hens, ducks, geese, dogs, cats.... Her study overlooks part of the Taw Valley, where the main road runs from Exeter to Barnstaple, and back in the 1600s Roundhead and Cavalier troops marched to and from battle. There are several friendly ghosts sharing the house and farm, and Helen regards herself as merely a temporary custodian of the lovely old house, not its owner.

First published in 1994, her passion, now, is her pirate character, Captain Jesamiah Acorne of the nautical adventure series, *The Sea Witch Voyages*, which have been

On The Account

snapped up by US-based, independent publisher, Penmore Press.

Helen became a USA Today Bestseller with her historical novel, *The Forever Queen* (titled *A Hollow Crown* in the UK) the story of Saxon Queen, Emma of Normandy. Her novel *Harold the King* (titled *I Am The Chosen King* in the US) explores the events that led to the 1066 Battle of Hastings, while her *Pendragon's Banner Trilogy*, set in the fifth century, is widely acclaimed as a more historical version of the Arthurian legend, with no magic, no Lancelot, Merlin or Holy Grail, but instead, the 'what might have happened' story of the boy who became a man, who became a king, who became a legend...

Helen is also published in various languages including German, Turkish and Italian and has written three non-fiction books, *Pirates: Truth and Tales; Life of A Smuggler in Fact and Fiction,* and as an avid supporter of indie writers, co-wrote a short advice guide for new writers, *Discovering the Diamond*. She is currently also branching out into the quick read cosy-mystery genre with her Jan Christopher series of Murder Mysteries.

Recognised by her stylish hats, Helen attends conferences and book-related events when she can, as a chance to meet her readers and social-media followers, although her 'wonky eyesight' as she describes her condition of Glaucoma, is becoming prohibitive for travel. She founded and runs the *Discovering Diamonds* review blog for historical fiction and is a regular blogger, Facebooker and Tweeter.

She occasionally gets time to write!

Website: www.helenhollick.net

Blog: www.ofhistoryandkings.blogspot.com

HELEN HOLLICK

Facebook: www.facebook.com/HelenHollickAuthor
Twitter: @HelenHollick
Email author@helenhollick.net
Newsletter: http://tinyletter.com/HelenHollick

Also by Helen Hollick

The Pendragon's Banner Trilogy
*The Kingmaking: Book One of the
Pendragon's Banner Trilogy*
*Pendragon's Banner: Book Two of the
Pendragon's Banner Trilogy*
*Shadow of the King: Book Three of the
Pendragon's Banner Trilogy*

The Saxon 1066 Series
A Hollow Crown (UK edition title)
The Forever Queen (US edition title. *USA
Today* bestseller)

Harold the King (UK edition title)
I Am The Chosen King (US edition title)

1066 Turned Upside Down
(A collection of alternative stories by a
variety of authors)

Betrayal
(Tales of Betrayal by twelve different
authors)

Jan Christopher Murder Mystery Series
A Mirror Murder
(published 2021)

Non-fiction
Pirates: Truth and Tales
Life of a Smuggler: In Fact and Fiction
Discovering The Diamond
(with Jo Field)

And
The *Sea Witch* Voyages
Sea Witch: The first voyage of pirate
Captain Jesamiah Acorne
Pirate Code: The second voyage of Captain
Jesamiah Acorne
Bring It Close: The third voyage of Captain
Jesamiah Acorne
Ripples In the Sand: The fourth voyage of
Captain Jesamiah Acorne
On the Account: The fifth voyage of
Captain Jesamiah Acorne
When The Mermaid Sings: a novella prequel
(How the young Jesamiah Acorne became a
pirate.)

BELLERAPHON'S CHAMPION

BY

JOHN DANIELSKI

Deep within each man, lies the secret knowledge of whether he is a stalwart or a coward. Three years an un-blooded Royal Marine, 1st Lieutenant Thomas Pennywhistle will finally "meet the lion," protecting HMS Bellerophon at the Battle of Trafalgar.

Not only will Pennywhistle be responsible for the lives of 72 marines aboard Bellerophon but their direction will fall entirely on his shoulders since his fellow Marine officers consist of a boy, a card shark, and a dying consumptive. If he has what it takes to command, it will take everything he's got.

In the course of battle, he will encounter marvels and terrors; from valiant foes to women performing miracles, from the skill of acrobats to the luck of the ship's cat, from a dead man still full of fight to a coward who has none. He and his marines will meet enemy élan will with trained volleys and disciplined bayonets. Most of all, he will meet himself; discovering just how dark his true nature really is.

Europe will be changed forever by Trafalgar, and so will Pennywhistle.

PENMORE PRESS
www.penmorepress.com

Fortune's Whelp
by
Benerson Little

Privateer, Swordsman, and Rake:

Set in the 17th century during the heyday of privateering and the decline of buccaneering, *Fortune's Whelp* is a brash, swords-out sea-going adventure. Scotsman Edward MacNaughton, a former privateer captain, twice accused and acquitted of piracy and currently seeking a commission, is ensnared in the intrigue associated with the attempt to assassinate King William III in 1696. Who plots to kill the king, who will rise in rebellion—and which of three women in his life, the dangerous smuggler, the wealthy widow with a dark past, or the former lover seeking independence—might kill to further political ends? Variously wooing and defying Fortune, Captain MacNaughton approaches life in the same way he wields a sword or commands a fighting ship: with the heart of a lion and the craft of a fox.

PENMORE PRESS
www.penmorepress.com

Midshipman Graham and the Battle of Abukir

by

James Boschert

It is midsummer of 1799 and the British Navy in the Mediterranean Theater of operations. Napoleon has brought the best soldiers and scientists from France to claim Egypt and replace the Turkish empire with one of his own making, but the debacle at Acre has caused the brilliant general to retreat to Cairo.

Commodore Sir Sidney Smith and the Turkish army land at the strategically critical fortress of Abukir, on the northern coast of Egypt. Here Smith plans to further the reversal of Napoleon's fortunes. Unfortunately, the Turks badly underestimate the speed, strength, and resolve of the French Army, and the ensuing battle becomes one of the worst defeats in Arab history.

Young Midshipman Duncan Graham is anxious to get ahead in the British Navy, but has many hurdles to overcome. Without any familial privileges to smooth his way, he can only advance through merit. The fires of war prove his mettle, but during an expedition to obtain desperately needed fresh water – and an illegal duel – a French patrol drives off the boats, and Graham is left stranded on shore. It now becomes a question of evasion and survival with the help of a British spy. Graham has to become very adaptable in order to avoid detection by the French police, and he must help the spy facilitate a daring escape by sea in order to get back to the British squadron.

"Midshipman Graham and The Battle of Abukir is both a rousing Napoleonic naval yarn and a convincing coming of age story. The battle scenes are riveting and powerful, the exotic Egyptian locales colorfully rendered." – John Danielski, author of *Capital's Punishment*

PENMORE PRESS
www.penmorepress.com